A Scarcity of Condors

of

Condors

a novel

SUANNE LAQUEUR

CATHEDRAL ROCK PRESS | NEW YORK | 2019

Suanne Laqueur/Cathedral Rock Press

Somers, New York

WWW.SUANNELAQUEURWRITES.COM

Publisher's Note: This is a work of fiction. Names, characters, places, and incidents are a product of the author's imagination. Locales and public names are sometimes used for atmospheric purposes. Any resemblance to actual people, living or dead, or to businesses, companies, events, institutions, or locales is completely coincidental.

Book Design by Ampersand Book Interiors

Cover Design by Tracy Kopsachilis

A Scarcity of Condors/ Suanne Laqueur. — 1st ed.

ISBN 978-0578611341

Author's Note

*I*T IS ESTIMATED THAT between 1973 and 1978, approximately 4,500 people from diverse backgrounds passed through the Villa Grimaldi detention center in Santiago, Chile: leftist militants, workers, students, men, women, girls and boys.

The first to pass through the gates were Baptist Van Schouwen Vasey, a surgeon, and Patricio Munita Castillo, a law student at the University of Chile. Both men were kidnapped on December 13, 1973. As of this writing, Van Schouwen Vasey remains disappeared. Castillo's remains were identified by the Servicio Medical-Legal.

A Scarcity of Condors is a fictional novel, based on historical events. Cleon Tholet's torture and interrogation in the Villa Grimaldi compound is a composite of actual testimony by detainees. His being imprisoned in November of 1973 is an intentional anachronism on my part. This, along with any other historical inconsistencies in the book, was taken with poetic license, and written with the utmost respect and regard for all of Chile's victims, survivors and Los Desaparacidos.

—SLQR
Somers, New York
September 30, 2019

For Moony, the river on which this boat sailed.

"I love you without knowing how, or when, or from where. I love you straightforwardly, without complexities or pride; so I love you because I know no other way than this: where I does not exist, nor you, so close that your hand on my chest is my hand, so close that your eyes close as I fall asleep."

—Pablo Neruda, Sonnet XVII

"Desaparecidos were not just murdered, but attempts were made to convince the whole world that they did not exist. This almost drove some families crazy. Legal documents were manipulated to the point that individuals really did disappear. Not just that their whereabouts were unknown, but that they didn't exist at all in the records...

"The attempts of families and friends to find the missing were portrayed as desperate attempts by crazy people to destroy the country through their lies. They were transformed into pariahs of society through the disappearance of the victims. Families looking for desaparecidos were seen as dangerous and problematic, not because of their political beliefs, not for their own values, but merely because they insisted in the existence of people that 'did not exist.'"

—Marisol Intriago,
director of the Special Unit of Forensic
Identification at the Servicio Medico-Legal,
an institute under Chile's Ministry of Justice, which advises
the courts on medical and legal matters.

PROLOGUE

SERVICIO MEDICAL-LEGAL
SANTIAGO, CHILE
JULY 2010

1

ISABELLA EBERHOFF SMILED ABOVE the report on her desk, her gaze caressing the page as if it were a beloved child's artwork or the revealed physique of a new lover.

> *The STR analysis revealed a very high degree of allele sharing among the two male profiles, heretofore known as I-14307 and I-29742.* **This degree of allele sharing suggests the individuals are closely related.**
> *The Sibship Index (SI) was calculated by determining the likelihood ratio of two hypotheses:*
> **Hypothesis-1:** *I-14307 and I-29742 are siblings;*
> **Hypothesis-2:** *The samples belong to two unrelated individuals.*
> *The SI was determined to be 5.6 million in favor of Hypothesis-1.* **In other words, the DNA evidence is 5.6 million times more likely that the individuals are siblings, rather than unrelated individuals.**

Isabella turned the page and tucked her hair behind her ear. The siblings being male gave the lab an advantage. The Y-chromosome replicated itself exactly when it passed from father to son, leaving a trail of genetic pebbles through generation after generation.

Anticipation rising in her chest, her eyes scanned the next section, which summarized the DNA profile of Lot 97-M: nineteen male bone fragments exhumed from a mass grave in 1991. The comparison of this DNA to I-14307 and I-29742 could put a forty-year mystery to rest.

> *We generated a 17 Y-STR loci profile using DNA from Lot 97-M,*
> *I-14307 and I-29742.*
> *We observed an exact match between all three males over all 17*
> *markers. The loci are:*
> *DYS456 (16 repeats)*
> *DYS389I (13 repeats)*
> *DYS390 (24 repeats)*
> *DYS389II (29 repeats)*
> *With the likelihood ratio being 6.1 million times more than if*
> *these samples were from unrelated individuals,* ***it is the conclu-***
> ***sion of the team that Lot 97-M is the biological father of both***
> ***I-14307 and I-29742.***

Isabella drew in and exhaled a long breath, then checked her watch. It was close to seven o'clock on the west coast of the United States. Nearing ten on the eastern seaboard. Two brothers on opposite sides of the continent, each unaware of the other. Unaware that she, from the other side of the equator, could reunite them.

In case I-14307 was an early-to-bedder, she opted for the brother on the west coast. Her heart thudded as a connection was laid from Santiago to Seattle. Her stomach prickled as the phone rang. These were the last seconds of I-29742's life as he knew it. A touch of his finger to the screen of his phone would change everything.

The smile curved up her mouth as she patted the report's pages. You could guess at the truth. You could hypothesize, you could hope, you could pray, or you could believe the hunch in your gut.

Isabella Eberhoff, director of the Special Unit of Forensic Identification, wasn't in the business of hunches found in the gut or hope found in the heart. She was in the business of the truth found in bone matter.

And at the end of the day, the bones never lied.

I-29742 answered on the fourth ring. "¿Diga?"

"Buenas noches. ¿Es Jude Tholet?"

"Sí."

"It's Isabella Eberhoff with the Medical-Legal Institute in Santiago. I have news…"

JUDE THE OBSCURE

"The beggarly question of parentage—what is it after all?
What does it matter, when you come to think of it,
whether a child is yours by blood or not?"

—Thomas Hardy, *Jude the Obscure*

THE VERB

*T*HE CONTENTS OF JUDE Tholet's wallet were what you'd find in any man's daily essentials kept folded in back pocket. Driver's license, credit cards, insurance card, two condoms, an emergency $20 bill. His green card, of course, in accordance with Section 264(e) of the Immigration and Nationality Act. He was a rule-follower by nature, but being the child and grandchild of refugees, his chromosomes had an extra be-prepared gene. An inherited propensity to keep his eyes on the exit signs, ready to make a run for the border at the first sign of trouble. He had zero cause to worry about his permanent residence status, but he was never without his papers and a plan.

In a secret slot of his wallet, Jude carried something slightly unique. A slip of folded paper, born of a page torn from a paperback copy of Scott Spencer's *Endless Love*. Now cropped to the first half of the first sentence of the first chapter, its active verbs underlined in red pen:

> *When I was seventeen and in full obedience to my heart's most urgent commands, I <u>stepped</u> far from the pathway of normal life and in a moment's time, <u>ruined</u> everything I loved.*

Below, in fine black pen, Jude wrote his revision:

> *When I was seventeen and in full obedience to my heart's most urgent commands, I <u>was stepped</u> far from the pathway of normal life and in a moment's time, everything I loved <u>was ruined.</u>*

Jude Tholet learned a hard lesson about physical grammar at age seventeen: the noise of breaking bone was made distinct by the verb being transitive or intransitive.

I broke my leg made one sound. *My leg was broken* made entirely another.

If you broke a bone, it became an experience.

If your bone was broken, it became your identity.

Jude grew up knowing his father walked with crutches and occasionally used a wheelchair because he'd broken both legs. But it wasn't until his early teens that he learned Cleon Tholet didn't trip down some stairs, or slide into home base, or ski off a trail or foolishly jump off a roof to a swimming pool below. Cleon had no ownership in the verb. He did not break his legs.

His legs *were broken.*

While a political prisoner in Chile, Cleon endured six weeks of interrogation and torture in the Villa Grimaldi detention center. He was thrown back onto the streets of Santiago—literally thrown from the back of a jeep. The soldier driving ran him over, breaking every bone in his legs.

Cleon's bones were among thousands broken in detention centers where Chileans were tortured, beaten, maimed and murdered in the vicious tornado of government upheaval later known as Operation Condor. By fourteen, Jude knew that thousands of people in Chile did not disappear under General Augusto Pinochet.

They *were disappeared.*

Jude possessed an exact replica of his father's Y-chromosome. The sound of intransitive breakage and disappearance coded into every cell of his body from birth. Instead of being thrown into the street, he was held upright against a playground's chain link fence. In the role of a soldier with a jeep was a neighborhood boy with a baseball bat. The code name for an operation was replaced by a Chilean thug with the nickname El Cóndor.

Jude read Scott Spencer's novel while his broken leg healed. He tore out the first page of *Endless Love* with its provocative first sentence and edited the verbs to mirror his experience.

I was stepped far from the pathway of normal life and in a moment's time, everything I loved was ruined.

THE CHAIN LINK FENCE

*J*UDE SAT ON A picnic table, staring at the chain link fence surrounding one of the playgrounds in Vancouver's Central Park. Forest green diamonds stretched taut between the iron uprights.

In his high school days, the playground was enclosed by a dilapidated, rusty barrier with more gaps than links. It made a tired, saggy twang as Jude's body bounced off it, the night he was stepped far from the pathway of normal life. The metal went on complaining as he wrestled in the single-minded grip of two senior jocks. A third boy called Juan-Mateo Díaz stood looking on. A six-foot-five champion pitcher whose arm span earned him the nickname El Cóndor. His Louisville slugger was tucked under one mighty wing and a cloud of cigarette smoke circled his head.

Feet planted wide on the bench, elbows on knees, thirty-six-year-old Jude stared down the new fence around the old memories. He slid down from the table, walked the few steps to the approximate place where his best friend Fernando Paloma had sprawled that night, unconscious after Juan-Mateo bunted his head.

Jude's foot moved through the dry leaves and litter, looking for…

What? A sign? An artifact? Some fragment of forensic evidence they missed?

He walked to the fence and put his back against it, bouncing a little. His hands went to fists and shoved deeper in his jacket pockets, resisting the urge to extend along the chain links. Re-enact how the Condor's lieutenants had pinned him like a butterfly in a tray, holding him wide open.

He closed his eyes, remembering.

"I'm gonna kill you, faggot." Juan-Mateo spoke Spanish, which Jude understood perfectly.

I'm fucked, he thought, right before the Condor's fist smashed into his cheekbone. His brain exploded in yellow stars.

A punch to the stomach, making Jude double over, winded and nauseous.

"Your people should've stayed in Poland to burn, Jew-boy."

"Son de Austria, hueón," Jude said through his teeth.

They're from Austria, asshole.

He snapped his buckling legs together to narrowly avoid a knee to the balls. Juan-Mateo put a few more punches into his ribs and head, punctuating his threats.

"Why don't I finish the job they started on your old man? They broke his legs? Should've broken his skull, then his fucking *cola* son would've never been born, po?"

Jude's labored, heaving breaths froze in his lungs as Juan-Matteo picked up his bat and took a few practice swings.

"You like being on your knees so bad, faggot? Let's see if I can put you there permanently. Hold him."

"Hey, man, that's enough," one of the goons said, his voice shaking.

"Basta, Cóndor," the other cried. "This is out of hand."

"Shut up." The air whistled around the slice of the bat and terror flooded Jude's body. He knew exactly what was coming and only these two wingmen could save him.

"Don't let him do it," he said between heaving breaths.

"I said fucking *hold* him."

Jude left himself. His consciousness seized its papers and fled for the border of his body. From far above he watched El Cóndor feint a swing at Jude's head, then pull back and come in low instead. He heard one of the henchmen give a garbled heave at the visceral, crunching thud of the bat against Jude's left shin, followed by his own scream echoing across the empty park.

He would always claim, truthfully, that he didn't remember the pain of the moment, but he never forgot the sounds. The whistle of air around the bat. The gag. The scream. And the distinct noise made by intransitive breakage. The two guards dropped his arms and he crumpled to the ground, shrieking in a way he didn't know was possible. Moaning and vomiting as Juan-Mateo advanced, tapping the bat in the palm of his hand.

"Hey, cola. How'd you like this woody up your ass?"

Jude dug fingers into the cold dirt and tried hard to die. At the hospital, nurses would discover four of his nails were torn down to the quick and embedded with dirt and blood.

"I want to see you deep-throat this baby," Juan-Mateo said. "You'll suck dick even better after I take your teeth out."

As Jude tried harder to will himself out of existence, his blurred vision focused an instant on Fernando, still sprawled in the leaves. Jude was sure he was dead. If he'd known today would be the last time he'd kiss and touch Feño, he would've made more of it. Said more. Did more.

Had more.

Twenty years later, the adult Jude opened his eyes and looked toward the parking lot, from whence came his salvation that horrible night. A husband and wife walking their dog, innocently passing through the park just as the Condor hit his grand slam. They could've sensed the altercation, heard the shouts and screams and hurried away, minding their business, not wanting to get involved because technically the park was closed and they were trespassing. Instead, the good neighbors investigated. They crossed the parking lot and called, "Everything okay?"

Obviously nothing was close to okay. The Condor and his fledglings took off. The wife went running for a payphone. The husband yelled louder, "*Hey,*" and then, in an extraordinary and fortuitous turn of events, he let the trained German Shepherd off the leash and gave a terse command.

Jude didn't hear the order. He only saw a barking, snarling streak of tan-and-black fur *jump* the chain link fence and barrel at the Condor, taking him down like a linebacker.

Going into shock, Jude thought it was a wolf. His mother's name was Penelope, but all the women of the Chilean ex-pat community called her Lupita. The little she-wolf. Through the narrowing tunnel of his vision, Jude saw the endearment made manifest, coming to his rescue with a jaw full of snarling teeth and…

He woke up ten hours later in the recovery room of Burnaby Hospital, his lower leg pinned and screwed back together. Feño had a severe concussion but was expected to recover. The Condor was in custody and two police constables from VPD were waiting to talk to Jude.

It was over.

Or rather, that part of the ordeal was over.

Jude's mother liked to say parenthood was constantly trading one set of problems for a new set of problems. Jude was released from the hospital and another pair of crutches came to live in the Tholets' house, along with a new set of problems.

Neither he nor Feño went back to Killarney Secondary School. Jude was home-tutored while his leg knitted. Feño's family whisked him away to boarding school in Victoria—an elegant euphemism for a Christian mental health facility that specialized in conversion therapy. He wasn't allowed to call or write Jude, wasn't allowed visitors.

All that long, lonely summer, Jude stayed ensconced behind locked doors and windows as the civil suit against Juan-Mateo Díaz grew more contentious. The conservative, Catholic community slowly made the Condor's crime into Jude's character flaw. The contention turned to violence and the Tholets finally left in August, fleeing not only Vancouver but the country. Putting an international border between them and the ordeal. Starting over in Seattle.

Feño emerged from the facility in Victoria a converted man. To his credit, he came to Seattle to formally break up with Jude in person.

Jude never saw him again.

His leg healed and his gait smoothed out, but stress and anxiety liked to manifest in his left shinbone, making him limp when he was upset.

He never went back to Vancouver.

Until today.

He pushed off the chain link fence and walked toward his car, favoring his left leg.

THE WIDOW

*T*HE SUN STREAMED THROUGH the stained-glass windows of Corpus Christi Church, splashing over the preponderance of wood and emitting the dry, baked aroma of a sauna. It mixed with the sickly-sweet smell of the lilies and carnations heaped on Fernando Paloma's casket. A pregnant woman in the pew ahead of Jude's finally slipped out for fresh air, a tissue pressed to her mouth.

The priest droned. Feño's stepfather read the eulogy. Communion was taken. A hymn warbled. Jude sat tight and still in his pew.

You can go, his conscience told him. *The record reflects your presence. You don't have to stay any longer.*

But some stubborn resolve sat in his lap, determined to see this through to the end. Committed to finishing strong, Jude flung his ego on the altar of mercy and went down the receiving line after the service. He shook the widow's hand and introduced himself, adding, "Feño was my best friend in high school."

The entire line went silent.

I told you to go, his conscience reminded him.

"Oh, you're Jude," the widow said. She was a California blonde, her red-rimmed eyes the thin blue of an early spring day. Cold and sullen on top of the unspoken question: *So you're the one who used to fuck my husband?*

"Yes, I am," Jude said. "I'm so sorry for your loss."

"Move along, Tholet," Feño's stepfather said in Spanish.

No Paloma offered to shake hands as Jude moved along. The eldest son, Hernán, ignored him. Middle son Patricio did some macho posturing, muttering loudly, "You got some nerve showing your face here, cola." The woman next to him put a calming hand on his arm, glaring at Jude for this intrusive disturbance. Jude murmured his condolences down the rest of the line and exited the church, limping a little.

Made it.

Done, his conscience echoed. *You don't have to do this anymore.*

This time, he believed it.

"Jude?"

He turned to see a woman in a black dress with a piece of black lace pinned to her hair.

"Jude, is that you?"

He raised a hand, brows furrowed at the name dangling just out of his reach.

"I'm Feño's cousin. Brenda Salazar. I mean Brenda—"

"Ronco," Jude said, as a seventh-grade taunt elbowed him in the back.

Brenda Ronco. Rhymes with bucking bronco.

A tired shame winced behind his eyes, remembering Brenda was one of the few decent members of the Paloma clan. She gave him a plump, warm hug. Her hand rubbed a firm circle on his back and her presence restored order in the world. Even her perfume evoked a common-sense compassion.

Eau de Just Be Nice.

"I haven't seen you since…" Her hand turned over in the air.

"Since the time of which we will not speak?"

"Give or take a few days."

"I haven't been back here, no."

"At all?"

"Well, once or twice to sign legal paperwork. You know." His own hand made a circle in the air.

She switched to Spanish. "But you came back for Feño."

"For closure."

She sighed. "As you can see, forgiveness runs deep in my extended family."

"I did nothing that warrants forgiveness," Jude said, a little too sharply.

"I know."

"Sorry, Bren. That wasn't directed at you."

"I understand."

"Emotional day."

"Of course," she said, touching his arm. "They treated you like shit in there, and for what purpose? Feño is still dead. God, what a fucking waste."

"Mm."

"Some people are incapable of evolving," Brenda said, with a glance over her shoulder. "Emotional Neanderthals banging rocks together."

"It's all fear-based," Jude said. "Gay cooties in the presence of the children. And I guarantee at least one macho prick in there got a hand job from a buddy in college and liked it."

Brenda's smile cringed.

"Sorry," he said again. "I think I left my filter in the pew."

"Except you're right," she said. "I mean, I don't know about the hand job thing, but it's definitely fear-based. It takes so much *effort*. Good lord, the time and energy spent hating, they could… I don't know, build houses or something." Another big sigh and she bit her lip, hesitating.

"What?" Jude said.

"Where are you living now?"

"Seattle."

"Do you still play piano?"

"I'm a company pianist with Pacific Northwest Ballet."

"Oh, that's great," she said. "You were so talented. Are so talented, I mean. I left my brain in the pew."

He laughed. "The game I used to have keeps getting better."

"I remember the best parties were always at a house with a piano and you would play and play. Everyone gathered around like it was an Irish pub, shit-faced and singing."

Again, Brenda's face twitched, hesitating around something she obviously wanted to say.

"Tell me," Jude said.

"Feño was never the same after the conversion therapy."

A bitter chuckle snorted out his nose. "I think that's the purpose of conversion therapy."

Her face flushed.

Would you knock it off, he chided himself. *She's being kind and you're throwing it back in her face.*

"He always struck me as a man on auto-pilot," Brenda said. "Like he could take it or leave it. Even when he went into remission those couple of years, he had none of the life-is-short-embrace-every-minute attitude. When he relapsed, he could've participated in a clinical trial for a new drug regimen. He chose hospice instead. He was just *done*."

"It's hard work being straight when you're gay," Jude said.

God, man, would you just shut up?

Brenda took his hand. "I'm so sorry."

Jude was helpless to answer. He could only nod, lips rolled in tight.

"Nobody in there will say it but I will, Jude. You were the love of his life."

He squeezed her fingers. "Thank you."

HE CAME ALL THIS way and if he was going to do it, he might as well fucking do it. So he left Corpus Christi and drove past Killarney Secondary School, which was fat with new wings, sleek with renovations and depressingly unrecognizable. He went down Ormidale Street to see his old home. A spot at the curb beckoned, so he parked and got out to get a good look.

Butter yellow in his day, the house had faded to a tired buff, its white woodwork shabby and peeling. A low, wrought iron fence surrounded the yard and within, all Penny Tholet's beautiful gardens had gone to grass and weeds. Jude looked up over the porch's gable to his bedroom window, peering through the curtained glass to his youth.

"Can I help you?"

Jude jumped in his shoes and spun to face a woman walking a dog, her brow pulled tight and her posture defensive. He moved quickly away from what was obviously her front walk.

"Hi," he said. "I used to live here. I was just looking and remembering."

"Oh," she said, still wary. "Long time away?"

"Twenty years. It looks smaller. I think because those trees are bigger."

She smiled now. "And you're bigger."

"That, too. Do you mind if I take a picture to show my parents?"

She didn't. She didn't invite him in, and if she had, he would've politely refused. Nothing he needed was in the house.

All clues are on the ground, he thought, walking down the sidewalk a few steps. He looked back to ascertain the woman had gone inside, then reversed course, eyes sweeping the curb, searching for the exact place his father's car had been parked one ordinary morning. Or rather, the new ordinary: Cleon taking Jude to physical therapy instead of school. Jude being schooled at home because he'd been outed by El Cóndor and now he had a broken leg and a target on his back. His house transformed into a bullseye's center circle and rare was the day it didn't take a hit. Death threats in the mailbox. Promises by phone to break Jude's other leg. Bricks through the windows. Tires slashed. Swastikas spray-painted across the driveway. Homophobic slurs in English and Spanish left on the garage door.

No fresh graffiti was visible that newly ordinary morning. Only the merest trace of royal blue letters power-washed away by Cleon. A whispered *faggot* echoing off the concrete.

Cleon opened the passenger door and took Jude's crutches. Jude sat sideways, then pivoted and eased in his casted left leg, then his good right one. Cleon shut the door. He opened the back door, put the crutches on the seat, shut the door. He came around to the driver's side and got in, easing his own bum legs behind the steering wheel and stowing his cane. He started the engine. Because it was humid, he turned on the A/C. Because it was rainy, he flipped the wipers. Because the glass was grimy with damp pollen, leaf matter and bird droppings, he pulled the wand to spray some washer fluid.

And then the windshield was covered with blood.

"What the…" Not understanding, Cleon pulled the wand again. More blood spurted. The wipers scraped arches through the viscous red and flung it aside, splashing it onto the hood, the sidewalk and the street. Still not understanding, Cleon pulled the wand a third time and now Jude shouted, "Papi, *stop.*"

He went on crying out. He couldn't stop saying stop. The word rolled over and over in his screaming mouth as he fell sideways in his seat, curled on the armrest howling and sobbing, arms over his head and hands clawing at his temples, yanking at his hair. Beside him, Cleon hunched over the wheel, fists pounding the rim in time to Jude's "Stop…stop…stop."

Stop. You don't have to do this anymore. You're done.

Just stop.

The police lab determined it was pig blood. Not human. Not infected with HIV, as a note taped to the inside of the hood attested. Detectives couldn't pick up any fingerprints from the note or the car. It was a clean, dirty job.

Jude's eyes searched the street, the curb, the sidewalk, but he found no traces of blood or spray paint. A combination of time, rain and scrubbing had erased the evidence from the ground.

He got back in his car and took a last look down the street through his clean windshield. His fingers hesitated around the control wand, then he gently pulled it forward, exhaling as clear wiper fluid sprayed onto the glass.

"All gone," he said softly. "You're done."

He drove through the housing co-op on School Avenue. The unit where Feño lived was completely concealed by trees and shrubbery. *Nothing to see here,* it told him. He turned down the street where his friend Hewan Bourjini once lived. Trees had been cut down on the property and the house begged to be noticed.

See me, it shouted, as Jude slowed the car to take a picture, which he texted to Hewan:

Greetings from 666 Memory Lane.

She replied with a picture of Linda Blair in *The Exorcist,* her head poised atop her shoulder blades and spewing green vomit.

My sentiments exactly, Jude replied.

23

Are you OK? Tell the truth.

I'm all kinds of OK. Promise.

At work but call the shit out of me tonight. I want to hear all the pukey details. XOXO.

He got a milkshake at Tomlinson's Café because it would be illegal not to. With the thick icy taste of chocolate in his mouth, he drove back to Central Park, locked the car and took a certain trail into the woods. He had one last thing to check off his list.

Walls of Douglas fir, western hemlock and western red cedar closed in. Taller, thicker and denser than he remembered. He skirted clumps of blackberry bushes and waded through sword ferns. His hand trailed across rough bark while his eyes scanned the trunks. His ears full of Feño's wicked promise: *I'm going to make you come against every one of these trees.*

After each conquest, Feño took his pocketknife and carved *J/F* in the bark.

He was your dear friend.

He was never the same.

You were the love of his life.

And he was done.

Jude searched and searched for their memorials. Just when he thought they'd all been culled or swallowed up, he found one.

"Hey," he said softly, feeling his smile stretch wide and true. "Here you are."

His fingers traced the letters, now twenty rings farther from the tree's center.

It's all right, he thought.

You're done. You don't have to do this anymore. Neither of us do.

We can both go back home and be ourselves now.

We're free to move on.

❧

HE CROSSED THE BORDER, then stopped in Blaine to get gas and text his mother.

All is well and uneventful, he typed. *Safe on this side again.*

Thank you for letting us know, Penny replied. *Do you still want to come for dinner, is it too much?*

No, not at all. I want to.

Come around seven then. Drive safe, querido. I'm proud of you for going.

Jude slid behind the wheel, put in his ear set and dialed his therapist's number. He got Phil's voicemail and left a message as he pulled back onto the road.

"Just checking in," he said. "As promised. I'm on my way home. Alive and intact. Got some token shit from the family, which I'm not taking personally. Got some unexpected kindness from an old classmate, which I'm taking with me. So... Honestly, it was all kind of anti-climactic. I came, I saw, I brooded. I visited all the proverbial graves. I feel all right. Pretty good, actually. But you know me, my most intense emotions run on a forty-eight-hour delay, so I will still see you Monday morning. As promised. Ciao."

He turned on the radio. The miles fell away behind him and he felt more than pretty good. A warm peace had coiled up in his chest, both strange and familiar, like a classmate whose face you knew but name you'd forgotten.

He breathed in deeply, positive the oxygen was reaching new parts of his lungs and stomach.

I feel good.

The exhale was tight with anticipation.

I feel ready.

It's time. Let's go. Let's do it.

His eyes glanced to the empty passenger seat, imagining a travel companion. His fingers drew along his thigh, conjuring a hand to hold. He thought about a face to go with the hand and for once, it wasn't Feño's face. Or any of the boyfriends who came in and out of Jude's life, leaving no impression and making no difference. He drew another deep breath, exhaled and thought about the iconic news footage from the fall of the Berlin Wall. A crane lifting out a section of the notorious barrier and opening up the world. Hands reaching across, bodies slipping through. One story ended and a thousand new ones begun, because the winds of change blew and it was time.

It's time.

He twined fingers with his invisible passenger, wanting someone. Every breath taken, a brick in his wall loosened, opening to someone. Every mile he put between him and Vancouver was a hand he reached toward the possibility of someone.

I want someone.

His phone chimed and he quickly glanced at the text from Phil: **Got VM, see you Monday. Looking forward to it.**

"So am I," Jude said to his crystal-clear windshield, holding hands with the future.

Looking forward and moving on.

THE SHE-WOLF

*O*N THE MORNING OF October 17, 1973, Cleon Tholet was arrested on the streets of Santiago. After being detained five days at the Estadio de Chile, soldiers transferred him to the Villa Grimaldi detention center, where he endured six weeks of brutal interrogation and torture. When he was transported again, this time to the Estadio Nacional, he weighed one hundred and fifteen pounds and his dark hair had gone the color of dust. Manhandled once more into an army jeep, he was driven around for an hour, then dumped onto the street in Santiago's red-light district.

No one dared come to his aid as soldiers administered one final beating. Prostitutes, madams and pimps peeked from behind doors and windows as Pinochet's men climbed back into their jeep and started the engine. They drove off, not around Cleon's body, but over it, breaking every bone in both his legs.

As a boy, Jude couldn't believe his father didn't remember the moment when he was crushed beneath the wheels. Of course, the very young couldn't grasp how trauma rearranged memory. How the human brain consciously decided when to cover its eyes and turn away from certain events, refusing to let them be written in books of life. Jude didn't understand until his own leg was broken and his mind turned its back and refused to acknowledge. Overnight, his bond with Cleon deepened past filial to the profound devotion of war mates.

"So we're compañeros now," Jude said, while still in the hospital recovery room.

"Yes." Cleon gathered him in arms and held him tight. "We are."

It was all that could be said and at that moment, all Jude needed to hear. Beyond Cleon's embrace, he sensed the plate armor of his mother, sister and brother sliding into place, rolling the five Tholets into a tight ball, like an armadillo. Jude at the center, cloaked in the unique courage and resilience of his people. Keenly aware they would kill for him, and he for them, and from now on, family was the only thing he could trust in the world.

⌒

OUT OF CLEON'S SIX complicated, messy fractures, all but the right tibia knitted properly back together. The right shin bone rejected internal fixation with titanium screws, so doctors backed everything out and did an external fixation, pinning the bone from the outside in.

The leg stubbornly resisted skin grafts and electromagnetic bone stimulation. It sulked through physical therapy and its painful mood swings were more unpredictable than a heartbroken teenager's. A glutton for attention, the tibia got into a co-dependent relationship with Cleon's ankle, then invited his knee for a threesome, which made his hip jealous. After forty years of managing the orgy of chronic pain, Cleon took the extreme measure of having his hopeless limb amputated below the knee, followed by a double hip replacement.

"Look at that now," he said to Jude, six weeks post-surgery. Standing on his left foot, he flexed and extended his right knee, showing off his new prosthetic.

"Papi, that is one handsome leg," Jude said, bending to touch the glossy black plastic that made up the calf. "Look at that, they even give you some muscle definition."

"I can get it customized," Cleon said. "I found websites that will airbrush anything you want on it."

"What, like lightning bolts?"

"Why not? Look at the range." Still holding Jude's shoulder, he made circles with his calf, clockwise and counter. The black plastic smoothed into a titanium ankle that fitted into a false foot, smartly dressed in a tennis sock and Nike sneaker.

"How's the knee feel?"

"Fantastic."

"You're like the bionic man."

"And, wait for it…" Cleon let go of Jude's shoulder and put all his weight on his false foot. Arms extended, he lifted his left foot off the floor and balanced. Only a couple seconds before he grabbed onto Jude again. "I held it longer at therapy."

"I believe you. This is amazing. Let me see you walk. Give me your best runway."

Cleon walked slowly down the little hall. The lateral tilt in his hips would never straighten out. He would always limp, but the gait on the artificial leg was confident. He pivoted slowly to face Jude again, ran a hand through his white hair and raised one eyebrow.

"Caliente," Jude said. "Muy macho."

"Now we can both set off alarms at the airport."

Jude laughed. He had an intramedullary nail and four screws in his own leg. Some TSA agents at Sea-Tac knew him by name.

Penny Tholet came around the corner and kissed Jude. "No more showing off," she said, putting Cleon's cane in his hand. "Rest it. You need to ice?"

"I need nothing." Cleon's hand threaded through Jude's hair and gave his head a little shake. "It all went okay today?"

"It went fine. I think I left a lot of shit behind, too."

"Good, good, come sit." He tucked his hand around Jude's elbow and pumped the cane like a drum major as they walked, until Penny's glare made him set the tip down.

They sat in the kitchen, drinking wine and nibbling. They all spoke Spanish: Cleon with the mushy accent of a Chilean native, Penny with the inflection of a Western Canadian who learned the language as a young adult, and Jude's weird blend of the two. Out and about in the world, he made his Spanish sit up straight and behave, but at his mother's kitchen table, he let it be a mess.

"How did the house look?" Penny said.

"Old," Jude said. "You could barely see it from the road because all those pines grew old, too."

"Good," Cleon said. "Let it stay hidden."

He leaned to scoop up Walter, his chihuahua, and daintily fed him a cracker. Sitting in Cleon's lap, the little dog was even more miniaturized. Cleon's broad shoulders and barrel chest overflowed the kitchen chair. He was top-heavy by design, compensating his weak and painful legs by maximizing his upper body strength. One of Jude's earliest memories was watching Cleon do wheelchair pull-ups in their detached garage. Strapped into the seat, hoisting himself aloft, wheels and all.

Jude would hold his father's feet while he did pushups on his thumbs. Cleon could crack walnuts in one palm. His torso was magnificent when clothed and in the summer months, he kept himself carefully concealed. He wore long shorts to the pool or beach, way before jams became popular. The length hid scars where leg bones were broken by jeep wheels, then re-broken by doctors. A perpetual T-shirt hid the livid marks from chains and live wires on his chest and back.

Jude learned both the art of physique and the art of obscurity at his father's knee. He worked out obsessively after his attack and concealed the provenance of his own scarred leg with fish tales instead of clothing. A motorcycle accident (he didn't own a bike). A skiing mishap (he didn't ski). A skydiving incident (oddly, the fib most people took at face value).

"Are you ashamed of what happened to you?" his therapist asked.

"No," Jude said. "It's just such a drag to explain. Literally. I don't like dragging all that shit into the open and talking about it. It isn't pleasant for anyone involved."

"But it's the truth."

"I'll tell that truth to the people who need to know it."

Phil looked steadily at him. "While you make sure those people are few and far-between."

Fucking Phil. He'd been shrinking Jude's head since Jude was seventeen. Before Cleon and Penny searched real estate listings in Seattle, they researched adolescent psychologists who specialized in trauma. Jude had an appointment before the moving van even arrived. The first two therapists were duds but something clicked with Phil. Jude went to him once a week his entire senior year of high school. Every three months during college. Then as needed in his adult years. Phil was the one non-family member Jude was utterly, brutally honest with. Phil knew all Jude's tricks and tactics and bullshit. He let Jude get away with zippity-doo-dah.

Which was a blessing in its own sucky, cursed way.

"Did you see anyone else you know?" Penny asked.

"Nobody," Jude said. "But I wasn't looking too hard."

She patted his hand. She'd recently taken the plunge and cut her hair off. The pixie cut looked fabulous on her, but her hand kept going nervously to the back of her neck, where her own scar from Chile was now revealed. A long, raised welt ran from behind one ear almost to her nape, the souvenir of a soldier's rifle butt. At least she thought it was a rifle butt. She was hit from behind and the blow sent her into early labor with Jude.

Like her son and husband, Penny had a significant gap in her memory. Only a few fragments of Jude's birth stayed on the record, recollections that languished as the years went by. Inwardly, Jude regarded the scar with a mix of pride and awe. Out loud, he teased Penny about not remembering and she'd shrug it off, quipping, "At least the son of a bitch saved me an anesthesia bill."

Lucille Penelope Cambie was plump and round-faced, with the same sweet, tilted-chin serenity as the Queen Mum. She loathed her first name and permitted only a select few to acknowledge its existence. Growing up bright and shiny in Vancouver, she was Penny. During her life as a civil servant in Chile, her circle of *Santiaguinos* detected the ferocity beneath the placid exterior, and they shortened Penelope to Lupita—the little wolf.

It was Lupita who survived Pinochet's coup, fighting for her disappeared mate and her one vulnerable cub, engineering their flight back to Vancouver. As more and more Chileans fled the murderous regime, the British Columbian port city amassed a thriving ex-pat community and Lupita became queen of a new pack. Waiting at the airport, baby Jude in a stroller, welcoming refugees off planes. Organizing. Administrating. Advocating. Settling. Devoted to the people of her adopted country with her flat-toned Spanish and every drop of her Anglo-Saxon blood.

When the Chilean community turned against the Tholets in the wake of Jude's attack, the family took it hard, but the She-Wolf took it hardest. The second coup on her life broke the floor from under her feet and she spent two weeks at Swedish Behavior Health in Ballard, Washington. It took months for her to regain her footing as Penny. Never again wanting to be called Lupita by anyone. She recovered her shiny sweetness, but it was the pale green of aged copper, weathered by the elements and underlaid with the tiniest current of mistrust. A sadness lingered behind her eyes, but it could quickly turn to a snarl if she felt her family was being threatened.

She was never the same, Jude understated.

But which of us was?

The front door exploded open. "Hello," his sister yodeled over the stamp of wet boots.

Jude smiled, his question answered.

THE NOUNS

*S*ERENA THOLET'S REAL NAME was Suzanne. She became Serena when it became evident nothing, absolutely nothing phased this extraordinary child. She was six when a neighbor's house caught fire on Ormidale Street. The blaze spread and consumed the Tholets' backyard shed and Serena's playhouse. Amidst the chaos, Serena stood at a distance, placidly watching the firefighters, and said to the chief, "Well, this is a revolting development."

It became one of the family's mottoes. When life threw a curveball or thrust a wrench in the gears, a Tholet would sigh and declare, "Well, this is a revolting development."

Serena was the one you wanted on the scene of an accident, during a crisis, in the midst of tragedy. She worked a suicide hotline in college, volunteered in New Orleans after Hurricane Katrina, and received a citizen's citation from the mayor of Seattle when she helped a woman deliver her baby on a bus.

She swept into the kitchen, followed by her new boyfriend, Giosué. Jude's curiosity sat up. He hadn't yet met this Italian beau, but he was already a little obsessed with the name Giosué.

Jossuway.

Now that was a name that would sound good in the dark. And the owner was rather easy on the eyes, too.

Jude had a habit of crushing on his sister's boyfriends.

"Hey, Jude," Serena said, throwing arms around him. "Don't make it suck."

"Nice 'shmere," he said, caressing the back of her cashmere sweater. "Can I borrow it?"

"Get your own," she said. "Mami, I saw stork balloons on the Nouns' porch, did they have another baby?"

"They didn't have a giraffe."

"Who are the Nouns?" Giosué asked.

"Neighbors down the street," Jude said. "We call them the Nouns because they name their kids things. Liberty. Courage."

"Are those boys or girls?"

"Girls."

"Nation and Pride" Penny said. "Those are boys."

"What's the newest one?" Serena asked.

"Boy," Penny said. "Rodeo."

"Rodeo's not a bad name, actually," Jude said.

"Yeah, for one of the Village People," Serena said, pouring two more glasses of wine.

"Ridiculous names," Cleon said. "All of them. If their surname were a simple noun, too, maybe they'd work. Rodeo Brown. Nation Green."

"Those are adjectives, Papi."

"Their last name is Wiesnewski, for fuck's sake," Cleon cried. "Who names their kid Rodeo Wiesnewski? Excuse my French," he said to Giosué, whose laughter and wine were about to come out his nose.

"We're kind of a weird bunch," Jude said, handing him a napkin.

"Well," Serena said, rummaging in her big shoulder bag. "Speaking of family and weirdness and names, I have a surprise."

She pulled out four boxes, each emblazoned with the logo of a popular ancestry website. "I bid on them at a silent auction. It'll be fun."

"What do these do?" Cleon said, turning the box over in his hands.

"DNA testing," Jude said. "You find out your ethnic heritage."

"I'm Jewish."

"Ah, but how much Jewish?" Serena said.

Cleon held a hand level with his eyes. "This much?"

Penny was breaking the seal on her box. "Well, we already know I'm an homogenized Anglo-Saxon," she said. "Will this tell me how many shades of white I am?"

"To the fraction," Serena said.

"My family took one recently," Giosué said.

"Let me guess," Jude said. "You're Irish."

"Dude, my mother had some serious explaining to do."

Jude laughed. He loved a player. And *dude* in an Italian accent was seriously adorable.

"I'm joking," Giosué said. "No surprises. We're an old Sephardic family."

"From Venice," Serena said. "They do a big reunion every year. Our flight is already booked."

Giosué winked at Jude. "She only wants me for Venice."

"Well, I only want you for Venice, too."

The dude was nice enough to blush.

Serena opened her laptop on the table. "I made an account this afternoon. I have to make a tree for us and attach the kit numbers."

Cleon held up the tiny, sealed test tube. "Is this for sperm?"

Penny swatted him.

Jude held up his. "This could get messy."

"I needed two," Giosué said.

"Smartasses," Serena muttered above her clicking fingers. "It's for your spit. Fill it up to the line."

"I don't know if I can salivate on command," Cleon said, cracking the seal on his.

"I'm gay, I have to salivate on command," Jude said.

Penny swatted him.

"Just fill the damn tubes," Serena said. "Giosué, start reading me off the kit numbers."

"This is like a reverse toast," Jude said, trying to be suave as he let the saliva drip into the vial.

"To family," Cleon said, spitting.

THEY TOOK THEIR DRINKS in the living room where Cleon could put his leg up and ice his hamstring. Giosué, wine glass in hand, prowled the bookshelves and artwork before examining the magnificent gallery of family photos on one wall. Jude watched him draw a pair of reading glasses from his inside pocket and peer closer, taking in sepia portraits, old black-and-whites and modern digital photos.

Serena leaned to refill Jude's glass. "Stop fucking him with your eyes," she murmured in Spanish.

"Can't," Jude said. "Does he have a brother?"

"None who crave dick."

"Challenge accepted."

She swatted him. It was one of those nights when he'd leave his parents' house with bruised arms.

"Where were your Jewish relatives from?" Giosué asked Cleon.

"France a few hundred years ago. Migrated to Italy after they were thrown out by the reigning prick du jour."

"What part?"

"Place called Asti. In the northwest."

"I know Asti, sure. Your parents were born there?"

"My father, yes, but he lived in Vienna most of his life. That's him there." Cleon pointed. "No, the next one over."

Giosué studied the formal portrait of Jude's paternal grandfather. Born Feivel Tholet in Asti, he moved with his family to Vienna in his teens, where he became Felix Tholet. Both he and his brother, Louis, attended the University of Vienna, Louis to study art and Felix to study botany.

"They pursued the most genteel and useless of all genteel and useless degrees," Cleon said. "And both of them became rich men."

Felix eventually became the assistant director of the Botanical Gardens while Louis became a renowned sculptor. Felix married while Louis remained a bachelor.

"Bachelor in the biblical sense," Jude said. "Meaning he was gay."

The Anschluss came in March of 1938 and Austria was absorbed into Nazi Germany. By May, the Nuremberg Laws restricting Jewish business were passed. Felix was ousted from his role at the Gardens. Reading the writing on the walls, the Tholets fled to France, narrowly missing Kristallnacht.

"They couldn't have been safe there long," Giosué said. "Nazis invaded France, when, nineteen forty?"

"In June," Cleon said. "Round-ups began in May forty-one. Louis was arrested and my parents fled to Spain on false papers. They were there only a short time before they immigrated to South America."

"You were born in Spain or Chile?"

"Chile. In forty-two."

He was registered with Santiago's civil clerk as Carlos Luis, but neither the names nor their diminutives settled on him. Friends and family alternated between Carlín and León until his Uncle Louis dubbed him Cleón, which stuck forever.

"He ditched the accent mark when he came to Canada," Serena said. "Now it's Cleon, rhymes with neon."

"But enough about me," Cleon said, nodding his chin toward Penny. "Talk about the Canadian. She's the interesting one."

"How did you end up in Chile?" Giosué asked.

"My father was an engineer," she said. "He worked on a lot of international projects. After my mother died, I wanted a change of scene. Dad was working on the Pont Baldy dam in France, so I went with him and finished high school there. Then he took a job with the Franco-Chilean consortium that designed Santiago's metro system, and I tagged along."

Penny fell in love with Chile's capital city, completed her university degree and sat the civil service exam to land an administrative job at the Canadian embassy.

"She met Dad on the bus to work," Serena said. "They went to lunch and fell in love."

"Who does that?" Jude said.

"When you know, you know," Penny said.

"Really, that was it?" Giosué said. "One date and you knew?"

"Maybe two," Cleon said.

"Three," Penny said, now perched on the arm of his chair. "I definitely knew by that dinner at La Jonda."

"That unfinished dinner."

She swatted him.

"They went to lunch twice, they went to dinner, they fell in love and got married," Serena said. "Piece of cake."

"Then Pinochet took over," Cleon said. "And that was the end of cake."

"What a revolting development," Serena said.

A pause as Giosué judged the temperature of this opened furnace. "Is it true," he said slowly, "that Pinochet staged his coup on September eleventh?"

"Yes," Penny said. "Twenty-eight years to the day before Nine-Eleven in the States."

Giosué looked at Jude. "You must've been a baby when Pinochet took over, no?"

"Not even. I was born two months after, in November of seventy-three."

"I see." He drained the dregs of his wine and chewed it thoughtfully. "It's incredible. I mean, your family flees Nazi Germany for Chile. Then flees Pinochet's Chile for Canada. You move to the States and then, in a manner of speaking, you experience a third coup on Nine-Eleven. It's crazy."

The Tholets nodded as one, none of them choosing to mention 9/11 was their fourth coup.

It's such a drag, Jude thought, rubbing his left shin.

"When I first met Serena," Giosué said, in the chipper tone of an awkward subject change. "I pronounced your last name wrong. I was saying the T at the end."

"It's silent," Jude said. "Tholet. Rhymes with Swiss chalet."

"Oy vey," Serena said.

"Tell us you'll stay," Cleon said.

Giosué smiled. "Have a nice day."

"Olé olé olé." Penny stood up. "Let's eat."

THE SOCIAL POWER

*D*INNER STARTED WITH CEVICHE, from which Jude patiently picked out the cilantro.

"Give it to me," Serena said, holding her plate across. "Giosué doesn't like it either."

"Ugh, tastes like soap."

"Can't stand it," Jude said.

"Raw carrots taste like soap to me, too."

Jude pointed his fork at him. "Holy shit, yes."

"Did you know it's a genetic trait?" Serena asked.

"What?"

"Cilantro tasting like soap. It's a gene you have. Lots of taste preferences are genetic."

"Does your other brother like cilantro?" Giosué asked.

"It's difficult to know anything Aiden likes."

The sixth, empty chair at the table rolled its eyes, filling Jude with a wry guilt. He was tight as a knot with his sister, but his relationship with Aiden was complicatedly loose. Jude loved his little brother—of course he loved him, but only in the most general and fraternal of ways. Aiden belonged to Jude's tribe and if Aiden were in trouble, Jude would be there, he'd do anything. Which was the crux of the complication: unless Aiden was in trouble, which he never was, Jude had no motivation to be there and do.

"We don't really need each other," he told Phil once. "I love him because not loving him isn't an option. But he's not a personality I naturally gravitate toward."

They had nothing in common, no overlapping edges. Even if they had shared interests, Aiden's nature was to keep the world at arm's length and move in a universe of his own. He wasn't cold or cruel, he just seemed to be missing some essential wiring that made him *relatable.*

And yet, right when you wrote him off as an emotionless Vulcan, he shocked you. Jude woke up in the hospital after the Condor's attack to find Aiden sitting bedside, fast asleep with his head on the mattress by Jude's hip. His hand wrapped around Jude's wrist.

"He's been here two hours," a nurse whispered. "He won't leave."

Aiden didn't explain himself. He didn't ask questions, talk about the attack or how he felt about it. He simply posted himself at Jude's side and would not move.

Jude was in trouble and Aiden was there.

Thus Jude measured the relationship with his brother in intervals of cordial distance bordering on apathy, punctuated by intense moments of devotion and understanding. Aiden's work as an environmental researcher took him all over the world. Long stretches of time with no contact were the norm, but if something moved Aiden enough to reach out, Jude dropped everything and gave him his full attention. When Aiden retreated back behind his walls, Jude learned not to take it personally. He reached a point in his adult life where he accepted this was his brother's way and it would not change.

"Where is Aiden now anyway?" Serena asked.

"Last Skype call he was in the Galapagos Islands," Penny said.

Cleon shook his head. "He's back in Patagonia."

Serena patted him. "Of course, he let Papi know."

"He better." He pointed his fork at her. "And don't you dare not be where you say you are."

In their tender years, Cleon Tholet's children thought his vehement, obsessive need to know their whereabouts was just a weird dad-quirk. Penny wanted to know what they were doing, but Cleon only wanted to know *where.* He was the father who, if you didn't phone in to say where you were, called every single one of your friends or, worse, drove around the neighborhood looking.

"Just let him know," Penny said, after privileges were revoked or plans grounded. "It takes two seconds and does a world of good. When he isn't anxious, your life is beautiful."

Cleon did relax as his kids became adults and learned the root of his anxieties lay in the Villa Grimaldi: the long weeks separated from Penny, with no way to contact her. He didn't need a check-in between every point A and B, but he still liked to know their vacation itineraries and didn't rest until a call or text heralded safe arrival.

"You guys go sit," Serena said when they were done eating. "Jude and I will clear the table." Which was sibling-speak for *let's go in the kitchen and discuss my new boyfriend.*

"Isn't he delicious?" she whispered.

"Seems like a keeper."

Her expression turned wicked. "If you want him to eat out of your hand, go play some Billy Joel."

Jude laughed. "This is the first time you've given me permission to tempt one of your boyfriends."

"Because I'm a hundred percent sure of his persuasions."

"Challenge accepted."

A startled twitch in her face. "I will kill you."

"Dude, I'm kidding."

She whacked him with the dish towel.

"Again with the hitting. Stop *hitting* me."

"What, you going to tattle, little boy?"

"Mami," Jude cried, now backed against the refrigerator.

"Serena, stop hitting your brother," Penny called.

Jude grabbed the towel and yanked his sister into an armlock. "Ha. Who's your bitch now?"

"Let go."

"Tap out."

"Mami."

"You have to tap out, Serena," Penny called.

Serena tapped out and shoved Jude away. "Asshole."

"You love me."

"Go play."

Cleon and Penny had an upright piano that the humidity of Alki Beach was forever putting out of tune. Ears braced, Jude lifted the lid and played a few chords.

"Oh, don't make that face," Penny said. "I had it tuned last week."

Jude grimaced at her, then thanked Giosué, who set a cup of coffee on the piano's top.

"Serena told me you play in an orchestra?"

"Not quite," Jude said. "I'm a company pianist with Pacific Northwest Ballet."

"Oh. So you play when the dancers take class?"

"I started out as a classroom accompanist but now I'm what's called a rehearsal accompanist."

"Two extremely different skill sets," Serena said. "As Jude never tires of telling us."

"Do you ever get to perform?" Giosué asked.

"A few ballets have the piano onstage but for those, our principal pianist plays. I'd only go on if he were deathly ill. Which he never is, the son of a bitch."

"Well…" The Italian's expression narrowed and his voice dropped a tone. "I know people. I could make something happen. Some bad sushi, maybe."

Jude gave him a quick nod. "We'll talk."

"Play," Penny said.

He played "Penny Lane" because it was her favorite. Then he played "Let it Be" for Cleon.

AT AGE FOUR, JUDE was picking out tunes on the beat-up piano at the Chilean housing co-op. He started formal lessons at six. By eight, he was entering regional music competitions and winning. His talent was unquestionable, but it had no ambitions outside personal pleasure. He didn't want to be a pianist. He just wanted to play piano.

He was in middle school when he discovered the social power of music. He had lots of friends and was always invited to parties and events, but never felt quite included. Especially when his buddies started getting interested in girls, while Jude's interest was in his buddies. Sensing he was different in a potentially hazardous way, he kept to the fringes of school society, achieving a delicate balance of popular invisibility.

One night, he went to a house party where there was a piano. He touched the keys cautiously, half-expecting to be told not to, please, the host's parents would be pissed.

Nobody objected or even noticed. He sat down and because it was the holiday season and *A Charlie Brown Christmas* had just been on TV, he played Vince Guaraldi's iconic bass riff.

Head after head turned in his direction.

"Hey."

"Hey, man, cool."

"Charlie Brown."

"Play the rest of it."

"You know the rest of it?"

Suddenly he was surrounded. Suddenly his perfect pitch and musical memory and ability to play by ear, which seemed to be talents only adults appreciated, were cool.

"Hey, can you play Journey's 'Faithfully'?" a girl asked.

Sure, he could.

"You know 'Imagine?'"

He did.

"'Crocodile Rock.'"

"'We Are the Champions.'"

"'Come Sail Away.'"

The requests flew. Some songs asked for, others begged for, and a few thrown like gauntlets. He played them all and from then on, the piano was his calling card, his bodyguard and his manager. He didn't have to seek out company as long as a piano was present. As El Pianista, he was never without a topic of conversation. He could pick out a commercial jingle on the keys and create instant, smiling community.

Classical music would always be his first love, but in company he played pop, rock, show tunes and TV theme songs. People sat next to him on the bench, stood behind his shoulders, leaned on the piano top and sang.

"When I wasn't hiding in the closet, I was hiding under the piano," Jude told Phil.

"Well, there's a Freudian analyst's wet dream," Phil said, miming a horizontal keyboard across his lap. "The strong, solid barrier of wood and ivory hiding your genitals with definitive, black-and-white distinctions of tone and… Sorry, I forgot where I was going with that."

Fucking Phil.

⌐━━━━⌐

THE LAST NOTES OF "Let it Be" died away. Jude drank the rest of his coffee, then played the opening arpeggios of Billy Joel's "Summer, Highland Falls."

"Oh man," Giosué said behind him. "No *way*." He came to lean on the piano again, eyes wide and a smile of pure joy. "I love this song."

Jude winked, because the warm coil of *I want someone* was back in his chest and he wanted to flirt with it. He nodded encouragingly when Giosué sang the first line, shy and self-conscious, gaining confidence when Serena joined in. Jude played "Always a Woman" next, then Giosué asked for "Roberta" off *Streetlight Serenade.*

"Best tune about a hooker ever," Jude said.

"Now do your song," Penny said.

So he played "Hey, Jude," which he only enjoyed playing for a big group of people, the bigger the better. The song struggled with only three people singing. It didn't get under your skin and the sadness couldn't be made better. He stopped after the big build up into the falsetto scream.

"We don't need to na-na ourselves to death."

"Did you name him after the song?" Giosué asked Penny.

"His real name is Juleón. A young man who lived with us in Santiago came up with Jude as a nickname."

She took a picture down off the wall. In it, two men stood with arms around shoulders. One had his head thrown back, laughing. The other wore the smug expression of a well-timed joke.

"That's Ysidro," Penny said, indicating the laughing man. "He lived in the bungalow apartment on our property. He loved the Beatles. Didn't always understand the lyrics, but he loved their music."

"Who's this man with him?"

"His boyfriend. Tatán."

"Ah. Where are they now?"

"Disappeared," Jude said.

"Really?"

Penny raised and lowered one shoulder. "We've never been able to find out. Both men lived with us because they were estranged from their families. We had no next of kin to contact."

"I'm sorry," Giosué said, running his thumb along the edge of the frame. "Did you lose many friends?"

"We lost nearly everything," she said. "We boarded the ship in Valparaiso with a couple suitcases of clothes and a box or two."

"Jesus Christ."

Penny smiled at the Italian. "It's only stuff. I got on the ship with Cleon and the baby, that's all I cared about."

"But still..." Giosué shook his head. "It's an incredible story. Have you ever been back to Chile?"

"Never."

"No desire to," Cleon said. "Too many ghosts."

Sitting with his leg up and Walter in the crook of his arm, Cleon looked tired. His tank always dumped its fuel abruptly in the evenings and though he remained pleasantly attentive, he said less and less. The light from the lamp backlit his soft, sleepy face and shone through his white hair. Giving him a weird transparency that made the coil of peace in Jude's heart tighten. Soon it would be a serpent, intent on squeezing all his newly cultivated joy into pieces. His most extreme emotions were on a forty-eight-hour delay and the clock was ticking.

He sought comfort in the keys again, thinking it was a good thing he had that appointment with Phil on Monday morning.

THE AIRPORT

*A*S SHE WASHED THE last of the dessert plates and coffee cups, Penny Tholet kept turning her head into her shirt collar. Giosué's aftershave lingered in the fabric from when he hugged her goodbye. His questions lingered in the living room, too, still posed thoughtfully in front of the gallery of family photos.

"Pen, come see this," Cleon called.

"I thought you went to bed?"

"I just checked my email and Aiden sent me something."

"Our Aiden?" Penny wiped off her hands, interested. Any missive coming from their reclusive younger son was something of an event.

Cleon sat at the desk in a nook of the bungalow's living room, splashed with blue light from the computer monitor. Penny slid arms around him from behind, pressing her cheek to his. His stubble pricked her skin as her eyes swept the screen, brows furrowing as she read Aiden's typically terse intro—*Hey, thought this was weird*—followed by an article from the *Vancouver Sun.*

> *Groundbreaking Ceremony Set for Park Renovation Project*
>
> *The City of Vancouver is gearing up for the playground renovation of Central Park with a special groundbreaking ceremony.*
>
> *The celebration is to introduce the plans for the new skate park, running trails, bike path and playground equipment. Molinero Construction—a family-owned business in Vancouver for nearly forty years—both financed and designed the project. Upon completion, the park will be renamed Fernando Paloma Memorial Park, in honor of the owner's stepson who died of cancer last week.*
>
> *Mayor Edward Sullivan, along with City Manager Lorenzo Acevedo and other officials, will be in attendance to commemorate the breaking of ground.*

"The new playground design will enhance the current park environment, while providing safe and challenging play and community building opportunities for residents and visitors alike," said Mayor Sullivan in a press release.

"It's a tribute to everything our brother Feño was," said Fernando Paloma's older brothers Hernán and Patricio. "An incredible athlete. A hardworking man. Amazing husband and father."

"Feño never showed any weakness," said Andrea Molinero, the company owner and Fernando's stepfather. "He was strong right until the end of his life, devoted to his family and God."

"Methinks the brothers doth protest too much," Cleon said. "Athlete. Man. Husband. Father."

"Strong until the end. No weakness."

"Jesus Christ, even in death, they're trying to make him something he's not. They should name it Fernando Paloma Was Straight Park."

Beneath the copy was a color rendering of the planned renovations. Penny sucked her teeth, noting the new playground would be located clear on the other side of the park from where Feño and Jude were attacked by Juan-Mateo Díaz in 1990. Andrea Molinero made sure the equipment and trails would be safely distanced and unsullied by the disgraceful love affair in which he'd declared Jude predator and Feño innocent prey.

They were both targeted, Penny thought, the old anger licking at the edges of her vision. Every time she thought of her son and his lover walking out of the woods, no doubt tousled with sex and secrecy, and into the Condor's ambush, her stomach turned over.

"It was what you'd call a revolting development," Jude said later. Much, much later when he could make ironic comments and even joke about the night his leg was broken.

Beneath the landscape rendering were two black-and-white photographs. A formal yearbook portrait of Feño Paloma next to a candid shot of him with his wife and two children.

The adult Feño was a stranger to Penny, but she recognized the boy in the yearbook photo. The handsome face was inextricably tangled with viscous, vivid memories of their last, harrowing year in Vancouver. And tangled up even tighter with Jude.

BY MAY OF 1974, eight months after Pinochet's coup, Canada had issued over a thousand VISAs to Chilean refugees. The earliest arrivals in Vancouver were either politically prescient or privy to information that let them slip out before Pinochet's coup. Next came those who managed to bash their way out via embassies and consulates, or flee across borders, hidden in cars and trucks. Some made their way to the coast and escaped by boat. Their own boats, or else they obtained or bribed passage on a foreign vessel. In some dramatic accounts, exiles stole the first pleasure craft they saw and weighed anchor, sailing up the coast to Peru and never looking back.

Vancouver's ex-pat community memorized Chilean airline schedules and went in groups to the airport to welcome refugees. They shuttled them to hotels provided by the government. They obtained medical attention for the tortured, the sick, the traumatized. Passed out pamphlets and guides in Spanish for the newcomers to find their way around the city. Lists of phone numbers were shared so exiles could call for a ride or a translator.

Where Penny went, Jude followed. From sling to stroller to toddling feet, he was at her side during meetings and demonstrations and events. A sparkling, tender-hearted little boy, he could think of nothing more fun than going to parties at the airport and waving hello to people.

He was five when Feño Paloma arrived in Canada. By 1978, Pinochet's regime of terror was systematic. Survivors of the detention centers were more frequent among the arrivals. They were assisted off the planes, missing fingers and ears, faces scarred, noses broken, bodies twisted. They used canes and crutches or needed a wheelchair.

Feño's mother walked off the plane unaided, her face swollen and bruised, each step obviously sending a spasm of pain through her slight body. She lurched like an automaton along the welcome line, her papers clutched in one hand, a little boy's wrist in the other. Behind her trailed two teenaged boys, also with blackened eyes, swollen lips and a constellation of healing cuts and lacerations across their young faces.

Penny learned later both these boys, along with an older brother and sister, were tortured in front of their parents. The older siblings did not survive.

Penny kept her manner calm and unthreatening as she moved to the lost, incomplete family, a hand extended.

"Bienvenida," she said. She and her compañeras never said *welcome home* to these traumatized refugees. This was not home and the exiles couldn't even be sure the situation was trustworthy, let alone well. The past was barely behind them and the future insurmountable. All they wanted were the practical logistics of here and now. Where did they go and what did they do next?

"We're here to help you," the welcome brigade said, moving through the stunned, exhausted crowd. "We're going to take you to a hotel so you can get some sleep. It's all arranged and taken care of. Are you hungry? We'll get you something to eat. Does the baby need a bottle? Formula? If you need a doctor, we'll help you find one. We'll come back to see you tomorrow. We'll make a plan. We'll be here. We'll help you."

The broken mother wept in Penny's arms while her littlest son sat on the floor at her feet, wailing. The two older sons stared at Penny when she told them she'd help. One boy's gaze narrowed in sheer defense, as if the offer of assistance were an insult. And who could blame him?

No longer surprised by extreme reactions, Penny calmly asked their names. The wary-eyed son made introductions—he was Hernán Paloma, the middle boy was Patricio. The little one was Fernando, or Feño. Then Hernán's bruised eyes fell hard on the woman still in Penny's arms.

"My mother is called Graciela Toro," he said. "Our father is dead. He's not coming."

The open hostility in his voice made Penny's arms tighten around Graciela, sensing Hernán's vitriol was aimed at his mother, not the situation.

Jude looked around the distraught group, frowning. Then he plopped onto the floor and put arms around his weeping compañero.

"Don't cry," he said. "We're nice. Don't worry."

By the time the luggage and logistics were sorted out, the two little boys were still sitting on the floor and Feño was asleep on Jude's shoulder. Penny took a mental snapshot and in later years, asked the boys if they remembered the night at the airport. Both said no, but not before exchanging a tiny, surreptitious glance that told Penny they never forgot.

⌒

"THEY REFUSED TO ACCEPT him," Cleon said. "So they give him a playground and that just makes it all better."

His arms were crossed tight over his broad chest, his face unreadable.

"How do you feel?" Penny asked.

It was the most intimate question she could pose of her husband. Cleon Tholet was a heavily medicated man. He had pain meds and sleep meds and in the past three decades, he'd been on eleven different antidepressants. His Seattle psychiatrist had finally found the right cocktail and dosage to hold Cleon in balance, determining he functioned best when the balance was tipped toward detachment.

Cleon wasn't aloof. Not ambivalent or apathetic. He simply carried a slight air of checked-out-ness. He coasted above extreme situations, whether crisis or celebration. He rode straight down the middle. He never got too upset, he never got too jubilant. The latter was a sacrifice to avoid the former.

"How do I feel," he said. "Let's see. Sad, sure. He was a sweet, good boy and too young a man to die. Frankly, I'm pissed his family has so many stubborn, intolerant assholes in it. These little passive-aggressive digs in the article make me sick."

"Micro-aggressions," Penny said. Serena taught her that expression.

"But Jude went back for the funeral, which makes me proud. We were together tonight, which always makes me happy."

"Wasn't it nice?"

"I don't have a word for what it was. And all the wordless things together at one time leaves me feeling quite...ordinary."

Penny reached and turned off the monitor. "Come to bed."

He smiled. "I don't have a word for that, either."

She held out a hand, feeling nothing but gratitude the right cocktail had made Cleon check back into the bedroom. After a bout of long, lonely years, she never tired of welcoming him home to her.

CLE◉N

*Y*OU ARE FIVE YEARS *old when you see your father cry for the first time. He sinks into his easy chair, his face in one hand, the other hand clutching the telegram from the International Red Cross.*

"Who is it?" your mother says, unshaken in her belief that telegrams only herald death. "Who's dead? Who died?"

But this is a rogue telegram: your father's brother, thought dead in the concentration camps of Europe, is alive.

You're five. You think a concentration camp is a haven in the woods where people go to think deep thoughts. You've never seen Europe, having been born here in Santiago. You do know what excitement is. The house bursts with joyful anticipation during the three weeks it takes Uncle Louis's ship to cross the Atlantic. Your father plots the day's distance on a map in his study. A line of pins starting in the bulge of Turkey, squeezing through the Strait of Gibraltar and across the wide expanse of blue paper, heading for the curvy land bridge connecting North and South America. Through the Panama Canal and along the rump of Colombia, Ecuador and Peru. Creeping down the spine of the continent until finally the day of arrival is here.

You drive to Valparaiso to meet the ship—Papi, Mami, your sister Gloria and you.

You're too short to see over the masses of people lining the piers. Too big for Mami to carry. You hang onto the belt of Gloria's coat, terrified of being swept away to sea with no line of pins to mark the way. You know Uncle Louis has been spotted when Papi starts to cry again.

You've never seen two men hug so long. They kiss each other's cheeks, hold each other's heads and mop each other's faces. Finally, Papi comes walking toward the family, his face soaked with tears, his brother's hand clasped tight and raised between them, as if they've won a great race.

Uncle Louis and Mami hug a long time. The tall man then bows from the waist and kisses Gloria's hand.

"And this is your nephew," Papi says. "Carlos Luis. He's named for Papa and you."

With the same bow from the waist, your uncle shakes your hand. "Thank you," he says in German. "For keeping our names safe."

Louis's face is thin as a banana. His clothes hang off his shoulders and drag around his mismatched shoes. His hair is dirty and his teeth are broken. But the eyes behind the thick glasses are pale green and when he smiles, two creases flicker in his gaunt cheeks.

Papi is crying again. His arms open wide and gather Uncle Louis in tight. A passing news photographer snaps their picture and asks their names. The brothers ignore him and keep holding each other. They're so still for so long, you think they might be sleeping standing up.

You are five.

You think, If I am ever lost, I want to be found like this.

THE RAGTIME

*T*HE VANCOUVER POLICE COULD never prove someone from the Condor's family put the pig blood in Cleon's car. They couldn't solve any of the acts of vandalism and harassment against the Tholets. But the speed with which the Díazes agreed to the new settlement and liquidated their assets to pay out, was proof enough. After court and attorney fees and taxes, Jude walked away from Vancouver a startlingly well-off young man.

He wanted the family to split the money—everyone had suffered and should share equally in the reparations. Cleon and Penny firmly but gently insisted the settlement was his, and they put it into trust until he was twenty-five. When he achieved his majority, he paid off his siblings' student loans. He bought his parents' house in Alki Beach and his own place on 15th and Olive in Capitol Hill.

He reconfigured his townhouse's skinny layout to put all the social space on the ground floor, where his father could walk in at street level and not have to deal with stairs when he visited. His bedroom and bath were on the second floor and on the third his music space—soundproofed so his neighbors didn't have to endure the endless repetition and frequent cursing.

The Tholets joked that it cost Jude so much money and stress to hoist his baby grand piano through the windows, he was never moving again.

Tonight, Jude sat at the piano with the score to *Elite Syncopations*, Kenneth MacMillan's quirky ragtime ballet set to music by Scott Joplin. The company danced in skin-tight art-deco costumes while a scaled-down orchestra played onstage. Pacific Northwest Ballet's principal pianist, Dae-Hyun Cho, had his own natty costume and conducted from two pianos, one specially prepared to produce a tinny, rinky-tink sound.

One day, perhaps with the help of Giosué's bad-sushi connections, Jude might play the ballet. Until then, he was relegated to Dae's page-turner. Which didn't suck. His costume came with a really boffo hat.

He played Joplin for an hour, attacking the syncopated rhythms, insouciant and sloppy, ignoring any clunkers. This hour at the end of every day was only for the joy of playing. No repetition, no perfectionism, no making himself crazy. It was his soul's version of "Taps," bringing the day to an end.

He went to close the cover, then slid it back and played "Summer, Highland Falls" again.

Suspended between sadness and euphoria, he went to bed but didn't sleep. He gazed at an empty space on the wall that filled up with a vivid recall of steamed-up windows and Billy Joel on a car radio. Feño in the back seat of his Subaru wagon, Jude kneeling across his lap. Naked as birth, sweaty and taut, caught up in a tight fist of adolescent desire.

❧

"BABY," FEÑO SAID THROUGH a moan. "It's so good."

Jude threaded a hand through Feño's hair to pull his head back on the seat. That smooth, tender neck open to the night and Jude's hungry mouth. He sucked on the salty tang, tasted the pulse fluttering under his tongue. Then he rested forearms on either side of Feño's head and they stared as Jude pushed through the tunnel of Feño's slick hands, not blinking, barely breathing.

"So good," Feño said again. He was verbally fearless during sex, while Jude's words often deserted him.

"Fucking crazy about you." Feño's head wobbled side to side. His damp, tousled profile, eyelashes thick crescents on his cheekbone as his mouth closed around Jude's skin, careful to leave marks only where no one could see.

"They'd kill us if they knew," Feño whispered. "My people would, anyway."

"Not mine," Jude said. "We could tell my parents. They're fine with me, they'd be fine with you, too."

Feño's mouth strained against the night and his eyes shone wet as he shook his head. "We can't tell anyone."

"Listen. A gay couple lived with my parents in Santiago. They trusted my parents. They were safe with them. You will be too."

"No."

"You're safe at my house, Fen. We can be us at my house."

"No. It's only safe if only you and I know." Feño's hands grabbed hard at him, jerking and pulling and fingers clenched in Jude's hair. "Promise me you won't tell anyone."

"We can—"

"No. We can't. They'd kill me if they knew I was…"

"Gay."

"Don't."

"You can say it here."

"Stop. Just kiss me."

Jude knew Feño was being dramatic and dire. But Christ, they were seventeen, hot-blooded and hiding it from the world, thriving on being dramatic and dire. It was their fucking job.

And it felt so goddamn good.

"Am I hurting you?" Feño whispered. He always asked at least once.

"No," Jude said, moving deeper down on him.

It hurt when they first started having sex. Holy *shit*, the first time hurt like hell.

"Forget it," Feño said, watching Jude wince back into his clothes afterward. "We're not doing this again."

"I'm all right," Jude said through a clenched-teeth smile.

"Bullshit. No way, Jude, I can't deal with it hurting you."

He was adamant and Jude had to respect it, knowing where his friend was coming from. No word existed for the sexual abuse Feño's sister and mother suffered in the Estadio. As a child, Feño understood what rape was before he learned where babies came from. Within the struggle of being gay, he had *extremely* set ideas about sex and no quarter for violence, ugliness or pain.

Jude respected the rules, but he gently leaned on them. The sex hurt, but at the core of the rocky discomfort was a fascinating, complicated vein of pleasure. He wanted to tap it. Just as sports and music were skills born in repetition, he sensed time and practice were the keys here. He knew well the process of breaking down a musical phrase and coding the information into muscle memory. Feño put hours of training into athletic skill. Why would sex be any different?

"It hurt because we didn't do it right," he said. "We need to get some slippery stuff."

Feño put up his palms, shaking his head. "I'm not getting it."

Jude had identical reservations. He could buy condoms without being self-conscious, no problem. Lube was something else. That shit was over in the feminine hygiene aisle and with half the cashiers at Lawson's being classmates, no way was he throwing a tube of KY down with his shaving cream and gum. He considered shoplifting, but the risk of fatal humiliation was too great. He would literally *die* if he were caught. He opted to swipe what he found in his mother's bedside table drawer and let the chips fall under his own roof.

He didn't reveal the lube's provenance to Feño—the guy had enough mommy issues as it was.

"Come on, let's practice," Jude said.

One careful, patient encounter at a time, he figured things out. It worked best when he was on top and controlling the pace. It worked even better when they were both on the edge of coming before he let Feño inside him. He learned to go as slow as possible, then go slower. To use as much lube as he thought he needed, then use more. If he positioned himself this way, he could go a tiny bit faster. If he angled that way, he could go a hair deeper. He experimented, calling the shots, and kept Feño's trust by always stopping if it hurt.

It got better. Then it got good. Then one night, it got something damn close to perfect. It clicked. It went. It worked. It did. It was amazing.

"I love this," Feño said, holding Jude's brow against his. "I love your body. I love how you feel around me. Jesus Christ, I can't take it."

"I can," Jude said, sinking down on Feño's hips, letting the pressure build in his belly and groin. Floating on the quiet intensity of being so in love, he was out of words.

"Am I hurting you?"

"No." His body was utterly relaxed. No pain. Only an intense, tickling, buzzing pressure deep within.

"I don't understand," Feño said. "I fucked girls and it was like brushing my teeth. With you… I don't know why I'm like this. Is it guys, or is it you?"

"Me."

"It scares me so bad, man."

"It's all right."

"I don't want to be gay. I just want you."

In later years, Jude blamed himself for not reading what Feño painted on the wall in five-foot high letters.

I don't want to be gay. I just want you.

What was obvious to an enlightened adult was sweet music to a horny, dramatic teen's ears. Instead of heeding the warning, Jude ate it up and begged for more.

"Say you want me," he whispered.

"Want you so bad."

"Say it again."

"I want you all the time. It's all I think about. Walking around acting like I'm one thing when in my head, you're the only thing. I want you all to myself. All day long, all I want is to get you alone. Put my head on your shoulder and get inside you so I can feel like me."

"You are a greedy fuck."

"I am," Feño said. "So give me more."

THE DRAMA

"We HAD NO BUSINESS making love like that," Jude said to Phil.

It was Monday morning and Jude's most extreme emotions were up bright and early.

"I was fucking seventeen. Who communicates on a sexual level like that at seventeen? Jesus Christ, I was bottoming from the top. I didn't even know what that *meant* until I was in my twenties."

Phil nodded. It wasn't anything he hadn't heard before, but he always listened as if taking it in fresh.

"How did it work?" Jude said. "Why did it work? How did we not, in our cluelessness, hurt each other?"

"Hurt each other physically or emotionally?"

"Both," Jude cried, affronted by the world. He took a breath to calm down and be reasonable. "Put the physical stuff aside. With enough patience and lube you can always figure that shit out."

"Don't dismiss what was a genuine affinity for each other," Phil said. "Seventeen or not, you had something special and it let you communicate well about sex."

"Which brings me to my point. Where was the miscommunication? Where were the stupid misunderstandings, the arguments, the drama and angst?"

"You were in hiding," Phil said. "Maybe if you'd been free to be lovers in a normal, accepting environment, you would've been free to..."

"Free to what?"

"To fight? To... No, that makes no sense. Put a pin in that idea, we'll circle back."

Jude never admired Phil more than when he lost his train of thought or struggled to articulate something. It kept Jude coming back to the couch, no matter how painful what was unpacked there. He and Phil were collaborators, panning the muck for nuggets of truth, often throwing back buckets of unused, unfinished thoughts.

"I feel so fucking sad, man," Jude said, slumping against the cushions. "It's like grief."

"Because it *is* grief. Let's have Captain Obvious weigh in. You went back to the place you were viciously attacked and bullied and discriminated against. That alone is haunting. You don't shake that off overnight. But let's say Vancouver had none of those traumatic ghosts. You still went back to your estranged lover's funeral. I think that would leave the most enlightened saint reliving memories and regrets and feeling unspeakably sad. Feño was thirty-six years old, he left a wife and two kids and a secret side of him unresolved. It's a tragedy."

"We were so young," Jude said. "How the hell did we operate on such a plane of affinity when we were fucking babies? And how..."

Phil's eyebrows raised, as they always did when Jude was getting to the issue truly bothering him.

"How can it still feel like last night? How is sex from nearly two decades ago more vivid than sex I had two, six, I don't remember how many months ago?"

"What do you think the answer is?"

"I know what the answer is. We've unpacked this a hundred times. It's vivid and memorable because I was in love with him. Because I let him so close to me. Because I was fearless and trusting. And the subsequent question isn't 'Will I ever feel like that again?' but 'Will I ever let myself feel like that by letting someone close to me again?' I know this, Phil. I know the choices I made after I left Vancouver."

Jude spent his senior year of high school in heartbroken, traumatized celibacy. As a freshman at the University of the Pacific, he eased back into the game by presenting as bisexual, but only having intercourse with girls. It was almost comically dishonest and it felt like brushing his teeth, but that was fine. Even preferable.

Finally his sexuality asked if he'd had enough of this nonsense, and he had. He also had new and *extremely* set ideas about sex, the first one being his identity as a top. A total top. No versatility, no negotiations. He had zero desire to recreate how he'd been with Feño. Even less desire to ever let anyone that close to him, let alone inside him.

Maybe someday, he conceded. *But not today.*

After a few years, his inherent nature asked if he'd had enough of that nonsense as well. He was older now, a little wiser, with a significantly shrunken head that made swallowing hard truths palatable: he was no more a total top than he was heterosexual. He could still have set, constructed ideas about sex, but it was stupid not to be himself within their walls.

The UP campus was inclusive and tolerant, minds were open, male bodies were hot and out and there for the uninhibited taking. Jude ought to have turned into a cold-hearted, hot-blooded dog, out to fuck anything that would hold still.

But that wasn't Jude's way. Still shaken by the attack, he opted to be out-ish. He kept his closet door open, but the law of the land within was Tell Only If Asked. He picked his partners carefully, avoiding the dogs. Though his heart was averse to love, his body would always need and equate some kind of emotional connection with intimacy. He was wired to think of sex as something beautiful and profound. Horizontal ballet. A symphony of body and mind.

He was often disappointed nobody shared this philosophy.

"It's not a philosophy, it's a Catch-22," Phil said. "You don't want love, but you don't want casual sex either. You don't want lovers to abandon you in the morning, but you won't let them get close to you at night. You want sex to mean something, but you keep the parameters impossibly narrow and can't communicate what they actually are. It's not nothing, it's not everything. It's this immeasurable unit of something."

Fucking Phil. He never lost his train of thought when he was right.

In adulthood, Jude was the worst kind of serial monogamist, getting into dozens of relationships as a means to justify the constant physical intimacy he craved. He didn't like the concept of fuck buddies, so he invited far too many men to live with him, far too soon after meeting. None stayed long. Most of them left because Jude didn't know what the hell he wanted.

"Love isn't a bed and breakfast," fucking Phil said.

The longest of these beneficial friendships was with Christian Largo, a percussionist with PNWB's orchestra. They were together two years and to the outward eye, they were a relationship goal. They clicked on an intellectual level. Music was practically a third body in their bed. Chris had endured some vicious bullying in school and knew what it was like to step outside the front door and brace yourself. To constantly and subconsciously be on your guard.

Maybe that was the problem: each was so careful not to upset the other, that neither particularly inspired the other. Jude and Chris were faithful. They were even devoted. But Jude couldn't honestly say they were in love.

His best friend Hewan Bourjini ended up saying it best: "You're sort of two dogs who own and feed and walk each other."

They owned each other, it was true. Identical granted was taken. They were equally complicit in the complacency, but at least they didn't fight about it. It was company. Another body in the house. Guaranteed sex. Someone to fetch a roll of toilet paper if you were caught short. A warm tush in bed.

When Chris took a job in Amsterdam, Jude didn't mourn. A week of outraged pissiness and a few sulking, tush-less nights, and he was over it.

"You put your relationship to sleep," Hewan said.

At thirty-six, Jude was still out-ish, letting his left shin bone dictate his identity. Telling if asked but not flying his rainbow colors. He volunteered with Seattle Pride, but always in the back office. He worked tirelessly to organize the yearly parade in Capitol Hill but didn't march. He gravitated toward guys who were smaller than him. Less confident than him. Softer and shyer than him.

"Guys you can boss around," Hewan said.

"I don't boss them."

"You do like to call the shots."

"I don't like aggressive men," Jude said. "Being the victim of a hate crime will do that to a person."

They owned each other, it was true. Identical granted was taken. They were equally complicit in the complacency, but at least they didn't fight about it.

"It's important to you to feel in control," Phil said now. "It's not a character flaw. Neither is gravitating toward a certain personality type."

"I know."

"Believe me, man, I know it can be a blessing and a curse to have a first love that was so beautiful."

"Was yours?"

Phil smiled as his eyes circled the ceiling. "Took forever to get over the standard she set."

"Feño set a fucking impossible standard. I want to feel that way again, yet I do so much to keep from feeling that way."

"It's hard to pursue something you keep off limits."

An interval of silence, prickly with overlapping thoughts that snagged Jude's mind this way and that. Somewhere in this tangled briar patch was the thing bothering him. He sat still and waited.

"Remember my freshman year of college," he finally said, "when I had to come home and make an emergency appointment with you, because I was freaked out from a gay porn movie I watched?"

"I remember. You were shook up."

"Bad. It was worse than a horror movie lingering around. The imagery literally made me sick. Offended me in a way that was visceral. I had to physically get away from it, my dorm room, the campus, the entire state of California."

"You fled from it."

"Yeah. It was under my skin and in my bones." He raised one forearm. "Look at the hair sticking up. Even talking about it now is disturbing."

"Why? What upset you?"

"We already went through—"

Phil held up a hand. "You brought it up, which means it's bothering you. So pretend we didn't go through it."

Jude rubbed his arms, trying to settle down. "It was ugly. It was nothing I identified with. It was so full of hostility. I thought I'd be watching two guys make love, but they weren't even being nice to each other. It was like they were fighting with their bodies and their words. Trying to touch without being touched. Each blaming the other for making them like this. *Fuck you for making me want to fuck you. I'm going to fuck the desire to fuck you right out of you.*"

"It's porn. Porn is never reality. It's rarely nice and even more rarely about making love."

"But it's all I had," Jude said. "I had nothing else to go on. No books, no movies, no love stories, no openly gay celebrity role models. No mainstream litmus test of what two gay men who loved each other did together."

"Extremely fair point," Phil said. "You're right."

"All I had was my experience with Feño and this repulsive movie. Polar opposite depictions of intimacy and I'm stuck in between, nineteen years old with not a whole lot of nuance. I thought, *These are my choices. Intense beautiful lovemaking that ends in heartbreak and bone-break, or two gay men pissed about being gay and fight-fucking it out of their systems.*"

"No wonder you went running from it. To the safest place you knew."

"God, I came home despairing at what my options were. I went back to school and tried to date, but aggressive come-ons with all the crass language turned me the hell off. Bunch of buddies started calling me Jude the Prude. Which wasn't accurate. I wasn't prudish about sex. I just didn't like when guys were over-the-top and provocative. It only reminded me of the porn images still under my skin."

"And the less aggressive come-ons?" Phil asked. "With kinder, gentler guys?"

Jude sighed. "Those encounters reminded me of different things under my skin." He exhaled long, took off his glasses and rubbed at the bridge of his nose. "I fight off everything I want so bad."

"Mm."

"I want someone."

Phil's hand turned over in the air.

"I want someone the way Feño was a someone."

"I don't think I've ever heard you say it so simply and honestly."

"Maybe because I'm done. All this nostalgia and sadness for Feño. The residual fear of being targeted. The conflict of inviting people to knock on a bolted door. It's old. It's boring. I'm tired of it."

"Tell me more."

"Too much effort," he said, remembering what Brenda Ronco said at Feño's funeral. "I could take all this passion and build a house instead."

Phil's eyebrows raised.

"Maybe that's it," Jude said slowly. "Maybe I'm ready to let my house be a home."

Phil mimed a mic drop. "That," he said, "is a tremendous statement."

Jude's heart thumped hard, filled again with warm, coiling optimism. "Thank you."

"But as we know, talk is cheap."

"I know. Walking is also involved."

"And risk, pain, trust. Are you ready to be vulnerable?"

"I feel ready for something. I'm done with this narrative. Once upon a time, I was the victim of a hate crime. My family was targeted, the community turned against us, we fled the country. I unpacked all that shit with you. The betrayal and the abandonment and the trauma and the anger. I survived to be a functioning adult. My everyday life is rich but my love life is a third-world country.

"I was driving back from Vancouver this weekend, thinking about everything. And for the first time I realized I don't like the ending of this story. I mean, I don't like it ending here. I survived to be a functioning adult. True. And. Dot-dot-dot. Who do I want to be now?"

Phil smiled. "Of all the great Tholet Family Mottoes, that's got to be one of the greatest. *True. And. Dot-dot-dot. Who do I want to be now?*"

"It's the antidote to revolting developments."

"You look right on the edge of something big, my friend."

"I feel it. I feel excited. For real, I'm like buzzing with it."

The session was over and Jude had a foot out the door when Phil called to him.

"Listen, if the sadness comes back to visit later on, or even an hour from now? Don't beat yourself up. It's not a setback. It's being human."

"I don't think it will," Jude said. "But thanks."

Naturally, fucking Phil was right.

And naturally, Jude lay awake another night with Feño's ghost. Remembering. Regretting. And beating himself up.

THE SOCIAL PYRAMID

*L*IKE MOST CHILDREN OF the Chilean exiles, Feño Paloma was a damaged soul, the circuits of his young brain scrambled with terror and uncertainty. He had trouble eating, slept poorly, was afraid of the dark, afraid of the police and afraid of change. He had two traumatized older brothers and often found himself in the crossfire of their mood swings. But it was his mother's volatile emotions he feared most. He did everything in his young power to assuage her fears. To be her golden boy and personal savior. A vessel of goodness and innocence and hope. A sign the world could be redeemed. Even beautiful.

It was an exhausting job for a child, and he found the bulk of his respite in the Tholets' house on Ormidale Street, often falling asleep on Jude's shoulder as they watched TV.

Had Jude thought more of Feño's tactile nature during those tender years? He couldn't remember. Feño liking to lean on him was a natural law of the universe. Him liking it was another immutable law.

Their paths diverted in middle school, when sports intensified and drew lines through the social ranks. Jude had no interest in athletics but Feño found security, freedom and recognition on the soccer field and the baseball diamond. His coaches became his father figures, his teammates his dependable brothers. He bloomed and thrived, regaining his appetite and his rest and discovering a goodness that made his mother beam with pride.

He was no longer a fixture in the Tholets' house and if Jude missed him, it was in a nameless, instinctive manner. A frequent glance to one side or the other, looking for a loving, lawful presence, a tangible weight on his shoulder that wasn't there. Puzzled why its absence made him wistful. He wondered what might take its place, where something else like it could be. It certainly wasn't in girls, who were starting to notice him. And he noticed he didn't much care.

By the start of high school, he knew a deeper meaning lay in his hidden stash of men's underwear ads torn from the Sears' catalog, and teen idol pictures torn from Serena's magazines. He had a better idea of why he missed the feel of a boy's head on his shoulder. He knew his obsession with Sting and Bryan Adams and every member of Duran Duran wasn't entirely musical. Girls kissed him and it felt good, the way a back rub felt good. But when he thought about a boy's mouth pressed to his, he got light-headed, flustered and horny.

When the thought first identified itself—*I think I'm gay*—he didn't get scared, he got ready. He knew being gay could make his life miserable if anyone found out. Being gay could get him hurt. He had stay one step ahead.

Jude Tholet was smart. More than smart, Jude was wily. He used all his cunning and intellect to delay his sexual persuasion and pass for straight.

He had some natural advantages. Looks, for instance, the favored currency of social economy. He was dark and dimpled with bright blue eyes, but the azure gaze was partially obscured by his glasses and his ears stuck out a little, which made him approachable. Height was another blessing. Height was power. But instead of throwing his stature around, Jude cultivated a modest, graceful manner that put people at ease. He wanted a reputation of self-effacing decency to precede him.

Nothing to see here. Never mind me. Let's talk about you.

Jude had always been fearless around girls, because they had nothing he wanted on a sexual plane. He saw through the double-talk and manipulations that infuriated his male classmates, and he became an interpreter, ambassador and matchmaker. If you liked a girl at school, you got Jude Tholet to chat her up, drop your name and report back. If you wanted to approach a chick at a party, you got Jude to cross the room with you and start up a conversation.

Still, he made damn sure he was seen flirting. He went on dates, in groups when he could and alone when he had to. He pretended girls flustered and frustrated him. Around his buddies, he did a requisite amount of bitching and moaning how hard up he was, what a cold cocktease she was and what a loser she blew him off for. Not enough to be obnoxious. Just enough for the record to reflect *straight*.

"It must have been exhausting," Phil said, listening to tales of Jude's performance.

"It's exhausting in hindsight," Jude said. "At the time, it was just my life. Maybe because I subconsciously knew the alternative of being out would be a worse kind of exhausting."

The straight act did get easier when Hewan Bourjini moved to Vancouver in his sophomore year. They fell in fierce, soulful, best-friend love, then fell into cahoots and become a bearded couple. They went everywhere and did everything together, arm in arm, holding hands, carrying on. Openly hugging and easily kissing in school hallways and weekend parties. Always hanging out and yakking it up and being everyone's relationship goal before relationship goals were a hashtag.

"You guys are so sweet."

"You're like best friends."

"You're like an actual couple."

When Hewan met boys she wanted to date, she and Jude staged a breakup. Then Jude could play the role of the heartbroken, moody swain licking his wounds. It excused him from the dating game. He was on the rebound. He wasn't looking for anything serious. He was concentrating on his music and his schoolwork. Love sucked. Girls were trouble. He milked it until Hewan's relationship ended and she and Jude got back "together." The convenient cycle repeated at least three times during high school.

Phil laughed when Jude told him this. "What couple didn't break up and reconcile at least three times in high school?"

Feño, in the meantime, was a foot soldier in the army of an alpha male named Juan-Mateo Díaz. El Cóndor. His athletic machine ran on testosterone and machismo, rolling like tanks over the battlefield of high school. They could be carelessly cruel to girls—arbitrarily destroying reputations by choosing who was madonna and who was whore. They could be vicious to boys, particularly any male who showed the slightest degree of effeminacy. Or even boys like Jude, who had steady girlfriends but were suspiciously artistic and musical. Boys who played instruments and sang and knew the lyrics to show tunes. Boys who actually danced at school dances. Boys who put a little *too* much time into their appearance and spent a little *too* much time with girls a little *too* effortlessly.

Feño moved on the fringes of this gang of egos. Careless cruelty was not in his nature and Jude guessed Feño's enviable athleticism gave him a certain amount of leeway with the Condor. Feño made his bones and showed his loyalty on the field, so he didn't have to do it in the cafeteria.

When Jude passed by El Cóndor's clique, he and Feño caught eyes and jerked their chins—*Hey, I see you, I know you*—but said nothing. They were on duty, with roles to play. If they ran into each other alone, they stopped and took the time. They caught up, laughing and joking around. Then they moved on, but not before Feño said "Adiós" and with a funny little smile, poked a finger in the ball of Jude's shoulder. As if silently adding, *I'll be back. Hold my spot.*

The idea it was a flirtatious gesture never entered Jude's mind. Feño was straight like the sky was blue. As far as Jude was concerned, *he* was the only gay boy in the entire school. He had a wall between himself and his male classmates and he stayed the fuck on his side. He crushed on untouchable men in the movies and on TV. He changed pronouns in song lyrics and fantasized to his hidden stash of magazine pages. This was his life and he imagined, even counted on it being his life until he went to college. Exactly what would happen then he wasn't quite sure, but he believed he'd be among people who'd outgrown high school nonsense. Open-eyed, worldly intellectuals who lived and let live. It would be different. It would be better. He just had to get through these last couple years of bullshit.

Then one day, Jude bumped into El Cóndor in a crowded hallway.

"Mira por donde vas, maricón," Juan-Mateo said.

Watch where you're going, faggot.

The word rolled off Jude's back. He knew by some unspoken law, Juan-Mateo was required to say this. So toxic was his brand of machismo, he had no concept of accidental touch. If a female inadvertently brushed him in passing, she was a whore who wanted him. If a male did it, he was obviously gay.

Mira por donde vas, maricón.

Homophobic slurs had their own hierarchy. Maricón meant fag, yes, but any guy who bumped into you was maricón. A friend you were pissed off at was maricón. A friend you were giving good-natured shit to, a car that wouldn't start, a lost object, lousy weather, a bad situation. Maricón was a Swiss Army knife slur, just like hueón ran a useful gamut from buddy to asshole.

The epithet *cabro* carried a little more provocative weight. Same with *coligüe*, which came from the Mapuche language. If El Cóndor said "Mira por donde vas, cola," then Jude was in deep shit. If you called a guy cola, you were alluding not only to his deviant sexuality, but all the culturally approved discrimination that came with it. *That guy is gay, I denounce him and declare open season on his ass. Have at it. He deserves everything he has coming.*

Feño Paloma laughed. "Maricón? Him?" He whacked El Cóndor's arm. (It was permissible to slug, smack and punch your male friends.) "El Pianista gets more pussy than all of us."

Now Juan-Mateo had to save face on two fronts. "Yeah, he gets it with your mother."

This was a mistake. Mothers and sisters were fair game in trash talk, except if they had been detained, tortured or disappeared back in Chile. Survivors of Pinochet's terror were off limits. Even the white boys knew that.

Feño Paloma's older sister was disappeared and his mother was a shattered woman who'd suffered unspeakable things. El Cóndor had violated the code. As he and Feño stared each other down, his men exchanged troubled glances. It seemed equally unlikely Feño would throw a punch or Juan-Mateo would apologize. The phalanx quietly broke up, mumbling excuses of one kind or another, and made off in different directions. Feño, silent all this time, was slow to take his gaze off Juan-Mateo, a corner of his upper lip twitching.

"Vámonos, Tholet," he said. "It stinks in here."

He started walking. Jude shrugged a cool shoulder at the disgraced general and followed. Years later, he would wonder if, watching the two of them walk away, a seed of an idea was planted in El Cóndor's mind and watered with a trickle of revenge. But that was later. This was now. And things were about to change.

"Sick of his bullshit," Feño said. "A lot of us are."

"Yeah?"

"Fucker saying shit like that when he wasn't even born in Chile? He needs to watch his step. Anyway, what's up, hueón, haven't seen you in a while..."

They walked along, threading through clumps of students, squeezing by in stairwells, talking and catching up the way they always did. Laughing and joking as usual. Feño paused outside the locker room door and gave his customary adiós. His finger reached and poked Jude's shoulder. Then it held still. A single beam of pointed energy pinning Jude to the cinderblock wall.

And something was different.

"Want to hang out tonight?" Feño said.

Then everything was different.

Jude swallowed and it sounded like a tidal wave in his ears. Above the thud of his heart he heard his voice answer, "Sure."

Sure, Jude wanted to hang out.

All at once, he wanted many, many things.

He's beautiful, he thought. *When did that happen?*

"Can we hang at your house?" Feño said. "I need to get away from mine."

If he'd asked Jude to set his house on fire, Jude would've obliged. As Feño disappeared through the locker room door, the lingering touch of his fingertip held Jude frozen to the wall, staring after, flooded with wanting.

"Well, this is a revolting development," he said softly.

THE SHOW MUST GO ON

*P*ENNY ORCHESTRATED THE THOLETS' flight from Chile, but it was Cleon who scythed a path out of Canada. At the time of Jude's attack, the University of Washington had been courting Cleon for years, to teach at the Jackson School of International Studies. The offer was attractive, but Cleon had a strong aversion to pulling up roots and an even stronger antagonism toward America: it was Richard Nixon and Henry Kissinger who engineered the coup in Chile and put Pinochet in power.

"Kissinger can eat shit," Cleon famously said, which impressed Jude because "eat shit" was a phrase his father did not suffer gladly. Cleon had a colorful vocabulary and could swear in three languages. Neither he nor Penny minded their kids cursing in the house. Gross epithets, F-bombs, bullshit, horseshit, ratshit and batshit were bandied about with impunity. But once, in a heated argument with Serena, Jude told his sister to eat shit and Cleon hit him. Not an admonishing swat on the arm but a full blown slap across Jude's mouth.

"Don't *ever* let me hear you say that again," he said, with a finger in Jude's pounding chest and an iron tone that would brook neither discussion nor disobedience. Stunned speechless—his father had never hit him before—and more than a little afraid, Jude filed the rule under *Weird Papi Quirks* and without question, never uttered the words again.

After the incident with the blood on the car windshield, Cleon decided he could forgive America without forgetting Kissinger's deeds, and he accepted the job opportunity at Jackson as reparations. He took the university's relocation assistance, took everything offered and took his family out of Canada.

The Tholets spent their first month in Seattle living on top of each other in temporary housing. When Penny went to open houses and viewings, she took Jude with her. He wasn't a willing companion. Given his way, he'd hole up in the room he shared with Aiden, plug into his Walkman and pine. But Penny was having none of it. She pushed him into the driver's seat and made him explore the city with her. He grunted and moped through house after house and, much later, marveled his mother didn't throw him off one of Seattle's many bridges.

When the realtor led them over the threshold of a contemporary dwelling on SW Rose Street, Jude's pissy mood did a double-take and let out a startled, *Whoa.*

"Wow," Penny said, walking into the living room. One side was all windows, looking over the Sound. "Look at that view."

But Jude only had eyes for the baby grand piano. Its curved, matte black box was angled toward the fireplace, the bench kitty-corner to the sectional couch. A Wittner 813M metronome perched on the deck like a little pyramid. Sheet music for Chopin's *Nocturne in A-Minor* open on the stand.

Hello, hello, hello, it said. *You're here. I've been waiting. Come sit. Stay a while.*

"The owners are willing to negotiate the piano into the price," the realtor said. "Between us, you'd be doing them a favor keeping it. I don't suppose you play?"

Jude looked over, his breath tight in his chest. "Yes," he said, in the most pleasant voice he'd used all day. "I play."

His eyes finally took in the view outside the windows. Crisp white woodwork framed a dripping, gray and green vista. The moody weather, which until now had depressed him, felt romantic and full of longing drama, begging to be filled with music. He looked back at the room, noticing it was simultaneously spacious and cozy. The stacked stone hearth was dark and empty, but a fiery scenario kindled in Jude's mind. He saw Penny on the couch, absorbed in a book. Serena flipped through a magazine, a strand of hair coiled around her index finger. Aiden sprawled on his stomach on the rug, socked feet kicked up behind as he made his endless lists and calculations. Cleon in the handsome leather recliner, taking a little siesta. While Jude sat at the piano and played and the rain fell down the windows, washing everything cool and clean outside, warm and content inside.

"Where are the closest middle and high school?" Penny asked.

"You're five minutes from the Denny-Sealth campus and it's a twenty-minute drive to the University." The realtor's gaze turned on Jude, sly and expert. "Chief Sealth High School has an outstanding music program."

Oh please, Mami, Jude thought, a lumbering, angry teenager reduced to toddler negotiations. *Pretty please. I be nice. We stay here.*

He engineered a massive attitude adjustment, bribing fate like a child in the weeks before Christmas. He wanted that house and wanted that piano and wanted that view and if it took slapping a cheerful face on all his brooding rage to get it, he'd be Little Mary Fucking Sunshine.

Two decades later, Jude was again bribing fate with good behavior: *I be nice. You send someone.*

He invested in his side of the bargain by hitting the gym every night, hauling out his closet and indulging in some much-needed retail therapy. A good haircut, some trendy new glasses, contact lenses to switch it up. He still wanted to present as decent and self-effacing, but instead of *nothing to see here,* he tried to project *something to see here.*

Here it is. It's not all that, it's got a lot of weird quirks, but give it a look-see.

Fate threw him some softballs pitches. For years, he'd given free piano lessons at the Boys and Girls Club of Seattle. One of the volunteers asked him out for a beer. They went and had a beer. Jude had another long-standing gig playing piano at the Hilton's Sunday brunch. A new bartender asked him out. They went out. He had dinner with a librarian at the Music Hall. Caught a movie with the cute file clerk at his dentist's office. When Pacific Northwest Ballet did an assembly at a local elementary school, Jude left with an art teacher's phone number in his pocket.

He served up a positive attitude on the dates. An *I want someone* attitude. None of the dates were electric, but none sucked. Nice guys, all of them.

But no someones.

<hr />

JUDE HAD SUFFERED FROM White Coat Syndrome since he was a child, when merely entering the pediatrician's office made him teeter on the edge of tears. His intense aversion to doctors worsened when his leg was broken and followed him into adulthood. While he'd outgrown the anxious crying, the nurses at his practice knew not to take Jude's blood pressure at the start of an exam, but rather wait until the end when he'd calmed down.

Clinical settings made him nervous but his loathing of hospitals could only be described in psychological terms. He was proud of his track record in staying out of the ER. No more broken bones, no stitches, no freak accidents or illnesses.

Until tonight.

With a rattle of ball bearings, the curtain surrounding Jude's bed drew back and Hewan Bourjini put her head around. "Shmoopy, you broke your streak."

"Hey." He tilted a sullen cheek toward her kiss. "Thanks for coming."

"You all right?"

"I'm just annoyed. And my phone's dead so I'm bored out of my mind. Did you bring a charger?"

"Mmhm. You know, I'm kind of loving this look you got going."

"Stop." He was still in his zoot suit costume for *Elite Syncopations* and feeling like a complete moron.

"Let me see you with the hat," Hewan said, picking it up off the rolling side table.

"Do not put the hat on me. I will kill you."

She put it on her own head and inspected his left foot, propped up and packed in ice. "Is it broken?"

"No, but I tore the shit out of a ligament."

"I'm sorry," she said, patting his knee. "It was your big break, too."

Dae-Hyun Cho's wife had gone into labor this afternoon and ended up having an emergency C-section. Which meant Jude had to go on in *Elite Syncopations*.

It went well. Shit, it went terrific. Performing and conducting onstage, in costume, with the helm of the ballet in his hands, Jude was playing impeccably and having a blast. But in the middle of "Cascade Rag," he misjudged the edge of the risers, took one too many steps back and fell off the platform.

A collective gasp onstage and in the house, followed by nervous, shushed laughter and a scattering of applause from the balcony. The musicians were professionals and kept playing without their captain. The dancers were equal pros and masters of improvisation. They scooped up Jude, adjusted his hat and hoisted him back on the platform with much camp and ass-patting. Jude camped along while inside, he was mortified. And in more than a little pain from landing badly on his left leg. The ankle was throbbing, sending lightning bolts up and down his shin and an echoing ricochet off the walls of his skull.

I broke it again.

My leg's broken.

I broke it.

It was broken.

He conducted the rest of the ballet on autopilot, nauseous with pain and anxiety. Instead of taking his curtain call with the company, he took a cab to the hospital. X-rays showed no fractures to the pinned-and-screwed tibia. The fib was perfectly fine but he'd definitely torn an ankle ligament. He also had the mother of all panic attacks, bad enough for the resident to order an EKG. Jude's heart was fine, but at the nurse's insistence, he called Hewan for a ride home. And a change of clothes.

"Here," she said, handing over the backpack. "I brought the three Cs: cashmere, charger and candy bars."

"Thanks." He moved the ice packs and carefully swung his legs sideways off the bed. He slid off the costume's electric trousers and handed them to Hewan. He had no more issue undressing and dressing in front of her than he did in front of a mirror. She handed him jeans and folded the rest of the suit.

"Isn't this familiar," he said, glancing up as he tied one sneaker. "You being at my bedside?"

She snorted and brushed his hair off his forehead. "Like we need to re-live those Hallmark moments."

When the Tholets fled Vancouver, the sole backward glance Jude gave was at his best friend, his devoted beard and fiercest advocate. He still had shoeboxes of letters he and Hewan wrote during his first year in Seattle. None were less than ten pages, handwritten on both sides. In between the letters, they made and sent mix tapes. They did their college searches together, visited University of the Pacific together, applied together and each promised not to accept unless the other was. They both got in, suffered two lowerclassmen years in separate dorms before reuniting in an off-campus apartment. After graduation, they both went back to Seattle. Work and commitments and relationships reduced the time they spent together, but not their bond. No matter what life threw at Jude, three things remained constant: his family, music and Hewan.

When his blood pressure came down from the ceiling, he was discharged and Hewan took him home. He ran a gamut of friendly ribbing the next day at work, alternately teased and consoled. A reviewer in *The Seattle Times* was kind enough to praise Jude's piano playing before mentioning the half gainer off the platform, playing up the spirit of rah, rah, the show must go on. The embarrassment of the incident was behind Jude now. But something else was wrong.

The prospect of being on crutches for a month put him in a pathologically foul mood. It was more than the injury being an impractical stick in the wheel spokes of daily life. More than being locked into a walking boot, hopping up and down the stairs of his three-story townhouse. More than the hassle of getting to work, getting comfortable at the piano, going to lunch and negotiating the kitchen and shower. The host of non-life-threatening but pain-in-the-ass negotiations were nothing compared to the persistent echo in his head. He couldn't shake it.

I broke it.

Something's wrong.

This is wrong.

I'm broken.

I'm wrong.

He was back in Phil's office, triggered and demoralized and depressed. Losing weight. Either sleeping poorly and waking from nightmares about the Condor, or sleeping well and waking from intense, erotic dreams about Feño. Both circumstances rattled his soul, until he was reaching for meds he hadn't touched in years. Feeling he was a boy starting out on the road from Heartbreak Hell, instead of a man at the well-deserved end of the journey.

And frankly, he was pissed about it.

"We had an old mantra," Phil said. "I don't know if it's still in your rotation. *I don't want you to suffer.*"

Jude exhaled a sulky breath. "Yeah, I remember that one."

"It's a good one. Dust it off. If you need to wallow, wallow. But don't beat yourself up. Feño's funeral could be giving you delayed permission to grieve. Hurting your leg is just really rotten timing. You don't have to tie the two together, but I understand how it's hard not to."

"If I fell on the other leg, it wouldn't be so bad..." Jude trailed off, feeling like holy shit. "I don't know where I was going with that."

"Jude, what's the matter?"

The question sounded disingenuous but it was another of their mantras. A cue to either dig in and find the damn matter or, more often, acknowledge the matter lying right out in the open.

"It hurts," Jude said.

Phil nodded. "Still."

"Yeah. All this time and it's still in my bones."

"Mm."

It's all wrong.

I'm broken.

The Condor broke me. Feño's family broke him.

"Jude?"

I was stepped far from the path of normal life.

Feño and I didn't break up, we were broken up.

His eyes swam and his nose burned hot inside. "How we were broken up was so wrong," he whispered.

"Say again?"

"Nothing."

"Dude, don't nothing me, it insults both of us. If you want to talk about Feño, talk about him."

He dragged a rough hand across his face. "You already know all this shit."

"It's not about me." Phil leaned forward a little. "I don't want you to suffer. If you have to do this, we can do this. But I don't want you to suffer."

THE PICNIC TABLE

*J*UDE AND FEÑO WERE hanging out in all their free time. Going to parties or, more often, hopping in the car and going nowhere. Criss-crossing Vancouver, they sang loud to the radio and during the commercials, they talked. Safe topics at first: school politics, neighborhood dirt, music. And eventually, inevitably, sex.

"You ever do it with a girl?" Jude asked, then wanted to punch himself in the mouth.

Idiot, who else would he do it with?

"Sure. You?"

"Sure," he said, lying. "Lots of times."

A few blocks of silence.

"Actually, I'm full of shit," Jude said. "I've never done it."

Feño laughed. "You're not missing much."

"Huh?"

His shoulders gave an exaggerated shrug. "Sex is weird. Or maybe I'm just weird. But it wasn't what I thought it would be."

"Oh."

"I have a hard time doing it without thinking about…"

"About what?"

But Feño shook his head and changed the subject.

Little by little, the conversation on the drives went deeper. Until the boys were sneaking into Central Park to walk the trails and keep talking. Loitering on the playground and picnic tables. Sometimes Feño had pot, which made them brave and expansive, and they began to tell their parental war stories.

"I don't know what my father did or had or knew," Feño said, as they sat on the swings one night, passing a joint back and forth. "But Pinochet wanted it. They tortured my mother in front of Papi to get it. Then they tortured my brother and sister in front of *her.*"

Jude steeled himself, sensing he was being tested. Was he worthy of this information? Could he be entrusted to honor it? Dry-mouthed and stomach churning, he asked what the soldiers did.

"You really want to know?"

"If you want to tell, I want to know."

Feño pushed off the ground to start swinging, telling his story at the apex of each pendulum arc.

"Beatings and shocks," he said, swinging forward. Then backward, "Every day, in front of my parents."

Back and forth. "They threw vinegar on Pato's whip marks. They put Hernán in ice water for hours. And they pulled Oliva's nails, one at a time."

Toes to the sky: "Then they made my brothers rape my sister. Each of them had to do it, or they'd shoot my father."

Heels to the sky: "Then the soldiers took turns with Oliva to show how it was done."

Forward: "They made my oldest brother Cristian rape my mother."

Backward: "He hung himself in his cell afterward."

Feet up again: "Then the soldiers took turns with Mami."

Knees bent sharp: "And when they got tired of her, they gave her to the dogs."

He skidded to a stop, sneakers dragging in the dirt. "The soldiers trained their dogs to rape women." His hands stayed clenched on the chains as his gaze stayed on the sky. "They put mice up her concha. Both her and my sister. That's how Oliva bled to death, from mice scratching and biting inside her."

Jude's body did about eight things to repel the information. Winced, cringed, shivered, flinched and gagged. He'd heard such tales before. Not told to him but overheard in whispers from someone who'd heard from someone who knew someone. Horrific, unbelievable ways Pinochet's soldiers devised to rape women. But always third-hand accounts. Never from someone Jude knew.

"That's when Mami talked," Feño said. "She broke. She told them what Papi was doing, what his campañeros were doing, where people were hiding. She told them everything she knew."

"Lo siento," Jude murmured, because what else could he say?

"I swear, hueón, it's like Mami will never get rid of that animal inside her. She walks around like she can't stand to be in her own body. Like she can still feel a mouse skittering around and clawing inside her. It never stops. She can't stand herself and I don't know what to do about it."

"There's nothing you can do. It wasn't your fault."

"You know how I know all this shit? Because Pato and Hernán told me. To make it clear what they suffered and what I didn't."

"You were five. Your aunt was hiding you and—"

"They made sure I knew they didn't break but Mami did. That they... I don't know, they took it like *men* or some shit. They treat Mami like a traitor. I've heard Pato call her a whore to his friends. I just stay the hell out of their way because they're so fucking angry and damaged, they'll punch your lights out for saying good morning."

"Jesus, Fen, I..." He shut his mouth and said nothing.

"I look at Mami and nothing looks back. The older I get, the less I'm her son and more another man who can hurt her. She flinches at everything I say and do. Like she's waiting for me to act like Pato and Hernán. Ever since I grew taller than her, she goes stiff if I hug her. I don't know how to fucking be around her anymore and sometimes I think..."

Feño's twisted in the swing, gazing up at the tightening spiral of chains. "Like, when I'm with girls? Having sex? I can't...*not* think about what happened to Mami and my sister. What my brothers were forced to do to them. How they call her a broken whore now. I get with a girl and all that shit is looking over my shoulder, you know?"

"Yeah, I know."

He gave a little laugh and let the chains unwind, spinning in circles. "No you don't, you pure virgin."

"I'm not that pure. And I get what you're saying, it makes sense. I don't think it's anything wrong with you. You just... You're aware of how sex can be a weapon. You give a shit. You want it to mean something. Or at least not be fucking damaging."

"Or maybe I'm just weird."

He dragged his feet to stop again. His gaze held Jude's and it seemed he was sinking a lot of weight into the word weird.

Is he trying to tell me something?

He can't be.

"How does your stepfather treat your mother?" he asked.

Feño snorted. "I think Mami married him because he's got such a dominating personality. He makes all the decisions, she just has to stay alive and show up. Her life is so pathetic, hueón. I hate it. I hate what they did to her. And I hate what it's done to me. Or shit, maybe it was already done."

"Already?"

"Yeah. Maybe I was born like this."

Born like what, what is he saying?

Feño's stepfather was rabidly religious. One more reason it couldn't be possible Feño was looking at Jude this way. Mirroring all the confused wanting coursing through Jude's veins. Choking his breath. Prickling his limbs. Getting him hard.

I'm so hard for you. The words were rocks in his mouth, piled on his tongue and knocking against his teeth. Struggling to control them, he got off the swing and went to sit on top of a nearby picnic table.

"Do you remember the airport?" Feño said. "Your mom always asked. I don't know why I said I didn't when I did."

"I remember."

He remembered the cool linoleum under his butt, criss-crossed legs lopsided and smushed as he wormed close enough to Feño to put arms around him. He remembered the up and down heave of Feño's body and the hiccupped, irregular sound of sobs trying to be choked back. The shivering into stillness and silence. The whispered, measured breath of exhausted sleep and finally, the heavy, relaxed weight of Feño's head.

"Is that why you always poke me here," Jude asked, touching his shoulder.

Feño climbed up to sit on the table now, three feet of space between them. "I just remember next to you being a safe place. The first safe place I felt in a long time and I wanted to stay there. Sometimes...I miss being there."

Jude couldn't breathe. This conversation couldn't be happening. The word-stones in his mouth were not busting through the dam of his lips and he was not, oh no he was definitely not saying now, "You can come visit if you want."

The longest moment of his life passed. A naked, dangerous stretch of time that let him taste how thoroughly he'd just fucked up his life.

I need to get out of here. I need to run away. I can't go back to school tomorrow. He'll tell everyone. It's over. I'm dead. It's open season.

His body clenched, poised to make a run for it, then Feño slid closer to him on the picnic tabletop.

He's not, you're imagining this.

His head leaned on Jude's shoulder. Soft and tentative at first, then, with a sigh, heavy and relaxed.

No. No I am not here this is not real this is not this is not this is not.

Feño sighed again. "Thanks."

"Mm."

Don't hurt me. Don't tell. Don't say anything. Don't do this. Don't stop.

As Feño's scent filled his nose, his heart screamed behind the wall of his chest. His fingers twined tight and locked between his knees because if freed, he'd run a hand along Feño's leg. He kept his gaze straight ahead because if he turned his head, he'd bury his mouth in Feño's hair. He was being tested. This was a sting and any minute, people would spring out of the trees, surround him with torches and pitchforks. Yelling, *Die, filthy cola!*

He wouldn't dare move. He would not touch Feño.

If I touch you, I will die.

If I don't touch you, I will die.

The time slipped past, measured in heartbeats and denial.

I am so hard for you and this is not happening.

"I could fall asleep," Feño said.

"Yeah, I have that effect on people."

Their laughter eased the tension in Jude's chest a little but the night remained surreal and untrustworthy.

And hard, so fucking hard.

Feño turned his head, pressing his nose into Jude's bicep, then turned it back and burrowed closer. "Que quiero besarte."

I want to kiss you so bad.

Jude had still been staring straight ahead all this time. Now his head dared to turn. Down and to the side, until Feño filled his peripheral. "What?" he whispered.

"You heard me."

This isn't real. This is not happening. This is a trap. Do not trust it.

Feño's chin tilted up and his lips lightly brushed Jude's jaw. "Look at me."

Jude half-turned on the tabletop, dropping his shoulder so Feño had to pick up his head. He looked Feño in the eye and said, "Are you fucking with me right now, maricón?"

Because if this was a trap, let the record show he didn't fall for it. If it was a test, let it be known he passed.

"No," Feño said. "Are you afraid right now, maricón?"

Jude gave a tight swallow, still not trusting any of this. "Yeah."

"Me too."

"Afraid of me?"

"Everything but you."

Their bodies leaned in a millimeter, testing the strength of the night.

Jude asked, "When did you know I was...?"

"When I said I wanted to kiss you and you didn't punch me out."

Jude's body felt like one giant sob wrapped in joy smothered by terror. "Are you…?"

Feño pulled in a ragged breath. "You tell me."

They leaned in more, each flicking eyes to the other's mouth and back up to stare.

Then they kissed.

Everything below Jude's mouth and jaw melted as everything in the whole wide world threw its head back and screamed at the top of a roller coaster arc, then shut its eyes tight and plummeted over the edge.

"Think about you all the time," Feño said.

Lips tingling, Jude heard his floating head ask "Why?"

"Because I'm not what anyone thinks I am. I don't feel the way they think I do. I don't think the way they want me to. I'm nothing they want me to be. What I am is when I'm with you."

This is not happening.

They kissed again. Harder this time. Committing to it. Opening to teeth and tongues and letting the moans fall out of their throats. Feño's hands pulled Jude in, pushed him down on the table, pressed him tight and held him fast.

This is not happening.

"If anyone finds out," Feño said, blocking out the sky.

Jude braced himself. Only one thing could possibly follow. "Don't say it."

"Don't say what?"

"That you'll kill me if I tell anyone."

"Shut up." Feño kissed him. An edge of anger in his mouth, teeth closing on Jude's bottom lip and tugging. "I want to do a lot of things to you but killing isn't one of them."

His hand spread wide on Jude's brow. The other slid down Jude's chest, across his stomach and on top of his jeans. It crept a little further and squeezed.

Jude cried out, his feet rattling on the table's bench, his hips bucking into Feño's palm. "This isn't happening."

Feño unzipped him. "Yes, it is."

THE ETHNICITIES

*O*N NEW YEAR'S DAY, the Tholets gathered at the house in Alki Beach. After brunch, Serena pulled a handful of five-by-seven envelopes from her shoulder bag. "Dun dun *dun*," she sang, passing them around.

"What are these?" Jude said.

"The results of that DNA test we took. Remember?"

"Oh yeah."

"You totally forgot," Giosué said.

"I know. All that spitting and sperm. It's so unlike me."

"Ready to meet your maker, Papi?" Serena said.

Cleon made a face. "We've met."

"This last one is Aiden's. He said I should open it for him."

"Can't believe you got Aiden to spit for you," Jude said.

"All boys spit for me."

"Ditto."

Penny sucked her teeth as she ripped her envelope's flap. "I hope this shows me how I raised such disgusting children."

"Our level of crass is definitely genetic," Serena said.

They pulled out the invitation-like cards and the kitchen downshifted into thoughtful quiet.

"Oh my God," Penny said. "I'm white."

"Shut the front door," Jude said.

"Off-white. Eggshell white. Winter white. Linen white. Pale white. I'm shocked."

"No really," Serena said. "What does it say?"

"British, seventy-four percent. Ireland, Scotland, Wales—sixteen percent. Scandinavia, eight percent. Germanic Europe, two." She put her card down as if revealing a royal flush. "How about you, querido?"

"Sixty-nine percent European Jewish," Cleon said. "Twenty percent Germanic Europe. Six percent France. Five percent North African Jewish." He tossed the card down next to Penny's. "Sephardic."

"Sephardim," Giosué said, holding up a palm. Cleon smacked his against it. Jude stared at his card, not understanding.

> *Iberian Peninsula: 44%.*
> *Italy: 30%.*
> *Greece & the Balkans: 15%.*
> *France: 11%.*

"Me and Jude are probably the same," Serena said. "I'm forty-three percent European Jewish. Is that what you have?"

"No," Jude said.

"And twenty-five percent British. Then all the rest are little percentages."

"Um," Jude said.

"Damn, I don't care if it's nothing shocking. I still have chills."

"Serena?"

"Jude, what's the matter?" Penny said.

All eyes turned on him.

"Something's wrong."

"What?" Serena reached across for the card in Jude's confused fingers. For a second he held it back from her, his heart kicking up a beat.

Something's wrong.

He let it go. Watched her read it.

"What the hell?" she said. "This isn't right."

It's broken, Jude thought.

"What does it say?" Cleon asked.

"Forty-four percent Iberian Peninsula? Thirty percent Italy?"

"How much Jewish?"

Serena looked up, then down again. "None."

"What?" Penny said.

"Fifteen percent Greece and Balkans, eleven percent Fran— This can't be right."

A slimy beat of silence. Serena opened Aiden's card and read off the ethnicities, which were identical to hers with slightly different percentages. She fanned all the cards on the table before her. Cleon and Penny's side-by-side. Jude, Aiden and Serena lined up below.

One of these things is not like the other, Jude thought.

A SCARCITY OF CONDORS

"Well, that's a little fucked," Cleon said, clearing his throat. His gaze on Serena was heavy and hopeful. Waiting for the logical explanation he was sure was coming.

"They must've mixed up the kits," she said. "These have to be someone else's results."

"Or I'm someone else," Jude said, looking at Giosué because he couldn't meet anyone else's eyes.

"Juleón." Penny's hand closed around his wrist. She only used his full name when he was in a fragile state. Reminding him his name was made from the two people she loved best in the world—her husband and her mother, Julia.

He shrugged and smiled but his lips were numb. His tongue too big for his mouth and his thoughts too big for his skull.

Something's wrong.

"Jude, this is just a mistake," Cleon said.

"Human error," Serena said. "We'll take another one."

"We?" Jude said. He couldn't say or think more than a handful of words at a time.

Something is broken.

"We," Serena said, her eyes flicking around the table. "We'll all retake it."

Cleon and Penny nodded with a little too much enthusiasm.

The evening clutched to hold itself together. Jude tried hard to laugh and joke and speak of pleasant things. To affectionately tease Serena and dodge her swats. To almost-flirt with Giosué. To play the piano and be himself. But it was himself sitting like a cold stone in his stomach, making it next to impossible for him to interact with his parents.

Iberian Peninsula: 44%.

Italy: 30%.

He picked a piece of cilantro out of his rice and beans, remembering its soapy taste was a genetic trait. He gave it to Serena, who detected no such taste.

He'd never given much thought to being the blind bat in a family that could see in the dark, but now his glasses weighed heavy on the bridge of his nose.

European Jewish: 0%.

His muscles and bones tingled, measuring his lean, six-foot-one frame and comparing it to Penny and Serena's petite plumpness. To Cleon's barrel-chested five-foot-nine and Aiden's spare five-seven.

He blinked his eyes. Two bluebells in a bouquet of brown gazes.

One of these things is not like the other.

One of these things is wrong.

HE COULDN'T SLEEP THAT night. He went upstairs to the piano but sat still on the bench, playing only random notes.

Something's wrong.

He stood before a wall in his living room, where hung his copies of the old family photos. He took each one down, slowly going through his history. Scrutinizing his birth story, looking for holes.

His father was arrested in October of 1973. Penny was seven months pregnant, alone in the house in La Reina. Well, not entirely alone. Uncle Louis lived in one of the bungalow apartments on the property. The other was occupied by Ysidro Sepúlveda and Tatán Álvarez, the gay couple taking refuge in the haven of the Tholets' hearts.

As a unit, they went every day to the Estadio, trying to get information on Cleon. They knew he was in there. The lists of prisoners' names were posted outside. One day, Cleon's name was crossed out. "Transported," was all the family was told.

Pinochet's chokehold on the country tightened. The soldiers came to La Reina one November day, looking for dissidents, leftwing sympathizers and foreigners. They dragged Penny and her neighbors into the street, lined them up against property walls and staged a mock firing squad. Staged it not once but three times, until women were screaming and children were pissing themselves in terror. Then the power-drunk soldiers stopped mocking and started shooting.

Penny, eight months pregnant, watched as her husband's beloved Uncle Louis was gunned down. Then a rifle butt to the back of the head knocked her out cold. When she came to, she was back in her house, with Ysidro and Tatán. The city was blacked out and under curfew. The phone lines were cut. With the two young men as amateur midwives, she gave birth to Jude on the living room floor.

"You must've been terrified out of your mind," Jude always said when the story was told.

Always, Penny gave a little shrug and a self-effacing smile. "I don't really remember. Just a little fragment here and there. Either the head injury kept any memories from imprinting, or the trauma decided to erase all the memories."

Jude of all people could relate to the bizarre things a mind did to protect its owner. He exited far out of his own body when the Condor broke his leg. He recalled little of the pain and fear of the moment. Just a fragment here and there. And of course, he remembered the German Shepherd jumping the fence because goddamn, that was something else.

He took down a photo of his college graduation. He stood between Cleon and Penny, looking at the camera while they looked only at him.

These are my parents.

So where is my Jewish blood? Where is my British?

Iberian Peninsula: 44%.

Italy: 30%.

Ysidro and Tatán got Penny and her newborn baby to the hospital. The hospital registered Jude's Chilean birth certificate with Santiago's civil clerk, but Penny had a second one registered with the consulate, making him a Canadian citizen.

I'm a Canadian citizen, a Chilean nationalist and a permanent resident of the United States.

I am me. Juleón Tholet, son of Cleon Tholet and Penelope Cambie.

He took down the picture of Uncle Louis. Thick dark hair, like Jude's. Heavy glasses, like Jude's. Tall like Jude, hopelessly myopic like Jude, dimpled like Jude.

Gay like Jude.

A wild, irrational thought: *Are you my father?*

What the fuck, of course not. Louis didn't have a fucking *affair* with Penny. He was an old man. Well, old-ish. But he was gay. He was castrated in Sachsenhausen, for fuck's sake. He couldn't impregnate anyone.

Then who did?

He imagined an ugly scene after he left his parents' house tonight. Cleon demanding answers as to Jude's parentage.

No.

Wait.

Jude's results showed no British ethnicity. Penny should be demanding answers from her husband.

But how can she if I have no Jewish ancestry?

He was confused as fuck.

"This is fucked," he said, his voice small against the wall of pictures, his framed diploma among them. His finger traced his name in somber calligraphy: Juleón Tholet.

I took my mother's name and your father's name and made you.

"But where is her DNA?" Jude asked his history. "Forty-four percent Iberian Peninsula."

That meant he was Spanish, right?

Spanish and Italian. Maybe Greek. A little French.

The soldiers came to La Reina. They roughed up my mother.

"Did they rape her?"

His brow furrowed tight a moment, then he shook his head, flicking off the disturbing thought. More impossibilities. She was already eight months pregnant. Furthermore—he played the scenario out—if it was rape and she lied about Jude's birth date or his age, he'd still have her DNA. He had nothing of Penny's. Nothing of Cleon's, either.

I'm not their child.

His mouth was bone dry. He'd work up some spit and take the test again. No logical explanation existed but human error. It was Giosué who typed the kit numbers into the website, after all. He probably transposed some letters and numbers. It was a mistake. Jude's second test would match Serena and Aiden, and this would be a hilarious story to tell someday, plus a spectacular reason to flirtatiously give Giosué shit.

He got back in bed, but before settling down, he took his phone and texted Penny. It was late, she wouldn't see until morning, but he needed her to know:

I'm so glad you're my mom and I don't tell you enough. I love you.

He sent it. Defiantly. Daring his DNA to contradict him.

He punched the pillows around, getting comfortable. He closed his eyes, drew a deep breath and exhaled.

The marrow in his left shinbone trembled.

Something's wrong.

85

 THE KINGS OF DEATH

*P*ENNY SLEPT BADLY AND as soon as light began to fill the bedroom, she got up and made coffee. She stood at the kitchen counter, listening to the drips and concentrating on the level of rising java, cup by cup, so she wouldn't have to think of anything else. Not until she was sitting on the couch, wrapped in a blanket. On the coffee table were the five DNA result cards. She looked through each one, ending with Jude's, then stared at the wall of family photos behind the piano.

This is your family.

It's a mistake.

These have to be someone else's results.

Human error.

She drew a long, shaky breath past the knot of anxiety in her chest. Took a long sip of coffee, hoping to dissolve it with heat.

44% Iberian peninsula.

30% Italy.

"It makes no sense," she said across the rim of the mug. She dropped Jude's card, got up and walked closer to the wall, studying the old photos, looking for new clues.

Her mother's eyes stared back at her, soft and liquid. Julia's death ripped a hole in Penny's life, but it also put Penny on a trajectory toward Chile and the man who would become her husband.

Her fingertip traced her father's square head and blunt, earnest expression. When the Tholets fled Santiago, it was into the haven of Walter Cambie's home.

This is my home, this is my family. This will never change and this is all that matters.

Except…

She chewed her fingernail, staring at the face of Louis Tholet, Cleon's uncle. It took two years after he was liberated from Sachsenhausen for the Red Cross to track down his brother in Chile. He arrived in Santiago in 1947 and lived with the family until the day he died, which was the same day Jude was born.

November 25, 1973.

Springtime in Chile, but Pinochet had the country frozen in terror. Most of Santiago's radio stations had gone silent and some TV channels showed only static. Irregular blackouts rolled across the bowl of the city, plunging it into even deeper darkness.

Cleon's name was crossed off the list of prisoners posted outside the Estadio. The guards said he was transported but wouldn't say where. They were lying, for all Penny knew. Cleon could be dead. And she was going mad. Sick and sleepless, pacing the rooms of her house in La Reina. Some nights, Uncle Louis shuffled over in slippers to light the kettle and share the misery. Sometimes the light went on in the bungalow where Ysidro and Tatán lived, then one or both came over to pace.

Her mouth bitter with coffee and confusion, Penny studied the picture of the young gay couple. Nothing in their gregarious, thrown-back heads attested to their neighborhood nickname: Los Reyes de la Muerte. The Kings of Death. Tatán was an undertaker and Ysidro a memorial mason. Tatán prepared the bodies for burial. Ysidro marked the final resting place. Each was the heir to a family business and the families had worked together for three generations. Ysidro and Tatán had known each other since the playpen. They'd been in love since they were sixteen.

November 25, 1973. The day the soldiers came to La Reina. The last day of Louis Tholet's life. The day the Kings of Death became schooled in the business of birth.

Penny could give the day a title, but she couldn't remember all its events. When she attempted to recreate an hour-by-hour timeline, she felt fraudulent. An unreliable narrator. Unable to distinguish what were authentic memories and which were embellished. Or invented.

The soldiers came to La Reina, looking for dissidents, socialists, foreigners, communists, troublemakers. Or anyone associated with such people. Neighbors were dragged from their homes, Penny and Louis among them. The soldiers lined them up against a high brick wall and staged a mock execution.

Penny's hand went to the back of her head, fingertips walking along the scar at her nape. One of the soldiers rifle-butted her. She went down. Then she went out.

When she fluttered back to consciousness, she was on the floor of her house, riding the waves of active labor. The sun had gone down and the house was in total darkness. Santiago was blacked out again and before leaving, the soldiers had cut the phone lines.

After sunset, the city was under a curfew. The army and DINA, Pinochet's secret police, had carte blanche to arrest anyone on the streets. Penny couldn't leave the house, couldn't leave the unspeakable pain that had her by all four limbs and her head. So she blacked out again. Clawed her way up through the darkness only to scream in agony and retreat.

In and out of the dark. Her memory fell into smaller and smaller pieces. Different shades of black. Snippets of sound. It was a movie from a dream she'd read in a book about someone else's past life.

Jude was born on the floor of the house in La Reina, attended by the Kings of Death.

The coffee mug shook in her hands now, because she didn't remember giving birth. Not remembering was part of the story. It could be funny and ironic, or horrifyingly dramatic, depending on how she told the tale. But she'd never considered the ramifications of that blank space in the narrative. She had no reason to.

Until now.

44% Iberian Peninsula.

30% Italy.

0% memory of giving birth.

She remembered waking up in the hospital. She emerged from darkness into a daytime-bright, white room and wondered if she were dead. She turned her head a fraction to the side and the resulting pain made her wish she were dead.

"Descansa," a voice said over the pounding clang between Penny's ears. "Rest now. Just rest."

"¿El bebé?" Penny cried, and then gagged with the pain of crying.

"Lie still now, señora. Hold your head still. You have a serious concussion."

"The baby?"

"He's resting."

"He?"

"Es un niño, sí. Close your eyes now."

She tried to sit up instead. Wailed from the agony of her fractured skull, then vomited. She went on retching with her eyes closed, whispering "¿Niño?" between heaves.

"Está en la guardería, señora. Ahora, descanse."

She retched and rested. She dreamed of soldiers. Rifles cocked and aimed at the row people against the wall. Louis Tholet on his knees, staring straight into the line of fire. Finally hunted down, he was unafraid to face his killers. He'd been here before.

Penny woke and retched. Fell back and rested under the soldiers' aimed rifles. Woke again, crying for her baby and finally, they brought him to her.

"There's your beautiful mami," the nurse said, sing-song under her breath. "There she is."

Swaddled tight to the chin like a burrito, he was laid next to Penny's aching head. She rolled carefully to face her son and put her hand on his chest. Two straight-lined eyes beneath the cuff of a knitted cap. Little mouth sucking at the air, tongue thrusting.

"He's a bear," the nurse said, pulling a bit of the cap back to show a thatch of dark hair. "And señora, look. Look…"

Her fingertip caressed the baby's face. As his lips rooted, looking for milk, tiny indentations creased his cheeks.

"Tiene hoyuelos," the nurse said, laughing.

He has dimples.

<hr />

What was that nurse's name? Penny thought, huddled over the piano keys. She prided herself on remembering people's names. Names and birthdays.

She couldn't remember.

I don't remember giving birth.

I remember the soldiers in the street. Bullets ricocheting off stone walls. The children screaming.

Me screaming when they shot Louis.

I remember waking up. I remember throwing up. I woke up, I threw up, I slept again. Over and over. How many hours was that? Or days? I don't remember.

Thirty-six years and she never contemplated the role time played in the story.

I don't remember Jude being born. I don't remember being brought to the hospital. I don't know how much time passed.

How long before they brought Jude in? Hours?

Days?

I don't remember.

That nurse whose name I can't remember. She showed me his hair and laughed over his dimples.

Ysidro and Tatán came to see her. One held the baby while the other comforted Penny. Then they switched. Mother and infant passed from embrace to embrace. Tatán promised Louis would be buried in the Jewish Cemetery, with a rabbi to say Kaddish. Ysidro promised a beautiful headstone. The Kings of Death promised to keep going to the Estadio and asking about Cleon, doing anything and everything they could to find out where he'd been taken.

They passed tissues and passed the baby. Ysidro cradled the infant's head on his shoulder, singing "Hey Jude," his favorite song.

"So much hair," Tatán said, his index finger tight in the baby's grip. "He has sideburns."

All that thick, dark hair, Penny thought. *The blue eyes and dimples. And when Jude got his first pair of glasses, Cleon laughed and laughed. "I don't believe it. He looks just like Uncle Louis."*

"Querida."

Penny looked up, blinking away the past. Cleon stood by the piano, cane in one hand, her phone in the other, holding it out. "You had a text from him. I heard it ping last night. Late."

She took the device and read it.

I'm so glad you're my mom and I don't tell you enough. I love you.

She smiled above a warm cloud of tentative relief in her chest.

Cleon had gone to the kitchen to pour himself coffee. "Did you sleep all right?"

"Not really."

"Me neither."

Few were the times when Penny regarded her husband's injuries as injurious to her. Now was one of those times. She wanted a physical rescue. She wanted him to swoop in, crouch down and pull her into his arms. Hard enough to fall on the floor, where he'd fiercely draw her into his lap and rock her.

He couldn't swoop, crouch or throw himself to the floor. Couldn't tolerate her weight on his legs for longer than a minute. As he eased onto the couch, Penny held his mug. It was his favorite—an almost dainty stoneware cup with *Good Morning, Asshole* in elegant blue script.

She curled beside him. Walter put his paws on the cushions, all big eyes and quivering nose, but Cleon nudged the little dog away.

He couldn't swoop, but he could give Penny his fiercely undivided attention.

A long quiet moment passed.

"I've been thinking," she said. "How I don't remember him being born."

He put his big hand on hers. "We're getting upset over a fluke. A couple of digits got transposed, someone mis-typed."

"Cleon, if I walked out of that hospital with another woman's baby—"

"Shh." He squeezed her fingers. "You're getting way ahead of yourself. This is a fluke. Serena said they've processed over three million kits. It was bound to happen. Somewhere out there, a young, Spanish-Italian man is staring at his results, wondering what the hell is going on."

A hiccupped laugh in Penny's chest, the kind that could easily turn into a sob. "I feel terrible."

"It's all a simple mistake."

Penny clung hard to his strong grip. Her other hand worried at the scar at the back of her head, as if she could massage memory out of the old wound.

I don't remember Jude being born.

"One day soon, we'll be laughing about this," Cleon said.

Penny's eyes felt too wide for her face as she nodded, fearing it would be the kind of laughter that quickly turned to weeping.

CLEÓN

*Y*OUR SISTER GLORIA IS *wary of Uncle Louis's long, complicated silences, his anxious sighs and quick temper.*

You think he's wonderful. He knows everything. He's the one who renames you Cleón, after a great Athenian general.

Louis is a masterful storyteller. He never begins a tale with "once" or "once upon a time." Rather he begins with a German phrase: "Stell dir vor."

Imagine yourself.

Louis is a second-person raconteur, putting the listener in the role of the hero. He tells a story about you, not he or she, and he always tells a story precisely the same way. No deviations, no embellishments, no alternate endings.

He rarely tells what was done to him in Sachsenhausen, but he will talk at length about his mates, with whom he endured.

"Was ist das für ein Wort auf Spanisch?" he asks.

"Compañero," you say. "Mate."

Louis and nine other men in his block survived together.

"Some inmates had solitary tactics," he says. "We ten bonded forces. We made a minyan and we made our own covenant. Not to God but to survival. Ten men. One commandment: thou shalt survive."

Thou shalt survive, Arthur Faktor.

Thou shalt survive, Vojtech Friedmann.

And Jakob Bergmann.

Salomon Eckstein.

Boruch Irom.

Jolan Zolschan.

Hermann Bakker.

Szmul Korenbilt.

Zigfried Flechner.

And Louis Tholet, especially. Thou shalt survive.

"Together, we built a memory palace," Louis says. "A palace with ten floors. Ten wings to every floor. Ten rooms in every wing. In every room, ten stories. One from each man's life. A fortress of tales, rich and detailed, built into the walls and ceiling and floor and furnishings."

"And you remember them all?" you ask.

He nods. "As the only one who walked out of there alive, it's my job. I am the steward and caretaker of the whole palace."

One night when you are twelve, Louis sits in his comfortable chair, folds his hands in his lap and closes his eyes. You sit at his feet, watching and counting as he takes ten deep breaths.

"It's a simple front door to such a magnificent place," he says. "You knock ten times and speak the password: stell dir vor."

Imagine yourself.

"Imagínate," you say, because the old man has tasked you with helping him practice his Spanish.

"Imagínate." He smiles. "So. Imagine yourself on the first floor. You walk down the first wing. Come into the first room. Sit down to hear the first story, which is called Arthur Faktor Goes to the Circus."

You are twelve. Too big to cry. But the stories from the palace fill you with complex and unexpected emotion. You wish Louis would stop. You want him never to stop. You sit through three tales that night, charmed at the telling by heart, horrified at how they were learned by heart. You're both annoyed and grateful when your mother sends you to bed. You wait until the house is dark and still before you let down and weep.

Never again do you ask Uncle Louis about the memory palace. It is far too awesome a place, too full of unfathomable acts of survival, and you are unworthy to walk its halls. You could never achieve such a feat of architectural courage.

You are wrong about this.

Nineteen years later, while imprisoned in the Villa Grimaldi, you will build your own fortress of survival. But it's a palace with only room for one.

THE FONDUE POT

1

IT WAS FRIDAY NIGHT, which meant Full Frontal Fondue, a moveable feast Jude and his friends had been doing for years. Tonight, the festivities were at Hewan's place in North Beacon Hill. In addition to the requisite drinks and cheese fondue, she made a killer non-dairy artichoke dip she called cheese fondont.

Hewan was a witness coordinator for the Western District of Washington and worked mostly with victims of domestic violence. Her longtime partner was named Bert Gesundheit.

"For real?" Jude asked, the first time they met.

"For real," Bert said. "Go ahead, test me. Sneeze."

Jude faked an achoo.

"Myself," Bert said.

Bert worked at Seattle University's Center for Religious Wisdom & World Affairs. If there were a cooler title on a business card than Master of Divinity, someone would have to tell Jude what it was.

"Can I fall in love with him?" he asked Hewan.

"Feel free. You're my gay husband, it's only fair Bert be your straight-mate."

Bert had a harem of straight-mates. Everyone loved his gentle compassion and open ear. Deeply spiritual without being obnoxious, his casual but brilliant insights over the fondue pot could make the food fall out of your mouth. Bert only gave a sheepish smile and said, "Damn, I almost sounded like I knew what I was talking about."

Bert had an equal sign tattooed vertically on his right thumb. When he reached to shake hands, the tattoo reminded him to treat everyone as a peer. He had no hair on his head, a magnificent full beard and a PhD in hugging.

"Dude, what is *wrong*?" he asked tonight. "Your aura is fucked up."

"Everything is fucked up," Jude said, a PhD in misery.

"Come here." Bert wrapped arms around him, hands palpating along Jude's spine. "I'm not kidding, your aura is brown. Jesus, I'm going to have to smudge the house after you leave."

"Sorry."

Hewan put a glass of wine in Jude's hand. "What's killing you, shmoopy?"

If he were going to spill about the DNA test, now was the time, while he had Hewan and Bert to himself. But a weird, embarrassed shame had a chokehold on the story, begging him not to bring it up. Besides, the second test was at the lab. Serena paid extra for a rush job. When it all turned out to be a mistake, he'd have wasted a perfectly good bitch session.

"Residual hangover from Vancouver," he said. "I guess. All my issues are kicking my ass."

"That means they need attention," Bert said.

"B, I love you, but sometimes…"

Bert laughed and kissed his head. "You are a brave, beautiful and resilient soul. Let your issues sit in your lap and whine. Be patient. They'll get bored with you and leave."

"You almost sound like you know what you're talking about."

"Come here, slave," Hewan said, putting a cutting board and knife in Jude's hands. "Slice and dice while you're getting your ass kicked."

Hewan was ruled by common sense and compulsive list-making, and never coddled Jude's propensity for drama and exaggeration. She knew exactly what to do with his moods: give him jobs to feel useful, shower him with physical contact and not ask too many questions.

"You're doing great," she said. "I really don't see anything unusual about this funk. I can tell it sucks, I don't want it for you, I'd make it all go away if I could. But I'm not shocked you're feeling depressed."

"Telling you, Jude," Bert said. "You're right where you're supposed to be."

"I just want to move on from it already."

"You will," Hewan said, drawing her spatula through the melting cheese. "Bert's right. You'll get to a point where you've felt enough and you're bored with being blue."

"I thought I was bored with it when I was driving home from Vancouver. I was in this great place, looking forward and moving on."

"Well, you were wrong," Bert said. "Or to be nicer about it, you were misinformed. The optimism you felt was defective. The universe recalled it and will be sending you a better version. Optimism two-point-oh."

"Get the fuck out of my face."

Bert's laugh bounced off the walls. "Come on, that was good. You liked it."

His vegetables sliced, Jude tossed his glasses down on the table and scrubbed hands through his hair, sighing viciously. "Thing is," he said, "none of my relationships since Feño have felt like Feño. Do you get one chance at that kind of love? That adolescent euphoria of feeling everything to your bones?"

"Euphoria isn't sustainable," Bert said. "It's the candy bar breakfast of a relationship. Burst of invincible energy followed by a crash halfway through the day, and you crawl through the final hours doing the bare minimum."

"Well that's depressing," Hewan said.

"Love thrives on protein, not sugar."

"B, shut up."

"All right, smartass, what's your answer?"

"My answer is Jude, you are thirty fucking six years old," Hewan said. "You will never experience teen euphoria again. That ship sailed on your twentieth birthday, same way it does on everyone's twentieth birthday. The *SS Twentysomething Euphoria* didn't come in because your leg was broken with a baseball bat, which'll make anyone cautious. Now *Thirtysomething Euphoria* is on the horizon. And..." Her head tilted, one corner of her mouth smiling. "What would Penny Tholet say?"

Jude sighed again, hard enough to make the paper napkins flutter in their basket. "And. Dot-dot-dot. Who are you going to be?"

The doorbell rang, heralding the rest of the squad. Bert went to answer it and Hewan gave Jude a last squeeze.

"I love you always," she said against his head.

"I'm sorry I'm such a downer."

"You're human." She poured him another glass of wine. "And this ointment is sweet."

"The what is sweet?"

She shuddered. "Don't make me say it again."

"Ointment."

"Shut up."

"Moist."

"Jude, I will kill you."

"I'd like to point out that ointment makes the toilet seat moist."

She started whacking him with a dishtowel, screaming like Joan Crawford. "No! O-i diphthongs! Ever!"

FONDUE AND FONDONT AND the sweet ointment of friendship soothed him for the next few hours. But as soon as he sat down to practice that night, an enormous surge of emotion nearly toppled him off the piano bench. He gulped it back into his throat, where it stuck like a fist of iron.

"What the fuck," he said through his teeth, smashing both fists on the keys. "Fucking enough already."

Jude hadn't cried since he was seventeen. After the attack, he seethed, he raged, he brooded, he freaked out and threw up and melted down. But he never cried. He howled like a dog when blood spurted up onto the windshield of his father's car. He punched a wall once. Kicked things out of his way. He moped, sulked, picked on his siblings, snotted back to his parents, acted out and acted up.

He never cried. Not even after agreeing to see Feño one last time, so they could break up properly. *Especially* not after that.

He didn't cry now, but emotion was on him like a fever and he was mourning his youth. Abandoning the piano to reach up to high bookshelves for photo albums and yearbooks, dig in the closet for shoeboxes of notes and mementos.

I don't want you to suffer, he told himself. *If you have to do this now, we can do this now. But I don't want you to suffer.*

A photo turned over in his fingers. He and Feño in the woods of Central Park, leaning against one of their marked trees, looking up at the camera in Jude's outstretched hand. Bursting with life. Crazy in love. Eyes shining and sated. A freshly carved J/F in the bark above Feño's shoulder.

Jude's eyes were dry as he gazed on the last days of pure happiness before the Condor hunted them down.

He had to do this now.

THE GUN

*T*HEY BECAME SECRET LOVERS. Life became beautiful and dangerous.

At school, they kept their distance. Alone, they couldn't keep their hands off each other. The sneaking and the secrecy and the defiance made them even more crazed. They went at each other in cars, or in the woods at Central Park, or a half-dozen other hideaways they sussed out in Vancouver. Every once in a great, beautiful while, they were gifted an empty house for a few luxurious, feverish hours. Once, the planets aligned with both sets of parents out of town for a weekend, and they lived together for two days at Feño's house. Lying around in bed. Naked and tangled with the radio playing, every song an anthem written expressly for them.

During those precious, horizontal moments in a nest of sheets and blankets, Jude licked every inch of Feño's body. He was so in love, so besotted with the world and music and the whorl of fine hairs around Feño's belly button, he wanted to die. Not in despair or surrender. He wanted to resurrect. Explode out of this earthly shell and ascend to some higher plain where it felt like this all the time. Feño on him and in him and singing to him forever.

He didn't know such happiness existed.

"I'd fucking die for you," Feño said, an inky black silhouette looming over Jude. "I wish…"

"What?"

"I wish we could just be. I wish I could be with you without feeling like I'd be in danger. You know?"

"I know."

"Being so alert and aware and paranoid all the time. It's exhausting. This?" He gestured around his room, redolent with sex and sweat, the floor littered with condom wrappers. "This is fucking luxury. And I feel like I can't relax all the way into it because come Monday, I have to go back to being on my guard again." He settled on his elbows, taking Jude's head in his big hands. "I hate it. Soon as the bell rings for first period, the minute you're out of my sight, I start worrying if today's the day someone gives you shit."

"Not the day someone gives *you* shit?"

A flash of teeth as Feño's smile unfolded. "I can handle it."

"Because you have it," Jude said, biting along his neck. "Right?"

A chuckle within Feño's chest. "I always have it."

"Let me see."

Feño reached long for his bedside table and slid open the drawer. His hand came out filled with a milky, silvery glint.

Rossi 461 .357 Mag, Jude thought, like a prayer.

Braced on an arm, Feño offered the gun but Jude shook his head. He'd held it a few times. Its weight was a terrifying thrill but when he handed it back, his palm always felt slimy for a minute after.

He didn't like touching it. But he did like knowing Feño had it.

Sometimes at school, or in the car, or in the park, he'd casually ask, "You have it?"

Feño would answer, deadpan, "I always have it."

Really, Feño didn't do more than have it. He found the gun in the woods and instead of turning it into the police, he kept it. He liked it. It wasn't loaded and he didn't have the first idea how to go about getting it loaded. Or the need. It just lived in his drawer, making him feel better. Knowing it was there comforted Jude. And during that magical cohabiting weekend, he discovered making love in the Rossi's heavy, slick presence—even unloaded and impotent—was a *sick* turn-on.

"You know I'd kill anyone who tried to hurt you," Feño whispered in the dark.

He never got to make good on the vow, because he didn't have the gun the night he and Jude were ambushed by El Cóndor. It was in his drawer, doing nothing and comforting no one. And it took a long time for Jude to stop obsessively recreating the night of the attack, this time placing the Rossi in Feño's hand.

In Jude's early revisionist fantasies, the gun remained unloaded. Feño merely brandished its empty threat, de-escalated the situation and made the Condor take to the skies in terror. Nobody was hurt. Laced with the adrenaline of a narrow escape, Feño and Jude fell on each other like spoils of war, laughing and rutting in the playground dirt.

But after he gave Feño his breakup, his closure and his goodbye, Jude changed the scenario. Now the gun was loaded. Feño fired in the air. Again, just to scare the Condor. Nobody was hurt. But soon the dose wasn't enough to fix the addict. The scene shifted again, and Feño started shooting to maim.

Then to kill.

I'd kill anyone who tried to hurt you.

In each progressive version, Jude made Feño's aim train higher and higher along the Condor's body as he kept the promise. He shot Juan-Mateo's knees out. Then he shot him in the ass. In the back. Through the heart. At Jude's lowest point, Feño aimed highest and blew the Condor's head off, sending blood and brains through the diamonds of the chain link fence.

Jude added courtroom drama to the script, playing judge, jury and witness. It would be ruled self-defense. Feño would be sentenced to probation. Fine, maybe a little bit of jail in a minimum-security facility. Or time served. But then he'd be free, and he and Jude would run away to Toronto or Montreal and be together forever.

I wish he had it.

I wish he killed El Cóndor that night.

It took a long time to stop doing this.

<hr />

JUDE SAT IN THE dark, surrounded by souvenirs of the past. His eyes fixed on his own bedside table drawer, which never held a gun within.

Down low with nothing to aim for, he wished he had it.

THE WITCHES OF KILLARNEY

"**W**HAT ARE YOU READING?" Cleon said drowsily, reaching for the corner of Penny's book and turning it toward him. "Oh, you're reading me. How kind."

Cleon had written four books on human rights abuse in South America, but it was his magnum opus in Penny's hands. *The Witches of Killarney: The Women of Vancouver's Chilean Community.*

"Reading that for any particular reason," he asked. "Or is it just to bask in my pedantic bullshit?"

"I'm basking in your pedantic bullshit."

"I'm so glad I married you." He moved up closer against her hip and slid the stump of his right leg into the nest of warmth under her knees.

"Cold?" she asked.

"Mm."

"Put clothes on."

"Don't want to."

She tugged the comforter higher, leaned and buried her face in his thick, white hair for a long inhale. Then she went back to reading, resting a hand on Cleon's broad, bare back. Outside was damp, grey chill, with a mean wind off Puget Sound making the tips of lilac bushes scrape and rattle against the window. Inside was a snug siesta, with soft sheets, pillows piled high and empty mugs of tea on the side tables.

Penny believed in the power of taking to one's bed.

Once her children knew how to make a sandwich, she would occasionally announce to her family, "I am taking to my bed. Fend for thyself. I shall rise in twenty-four hours, a better woman."

To which Cleon, bless his soul, would always reply, "Impossible."

Penny would put out the Do Not Disturb sign. Amass every pillow in the house, stack books, magazines, snacks and the remote within easy reach. She donned soft clothing and ceremoniously placed herself between the covers. The ceremony was key, it highlighted the deliberate nature of taking to the bed, as did setting a time limit. A running clock told the world *I am having a breakdown, I shall return.* Without it, you were giving up.

"Mami invented self-care before self-care was a thing," Serena said.

Self-care. This generation had such good terminology. Penny would never say surviving the trauma of a murderous dictatorship would've been easier in the here and now, only that the language was better. Nobody knew what PTSD was in the seventies, now it was a household acronym. Maybe mental health and depression weren't completely de-stigmatized, but they were no longer spoken in whispers. Half the people you knew went to therapy, had been in therapy or joked they could use therapy. Television commercials hawked antidepressants more often than cold medicine. Penny would've given anything to have had just the vocabulary back in the seventies, let alone the prescriptions.

"I'm taking to my bed in self-care," she said to Cleon today, after a morning of boring errands and billpaying and housecleaning.

Bless his soul, he came with her. When the Sound was too rough for kayaking, he liked to make love in the afternoons, followed by a long nap.

It wasn't always this way. For two painful decades, their sex life had been erratic at best, non-existent at worst. One bad year in their thirties, they had intercourse exactly four times. The fourth time produced Aiden.

Penny had always been a sexualized creature and in Cleon she found a bespoke lover. She loved being married to him and she loved going to bed with him. Naturally after he was released from prison and they fled Chile, sex was out of the question. The man couldn't stand unassisted, let alone roll around under the sheets. He was ill, traumatized, learning to walk again, navigating a new homeland and a new language. They had an infant and were dodging all the wrenches of new parenthood. Sex? Sex was expendable ballast on this ship of madness. Penny would rather sleep.

But as the seas calmed and she got control of the vessel, Penny woke up. She wanted to go to bed with her man, her partner and best friend.

He didn't seem to want her. And it hurt.

In all other aspects, he was an ideal mate. Verbal with affection, with compliments on her appearance, praise for her accomplishments. Gratitude for how she helped him over the mobility obstacles, navigated him through health problems, soothed him down from anxiety and woke him up from nightmares.

"You saved me," he said, reaching out to touch her. Always hugging her, holding her hand, brushing her arm as she walked by. "Every day you've been saving me."

He never failed to tell and show her his love and she never once, ever, doubted he loved her.

But when it came to matters of the bedroom, Cleon was as disinterested as a fixed cat. Even when the interest was there, it carried an underlying current of take-it-or-leave-it. It was easy to blame the meds—doctors had warned decreased libido was a common side effect. But the things they prescribed to take the edge off, or rather, to give Cleon some kind of edge, didn't seem to work. Which made Penny sense something else was going on. Something deeper and more sinister spawned in the Villa Grimaldi.

"Did something happen?" she asked her husband carefully. Casually. Never in bed. Always in a neutral place with no distractions.

But as verbally lavish as he was with his love, Cleon was equally stingy with anything having to do with Chile.

"Leave it be," he said. "I know what you're asking and no, nothing like that happened. I don't want to talk about what happened. I don't want to bring it into this house. It's too clean."

He was forever describing their life post-Chile as *clean* and Penny couldn't get him to open up about that any more than she could get him to talk about the imprisonment. He knew he frustrated her, but his psyche was too far into this spiral to pull up out of it.

"I'm sorry," he said in the dark, when he didn't want to make love, or when his best attempt felt like the bare minimum. "I can't help it. I'm trying. I do what I can, I love you with everything I got, Pen. I swear..."

She was afraid if she pressed too hard, she'd push him away and be left with nothing. She had no other skills. No other language. She backed down, took the sex as it came, and threw her leftover passion into motherhood and the Chilean ex-pat community.

Life moved on a loop between her home, the co-op on School Avenue, the new co-op on Commercial Drive and the nearby La Quena Coffee House. In between mothering her trio of children, being a helpmeet to her husband, and caretaking the old farmhouse on Ormidale Street, Penny organized events. She presided meetings. She chaired committees. She welcomed, advocated, translated. Oiled wheels and paved ways. She kept her spare bedroom and bath cleaned and ready for any newly arrived exile who needed to put their head down for a night. She kept extra canned goods and bags of rice for any family caught short between paychecks. She raised awareness while she raised her children and took children of exhausted, traumatized parents under her wing. Among them Feño Paloma. Rare was the Saturday night he didn't sleep in Jude's top bunk, then sit at the Sunday table for pancakes or waffles.

"Do you two remember meeting at the airport," Penny would ask the boys, just so she could watch the minuscule exchanged glance before they answered, "No."

At the hub of the Chilo-Canadian neighborhood of Killarney was the housing commune on School Avenue. The hub of the commune was the large hall where political events and *penas*, social gatherings, took place. The penas allowed the exiles to raise their children in a Chilean atmosphere. Through food, music, plays and dancing, the kids were able to sustain their Spanish and remain aware of their heritage.

The penas were where Cleon got the idea for his first book. As a journalist, he was always looking for a good human story. His quiet, gentle-giant appearance, his attentive compassion and his ordeal in the Villa Grimaldi made him the ear that even the most reluctant survivors whispered toward. Thus Cleon Tholet, so loathe to speak of his own experience, became the curator of Killarney's collective ordeal. At every pena, you could find him at a table in some far-off corner, listening to an exile give their testimony.

Penny worried compiling so many blood-curling and abhorrent tales would send her husband into despair, but he seemed to thrive on the work. A holy purpose lay in being a witness and scribe. He was so enthused and consumed, Penny went all-in on the project, transcribing the tapes and typing endless drafts of the manuscript that became *Echoes and Exiles*.

It was a clunky, amateur publication, but the next pena was declared a release party, and nearly everyone in the neighborhood went home with his or her signed copy. The bit between his teeth, Cleon launched into his next book, *Inheritance of Fear: Women, Children and Human Rights in South America*. It reached a wider audience and took Cleon on a modest book tour through the academic institutes of British Columbia and Alberta. Then came his tour de force, *The Witches of Killarney: The Women of Vancouver's Chilean Community*. It won a Governor General's award, the Hubert Evans Prize and the Lionel Gelber Prize.

While Cleon reveled in success, Penny suffered in confused silence. She didn't know she harbored a survivor's guilt until acting as her husband's research assistant unleashed it. Every story she transcribed made her own pain more insignificant. Each account put to paper only diminished and dismissed every item in her catalog of horrors.

Her husband was arrested, tortured and nearly crippled for life.

But he was released and he is alive.

She was assaulted by soldiers in the street outside her own home.

At least you weren't tortured and gang raped.

She watched her husband's uncle and her neighbors shot in cold blood.

But you were not shot.

She was rifle-butted in the head and sent into early labor.

But your baby is alive. He wasn't tortured in front of you to get you to inform on your loved ones.

She had to flee the country she loved and identified with.

You fled to the country of your birth, straight into the arms of your rich father whose money greased the wheels and paved the way for your new life. You had your papers and your people. You spoke the language and knew the lay of the land. While hundreds of other exiles came with nothing and arrived at nothing.

Her husband rarely wanted to make love to her.

You have a husband. He adores you. Worships you. Never fails to tell you he loves you.

Other women you know will never feel their husband's touch, never hear those words of love again.

You suffered nothing compared to them.

Shut up and do something.

She did and did. Stifling the dissatisfaction and remembering it could be worse.

Then they got the call from the Vancouver Police Department.

Then they were standing at Jude's hospital bedside, gazing down on his broken body.

Then the Witches of Killarney turned on them.

And Penny could no longer do.

IN THE WAKE OF Jude's attack, Cleon took action while Penny fell apart. Not right away. Her habits sustained her as they settled in Seattle. She stuffed her pain under the mattress of her son's anguish. Staying strong and tight and silent because she suffered nothing compared to him.

Shut up and do something.

She did what she did best. She knew how to be a stranger in a strange land. She knew how to organize, preside, negotiate, advocate, oil, grease and pave. She did and did until the day they dropped Jude off at the University of the Pacific in Stockton. She cried the whole drive home, which was expected. But then she couldn't stop crying. She couldn't get out of bed.

She couldn't do.

Within two weeks, she was admitted to the Ballard campus of Swedish Behavioral Health, suffering a complete nervous breakdown. For the first time, she told her story to a pair of neutral, professional ears, who, for the first time, called it what it was. Her therapist underlined certain words in the narrative, acknowledging their horrible impact and not allowing them to be dismissed.

The women Penny worked tirelessly alongside and the women for whom she tirelessly worked had *turned against* her. It was a *betrayal.* The betrayal was a *coup* on her life. She didn't leave Canada, she *fled.* Again. For the *second time* she picked up her family and in a state of emergency with the irrefutably real fear of physical *harm,* she *escaped* the country she had looked upon as her *home.*

And *goddammit,* the loss of her sex life was *not* a fair or *acceptable* trade-off.

It was then Penny crafted a motto and personal credo: *True. And. Dot-dot-dot. Who are you going to be now?*

"I can't live like this anymore," she said to Cleon. "This is not who I am, this is not who I'm going to continue to be. When I come home, things have to change. No more telling me we're too clean to talk about what happened in Chile. It's time to get dirty."

She didn't believe in God but she did believe in a divine order. Things happened for a reason. Her breakdown gave Cleon his own come-to-the-divine-order moment, realizing Penny could no longer be and never should have been the basket in which he placed all his broken eggshells without revealing how they'd been shattered in the first place.

He began to tell her things. Or rather, he started by showing her.

"Under one condition," he said. "Not in the house. I don't want any of this associated with any part of our house. Not the kitchen table, not the living room floor, not the basement."

So they got a hotel room. Cleon brought a box he'd stored in the garage all these years, filled with dozens of sketches. Every piece of paper was an ear Cleon had whispered into, using pens and pencils as his voice. Over twenty years, he'd drawn a secret museum of memories. A gallery of nightmares. A stomach-turning display of torture and misery and agony and fear. One by one, he and Penny took them out and spread them on the hotel room floor.

They discovered their respective survivor's guilt, rooted in different experiences in Chile, bore the same poisoned fruit: *You are alive, while so many others are dead.*

You suffered nothing compared to them.

Shut up and do something.

"Let's try a new way," Penny said. "We get rid of shut up. We keep do something. Do something and be someone."

Cleon went for counseling, which he'd tried before, but this time he stuck with it. He found a psychiatrist who hailed from Argentina. Dr. Saavedra had witnessed death and detention and disappearance. She spoke all of Cleon's languages and understood the birthplace of his trauma. She helped leech out some of the silent, potent venom lingering in his bones. The unresolved grief for the loss of his beloved uncle Louis, whom he never saw again. The guilt for attempting to survive the Villa Grimaldi the way Louis survived Sachsenhausen, and failing.

"Failing how?" Penny asked.

"He made a palace with ten rooms," Cleon said. "He bonded with ten other men to survive and made himself the steward of their stories. I did it alone. I let no one else in. My palace only had room for one. I cared about my survival and mine alone, and…" He looked at Penny and forced up a secret that made his teeth chatter as it passed. "Dr. Saavedra says maybe I've been…unconsciously castrating myself for it ever since."

Penny went still and quiet. She cupped her hands, made them soft, and let Cleon set down the rotten teeth he was yanking from the jaws of the past. She held them a minute. Saw them. Weighed and measured them.

Then she handed them back.

They weren't for her to fix or keep. They simply asked their existence be acknowledged.

Not all the emotional gangrene could be exised from Cleon's soul, but thank God it was the early nineties and the emergence of third-generation antidepressants. It took time and patience, but finally Dr. Saavedra found the right combination and dosage of SSRIs that could hold Cleon's anxieties at bay without sacrificing his sex drive.

Penny and Cleon renewed their wedding vows and Seattle became the Florence of a marital renaissance. They discovered kayaking, which freed Cleon from the prison of his injuries, gave him physical movement and adventure and a new group of friends at the marina. He started art classes, a what-the-hell-why-not impulse that led to him re-creating the secret, one-room palace from the Villa Grimaldi. This fortress was an act of creative survival so extraordinary, Cleon's consciousness had declared it inconsequential. Un-noteworthy. He buried it and didn't think to dig it up until someone suggested he could.

It saved his life.

In a bizarre way, Jude's attack saved all their lives.

On the one hand, it seemed appalling to think so much beneficial change was conceived in the belly of a hate crime. On the other, if Jude's leg hadn't been broken, if the family hadn't pulled up stakes and fled Vancouver, if they hadn't come to Seattle, if Penny hadn't had a breakdown, if one of Cleon's colleagues hadn't referred him to Dr. Saavedra...

"Put down the pedantic bullshit," Cleon murmured, taking *The Witches of Killarney* out of Penny's hands and tossing it.

Like a creature from the primordial deep, his arms wormed around Penny's waist and dragged her down beneath the covers. Into the warm lair of their bizarre, golden-year rebirth, where they had a lot of time to make up for, a lot of revolting developments to reverse.

It was who they were now.

CLE◉N

*A*T THE ESTADIO DE *Chile, you and the hundreds of other detainees are kept in the stands, spectators to your own misery. You are utterly helpless. Your hands tied, your body's every move tracked by the muzzle of a machine gun. The lights are constantly on, so you lose track of time. You only know it's day or night by what the guards are eating.*

You eat nothing.

Thoughts of your wife tear your heart in two. You lament her name into the cup of your cuffed hands, whisper it in the tiniest, most secret folds of your mind. In public, to the world, she is Penny. Only you are allowed to use her real name, and in only tiny, secret, whispers.

(Lucy.)

(Lucy, my love, we were going to grow old together.)

You must survive. For her and the baby. And for the five days you're detained at the Estadio, you try Uncle Louis's way. You imagine yourself in a house and associate each room with a memory or anecdote of your life.

(It was supposed to be our life, Lucy.)

Stop that. Concentrate.

It's hard. Fear and anxiety make the roof collapse, the walls cave in and the foundation crumble.

You try again.

(Lucy, Lucy.)

Basta. Imagina.

A kitchen. The center of a house. Its heart and soul. A table and chairs. Sit down. Smell what's baking in the oven. Now think of a time in your life when you were happy. Tell a story.

Stell dir vor.

Imagine yourself.

It's 1963. You're twenty-one. Both the Beatles and the new neighborhood of La Reina emerge onto the scene, giving you a new home and a new obsession.

The Fab Four will never play any country in Latin America. Mexico is mad for "Los Bitles," but the country's dictatorship denies a concert to its children during the 1964 world tour.

1964? Shit, you've jumped ahead. No matter, this will be a saga, not a tale. So be it.

You and your friends beg, nag, cajole and convince the owner of the local record store to order the albums. Beatles lyrics are the first English words you learn and you teach them all to Uncle Louis.

"Lucy in a sky?" he says. "With diamonds? What's that supposed to mean?"

"Who cares," you say, hands behind your head, staring up at the ceiling, which transforms into an immense, indigo bowl of night sky, the stars arranged in the shape of a woman.

But no stars are visible over the Estadio because the lights are always on.

Your hands are tied. You're helpless, enraged and terrified. Lucy isn't in the sky. She's at home, pregnant like a berry and no doubt frightened out of her mind.

Lucy, you think, your cuffed hands trembling.

(Lucy, my love...)

THE SILENCE

*A*s the Tholets read the results of their second DNA tests, the kitchen became quieter than the space between symphony movements. Only the pitter-patter of rain outside. The tick of the clock as the appliances glanced sideways at each other and shrugged their shoulders.

> *Iberian Peninsula: 44%*
> *Italy: 30%*
> *Greece & The Balkans: 15%*
> *France: 11%*

The silence became unbearable. Penny was pale as ash, her mouth caught up in her hand. Cleon, who had been standing, sat down carefully, rubbing one palm against the other, staring into space. Serena's arms were crossed and her lips pressed into a razor-thin line.

They jumped in their chairs when Jude chuckled. "Well, this is a revolting development."

"Juleón." Penny's voice was a thick, choked bubble.

Jude reminded himself he hadn't cried since he was seventeen. His eyes were dry, but they burned hot when he looked at her. "You got a hell of a poker face, Mom."

Her cheekbones winced at the English. "I don't understand."

"Neither do I. I mean, wouldn't it have been easier to tell me I was adopted?" He flicked the card with the DNA results across the table. "You were busted six weeks ago, you could've come clean then."

"There was nothing to come clean about," she cried. Her hand gestured at the table. "I don't *understand*."

"It makes no sense," Cleon said, shaking his head. "I don't understand how this happened…"

And all at once, Jude was done. His entire life story bubbled up in a rage that made him want to turn the table over. He stood up and yanked his jacket off the back of the chair.

"Where are you going," Serena said.

"The fuck out of here."

"Jude, don't," Cleon said. "We need to talk—"

Jude whipped around, pointing a finger at his mother. "What the *hell* did you do," he said.

Cleon's face flushed and he pointed at Jude. "Don't talk to her that way."

Penny was in tears. "Juleón, please."

"Don't fucking Juleón me. Who the hell do you think you are?"

"Jude," Cleon said, raising his voice. "You're not adopted."

Jude turned on him. "Just how stupid do you think I am?"

He kicked the chair out of his way and walked out of his parents' home. His phone started blowing up before his car reached the end of Alki Boulevard. He ignored the calls and texts. At a red light, he powered down the phone and tossed it on the passenger side floor.

SAINT JUDE

"Judas (not the Iscariot) said to Him,
'Lord, what then has happened that you
disclose yourself to us and not to the world?'"

—John 14:22

THE APOLOGY

*W*HEN IT CAME TO his imprisonment in the Villa Grimaldi, Cleon was adamant about telling his children only what he felt they needed to know. Only what their ages and individual psyches could stand to hear.

Aiden's version of the story was stripped down to bare bones, because he was the youngest and because he moved in a world with little nuance. Serena's version didn't need much more teasing out, at least not from Cleon. His legs and his scars and his nervous quirks were enough of a plot outline. When she needed facts and details to fill the gaps in the narrative, she got them from her mother. She and Penny had always been two remnants from the same bolt of cloth.

"You are the sweetest, most serene child," both Penny and Cleon said to their extraordinary daughter. Except Penny always followed up with, "And how many kittens did you drown today?"

"None yet," Serena said, on a good day. Or, "Fifty-six," on a not-so-good day. On really bad days, she drowned tigers.

Jude's story started out the same as Aiden's, then gained height and weight as he grew up and began asking more complex questions. He took a page from his father's book of quirks and only wanted to know where his father was during the coup, not what happened there. He let strictly alone what went on in the Villa Grimaldi.

He disappeared it, Penny thought.

Sixteen was the year Jude came out to his parents. It was also the year he studied the Holocaust in social studies class. He already knew his great-uncle Louis had been in Sachsenhausen, and he knew Louis was homosexual. Now Jude was putting the two things together, both his sexual identity and his tender empathy firing on all cylinders.

"Was he deported for being Jewish?" he asked. "Or for being gay?"

He was alone at the table with Cleon and Penny, but his gaze instinctively flicked toward his siblings' chairs, making sure they were empty. These things were not meant for their ears.

"Both," Cleon said. "If he were a straight Jew or a gay Gentile, he'd be rounded up. He was both."

"Kind of a miracle he survived at all."

"Mm. Not many did."

"The Nazis castrated him?"

Cleon nodded as Penny collected plates and quietly took them to the sink. Always she and Cleon had been seamless in their handling of the children. Telepathically passing the baton between, across and within tough conversations. Each knew when to work together and when to discreetly retreat and signal to the other, *You got this one. I'll cover you.*

"Castrated, like...they cut it off?"

"They removed his testicles. He still had a penis."

"Oh." Jude's brow knitted, obviously trying to work out the anatomical repercussions. "While he was living with you in Chile, did he have a boyfriend?"

"That, hueón, was something of a mystery. If he had a lover or a partner, I didn't know about it. Pen, you recall?"

"No," Penny said. "He had lots of friends. They went to the movies, went to the theater. Came over and drank and played cards. But if he had someone special, he kept it hidden."

"Too risky," Jude said. "Maybe he felt Jews were safe but gay people were still fair game."

"Maybe," Cleon said. "To that end, he collected companions, not lovers."

"Man, that sucks. I mean that he survived Hitler only to end up gunned down by Pinochet. What the fuck?"

Neither Cleon nor Penny minded their kids cursing in the house (after what they endured, they were supposed to be offended by naughty language?), but all the careless bravado was swallowed up by the vacuum of Cleon's silence. The lull stretched out so long, even Penny glanced back to assess his expression.

This was 1989, when Cleon had exhausted the pharmacopoeia of second-generation antidepressants. He had to stop the Bupropion, because it gave him seizures. They tried Trazodone, which gave him the sexual appetite of Wilt Chamberlain, accompanied by a hostile irritability that made him utterly undesirable to be around, let alone sleep with. Now he was nicely tolerating Nomifensine. Meaning he was ambivalent in bed, but recognizable to his family.

He griped about the chronic dry mouth, and Penny watched as he drained the last of his Shaftebury dark ale in one gulp.

"¿Querido, tráeme otra cerveza, po?"

Jude fetched another beer and opened it.

"Chile has a dirty little secret," Cleon said. "A concentration camp for gay men up in the north. It's called Pisagua."

"A camp, a real camp? For gay people?"

"In the thirties it was, under Ibáñez. During the war, it expanded to include citizens of enemy nations. Then after the war, in forty-eight and forty-nine, they sent socialists, communists and anarchists up there." He raised his eyebrows over the end of the beer bottle. "Guess who ran the camp?"

"Who?"

"Pinochet," Penny said.

"The general? For real?"

"He was a captain then." Cleon took a long pull. "When he took over the country, he put his little camp in the desert back to use." He set the bottle down an inch from Jude's plate. "Solo un sorbo, hueón."

Small sip, buddy.

Jude took a taste and made a face. He liked being offered the sip more than the beer itself. "Nothing like the Holocaust could happen again, could it?"

The tick of the clock was immense as Cleon chewed on an answer to the two-headed question.

Could it happen again to Jews or could it happen again to gay people?

"Nothing like that will ever happen to you," he finally said.

But then it did happen.

When Jude came out from under the anesthesia, his face bruised and battered, his ribs broken, his leg pinned and screwed together, he looked at Cleon and said: "Ahora somos compañeros."

We are partners now. Compatriots. War mates.

Penny sank weeping into a chair, but Cleon didn't cry. His teeth were set, his eyes dry, his face a mask of stoic, revolutionary gravitas as he clasped palms with his son.

"I promised nothing like it would happen to you," he said. "I broke that promise. I'm sorry."

The apology was so ceremonious and formal, it was almost Japanese. A samurai unable to save face.

"Cuéntame todo lo que pasó en la Villa Grimaldi," Jude said. "Tell me. I want to know now. It can't hurt me now."

They were brave and beautiful together. Compañeros in the days after the attack, before the neighborhood turned against them. Then blood flew onto the windshield of the car and Jude ejected out of bravery, into a death spiral because it was happening. It was happening to him, in this place, in this day. Pisagua was next. Followed by castration. And then it would be death.

❧

CLEON SAT ON THE bungalow's back deck, staring out at the scrap of garden and rolling his phone over and over in his hand.

"¿Qué onda, querido?" Penny said. Rhetorically. The matter was Jude, of course. Jude inexplicably not being their biological child. Jude understandably walking out of the house two days ago. Jude ominously making zero contact since then. The last time they endured such prolonged radio silence from their son, he was on a flight to South Africa.

Penny brushed off a chair and sat. Carefully. As if a dramatic flop would break her bones. She pressed a hand to her chest, rubbing the gordian knot of shock and confusion that blocked her from taking a full breath.

Hey, Jude. The two-note Beatles refrain was inextricably tangled with her son's name, but now she couldn't get past *don't make it bad,* because this was terrible. The knot in Penny's chest yanked tighter because for all she knew, *she* had made it bad.

How did this happen?

How could he not be ours?

It was absurd. This was Jude, their first child. Born into abject terror, clutched in arms as they escaped Chile. Lying on his wounded father's chest in the hospital. Charming the passengers on the ship to Canada. Cleon's stay-at-home compañero in the early years in Vancouver. Father and son going everywhere and doing everything together, learning their new home and new langugage. Penny's little deputy at meetings and penas and airport runs. Their bright, kind, blue-eyed boy filling the world with music.

Jude wasn't theirs?

How did this happen?

"I don't know what to do," Cleon said, his voice hiding in the back of his throat.

"He just needs a little time," Penny said.

And I need time to figure out how this happened.

"I swear, if I lose that boy—"

"We are not losing him."

"He's disappeared."

"Stop it," she said, sharper than she intended, but that evil, intransitive verb had no business in this conversation. "He'll come around. He always comes back."

The look Cleon threw her was hard and hurt. "You can't say he always comes back when he's never gone away from us. Not like this."

This level of emotion was unusual for Cleon. Whatever he was feeling was important enough and strong enough to break past chemical bonds and shiver in his voice and demeanor. Which meant Penny had to corral all her crazed feeling, make it take several seats and shut up. Detach and let Cleon have the floor. It was his rare turn. She had to hold still and steady with open ears and hands. It was how they worked. It was how they survived.

"He's in shock," she said. "We all are."

Cleon looked down at his phone, lips pressed tight. "He won't answer me."

Despite her desire to be calm and reassuring, Penny felt a frisson of anger. Not answering was the cruelest thing Jude could do to his father. Unknown whereabouts were the cardinal sin of the Tholet children.

But Jude wasn't a child anymore.

And he's not our child.

Penny shook her head hard, flicking the thought away. These goddamn DNA tests changed nothing. They were still a family and their family rules remained in place.

"I know you want to get in the car," she said. "Go driving around the neighborhood looking for him. I do too. I'd go with you. But he's a grown man now, not a teenager. He's upset. You need to give him some time."

Feeling she was full of shit, Penny reached and took the phone out of Cleon's hand. "He's our son and I know him. He's not himself right now but he'll calm down, he'll come back and then we'll talk about it."

And until then, I am not thinking about it. This changes nothing.

She got up, putting the phone in her pocket. "Let's unplug and take the kayak out. The exercise will do us both good."

CLEÓN

*S*PECIAL BOOTHS ARE CONSTRUCTED *in the stadium. Inside, Pinochet's security services learn the mechanics of torture. Interrogation skills will come later. Right now, they practice applying the electricity, experimenting where and for how long.*

They practice and experiment on you.

You keep trying Uncle Louis's way. You build a house and ignore the screams. Ignore the cold and the hunger and the increasing filth and despair. Ignore that your turn is coming. Build your house. Furnish your rooms. You must endure. Thou shalt survive.

Try again. Imagine yourself. It's 1967. The Beatles release Sgt. Pepper's Lonely Hearts Club Band, *along with the double A-side single "Penny Lane" and "Strawberry Fields Forever."*

You're in love. This music is your life. You don't consider yourself an artistic man, although you're the son of a landscape designer and the nephew of a sculptor. You don't paint or draw or even doodle. Yet the music of the Beatles creates grandiose works of art in your head. Some songs are sweeping murals, others are miniature portraits. The village life normalcy of "Penny Lane" juxtaposed with the lucid-dream imagery of "Lucy in the Sky with Diamonds." The mundane and surreal blended to perfection in "A Day in the Life." Sandwiched between are odes to the beautiful simplicity of friendship, and a couple pledging devotion into old age.

(Forever, Lucy. Grow old with me.)

They call your name.

The electrodes are placed.

(Oh God, Lucy...)

Your house collapses.

You will not survive this.

THE SOBER JUDE

*E*LEVEN O'CLOCK ON A Tuesday night typically saw Jude in bed or heading toward it. Instead, he was in a booth at a Capitol Hill pub, heading toward his fourth beer.

I'm not my parents' child.

He'd never again use the word "stunned" lightly. He couldn't feel his face and he was sure the alcohol had nothing to do with it. One billion and seven thoughts careened through his brain, like an eclipse of moths around a light-bulb. *What the fuck* alighted on his shoulder, then flew off again. *I can't believe it* made loop-the-loops around his head, followed by a more sluggish *What do I do?*

What now?

Where do I go now?

He stared at the window. Sometimes through it, looking for answers on the street. Sometimes into it, catching his reflection in the window, unable to recognize his own face.

I'm not theirs.

So who am I?

What is my name?

"He's not worth it."

Startled, Jude looked the other way to see a man lounging against the booth. "What?"

"He shit on you. He broke your heart. Fuck it, things happen for a reason. He's not the one. This is happening because you're destined to meet someone better. I'm telling you, one day, you'll be lying in bed with the most excellent dude to walk the planet, and you'll look back on this night and wonder who that prophetic stranger at the bar was. I'll say you're welcome now."

Jude blinked. The guy kept smiling back, handsome and confident. A little too much of each, frankly. In Jude's experience, exceptionally good-looking men were either guarded as hell or entitled as hell, and this grinning tomcat exuded the latter.

"Do I know you?" Jude said.

"In the biblical sense? Not yet."

Jude stared, the hoppy air of the pub cool against his teeth and tongue.

"Close your mouth. It's making me have inappropriate thoughts."

Resisting the urge to check over his shoulder or point a finger at his chest, Jude said, "Are you hitting on me?"

"Are you available to be hit on?"

The sober Jude would roll his eyes and flick this lothario off like a horse-fly. Instead he leaned back on the alcoholic buzz and settled into his skin. Gaze holding still as he took a long sip of his beer.

"Don't lick your lips like that," the lothario said. "It's not helping get rid of me."

Not looking away, Jude licked his lips again. The guy's head tipped back with laughter, showing a rather lovely throat.

"You got game," he said, sliding uninvited into the opposite bench. "I knew you did."

"What's your name?" Jude asked. Since when were throats a lovely thing to him? This one looked meaty rising up out of a shirt collar, with a bristle of incoming beard through the soft skin. Delectable little adam's apple rising and falling as he said, "I'm Tage."

Jude frowned. "Tage?"

"T-e-j. Rhymes with page."

"Tej. Cool name. I like it."

A long staring moment before Tej raised an eyebrow. "See, this is where you tell me your name."

"I'm sorry."

"Your name is sorry?"

"My name is Juleón. Friends call me Jude."

He'd punch this guy out if he started singing the Beatles.

"Nice to meet you, Juleón," Tej said. "So what's going on?"

"How old are you?"

Tej winced. "Dude, seriously?"

"I'm thirty-six and just found out I'm adopted."

"Now I'm losing my erection."

A waitress materialized and collected Jude's empty glass. "Another one?"

"Please."

"Something for you, Tej?"

"I'll have what he's having. To soothe my wounded ego."

When she'd gone, Jude sat back and tried to assess his new company. "You're quite the force to be reckoned with."

"Thank you, I try. Now run the adopted thing by me again?"

"I would if I could get two thoughts to sit next to each other. So I'm obliterating all thoughts entirely. Or trying."

"I got a better means of obliterating thoughts. Without the debilitating hangover."

Again, the Jude that Jude knew, who hated this kind of come-on, was nowhere to be found. Tej was making him preen a little. Sit back in relaxed confidence and accept his due.

"What are you smiling about," Tej said.

"Normally, arrogant audacity turns me off. But I'm rather enjoying this pick-up."

"And this is my bare minimum effort. Can you imagine if I really turned on the charm?"

"I might combust."

"Hopefully."

As fast as the confident rush came, it left. Jude felt his face flame up as all clever comebacks deserted him. "I don't really have the wherewithal to spar with you right now."

"Do you have the wherewithal to fuck with me?"

"Dude... You can't say shit like that."

"Why not?"

Because it's giving me a hard-on. "Didn't your mother ever tell you not to talk to strangers?"

"Talking to strangers gets you laid."

"Jesus."

"Besides, we stopped being strangers five minutes ago. So let's stop talking and get out of here."

"Shut up."

Tej leaned his chin on the heel of his hand. "You're actually giving this some thought."

"What I'm thinking is you're insane."

And I'm kind of loving it.

"Come home with me," Tej said, unperturbed. "I'll make you feel better. You get a good night's sleep and things will look clearer in the morning. And if they don't, at least you got laid."

"I'm a lousy lay when I'm distracted."

"I'll have to work harder at holding your attention then."

Jude held still, knowing the slightest attempt to readjust the erection in his jeans would not only be detected, but remarked upon. "This is extremely flattering," he said. "But I don't go home with strangers."

Tej jerked his head toward the back of the pub. "We could go in the loo."

Jude lowered his laughing face into his hands. "Who are you?"

The waitress returned with their drinks. "Here you go, fellows."

Tej tugged at the pocket of her apron. "Rosie, I need a favor."

"What, baby?"

"I'm attempting to seduce this gorgeous gentleman and he's wisely being prudent about consorting with arrogant and audacious men he doesn't know."

"In other words, Tuesday."

Tej pointed a finger. "That was unnecessary."

"Sorry. Where do I come into the seduction scheme?"

"You already know everything about me. Can I ask you to please note his description?"

Rosie looked at Jude and winked. "With pleasure."

"Perhaps he'll give you his contact information. And if he goes missing in the morning or is found floating in the harbor, you report me to the police with all due dispatch."

"You are the dispatch."

"This is true."

Her empty tray on her hip, Rosie smiled at Jude. "For real, he's an EMD. He answers nine-one-one calls."

"No shit," Jude said.

"I do know where he lives. And all his secrets. He talks a big game but he's really a mush. You could do worse."

"Hey, hey, hey," Tej said. "I don't recall asking for this."

Rosie ruffled his hair. "Good luck. Both of you."

Jude watched her walk off. "Your sister?"

"I wish. So what do you think?"

But the second the word *sister* slid through Jude's teeth, it free-associated into siblings, lost children, unknown family and *who am I?* And then for fuck's sake, he was tearing up. What, he was going to fucking cry about this? He never cried. Not anymore.

"Hey." Like a curtain falling, the teasing dropped out of Tej's face. In an instant he went from unknown libertine to trusted companion. "Hey, it's okay. I'm sorry. You're legit upset. I'll let you be."

Jude felt an odd stab of panic at the thought of this guy *leaving* him anywhere. "No, no," he said, shaking the episode off hard and getting what shit he had together. "It's just… I'm a sloppy drunk."

"You're not drooling or slurring."

"Yet."

"I'm bold but I'm not stupid. I can see whatever's going on, it's hurting like hell. I'm sorry."

"I typically try much harder than this to make a good first impression."

"There's something to be said for getting your worst moments over with."

Jude raised his glass. "Welcome to my shit show."

Tej clinked his against it. "I've seen worse."

"Yeah?"

"Yeah. Anyone ever tell you you look a little bit like Daniel Westling?"

"Who?"

"Daniel Westling. Prince consort of Sweden."

"No."

"Well, I'll be the first then." Tej held up his glass. "Skål."

They drank, eyes locked over the rims of their glasses. Beneath the table, the slightest, tiniest pressure: the toe of Tej's shoe against the toe of Jude's. It sent a tiny current up Jude's calf.

"Don't look at me like that," he heard himself say.

"Like what?"

Like you want to fuck me.

"Like…that."

Tej reached and pushed Jude's glass back down to the table. "Come on. You're cut off and so am I. This was fun, but now let's find you a cab."

They didn't do-si-do around the bill. Each put money on the table. Jude pulled on his jacket and Tej went to retrieve his from wherever he'd left it. Outside, the air was icy and bracing.

"I think I'll walk a little," Jude said, inhaling deep into his stomach.

"I'll come with."

"You will?"

"If you don't mind."

"Okay?"

Tej crossed his arms, eyes flicking to the skies. "Don't look so surprised. You're nineteen kinds of gorgeous, but you also look like your life's been turned inside-out. I feel bad."

"I'll be all right."

Tej took a step in. "Don't misunderstand me."

"Mm?"

"My only goal tonight is to get you safe in a cab home. But it doesn't mean I don't want to get you naked."

Jude filled with curious and arrogant heat. As the cold night enveloped him, he was shocked steam didn't start rising off his body. "I see."

"And not for nothing, but I want that pretty bad."

"You don't even know me."

"Instinctive lust. It serves a certain purpose."

Son of a bitch, the heat switched off and Jude was freezing cold. And light-headed all of a sudden. He put a hand against the building's brick façade. "Oh man, I'm wasted."

Tej touched his elbow. "You okay?"

"I swear, I don't..." He laughed softly as he drew in breath after breath. "This isn't me."

"No, I think it is you. And I'm digging it."

"Bullshit."

"No really. And whatever's hurting you, I want to make it stop." The fingertips on Jude's elbow turned into a palm, then a warm, strong grip around his bicep.

"Who *are* you?" Jude whispered, staring at Tej's mouth.

Tej's smile—quick, wide and true—was a beautiful thing. "I'm just me."

Jude stared, caught up in the moment that wanted him to trust it so badly.

Tej leaned in a little. "It's me."

His other hand ran lightly through the hair above Jude's ear.

"Only me."

He closed the gap and rested his mouth against Jude's. Soft and neutral, letting Jude get used to his proximity. Jude closed his eyes and leaned into the kiss. Opened for it. Slid down it, falling through the darkness behind his eyelids.

"You taste amazing," Tej said against Jude's chin.

"So do you."

"Feel better?"

"Yeah. That was...rather head-clearing actually."

"You want to walk or find that cab?"

"Neither." He pulled Tej back in, turning them so Tej's shoulders were up against the bricks now. His fists full of Tej's jacket, he kissed him. Opening his mouth a little more, inviting the slide of tongue and the edge of teeth. Following it back into Tej's mouth, swallowing his breath, echoing back a sharp moan in his throat.

"Damn," Tej said, breathing hard. "I didn't think this would actually work."

"Now I know you're crazy."

Tej slid hands into Jude's back pockets. "Crazy also serves a certain purpose."

Jude planted his palms against the wall. Their eyes held a long moment, shoulders and chests rising and falling in unison. Breathing their way through a decision.

"Whatever you want to do," Tej said. "Nothing. Everything. Something. It's fine. I just want you to be all right."

"I think I just want you."

THE ORANGE

*J*UDE WOKE NAKED IN an empty bed. His watch read a little after seven. An orange, a business card and a note rested on the unoccupied pillow:

> *Well, I had ten kinds of fun. Gone to work. Left you a card so you can see I'm a respectable, contributing member of society. The card has some digits on it. If you punch them into your phone, magic things will happen.*
>
> *Lock the door behind you. And don't worry. You're going to be all right.*

Jude read the card next:

> *Timothée Jalil (Tej) Khoury, EMD*
> *Seattle Fire Department*

The corners of Jude's mouth pulled down as his eyebrows went up. "A fireman," he said slowly. His sister would be impressed.

Except she's not actually my sister.

He got dressed, made the bed and, unable to think of anything clever to put in a note, simply left his own card on the pillow.

It was a bit of a hike back to his neighborhood, but the morning was fresh and the sun sliced valiantly through the city's perpetual cloud cover. He opted to hoof it home, eating the orange as he went.

So this is a Walk of Shame.

Striding along the morning streets, boxers balled-up and stuffed in his jacket pocket, Jude took inventory of body and mind. Instead of empty and disturbed, he felt spectacular. Young. Strapping. Alive. All his upset downgraded into a manageable worry. Tej was right—lust served a certain purpose. Just what the doctor ordered.

Jesus, what a night.

Tej was a ruthless lover. Bold. Verbally fearless. Audacious and lusty. Teasing. Lewd. And Jude should've hated it. The things Tej whispered and his aggressive sexual drive should've repelled him.

He loved it.

This isn't me. I'm not like this.

Yet walking along, looking at his life story turned inside-out, his history erased, his slate blank…

Maybe I am, he thought. *Maybe this really is me.*

His pace was confident, his chin high. Slap his ass and call him Betty: he got propositioned by a gorgeous punk and he went for it. Seduced from hell to breakfast. Ravished by a smartass power bottom with a foul mouth, an irresistible throat and a surprising soft side in between the bouts of feverish fucking.

Jude's eardrums blushed, but an erection yawned and stirred to life in his jeans. *Yes? You rang? Is it on? Are we fucking again?*

He chided himself to knock it off, but his heart wasn't in it. He felt great. And grateful.

Thanks, kid. Whoever you are.

His smug mood saw him through the day, but the arrival of Cleon at his apartment that evening quickly deflated his euphoric balloon.

"Jude, open the goddamn door."

All the ambiguity of Jude's parentage instantly vanished. This was his father, come out looking when Jude's whereabouts were unknown. This was his father's fist on wood and his unique tone of voice that could not be disobeyed.

Jude opened the door.

"Don't you *ever* not answer me when I call or text you," Cleon shouted.

Jude blanched, twelve years old and in deep shit.

"Never again." Cleon's finger touched Jude's chest. "Don't you ever disappear on your mother and me like that. I don't care how angry you are, you keep that goddamn phone turned on and if I call, you *answer it.* Cachai?"

"Cachai."

The finger bore into Jude's heart. "Never again."

"I'm sorry."

"You should be. Now get in the fucking car."

"Why?"

"Because we need to talk about this."

"Why didn't you tell me I was adopted?"

"You're not."

"You and Mami aren't my parents."

"I *know*," Cleon cried through his clenched teeth. "And you're not adopted either."

They stared each other down. Cleon's eyes were wide and glassy, his unshaven face a pale shade of grey. He looked old. Worse, he looked frail. And he looked like he was *feeling*.

Jude was adept at reading the minuscule gradients within his father's moods, skilled at recognizing deviations from the norm. What he saw before him was a pendulum swinging too far off course. Cleon was off course. One look and Jude knew Cleon had forgotten his meds for about two days.

"Papi," Jude said, a sickening terror creeping through his bones. "What the hell happened when I was born?"

Cleon shifted his weight onto his cane and the other hand reached, trembling, to press flat against Jude's cheek. "Querido, I wasn't there."

"I know you weren't. Goddammit..." Gritting his teeth, Jude turned and walked into the living room. Slowly, so Cleon could follow.

"Jude, please. Come back to the house with me. Come home so we can talk about this."

"Give me a minute, all right? Jesus Christ. I just..." He took several long breaths, looking for something to focus on. Anything. "You need to take your meds."

"What are you talking... Oh." Cleon eased himself into a chair. "Shit."

"How many days now?"

"I don't remember."

"Since I walked out?"

"Possibly."

"Get back on the wagon, cachai?"

"Cachai."

Each dressing the other down seemed to settle an invisible score, and the room swayed into an uneasy balance. Jude sat on the windowsill, needing to stay distanced. "So, it sounds like I was switched in the hospital," he said.

Cleon nodded slowly. "They say to look for the simplest solution first."

"Mm."

Each rubbed a hand across the lower half of their face. Covering their mouths. Squeezing lips into a cupped palm. An ocean of thoughts roared between Jude's ears. The room screamed with things unsaid.

"You've been a gift to me all your life," Cleon said. "Starting from the first time they put you in my arms. You don't know what—"

"I know." Jude's voice felt like a dull, rusted blade in his mouth. "But how did I *get* in your arms? How did… Doesn't this bother you?"

"Of course it bothers me. Yes. Of course I want to find out what happened to my biological child but right now I need you to know that… Jesus Christ, Jude, you're my *son*. You are what's bothering me right now. The rest is… I don't know what it is. I'm lost."

"Yeah. Me too."

Jude had never been at such a loss. Never known this kind of confused, conflicted misery. Even at his lowest point of mourning Feño, even in the exhaustion of being closeted or the terror of being targeted by his community, he'd never faltered in his identity as a Tholet. Never doubted his parents' blood ran deep in his veins and would sustain him through whatever revulsions developed.

His fists clenched, desperate to wring out an explanation. Needing someone to blame. An enemy to vanquish.

"Do you ever feel vengeful?" he heard himself ask.

"How so?"

"For what happened to you in the Villa. Everything…" He made a lame gesture at his father's body. "Do you think about revenge?"

"Sometimes. It's a general vindictiveness though. I don't have a specific person I can arrange a vendetta for. Pinochet's dead." Cleon's shoulders flicked as he gave a bitter snort. "I admit I would've enjoyed shooting him in the gut."

"What about Captain Villarroel?"

Cleon's eyes narrowed as he drew a deep breath through his nose. Villarroel had been one of his torturers. Adept in both physical and psychological terror. His latter technique involved one bullet in the chamber of a six-shot pistol, pointed at Cleon's head during interrogation.

"I guess… If I were told to have at it, full immunity, no consequences…" His fingers lifted off the arm of the chair, folded one at a time into a fist and then relaxed again. "I'd think strenuously about it. Maybe. Sure."

"What about for Vancouver."

"Do I want revenge on Vancouver?"

"Let's say you were an Old Testament god and you could rain down fire and brimstone on a city. Send another flood or a plague."

Cleon's sideways glance was laced with concern. "¿Juleón, qué me estás preguntando, po?"

Po, along with cachai, was a beloved word Chileans tagged onto the ends of sentences. Or anywhere in the sentence they felt like sticking it. The whitest man on earth could go to Chile armed with only po, cachai and hueón, and he'd be hailed as fluent.

Jude was fluent. He grew up knowing by blood, he was a British-Canadian Jew but in spirit, he believed he was Chilean. He belonged to the community of exiles and their first-generation American offspring. Cleon and Penny gave years of their lives to build and better the neighborhood. Jude went with his mother to the airport to welcome Chilean refugees. He didn't know what the hell it was all about, he just figured it was what people did. And these *were* his people. He spoke their language, his sentences laced with po, cachai and hueón. He went to their penas, sang their songs, danced their dances and ate their food.

Then they turned on him. Exiled him.

"What am I supposed to do now?" he said softly.

Go looking for my people? Just so they can turn their back on me again when they find out I'm gay?

No way. I am not breaking my own leg and staging a deliberate coup on my life. Forget it.

"You've been nothing but a gift to me," Cleon said. "We'll get to the bottom of this, but know it will never, never change how much I love you."

Lips pressed tight, Jude nodded, staring down at his clenched hands.

"Juleón, you are my son."

"I know." Love for his father pressed against the backs of his eyes while the shadow of an unknown interloper lurked in the vague distance. Another father out there in the world. One who might change how he felt when he discovered who Jude was.

Jude wanted Cleon. Nobody else.

I don't want to be anyone else's son but yours. I don't want any other father to love me. I don't want to know that my name is anything but Juleón Tholet.

"Querido, come home with me now."

Jude went. Because it was what he did. Whenever he had a problem, he went home.

He wasn't sure how to handle the problem *being* home.

⁓

"It's all broken up," Penny said.

"I understand," Jude said.

"I don't remember giving birth, you know this. But I have no concrete memory of how I got to the hospital either. All these years, I said Ysidro and Tatán took me there because I assumed they did. But I couldn't swear to it."

"Tell me what you do remember."

"Waking up." A wry smile. "Throwing up. Everyone telling me to rest. *Descanse, señora, you must rest. The baby is fine. He's sleeping. Just rest now.* Falling back under. Waking up. And then finally, they brought you in."

Her eyes bright with frustrated tears, her palms opened to the ceiling. "They brought you to me. Swaddled up tight to your chin, that little cap tugged over your eyebrows. They put you down in the bed. Right next to me. 'Look at him,' the nurse said. 'Look how much hair he has. And look, señora, he has dimples. Look. Here he is.'" Her hands fell limp in her lap. "There you were."

Jude nodded, unable to speak.

"Juleón."

He nodded harder.

"You have to believe me."

"I believe you," he said.

He looked at Cleon, who'd been silent all this time. Silent and helpless because he wasn't there. He was in the Villa Grimaldi, being beaten with chains, shocked with live wires, forced into Russian roulette games. Thrown into the street and run over. A victim of relentless intransitive verbs. He couldn't corroborate or confirm Penny's story. He was off in his own hell, building a secret world in his mind to escape the constant terror and agony. That was his story and Penny couldn't corroborate it any more than he could hers.

They survived Chile together, but separately. A parental narrative crafted under torture and duress wasn't the most reliable, but it was the narrative Jude built his life on. The one he had to trust.

He'd never, *never* not trusted his parents.

"I believe you," he said again, closing his eyes.

But I'm not the baby my mother gave birth to.

I'm not the unborn child my father survived for.

I am someone else's hope and dream. My name shouldn't be Jude. I should not be here.

None of this belongs to me.

None of this was meant for me.

He opened his eyes and looked at the wreckage of his Penny's face.

It wasn't meant for her either.

"Mami." He inhaled deep, forcing the air in, stepping beyond his blinding bubble of outraged perspective and attempting to step inside his mother's.

Because this *was* his mother. Fuck the DNA, fuck the percentages. Fuck Italy and Iberia and every other ethnicity attempting to redefine the laws of his life.

"This must be killing you," he said. His voice dragged in slow-motion. The world had gone insane. "I mean, if I'm not… Then what happened to…him? Your real son. What happened to your baby?"

Penny doubled over weeping, fists in her hair. "*You're* my baby," she said, sobbing. Her voice rose up in a rage. "They almost killed you before you were born and they almost killed you in Vancouver. Twice I almost lost you."

"Querida, don't," Cleon said, moving stiffly to sit next to her on the couch.

"I am *not* losing you again. I am *not* doing this again. Never again. Not *one* more thing happening to my family, I cannot *take* another…"

Before Jude's eyes, Penelope Tholet turned inside-out. Flipped the coin of her bright, shiny nature. No longer Penny but Lupita. The She-Wolf screamed into her hands and Jude nearly threw his arms across his face, wanting to shield himself from that horrible, keening howl.

"No más. *Nunca* más."

For a moment, Jude thought the house would explode under her wrath. Then she slumped against Cleon's side, weeping through her palms. He wrapped arms around her and planted his chin atop her head, tucking her against his massive chest. The mighty barrel of his torso wobbling above his frail, broken legs. His fierce, dry gaze guarding his wife's pain. Their bodies creating a raw sculpture not of smooth, polished marble, but jagged black rock hacked from the volcanic spine of the Andes Mountains. Set atop a pedestal of broken bones.

Jude knelt between their feet, eyes wide and mouth parted in awe as he gazed at the Pietà of his parents.

THE VISUAL

*F*ROM THE DAY HE started at Pacific Northwest Ballet, Jude fell and remained passionately in love with his job. Despite the bonanza of gorgeous gay and bisexual men at PNWB, Jude did not date at work. He flirted and ogled and took every guy on the roster for a mental spin, but he kept his hands to himself for two reasons. First, because dancers, ladies and gentlemen, were certifiably crazy. Second and sacrosanct, Jude loved his work too much to inject it with relationship drama. This job was a golden apple that fell into his lap, and it deserved nothing but his pure, undistracted best.

He was ridiculously distracted today. The company was learning a new ballet, *Rakewind,* set to Mozart's *Requiem in D Minor.* The choreographer had flown out from New Brunswick to stage the work and Jude could not take his eyes off her. More precisely, he couldn't stop staring at her left leg, where a long scar ran from knee to ankle, just like his. Her hair was dark and wavy, just like his. No dimples, but holy shit, her preternaturally blue eyes were *just* like his.

The more he stared, the more absurdly obvious it became.

She could be his sister.

His gaze swiveled around the studio. Christ, anyone here could be related to him. When he walked down the street, he could pass a stranger with the same DNA. Highly unlikely, sure, but it could happen. In all his world travels, on any street in any city, he could've bumped shoulders with a cousin and not even known it.

You never knew. How could you know? *Someone* had to be related to him, why not this dark-haired, blue-eyed, scarred woman? Here she was. And she—

"Jude?"

He blinked. All eyes were on him, including the choreographer's.

"Come back to me," she said, smiling.

Positive she was signaling him, his heart gave the most idiotic lurch in the history of lurches.

"Can we take it from the *Confutatis?*" she asked.

"I'm sorry, I was… Sorry." His face hot, he began playing. A tightness crept into his throat, which pissed him off. The distraction was justified but this constant verge-of-crying shit was getting ridiculous.

With an effort, he buckled down and focused through the remainder of rehearsal, then skulked away to his lunch hour, avoiding talking to or even looking at the choreographer.

A creature of habit, Jude always lunched at the Utter Chaos Café, where his same waitress always held his same table. Typically he went over a score as he ate. Today, he pulled one of his father's books from his messenger bag—*Inheritance of Fear: Women, Children and Human Rights in South America.*

He had copies of all Cleon's works, dutifully displayed on his bookshelves and skimmed politely. Now his eyes volleyed back and forth through paragraphs and pages, looking for answers to questions he couldn't even formulate.

> …*Amnesty International has documented numerous cases of the disappearance of mothers and children, where the child was either born in prison or abducted with the mother. In Argentina, the greatest number of pregnant women and mothers of infants and schoolchildren were disappeared between 1976 and 1980.*

"Seventy-six is too late, Papi," Jude murmured. "What about earlier accounts? In Chile?"

> *During this period, pregnant women were taken to the Naval Training College in Buenos Aires, earmarked as the maternity unit of the region's secret detention camps. All pregnant women were attended by a doctor from the naval hospital. After giving birth, mothers were usually "transferred" (a known euphemism for assassination) while infants were sent to clandestine orphanages for adoption by childless couples in the armed forces.*
>
> *Evidence and documentation concerning the sale of some of these children is just surfacing.*

The hair on Jude's nape bristled. If it happened in Argentina, it could happen in Chile. Shit, maybe Argentina took lessons from Chile.

Hundreds of Argentinian babies have been reported as missing by grandparents and surviving relatives. The toddlers and older children abducted with their mothers have never been seen again. The grandmothers of these missing babies and children have formed an association, The Grandmothers of the Plaza de Mayo...

Jude's eyes stopped, widening. Not from the impact of the words, but from a most familiar combination of aftershave and skin tickling his nose.

"We meet again."

He looked up. It took him half a minute to finish chewing his last mouthful before replying, "We do."

Tej looked around the café. "I never come in here."

"This is my usual joint."

"Imagine that."

Jude closed the book and slid the glasses on his head back on his nose. "How are you?"

"At what?"

Oh my fucking Lord, here we go again.

"Apparently I'm really good at making you blush," Tej said.

"And I'm not a blusher."

"Well, they say to accomplish something every day, so thanks for helping me fill the quota."

"You're welcome."

They stared. The shared gaze immutable while beneath, each mouth rolled over and around and through a smile.

"See, this is where you invite me to sit down," Tej finally said.

"You want to sit down?"

"No, I just wanted you to ask."

"I think I like you better with my dick in your mouth. You're less of a smartass."

Tej blushed. He actually fucking blushed. "Now I will sit down."

Jude's eyes slid appreciatively against the grey sweater over a collar and tie. "You scrub up nice."

"I'm commando."

"Thanks for the visual."

"You're welcome." He turned the book toward him to see the title. "Well, this must be an uplifting read."

Jude turned it back. "Yeah. I mean, no. It's for… Nothing, never mind."

"Sounds engrossing." He took a chip off Jude's plate. "You do remember my name?"

"Tej. Rhymes with page. Do you remember mine?"

"Jude. Rhymes with one of the best fucks I ever had in my life."

Jude's neck and ears flamed up. "Liar."

"Hand to God."

"That wasn't even my A-game."

The gold flecks in Tej's brown eyes flared. "Challenge accepted."

Jude eased past flustered and approached hot mess.

Tej laughed. "I think it's my new life's mission to make you blush."

Jude could only shake his head, thinking, *You are nothing I like. I shouldn't like you. I have no business liking you.*

Tej's eyebrows knitted together. "Now what are you brooding about?"

"I don't know," Jude said. "You're making me blush, you're making me giggle. I don't know what the fuck is going on."

"Me neither. But it feels good."

"Yeah, you have a knack for making me feel better."

"It's my alternate life mission."

He held Tej's gaze, trying to be serious. "We just met."

Tej didn't look away but his wicked expression calmed down. "I know. Weird, right?"

"You're not even my type."

"Bullshit. C'mon, what's your type? Twinky bottoms who let you boss them around?"

"As opposed to bossy twinks who bottom from the top?"

"You loved it."

"I did."

They held eyes through one inhale and exhale.

"I kind of can't stop thinking about it," Jude said.

"And here I am."

"Here you are."

"I kind of can't stop thinking about it either. To the point where I staked out your place of employ and discovered you came here for lunch every day."

"Oh, so this was planned."

"Yeah. Kind of. Entirely. Yes."

"So you're a stalker as well as a smartass."

"I prefer to think that I go after the things I want. Aggressively and with smart humor."

"What if those things don't want you? Hypothetical question."

Tej leaned on his crossed forearms. "I'm bold but I'm not stupid. I know when to fold my cards and walk away."

Jude stared at Tej's wrist. A stripe of tanned skin emerging from the cuff of his sweater. A knob of bone next to his watch. The veins and tendons fluttering on the back of his hand. A small tattoo of a cross next to the name Raymond.

Was Raymond your Feño?

Tej took another chip. "In all seriousness, I do recognize you were in a bad way the other night. And I hope you're all right. Or a little righter than before."

"Thanks." Something about Tej eating off his plate touched him deeply. "I went back and saw my parents. They say I'm not adopted."

"What made you think you were?"

"We did one of those DNA spit kit things. I'm unquestionably not their kid. But they swear I'm not adopted."

"And you... I ask this respectfully, you believe them?"

Jude nodded. "I do."

"So what the fuck happened?"

"Dude, we have no idea."

"Sounds like you were switched in the hospital."

"Which sounds like a bad plot device."

"And yet here you are," Tej said.

"Here I am. With no idea who I am."

"Well, let me be first to say that is *fucked.*"

"Yeah."

"I'm glad you didn't share it on our first date."

Jude smiled. "Are we on a date?"

"Not yet. And why do you keep staring at my wrist like that, you coveting my watch or something?"

"The watch is nice, I'm just being nosy about Raymond."

"My brother. He died when I was four."

"I'm sorry." Jude hesitated, then turned the book over and tapped his finger on Cleon's photograph. "That's my father. Or should I say, the artist formerly known as my father?"

Tej leaned, studying the black and white photograph. "Huh."

"This is where you say I look nothing like him."

He looked up at Jude, then down at the cover. "I like his face." The gaze came up again, soft and shy. "And I like yours. And I need to get to work."

"Do all nine-one-one dispatchers dress as nice as you?"

"No. I made an effort because I was stalking you on your lunch hour."

Jude leaned hard on his arms, stretched across the table and kissed Tej's mouth. "A for effort."

"I did not see that coming."

Jude picked up his sandwich. "You're blushing."

"I am," Tej said, standing up. "Well done."

"Thank you."

"I'll never let you do it again."

"Challenge accepted."

⁓

STAGE REHEARSAL THAT AFTERNOON was for Jerome Robbins' *Dances at a Gathering*, set to eighteen pieces by Chopin. Dae-Hyun Cho played onstage for the whole ballet. In performance, Jude would be next to him, turning pages. Right now, he sat in one of the orchestra seats with his copy of the score, fingers playing along and taking last minute notes.

His muted phone vibrated on the armrest. It was Tej.

When am I going to see you again?

Jude smiled as he texted back: *You know where I eat lunch.*

You're going to make me wait?

LOL, I get the feeling nobody can make you do anything.

You made me blush.

This is true.

I won't beg. (I'm totally begging)

I want to see you too. Soon.

Soon? Does soon mean like tonight? Or as soon as you break up with your boyfriend who's not half as good in the sack as me?

LOL. No boyfriend.

Girlfriend?

Dude, WTF?

My track record with bisexual men is abysmal, I always lose out to the chick. If you're bi, please let's part as friends. I'm an arrogant ass, but a fragile arrogant ass.

With a jolt, Jude caught up to the music. He'd texted through three pages. He shoved the phone down in his bag and tried to be attentive, but now he was hornier than hell. Which was making it difficult to hold the score open on his lap.

Christ, who is this guy?

He was trouble. No question. An excellent temporary diversion, but not long-term material.

So why not embrace temporary? Have a fuck buddy to take the edge off all the shit going on?

He couldn't think of a good reason why not. Except Jude the Prude was clutching his pearls and fainting onto a couch. And Tej was crawling up to the chaise, eyes wicked and expression intent as he reached for Jude's belt buckle. Saying, "You're so fucking stressed, baby. Why don't you blow that load…"

Goddammit, he was behind two pages again.

He mentally slapped himself out of it and focused on the music. All the while his toes curled tight in his shoes and a little fold in his brain stared into space, imagining Tej calling him baby.

THE RULE EVER SINCE

"I'M SORRY I GOT emotional yesterday," Penny said. "I've been so tired la—"

"Mami, it's an emotional situation."

A hollowness in Jude's voice made Penny guess he was wearing his earbuds, probably driving home.

"A Benedictine monk would've freaked out," he said.

"I love you," she said. "I need you to know I love you and this changes nothing in terms of loving you."

"I know."

"You're a gift." It was an effort to keep her tone simple and honest. Not go overboard into maudlin and embarrass the both of them. "You were a gift to us from the beginning. It's not that we love you more than Serena and Aiden, but…"

"Ma, I know," Jude said. "I'm your firstborn. You fled a coup with me. It's kind of a bond. And I had you and Papi to myself almost five years before Serena was born. I understand."

Penny exhaled, sinking her forehead into the palm of her hand. Her rings were cool against her brow. She'd been running a low-grade fever the past twenty-four hours.

"They broke Papi's legs," Jude was saying. "And then they broke my leg. It was traumatizing. You had to flee twice. It makes sense, all right? You're entitled to some strong emotion here."

"I just need you to know I love you and you're no less my son than before."

"I love you too, Mami. And you *are* my mother."

"But if you want to go looking—"

"God, I don't know."

"—I support you. If you look or don't look, Papi and I will respect your decision. In fact, he thinks we might want to talk to a lawyer."

Cleon came into the kitchen. "Is that Serena?"

"Jude."

"Put it on speaker. ¿Qué onda, cariño?"

"¿Qué onda, Papi? You think we need a lawyer?"

"God, I don't know if we need one. I just want to explain the situation to one and see what they think. Cachai?"

"What kind of lawyer?"

"That's the thing," Cleon said. "I don't know. An international lawyer?"

"Family lawyer?" Penny said.

"Adoption lawyer?" Jude said.

At least we're laughing, Penny thought.

"You heading home?" Cleon asked. "No date tonight or anything?"

The tiniest beat of hesitation before Jude answered. "No, no date."

"Well, then rest well, cariño."

"I love you," Penny said, and hung up.

"He's such a good boy," Cleon said.

Her voice cracked open like an egg. "But who *is* he?"

She was crying again. Rotten, sulfurous tears she tried to stuff back into her mouth and stifle against the wall of Cleon's chest.

"Don't do this," he said, rocking her. A hand in her hair, caressing the scar behind her ear. "Don't do this to yourself. He's still our son. He'll always be our son."

She dragged a rough hand across her face. "But if I took another woman's baby—"

"You didn't take anyone. This is none of your doing."

"But what do I do now?" She flung a hand up, gesturing to the kitchen. "Is another woman sitting at a table, weeping and wondering? Is there a couple in Chile desperate to know what happened to their child?"

"I know. I know, honey. We'll figure this out."

"I feel responsible. Not for what happened but for what happens now. Don't you?"

"Pen, I don't know what to feel."

And of course, he was medicated to be that way. His attention was focused on her, his eyes burned with intensity. The hands in her hair trembled. He was upset. He was rattled. He was feeling this.

But he wasn't *feeling* this. Meanwhile Penny was flayed wide open, half expecting to see her intestines spilled in a writhing mess on the floor.

"If another mother, another couple has spent nearly four decades in pain, wondering what happened to their baby... If we have the means to stop it. To end the wondering. Let them know, he's here, he's alive, he's safe... How can we not?"

"I know."

"And I need to know where our child is. All our children. I want to know. I need to know. Don't you?"

"We should find out," he said, which wasn't quite the answer to her question. "We'll try to find out, querida. We'll do what we can. But we may never know."

"We have to try."

"We will."

She pushed at his steady strength, trying to get it to crack. He was supportive but she wanted him to be *dire*. To mirror her upset. At the same time, she relied on him not to splinter open. She needed him to be her complement, her polar opposite in temperament.

They couldn't both go crazy. It was the rule ever since they left Chile.

❧

BECAUSE CLEON WAS BROKEN in pieces and had to be moved carefully, the Canadian embassy in Santiago first handed the Tholets off to their sister diplomats in Lima. There, Cleon had the first of his eleven surgeries and was stabilized for the journey by ship to Vancouver. Penny's father, Walter Cambie, hired two private nurses and flew them to Peru to accompany the family home.

When the ship arrived in Vancouver harbor, Walter was waiting at the pier. He brought his secretaries and his lawyer. In his pocket he had business cards of doctors, diplomats and real estate agents. He had an ambulance for Cleon and a carriage for the baby. Like Mary Poppins' older brother, he scooped up Penny's fragile family and placed it in the stroller of his pragmatism and fierce organizational skills, bashing them through customs and formalities. Terse commands scything a path from harbor to hospital to home.

For the first year, home was Penny's childhood house on Balfour Avenue. It was a geographical necessity—Vancouver General Hospital was blocks away, a straight shot up Oak Street—as well as a financial one. They were flat broke. *Broke*. Penny had bribed every cent she had to get Cleon out of the Villa Grimaldi, leaving only a few shekels within the web of Walter's investment portfolio.

144

Cleon's money was in the Banco de Chile and Walter's legal team was trying to get it out. Meanwhile, the hospital bills multiplied and the baby was hungry. It galled Penny's work ethic to be under her father's aegis, unable to earn her own living because every hour was devoted to her husband, and the minutes between to her son. But she had no choice. She'd have to wait to unpack her pride.

Cleon spoke only rudimentary English but that was the least of his problems. He was a broken, sick man. And a hairless one: so infested with lice and fleas after his imprisonment, the hospital in Lima had shorn him to the skin. For a month, Jude had more hair than his father.

The humor in that would have to wait to be unpacked, too.

Cleon's leg bones were set and pinned, leaving him immobilized in traction, where the fluid could happily collect in his lungs and become pneumonia. His susceptibility to infection worsened by the removal of his spleen. The shock and trauma gave him only the slimmest chances of survival, and nobody even addressed the mental repercussions if he lived.

Bombarded with antibiotics, painkillers and sedatives, he slept long, motionless hours. Doctors said it was the best thing for him, but Penny watched her slumbering husband anxiously, afraid his rest was too deep, too peaceful, too much of a relief after the ordeal and he'd choose not to come back to her.

"Don't you dare," she whispered. "We have a deal, remember? We need and feed until we're sixty-four. You do not contemplate checking out until then."

As soon as she was allowed, she began bringing the baby to the hospital and laying him on Cleon's chest. The sight of Cleon's bald head rubbing against Jude's dark fuzz tied her heart in a knot. A flicker of a smile even as his eyelashes grew wet.

"He's so clean," he said, his nose against Jude's crown. He dropped a hand on the bedsheets, rubbing them between his fingertips. "Everything's so clean."

Holding his son, breathing in his cool scent, Cleon passed long stretches of time looking at the ceiling, with a fierce concentration that first amused Penny, then worried her.

"What are you looking at up there?"

"Nothing."

Cleon's sleep made her anxious. His staring was worrisome. But *nothing* absolutely terrified Penny. What happened in the Villa Grimaldi was not nothing. If allowed to label it as nothing, hide it away and ignore its existence, nothing would become something.

"You can tell me what happened," she said gently. "When you're ready. I'm not afraid. I want to know, so I can get through it with you."

Cleon's eyes closed and his cheek nestled Jude's temple. "Not now," he said. "It's so clean. Just let it be."

It killed her to see him so exhausted and complacent. So docile. He lost both patience and temper exactly once, when a dish of chocolate pudding appeared on his lunch tray for the second time. The first time, he'd sent it back with a polite but firm instruction, "Please, no chocolate."

Penny had never known him to be averse to chocolate. But she knew he and his cellmates had essentially been living in their own filth. She could hardly blame him for not wanting to see a container of whipped-up, brown custard with his meal.

When the pudding appeared the second time, Cleon divided. One side of his body soft and composed, tenderly holding Jude in a crooked elbow. The other side stiffened, reared up, seized the offensive dessert and threw it against the wall, narrowly missing the orderly.

"Sir," he cried, whipping around.

One half of his mouth still grimacing, Cleon held up a finger. "No chocolate," he said. His hand fell into his lap and he added softly, "Please."

He went from the hospital to an inpatient rehab center, learning to walk again. By the time he came home for good, Cleon could discuss medical procedure and rehabilitation protocol in perfect English but he couldn't say "pass the salt." Fortunately, he had a baby boy learning to talk. A growing tyke who thought all fathers walked on crutches and stayed home during the day, while mothers went out to work.

Penny trusted Cleon alone with the baby. In fact, alone with the baby was when Cleon seemed most himself. He was rarely without the child. The stroller doubled as a walker, keeping him balanced as he exercised his weak legs. He only went up and down the driveway at first. As his strength and confidence increased, he ventured onto Balfour Avenue's tree-lined streets, but didn't go far from the house. The world was still too dangerous, too full of the unknown.

Cleon learned most of his English by watching *Readalong*, *The Friendly Giant* and *Romper Room* with Jude. He cooked with the baby in a bassinet or later, in a highchair. He napped when Jude napped, placing the boy on his chest, heartbeat to heartbeat, hands spread wide on Jude's rising and falling back.

In bed with Penny at night, he didn't want to make love, didn't want to talk about Chile.

"Later, later," he murmured, drawing her hair over his face and inhaling. "It's too clean right now. Just let it be."

Penny would shower, then come to bed and press her breasts and belly against his scarred back, her leg over his dented, withered calf, his head cradled in her elbow and their fingers twined. This was the trade-off. Penny could leave him during the day and go out into the dark, dirty world where unspeakable things happened. When evening fell, Cleon wanted clean sheets on the bed and Penny's naked heartbeat against him.

Hold me all night. Do not let me go. Do not let me out of your sight again.

They loved each other terribly, and they endured. A two-person ship sailing through the vast ocean of the dark hours, in a ship bottom-heavy with things Cleon wouldn't talk about. Not yet.

"Later," he said in the dark. "These are things you'll never un-hear. It's too soon to tell them. Too soon and too clean."

CLE◉N

*Y*OU MUST SURVIVE THIS. *Build your house again. Pick up the knocked-over furniture, straighten the rugs, sweep the floor. Start again because thou shalt survive.*

Imagine yourself. It's 1970. A year of tremendous changes. Salvador Allende is elected as Chile's president. You have a weekly column in the Clarín. *Your parents decide to move back to Austria. The Beatles break up and break your heart.*

In the midst of feeling terribly sorry for yourself, you meet a woman.

Not a girl. A woman.

"Her name is Penny," you tell your uncle.

"Lane?"

"I don't know her last name."

"Take her to dinner and find out," Louis says. "If it's Lane, marry her."

You come home from the dinner having experienced something between an epiphany and an existential crisis. "Her last name isn't Lane," you say. "But her real name is Lucille."

Louis lowers both his newspaper and his glasses. "Nu?"

"She hates Lucille. Hates to be called Lucy. Nobody's allowed to call her either. She says most people don't even know what her real name is."

"But you do."

You don't answer. You're gone. In your mind, you follow Lucille Penelope Cambie to a bridge by a fountain. The world tilts beneath your feet like a rocking horse while thick marshmallow fluff fills your chest. Her sweet, simple face set against a night sky, flung with handfuls of diamond stars. You can find something about her in every Beatles song you know. You could love, need and feed this woman until you're one hundred and sixty-four.

"Lucy, will you marry me," you whisper one night as she rolls beneath you, plump and sweet as a strawberry.

She calls your name to the diamond skies, followed by "Yes."

Then the soldiers call your name.
It's your turn.
(Lucy…)
Your house collapses.

THE WORST SISTER

*J*UDE FINALLY CALLED SERENA. "Did I win the Oscar for Most Melo-dramtic Exit?"

"Not even close."

"Sorry about the scene."

"For fuck's sake, why are you apologizing?"

"Sorry."

"Stop it. I can't even…"

"I know. There are no more evens to can't."

"I love you."

"I love you too. None of that changes. I just don't know where to put all this."

"What can I do, can I do anything? Or have I done enough? I mean, this whole stupid DNA thing was my idea in the first place, I swear I could fucking kick myself."

"You know what, you're right. It's entirely your fault."

"I am completely and unquestionably to blame. I suck."

"Fuck you."

"Fuck me, everyone who looks like me, the horse I rode in on and every horse that looks like that horse."

"You're the worst sister ever," Jude said, his sadness full of laughter. "And I don't want any sister but you. I don't mean to be a sap, but I'm having trouble finding anything to say that isn't sappy right now."

"I feel terrible. Tell me what I can do."

"Walk me through this stupid ancestry website?"

They got on Skype. Serena was in her home office, and from the desk in the background, Giosué waved. "Hey, Jude."

Jude raised a palm. "Yeah, I know. Don't make it bad. I'm trying."

"Want me to get lost, I can go in the other room if you—"

"No no," Jude said. "Mi pesadilla es su pesadilla."

My nightmare is your nightmare.

Serena logged into her account and shared her screen.

"So those cards we got just show ethnicities," she said. "But once you link the test kits to your family tree, then it starts calculating relationships and finding matches. So you can see… Here."

SUZANNE MIRIAM THOLET'S DNA MATCHES

Relationship: Parent/Child
Cleon Louis Tholet
Shared DNA: 3,453 cM across 67 segments

Lucille Penelope Cambie
Shared DNA: 3,462 cM across 72 segments

Relationship: Full sibling
Aiden Walter Tholet
Shared DNA: 2,715 cM across 65 segments

"Ouch," Jude said. "I was prepared not to see me but still…"

Not only am I not like the others, I'm not even here.

"What does cM mean anyway?" Giosué asked.

"Centimorgan," Serena said. "It's the unit they use to measure genetic linkage."

"And segments?"

"I think they represent a common ancestor. I'm not sure. All the technical terminology makes my eyes glaze over."

Jude rubbed his chin. "So, to see who I'm related to, I'd have to make my own family tree and link my kit."

"Right."

"Okay."

"You think you will?"

"I'm not sure yet."

"Whatever you want to do, I'm there. I'll help you do something, I'll help you do nothing. All right?"

"All right. You'll be the first to know."

But as soon as they disconnected, he made an account. He'd do this much alone and decide where to go from there.

Once he was set up, he created a private family tree with one single box: Juleón Tholet, born 25 November 1973, Santiago, Chile. He attached his kit number to it.

Thanks, chirped a pop-up box. *Give us a few minutes while we find your DNA matches!*

He went upstairs and played the *Grand Valse Brilliant* from Chopin's *Les Sylphides.*

He came back down to his desk, jiggled the computer screen awake.

A new pop-up box squealed, *View your DNA matches!*

He went back upstairs and played the waltz again.

"Don't be a pussy," he mumbled. "Just look and see what's there."

What wasn't there was a parent/child match. Or a full sibling match.

Everyone happy? I came, I linked, I looked.

Nothing to see here.

Nothing except a list of a dozen usernames, grouped by generational proximity. 3rd-4th cousins. 5th-8th cousins. Moderate probability. Good probability. Excellent probability.

Extremely likely probability.

Who were these people?

As he scrolled, a red number popped up in the menu bar, on top of the envelope icon. He had a message.

> *From: John Pastorino*
> *To: J_Tholet*
> *Hey, cousin, we're a close match! My family's from Genoa. Your tree is private and I don't recognize your surname but I'd love to chat.*

Jude unconsciously reared back from the desk, filled with stranger danger.

Get the fuck away from me.

You're not my people.

He logged out of the account and shut the browser window. He wasn't ever going back in. None of it was his.

He looked at his watch—a little past six. He called Penny.

"Hey, can I come over?"

"Oh honey," Penny said. "Of course you can. Please come over."

ALKI WAS THE BIRTHPLACE of modern Seattle and had the feel of a California beach town with its bungalows and boardwalk. Jude found parking on 53rd and walked down Alki Avenue. One of the Nouns' children strolled toward him, importantly leading a rabbit on a leash.

"Hello, Mr. Jude," she called.

"Hey, Pride."

"I'm Courage."

"My bad, I'm sorry." He crouched down and held out fingers for the rabbit to sniff. "Is this a boy or girl?"

"Girl. We had to give away her husband and her bunnies but Mom said I could keep her."

Jude smoothed the quivering brow. "Well, she's real sweet. What's her name?"

"Spay."

"Brilliant." He stood up, knees popping. "Tell your mom and dad I said hello."

He watched the little girl walk away, the rabbit's cotton-tailed posterior bouncing beside her, thinking, *Courage says hello.*

Sounded like an album title.

A prim, wrought-iron fence enclosed the Tholets' bungalow, and the beds were crammed with tulips in popsicle shades of pink, orange and purple. The yellow front door opened before Jude had even closed the gate, and Penny was waving. Inside, she had boxes of papers and pictures stacked on the kitchen table, along with her laptop.

"You've been busy," Jude said.

"Busy is the new obsessed. Glass of wine?"

"Please. ¿Papi está en casa?"

"He's at the marina with his buddies. He said it would only be for an hour, which means he'll be back around midnight."

Jude shed his jacket and pulled out a chair. "So let's pretend we're detectives," he said. "Or archaeologists. Detach, be robotic and look at what we know."

One at a time, each document was examined and set to the side. Penny's Canadian birth certificate. Cleon's Chilean one, plus his expired passport. His Canadian citizenship papers. Their American papers. Photocopies of Jude's two birth certificates. One under the seal of the Chilean civil clerk, the other under the seal of the Canadian consulate in Santiago.

"When did you get this?" Jude asked, holding up the Chilean document.

"I left the hospital with it."

153

"And this one you filled out at the embassy."

"That's right."

"If I was switched, I assume it was at the hospital."

Penny drew the laptop closer. "I tried to look into documented cases."

"And?"

"It's not unknown but it's rare. I made a list." She turned the screen toward Jude.

> *1931, Albinusdreef, Netherlands: Agnes van Vegten and Lenie van Duyn switched at the Leiden University Medical Center.*
>
> *1951, Prairie du Chien, Wisconsin: Sue McDonald and Martha Miller switched in the hospital. Miller's mother Mary always suspected a switch occurred but did not pursue her suspicions for 43 years.*
>
> *1953, Heppner, Oregon: DeAnn Angell and Kay Rene Reed switched at Pioneer Memorial Hospital. Angell's mother insisted she had been given the wrong baby after nurses returned from bathing them, but her concerns were ignored. DNA tests confirmed.*
>
> *1953, Tokyo, Japan: Two baby boys switched at San-Ikukai Hospital. Became a Japanese "prince and pauper" tale.*
>
> *1966, Canary Islands: One of identical twin girls switched with another female infant in a state hospital.*
>
> *1971, Ottowa, Canada: Brent Tremblay and Marcus Holmes switched not in hospital, but within foster care through the Children's Aid Society of Ontario.*
>
> *1978, Wachula, Florida: Kimberly Mays and Arlena Twigg switched in the hospital. Dramatized as the TV movie* Switched at Birth.
>
> *1989, Johannesburg, South Africa: The sons of Margaret Clinton-Parker and Sandra Dawkins were switched.*
>
> *1995, Charlottesville, Virginia: Callie Johnson and Rebecca Chittum switched in the hospital.*

"Less than ten cases," Jude said.

"And none from malicious intent. The ones in Wisconsin and Oregon both had a mother who suspected something was off but didn't follow through for one reason or another. All the rest seem like random mistakes. Human error."

They were quiet a moment, no closer or further to anything.

"Pure human error," Jude said. "One nurse picked me up, another picked up your baby, and each was put down in the other's bassinet."

"That's the simplest story."

"Or it could've been a more malicious swap."

"How so?"

"I'm not sure but you know me, anything worth doing is worth overdoing."

She gave a sad smile. "I wish I remembered more."

"It's not your fault."

"I thought about hypnosis."

"What, you mean to try to loosen some memories?"

She shrugged, the color high along her cheekbones. "It's silly."

"Hey, if we're dealing with a plot device problem, why not try a plot device solution?"

"Does Phil do it?"

"I could ask."

They stared off into private thought. Jude tugged his lower lip, wondering what might be pried out of his mother's memory after nearly four decades. He wasn't sure he liked the idea of taking her back to that horrific day when she watched her neighbors terrorized and her husband's uncle gunned down. How could anyone ask her to re-live giving birth on the floor of her house with only two unqualified friends to help her. It would be as cruel as making Cleon go through his days in the Villa Grimaldi.

But it might give some answers.

She'd do it for me.

He squeezed his eyes closed, overcome with love and frustration. "I'm so sorry about all of this."

"It's not your fault. None of this is anyone's fault."

"I asked Papi if he wanted revenge on his interrogators. Or even Pinochet. Right now, I'd gladly time-travel to kill some of those people."

The backs of her fingers brushed his cheek. "That's not you, though."

Maybe it is, he thought. *Maybe this really is me. I dig aggressive lovers and I'm consumed with murderous revenge.*

He reached for one of the boxes and drew out a random handful of photographs. Black and white snaps with miniscule timestamps in their margins. 1965. 1967. 1971. Individual shots of his parents. Group gatherings with friends. Uncle Louis reading on the patio of his little bungalow. Ysidro and Tatán lounging against the side of a hearse, sharing a smoke.

"Which one was the undertaker?" he asked.

"Tatán. Ysidro was the memorial mason."

"He made the gravestones."

She nodded. "He did beautiful work. I never saw anything like his skill. He would chisel completely freehand. Maybe a little penciled mark to center the name and date, but no guidelines to keep it straight. He had a perfect eye the way you have perfect pitch."

"Perfect plumb."

She laughed. "Exactly."

"Did he do any sculpting, like Uncle Louis?"

"No, he was strictly an engraver." She leaned on her elbow, cheek on her fist, her face going all soft with memory.

"What?" Jude said. "What are you thinking about?"

"Ysidro had a record player in his workshop across the road, and you'd hear the Fab Four all day long. He'd take scraps of stone and chisel Beatles lyrics into them. Like something you'd find in a Homegoods or TJ Maxx today. A little block of granite with *Come Together* carved into it. Or a big flat paver, like…" Her hands shaped a rectangle of remembered space. "He chiseled *sitting in an English garden, waiting for the sun.* I put it next to one of the stone benches outside, in a big patch of California poppies."

"He chiseled all the lyrics in English?"

"Mm. Papi joked that he and Ysidro spoke terrible English but they were fluent in John, Paul, George and Ringo. We had dozens of those Beatles stones. In the garden beds, on side tables and the windowsills. Papi used one for a paperweight. I'll never forget because Ysidro botched it."

She took a pen and jotted on a scrap of paper, *Nothing's Gona Change My World.*

"Ysidro was mortified about the misspelling but Cleon wouldn't let him re-do it. He said, 'Nothing's gonna change my stone.'"

As Jude stared at the two-dimensional photograph of the gay couple, the anecdotes made them take on depth. "I wish we knew what happened to them."

Penny exhaled long. "So do I. Now more than ever. They both held you in the hospital. Ysidro was the one who came up with your nickname."

Jude put down the photograph. "Pretend I don't already know this story."

THE OUTCOME

*A*RRIVING IN CHILE IN 1941, Cleon's father, Felix Tholet, had dreams of getting into public park planning. When that didn't pan out, he opened a nursery and landscaping business, designing private gardens for upper-class families, among them the prominent Larraín family.

Felix's brother, Louis, made a modest living creating garden statuary, either on commission, or to sell at Felix's nurseries. In 1960, he entered into a business arrangement with the Sepúlvedas, an Italo-Chilean family of memorial masons. Louis sculpted ornaments for markers, obelisks and mausoleums, and designed Hebrew inscriptions for Jewish gravestones.

"It was fashionable in Jewish circles to say 'Tholet did the stone,'" Penny told Jude.

In 1963 the Larraíns' ranch was sold to the city of Santiago and developed as a suburban neighborhood, La Reina. Felix Tholet purchased one of the first plots for sale. He bought the adjacent plot as well, creating a satellite nursery that did a killing as the neighborhood grew.

"Louis bought the lot across the street," Penny said. "But he didn't do anything with it for years, not until Ysidro Sepúlveda suddenly needed a place to live and work."

"Because his family threw him out."

She nodded. "The Sepúlvedas wrote their laws in stone."

"That's when he and Tatán came to live with you."

"Louis had been using the second bungalow on our property as a studio," Penny said. "He cleared it out so the boys could live there... Funny I always say boys when I tell this story. They were only four years younger than I was. Anyway, they built a new masonry workshop on Louis' vacant lot. Tatán lacked the capital to start an undertaking business. He cobbled together a living driving a hearse for a funeral home and driving an ambulance for the city coroner."

"They were living with you the whole time you were pregnant with me?"

"Pregnant like a strawberry."

Jude's head tilted. "You always say that. What is that from?"

She shrugged. "Your father made it up."

"Tell me about Ysidro coming up with my name."

⌒⌒

A COLD, RAINY JUNE day. Late afternoon after siesta and Penny was making fruit empanadas. Ysidro sat at her kitchen table, deftly peeling apples.

"What will you name him?" he asked.

"You think it's a boy?"

"I come from a long line of witches. We know these things."

"¿En serio?"

Ysidro waggled his fingers in a circular motion around Penny's belly, murmuring some mumbo-jumbo. He closed his eyes, an open palm held a quarter inch from her flowered smock. "Boy," he said. "Absolutely."

"Are we making a wager here?"

"My honor doesn't allow me to wager when I know the outcome." He glanced at his watch, then back at her. "What will you call our boy?"

The plural pronoun touched Penny's heart while a funny superstition made her tongue reluctant. She took paper and pencil and wrote the name: Juleón.

"Juleón?" Ysidro naturally pronounced the J like a H.

"In English it would be Juleón," she said, exaggerating the hard J for him. "My mother's name is Julia. Then the last part of Cleón. The two people I love most in the world become Juleón."

"Your father won't mind?"

She smiled. "He doesn't want any grandson of his to be named Walter."

Ysidro laughed. "What if you have a girl?"

"Are you revising your outcome?"

"I'm predicting your next baby."

"If it's a girl, then either Julia or Suzanne. I haven't decided yet."

"Suzanne," Ysidro said, with authority. "It's pretty."

He checked his watch again. Not much bothered him, but he didn't like when Tatán was late getting home.

"Don't worry," Penny said.

"I'm not."

"You are."

His eyes looked everywhere but at her and the back of his neck reddened, highlighting the heavy chain necklace he wore. Off it, a saint's medal dangled.

Penny sat down and reached a curious finger toward the pendant. "Who watches over you, can I see?"

"Jude," Ysidro said, with the J like a Y. "Patron saint of lost causes. He protects people in desperate circumstances."

"Jude." She made the J hard. "I like that name, too."

His hand gestured toward her belly. "You could call our boy Jude for short."

"I could."

"Then he'd have his own song." In a voice husky but on tune, Ysidro sang the opening notes of the iconic Beatles tune. "I love that song." He warbled a couple more lines, the English lyrics mushy within his accent.

Penny put her chin on her hand. "Do you understand the words?"

"A little. I get make a sad song happy and make bad things better. What does letting someone under your skin mean?"

"It's an expression. When you're in love with someone and can't stop thinking about them, you say they've gotten under your skin."

"Ah. I know the feeling."

"What feeling?" Tatán said, appearing at the screen door, tousled and tired. As he came in, Ysidro leaned on the rear legs of his chair, gazing up and back. Then both their glances flicked toward Penny, who quickly invented business at the sink. The lovers were still getting used to the freedom to be affectionate within the walls of this house.

"What's your favorite Beatles song?" Ysidro asked his mate.

"Eleanor Rigby."

"Why's that?" Penny asked.

"It's a lament for lonely people. Eleanor and Father McKenzie could've had a beautiful life together but they—"

"He was a priest," Ysidro said.

"An English priest. They can marry."

"Punto."

"They missed each other, missed a chance to have a connection. All the priest can do is make sure she's buried along with her name. But it should have been his name."

"I'LL NEVER FORGET HOW sad he looked telling us about Eleanor," Penny said. "Fiercely sad. These were real people to him. He believed somewhere in an English churchyard was a stone chiseled with *Eleanor Rigby*, and a devoted clergyman who kept the grave neat and tidy. He was such a tender soul. He didn't think anyone should die alone."

Tatán's job was transporting Santiago's deceased. From the place where they died to the morgue. Morgue to funeral. Funeral to graveyard. Lamenting when he collected people who died alone. When those lonely people were buried, Tatán often attended, just so they'd have someone.

"Uncle Louis went with him," Penny said. "He had that same holy regard for death. Insisting nobody should go to their grave unwitnessed."

Whatever the deceased's affiliation, Louis would read Kaddish, the Hebrew prayer for the dead that celebrated life rather than mourning it.

"But who read Kaddish for Louis?" Jude said.

"Ysidro promised someone would," Penny said. "When he visited me in the hospital. He promised Louis would be buried in the Jewish Cemetery. He'd find a rabbi to say Kaddish and Ysidro would make the stone."

"And he did?" Jude asked. "That happened?"

"I don't know. But he promised and I have to believe." She smiled, dreamy with bittersweet memories. "He made you one."

"He made me a gravestone?"

She laughed. "No, I mean one of his Beatles lyric stones. A beautiful piece of rough, pink granite, chiseled with *Hey, Jude*."

"Really?"

"Mm. He left room underneath. Said, 'I'll add our boy's birthday when it's time.'"

"What happened to it?"

"I left it," Penny said. "I went back to La Reina just once, with an armed guard. He gave me twenty minutes to pack essentials and a handful of luxuries. A heavy piece of granite didn't qualify as either. I had to let it go."

"I wonder if he finished it. Along with Louis' stone."

"He did. I know he did. Not just because it was a promise to me, but because Sepúlvedas write their laws in stone."

Jude nodded slowly. "I didn't pay much attention to this story before but now, God, I wish I could meet them. For so many reasons. Jesus, they helped deliver me on the freakin' floor and..." He took off his glasses and rubbed at his eyes. "Not me, but him. Shit, I'm never going to get used to this."

"I know. It keeps tripping me up, too."

He looked up at her. "What should we call our boy?"

Her own laugh was half a sob. "Oh God, don't."

"I'm sorry. I'm trying." He passed her a tissue.

"You were meant to be my boy," she said, wiping her eyes. "Don't ask me how, but if I'm going to profess belief in a divine order, I can't cherry-pick what's divine and what isn't. You ended up in my arms in the hospital and I never had any inkling, any suspicion, any strange instinct you didn't belong there. I have no idea why my biological child ended up where he did... Or she did..."

Jude drew a quick, sharp breath. "That's a pretty brutal and brave admission. To say it might've been a girl."

"Well? It could have. The brutal, brave truth is I don't remember." Penny opened her hands to the ceiling. "Who would Serena and Aiden be without you as their older brother?"

Jude shook his head. Smiling a little but saying nothing.

"Why don't we call it a night, querido?"

As he stood up from the kitchen table, he blurted, "I met someone."

Penny blinked. "Did you now?"

"Yeah."

"Where?"

He laughed. "At a bar. Which sounds like a cliché, but he's not... He's different."

"How so?"

A long pause, Jude's face now filled with puzzled revelation. "I feel different when I'm around him," he said. "Or rather, I feel like I remember who I am. It's hard to put into words."

"Well, those words sound terrific." She kissed him. "I'm glad, honey. Go home and get some sleep."

 THE SEARS CATALOG

$\mathcal{P}$ENNY COUNTED FIVE AFTER the front door closed, then called her daughter. "Jude said he met someone."

"He said that?" Serena said. "Out loud? To you?"

"Word for word."

"Who is he?"

"No idea. Jude met him in a bar."

"Shut up. Jude *hates* bar pick-ups."

"He said it was different."

"If he's telling you they met, it's definitely different. I'm just relieved he walked back into the house."

"Well, Papi had to pull rank, go over there and beat on the door. You know how he gets when any of you kids disappears."

Serena laughed. She'd been grounded countless times for not phoning in her whereabouts or being where she was supposed to be.

"Did you come to any action plan," she asked. "Or you just kept company?"

"We kept company, looked at papers and pictures. Tried to look at the story from a new angle and see if we missed anything obvious. We talked a lot about Ysidro and Tatán."

"You never found out what became of them, did you?"

"They fled to Argentina. I know that much."

"And it wasn't much better there."

"Exactly, so they could have moved on."

"Or been disappeared."

"Maybe," Penny said. "Maybe I'll do a little looking around."

"Do you think Jude will look around?"

"I couldn't say, querida. We didn't go there tonight."

"How would you feel about it?"

"I think I would be all right with him looking. But if he finds people and they reject him, I wouldn't take it well."

"Reject him because he's gay?"

"I watched Chileans do it before."

"Punto."

"You know I love to say parenthood progresses by trading in one set of problems for a better set of problems. I don't miss the things that used to keep me up at night when you were teenagers, but worrying about Jude being treated unkindly or with outright malice… It's never left. He's thirty-six. Tonight he told me he met someone, and I smiled and said how wonderful. But inside, I chambered a round and put a perfect stranger in the crosshairs. Thinking, *You hurt him and I will kill you.*"

PENNY WAS STRIPPING THE sheets off Jude's bed one spring morning in 1988, annoyed he had neglected this chore for the second week in a row. The fitted sheet snagged on the far corner of the mattress and she yanked hard enough to pull it off-kilter from the box spring. A shower of paper fell to the floor, followed by a clattering thump. The latter came from a bottle of Nivea hand lotion.

Her irritation softened a split second, releasing as a wistful sigh. She grew up with two brothers—how many times did her own bottle of Jergens mysteriously go missing from her vanity? Another sigh, thick with the inevitable passage of years. Her sweet baby was a moody fifteen now. Almost taller than Cleon. Deep-voiced and hairy. No doubt crazed with hormones and consumed with sex.

She put the lotion on the bedside table. She picked up the scattered papers next and her stomach turned over.

Newsprint pages moved through her fingers, their margins ragged, torn from magazines. *Teen Beat. Tiger Beat.* Tabloid headlines thick with bold print and chipper with exclamation points. Actors and rock stars staring down the camera. Arrogant. Shy. Contemplative. Seductive.

All young men.

These were Serena's magazines.

With trembling hands, Penny picked up glossy, color pages from the floor. Torn from the men's apparel section of the Sears catalog. Some formal wear but mostly men in briefs and undershirts. Broad-shouldered, muscular. Expressions mild above crossed arms or hands on hips. Every bulge in every groin neat, compact and symmetrical.

She looked at the Nivea bottle. Then back to the images.

He's masturbating to pictures of men.

Fear coiled around her and she fought not to clutch the pages and wrinkle them. No doubt they were filed in a certain order beneath the mattress and she'd never return them properly. He'd know they were discovered. He'd know someone knew his secret.

Jude is gay.

"Oh my God," she said under her held breath. "I'm sorry."

I'm not sorry you're gay, she immediately amended. *I'm sorry I found out this way.*

Heart beating, throat clenched, she assembled the pages together carefully. *I'm sorry being gay is going to be so hard. I'm sorry this can't be normal. I'm sorry it has to be hidden.*

She crouched to pick up pages she missed. Clippings from the neighborhood paper that followed the school sports teams. Baseball stories accompanied by grainy black-and-white photographs. Each one about Feño Paloma's latest win.

"Jude, honey," Penny whispered, unable to stop the tears now. Jude crushing on his oldest childhood friend was so ordinary and predictable, it was tragic.

Please, she thought. *Don't let Feñó know. And if he knows, let him be kind.*

Her maternal instincts picked up a sword and tested its weight and edge. The She-Wolf's eyes narrowed at an enemy not yet revealed, seeking justice for a wrong not done. Not yet.

Be kind or else.

His life is going to be difficult enough as it is. You hurt him even more, you will answer to me.

She put everything back. The magazine pages, the lotion bottle, the mattress, even the sheets. When Jude got home from school, she dressed him down for the forgotten chore, but made no mention or hint of what she found. She wouldn't dare.

She told Cleon when they were getting ready for bed that night. His toothbrush froze mid-scrub and his eyes held hers in the bathroom mirror a long beat. Then he leaned and spit and came up nodding. "A lot of things make sense all of a sudden."

"What do you mean?"

"The whole business with Hewan Bourjini, for one. It always seemed a little too perfect to me. Deliberately perfect. Almost staged."

"Oh." She'd never given it a thought but now that Cleon brought it up, it was brow-smackingly obvious that Jude's longtime girlfriend was a beard.

Cleon wiped his mouth with a towel. "And he has no other male friends."

"Oh stop it, he has friends."

"Pen, he has male classmates and acquaintances. When was the last time he had a buddy over to hang? Who took Feño Paloma's place? No one. Jude's tightest with Serena and Hewan. Telling you, Pen, I'm surprised but I'm not."

"What should we do?"

"Nothing. We wait for him to share with us." He set his hands on the edge of the vanity and sighed, closing his eyes. "Christ, what's going to happen to him?"

They agreed not to confront him. This was personal, private and, above all, his story to tell. Instead, they did what they could to prepare the soil for whatever Jude might want to plant. Penny held tight and silent, biting her tongue. Hyper-aware of teenage cruelty that could easily turn into mob mentality. All the hours Jude was out of her sight, on his own and at the mercy of others.

Be merciful.

Be kind.

Or you will answer to me.

Her guard stayed up, her sword sharpened and at the ready. But even when you were prepared, you were never prepared. Penny harbored a niggling guilt she and Cleon hadn't handled Jude's official coming out the best way. To be fair, he sprung it on them at the end of a long, tiring day. But what were they expecting—an appointment?

She and Cleon were in bed with the news on. Penny was already half-asleep. Without preface, context or warning, Jude tapped on their door and sidled around the jamb, spilling a string of words across the foot of their bed. "Hey, got a minute I just want to let you know that I'll pay."

Penny repeated, "You'll pay?" just as Cleon said, "You'll stay?"

Exhaling at the two old fogeys he was burdened with, Jude crossed his arms and spoke with exaggerated enunciation. "I said, I want you to know I'm gay."

"Oh," Cleon said. "That."

Jude's arms dropped. "What do you mean, *that*?" So affronted, his still-deepening voice squeaked.

"We know," Penny said.

"You know?"

"We've known a long time."

"How?"

Penny's mouth hung open. She wasn't going to mortify him by mentioning the stash of magazine pages, but she had no backup plan. Instead she looked helplessly at Cleon, who looked encouragingly back.

You take this one, his eyes said.

Penny glared. *No, you.*

I'm good cop, he telegraphed.

That's why you should take it.

"Mom," Jude said. He only used Mom when he was annoyed with her.

"I don't know how," she said, holding up her palms. "I just knew."

"Why didn't you say something?"

"Like what?"

Oh my God, should I have said something? Did I screw this up from the get-go?

Parenthood: trading in one set of problems for a new set of problems. With no goddamn instruction manual for any of the problems.

"We didn't say anything because it's private," Cleon said, swinging his legs out of bed and reaching down for his crutches. "It's your private business and your story to share with us at the time you choose. So. It's time. You chose. And here we are."

"God, honey, all the color just went out of your face." Penny got out of bed. "Are you all right?"

Jude was still hanging on the door jamb. As she moved to him, Penny couldn't tell if he was going to burst into tears or burst into a run.

"We love you," she said, reaching out a hand, as if calming a feral dog. "We love you no matter what."

She put her arms around him. He trembled in his skin and didn't hug back.

"It makes no difference to me, hijo," Cleon said, a hand on Jude's head. "No difference whatsoever. Nothing changes. We're your family, this is your home."

As Cleon kissed his temple, Jude let his breath out and let go of the door-frame. "Okay."

"Is there anyone else?" Cleon asked.

"Hewan knows."

"No, I meant do you have someone?"

"Are you kidding?" Jude said. "I don't have a death wish."

"Well, when that changes," Cleon said. "You can always bring him here."

Jude's eyes made a circuit around the ceiling, skepticism in every line of his tall body.

"Listen to me, hueón," Cleon said. "I know this is hard and I know you feel isolated and in hiding. But Vancouver is one little corner of the world. When you go to college, the world is going to get bigger than you'd ever believe."

"You're going to meet a lot of people like you," Penny said. "I promise. It's not always going to be the way it is now."

Jude's gaze started to roll again, then stopped. He drew a deep breath and let it out slow. "I hope so."

Cleon took his shoulders. "It's going to be different someday. Someday soon. I promise. And you will meet someone. You'll bring them home and they'll be welcome here. Cachai?"

A gulped "'Chai," barely audible.

"Te queremos tanto," Penny said. "You're our boy, you're always our boy."

Then Jude put his head on his father's shoulder. "Estoy tan cansado."

I'm so tired.

"I know," Cleon said rubbing his hair. "It's exhausting to hide who you are and worry all the time. Not here though, po. Not in this house."

Lucky Cleon, the good cop. It was up to Penny to sit her son down the next day for a scathingly clinical discussion.

"Mom," Jude groaned, in between squirming and rolling his eyes and blushing to his hairline.

She crossed her arms on the kitchen table. "AIDS is legitimate concern to you now. You cannot ignore it."

"All right. Jesus, just stop saying the word anal already."

"If you can't say it you can't d—"

"*Mom.*"

"You have condoms?"

"Yes, I have condoms."

"Do you know how to use them?"

He answered through his teeth. "Yes, I know to use them."

She put up a finger. "You carry them and you use them. Every time."

Jude's mouth opened and quickly shut. Penny could see him culling the exasperated *I know* on the tip of his tongue. Swallowing the impulse and taking a breath. His shoulders squared for responsibility he now bore.

"I will," he said. "I want to be alive, too."

"All right. Torturous sex ed class dismissed. You're free."

Jude couldn't get out of the kitchen fast enough. Sighing heavily, looking forward to the next set of problems, Penny opened the fridge and mucked around for dinner makings. Leftovers were a thing of the past, since her three teens ate like linebackers. And were they out of milk *again*?

"Mami?"

Once more, Jude was curled around a door jamb. Smiling this time.

"Thanks," he said.

CLE◉N

*S*TART AGAIN BECAUSE THOU *shalt survive.*

Imagine yourself. It's 1971. You and Penny marry the same year John Lennon's Imagine *releases. Uncle Louis likes the title track, although he never bothers to learn the words. He accepts the gist of your translation, but he's content to jimmy the one Spanish word "Imagínate" wherever it fits and hum his way through the rest.*

"Imagínate la la..."

"There's no heaven," you say in English. "Come on, it's not difficult. 'Imagine there's no heaven.'"

"I see what he means in my head," Louis says. "I don't need to say it out loud."

In time, you will come to arrange certain things in your head so they don't have to be spoken aloud. Select emotions are permitted into your soul's melody as you see fit, and the rest will have to hum their way through.

But that's later.

Now, the soldiers are calling your name.

(Lucy.)

This time, you're not taken into a booth.

Handcuffed, your eyes taped under dark glasses, you're put into a van and taken to a new house. The Villa Grimaldi. Once an old colonial weekend home, but now the DINA—Pinochet's secret police—use it as a detention center.

(Lucy, how will you find me now?)

Things happen in the Villa Grimaldi. Things that defy imagination.

Things that don't fit into rooms of houses.

Things that cannot be survived.

THE POOR MAN'S REUBEN

*T*HE DOOR OPENED. TEJ stood in loose jeans and a T-shirt. Feet bare and a little stubble along his jaw. "As I live and breathe," he said, the brown of his eyes deepening and the gold flecks twinkling through like stars.

A two-by-four of pure desire smacked Jude in the chest, breaking open a piñata that cascaded into his belly and groin.

"I went way out of my way to be in the neighborhood," he said. "Thought I'd stop by."

Tej looked him up and down. "No flowers?"

Jude plucked a twig from the dead foliage in the planter and handed it over.

"You shouldn't have," Tej said, twirling the stem. Behind his legs, a cat meowed. He bent to pick it up.

"Are you busy?" Jude asked

"No."

A long staring moment which felt like the greatest game of chicken in the world. Tej's shoulder slid a little further down the door frame, as if he were settling in for the night. Jude moved a little closer. His fingertip reached and slowly drew up and down the placket of Tej's jeans. In full view of the street and its pedestrians. Not giving a shit who saw.

They stared, breathing the electric air.

"See, this is where you ask if you can come in," Tej said.

"Can I come in?"

"Thought you'd never ask." He gestured over the threshold. As Jude walked by, a fingertip caressed his neck and he was instantly and thoroughly hard.

Jesus Christ, what is happening to me?

"Nice place," he said, unzipping his jacket. "I noticed the other night, but I forgot to mention it."

Tej put the cat down. "You were distracted."

Jude laid his jacket on the back of a chair. It was a monumental effort not to take the rest of his clothes off. He'd never been so horny in his life. He doubted he appreciated or even comprehended what horny meant before tonight.

"Anyway, don't get ideas above my station," Tej said. "I'm house-sitting."

"Oh."

"Nothing here is mine so don't break any of it." He headed into the kitchen. "Including the cat."

Jude followed, sniffing at the buttery crispness lingering in the air. "What's cooking?"

"A poor man's reuben."

It was a beautiful sandwich, cut along the diagonal to show layers of ham, cheddar cheese and pickles. A single bite taken out of one triangle. A bottle of beer stood open by the plate, frosty around the neck and starting to drip condensation.

"Looks good," Jude said.

"It is," Tej said, taking a bite and chewing slowly. Perfectly comfortable in Jude's hungry gaze as the seconds dripped by. "What, my body isn't enough, you want my dinner, too?"

"Just your body."

Tej took another slow bite. "You totally want this sandwich."

"I don't."

"You do. You can't even meet my eyes, you're so fixated on my plate."

Not looking away, barely blinking, Jude put a knee down on the hardwood floor. Then the other. Not looking away, he unbuttoned and unzipped Tej's jeans. Reached inside to find what he came for. Above him, Tej kept eating, chewing slowly and deliberately. Never looking away.

"I don't want your sandwich," Jude said.

Tej kept eating, his free hand casual on the countertop, his ankles making no move to uncross. Their eyes stayed locked as Jude went at him. The game of chicken intensified. Tej blinked a little more rapidly. Swallowed hard as the sandwich hung suspended in his fingers. He reached for the beer bottle, took a long pull and then lowered it to Jude's level.

"Here," he said softly. "Make your mouth cold."

The dark, icy stout made Jude's teeth ache while the alcohol burned down his throat and into his belly. He wrapped his cool mouth around Tej's hardness again.

With a luscious thud, the poor man's reuben hit the floor and spilled open like a book. Up rose a tangy wave of mustard and vinegar and Tej's voice surfed above it.

"Baby…"

His eyes closed and his hand threaded through Jude's hair.

"Colder," he whispered, his head falling back, knuckles white on the counter's edge.

Jude drained the last of the beer, then slid up closer, got in tighter and with his ice-cold mouth, finished Tej off.

❧

"TELL ME ABOUT THIS?" Tej's fingers drew along the deep, livid scar on Jude's left shin. "I noticed the other night, but I forgot to mention it."

"You were distracted."

"Tell me."

"I broke it." Jude was too blissed-out and stupid with sex to use the intransitive verb.

"Well obviously. What happened?"

His endorphin-soaked brain spun the roulette wheel of trusty fish tales—motorcycle wreck, skiing accident, skydiving mishap—before deciding, *Fuck it.*

"Oh, what usually happens," he said. "Neighborhood homophobe took offense to my sexual persuasions, so he took a baseball bat to my leg."

Tej's hand closed tight around Jude's ankle. "Shut up."

"Shut down."

"Are you fucking kidding me?"

"Nope."

"What happened then?"

"Lots of things."

"I mean did anything happen to him? Is he in jail? Say yes."

"He took a plea deal, did two years. We sued the shit out of him in civil court."

"Did you win? Say yes."

"Settled."

"I know it's vulgar to discuss money, but I hope it was a tidy sum."

"Juan-Mateo's father owned a multi-million-dollar construction business. Let's just say my siblings aren't student debt-free by luck and my parents do not own beachfront property on Alki Avenue by accident."

"Good." Tej drew a finger along the scar, mumbling something in a different language.

Jude raised his head from the pillow. "What?"

"Nothing."

"What language was that?"

"Arabic. I was throwing down a curse on Juan-Motherfucker's progeny."

"Who are you?" Jude asked the ceiling, not for the first time that evening.

"Your future husband. Get used to it."

"Shut up." Jude's laughing mouth shaped the words but put no sound behind them because Tej was kissing up his thighs, breath warm and rough beard scratchy. "You're a persistent man, Timothée Jalil."

"Pardon your French."

"Do you speak French?"

"Oui."

"French and Arabic."

"Oh God, I'm gonna be profiled now."

"Forgive me, I'm a little obsessed with ethnic origins at the moment."

"Fair enough." He wiggled Jude's legs apart and lay between them, putting his cheek on Jude's belly button. "Guess mine correctly and you can sit on my face."

"You're Irish."

Tej's head lifted. "You're not even trying. Obviously my offer doesn't appeal to you. I'm insulted. Get out of my house."

Jude pushed his head down again, keeping a hand threaded in the thick, dark hair. "French and Arabic," he said again, envisioning a map of the Middle East. "Syria?"

"One over."

"Iraq?"

"The other way. Toward the cedar trees."

"Lebanon."

"If you were wearing pants, I'd call them smart."

"When did you family come here?"

"My father's eldest brother came in the early sixties. They're all vintners on that side of the family. Huge winery in the Beqaa Valley got them stinking rich. My uncle always had itchy feet and he wanted to check out the Napa Valley. He came first, started building the empire."

"When did you come?"

"Seventy-eight. Dad left first, to secure the way. Then Maman would follow with us kids."

"Was Raymond still alive?"

"No." A ruffle of sighed breath across Jude's stomach. "My little sister died in a bombing, just before we left."

"Shit, I'm sorry."

"Thanks."

"Are you out to your parents?"

"Yes."

The terse tone made Jude hesitate. "How is it?"

"Cool."

"Cool like groovy, or cool like cordial?"

"Cordial."

"Ah." He said no more, kept running his fingers through Tej's hair.

"Actually, that's a lie. I don't talk to my parents."

"Ever?"

"My father not at all. My mother rarely, and only through my sister, Mireille. She's the hero in my sad story."

"She's an ally. You're the hero."

"Great, I'm in bed with Joseph Campbell."

"You love it."

"I do." Tej's hand ran from Jude's rib cage, down the trunk of his body to his knee. Then up again. "I'm glad you came by."

Jude closed his eyes and slowly exhaled. "So am I."

The buzz of the doorbell made them both jump.

"Did you order take-out?" Tej said.

"Not me. You have other lovers in the neighborhood?"

"It might be my ex-wife." He laughed and dodged the pillow Jude swung at his head. "Kidding. I don't know." He pulled on jeans and walked out of the bedroom, smoothing his tousled hair.

Jude brushed away condom wrappers and rolled onto his stomach, wrestled the lube bottle out from under his chest and flung it aside. "Good fucking lord," he whispered, grinning into the pillows.

Through the cracked door he could hear mumbled conversation. It was definitely a female voice. Now Tej was coming back down the hall.

"Hold on, hold on, I got a naked man in here." He peeked in. "It's my sister. She's cool, you can come out."

Jude got up, tugging at his own hair.

"Put clothes on," Tej said. "She's not *that* cool. And don't blush. That's my department."

In the bathroom, Jude washed his hands and face, took a swig of mouthwash. Studied his reflection in the mirror. Tried not to look like someone who just fucked the shit out of your baby brother.

Before his eyes, he flamed up red.

THE DELIBERATE CRUELTY

1 N THE LIVING ROOM Jude was greeted by a lovely, meticulously groomed woman, introduced as Mireille.

"It's so nice to meet you," she said, and then turned raised eyebrows to Tej. "This is an improvement."

Glaring, Tej closed his fingertips around the air with a hissed, "Shh."

"What? It's nice not to see you with a pouting, tattooed college boy for once."

Tej replied in one of his two languages. Mireille answered in the same. As the siblings bickered, Jude slowly knelt down. At Mireille's feet was a dog. Perhaps the most amazing dog Jude ever saw. A dog that redefined the definition of dog. Jude wanted to punch the cat, this dog was so fucking cute. And when this incredible pooch trotted forward and greeted him like a soul mate, Jude felt something beyond pleasure. He felt chosen.

"Look at you," he said, laughing as the dog circled between his crouched legs, sniffing and nudging before settling down and leaning on him.

"That's Samson," Mireille said.

"We love him," Tej added, and headed into the kitchen.

"Look at you." Jude couldn't take eyes or his hands off this creature. His fur was a gorgeous, smooth caramel with a patch of white on his chest and the toes of one paw. His tail and ears were chocolate brown, the latter folded neatly forward beside his square head.

"God, this is one handsome dog," Jude said. "What breed is he?"

"He's the offspring of a Beagle and a Boxer-Lab," Mireille said. "He's got that blunt-face silhouette but he's not as jowly as full Boxers. And he's a nice size."

Not satisfied with leaning, Samson started crawling up Jude's chest, panting contentedly, hinting he wouldn't mind be carried.

"He doesn't seem to like you," Mireille said.

Jude stood up, arms full of puppy love. "Do you take checks, or do you prefer cash?"

"You can't afford him."

"Try me."

"Anytime you want to babysit, feel free."

"He's my babysitter," Tej said, coming out of the kitchen with a tray in his hands and a bottle of wine tucked under one arm.

"So how'd you two meet?"

"He picked me up in a bar," Jude said to Samson's curious face. "Didn't he? Yes, he did."

"Must've been a Tuesday," Mireille said.

"Hey." Tej looked up from pouring. "You and Rosie need to cut that shit out."

The tray had a bowl of salted almonds and another of green grapes, which Mireille warned not be fed to Samson. "They're incredibly toxic to dogs, as I learned via a five grand veterinarian bill. So, Jude, are you a Seattle native or newcomer?"

"I moved here in high school. From Vancouver."

Mireille leveled her gaze at her brother. "Canadian. Definitely an improvement."

"Well you told me I had to start making better choices, so I stood in a bar and asked for countries of origin."

"Actually, I was born in Chile," Jude said, scratching Samson's chin. "Wasn't I?"

"Shut up," Tej said around a mouthful of almonds. "I did not know this."

"Well, we just met."

Tej tilted his head in the direction of the bedroom. "We also just had a long getting-to-know you conversation, so how did Chile not come up?"

"If you guys are going to have your first fight, I can leave," Mireille said, then laughed when Jude widened his eyes and clutched Samson tighter. "Or not."

Tej looked poised on the edge of a question, which Jude could tell involved the DNA test and the switched-at-birth story and the new Chile information. He shook his head just the tiniest bit.

I don't want to get into it. Okay?

Tej's chin gave a tight rise and fall, and he only said, "Great, Miri, now he's only going to want me for the dog. Thanks for coming by."

Mireille Khoury had a master's in Oh Never Mind Me, Let's Talk About You. Jude did glean she was an interior designer, but she could've been a hell of a therapist. Plus Samson acted like some kind of muscle-relaxing truth serum and before Jude knew it, half his life story was on the coffee table. Not just a neat, encapsulated version but deep, intimate memories and recollections of his childhood.

"This is so interesting," Mireille said, kicking off one of her flats and tucking her foot underneath her. "What was it like being your father's child? I mean, did you and your siblings know what happened to him?"

"We knew, sure," Jude said. "But we didn't learn in one sit-down session. I remember it all being kind of gradual. Like we were spoon fed age-appropriate versions of the story. Real simple at first—bad men hurt Papi, but he's all right now. His legs don't work so well, but he got away and nobody can hurt him or us ever again. As we got older and could understand the political background and who the bad men were, we learned more of the details. Learned he'd been tortured..."

Learned my mother was roughed up when the soldiers came to La Reina. They shot Uncle Louis, rifle-butted Mami in the head and she gave birth to me on the floor of the house.

Or rather, she gave birth on the floor, but not to me.

"Anyway," he said slowly. "We knew. It made us an incredibly tight family. My father was protective of us, but we were just as protective of him. He definitely had his trigger points. Things or situations that instantly made him upset."

"Like?" Mireille asked.

"He'd never go to a stadium. Not for a sporting event or concert. Police and soldiers made him really nervous. He was a perfect driver. I mean a textbook, *impeccable* driver, because being pulled over could be a psychological ordeal. Once, leaving for a vacation, we were walking into Sea-Tac and a couple of on-duty soldiers were coming out. Full metal jacket, armed to the teeth, German Shepherd on a leash. My father was on his crutches, so one of the soldiers held the door for him. Perfectly polite, 'I got it, sir, take your time.' Papi broke out in a sweat. I watched him look over his shoulder a good five minutes after, seeing if they were trailing him."

"Jesus," Tej said, shaking his head.

"And he always needed to know where we were." Jude shifted in his chair, rearranging both Samson and his lingering guilt. The deliberate cruelty in putting Cleon into radio silence was sour in his stomach now. It was a beyond shitty thing to do.

"We had a bit of an argument recently," he heard himself say. "I didn't speak to him for a couple days. Didn't answer his calls. He practically broke my door down and tore me a new one." His cheeks prickled warm as he smiled at Tej. "Which I deserved."

Why am I telling him all this?

Tej nodded, tousled, handsome and thoughtful.

"Unbelievable," Mireille said over the rim of her wineglass. "Have you ever been back to Chile?"

"No. Not my parents or sister, either. My brother's an environmental researcher and his work will often take him to South America. But mostly to the Chilean coast and Patagonia. I don't think he's ever been to Santiago. Or feels a desire to."

"Mm. We've never been back to Lebanon, either."

"Wait, you did that Mediterranean cruise," Tej said. "Greece, Cyprus, Turkey, Israel. Didn't it stop in Beirut?"

"It did," Mireille said. "But I didn't get off the boat. Hell, no."

"How old were you during the war?" Jude asked.

"Eight when it started. Ten when we left. And call me a wimp, but it took so long to get over those bad memories, I didn't even want to stand at the ship's rail and look at the damn place." She stood up and wiggled her shoe back on. "Unfortunately, I need to get going. Tej, help me get the dog back."

Jude sighed, got up and gave Samson over. "If you go on another cruise, I'll dog sit. Free. I'll pay you to watch him."

She laughed and kissed his cheek. "Deal. So nice to meet you." She glanced at Tej, then back at Jude. "I mean *really* nice to meet you."

"Fiche le camp, cherie," Tej said loudly. "Door is that way."

She left still laughing, Samson trotting behind, leaving Jude bereft.

"From now on, I really do only want you for the dog," he said. "Let's just make it clear."

"Last time I let Miri drop by with her voodoo pooch." Tej turned the locks and was about to slide the chain across when he stopped. "Well, look at me presumptuously bolting us in for the night." He glanced back at Jude. "Do you want to stay?"

Their eyes held. Tej's gaze was like warm maple syrup, up to no good as it dripped down Jude's body. An impossible mix of angel and devil beneath thick, sleek brows. One side of his mouth smiling through his beard growth.

Jude had an appointment with Phil early tomorrow morning. Then a full day's work, including a new ballet with a bitch of a score he hadn't practiced.

Tej reached and drew his finger down Jude's stomach. "See, this is where you say thanks, but it's a school night and maybe another time, you'll call me, yadda yadda."

Quivering in his skin, Jude exhaled. "Can I borrow a toothbrush?"

 THE ELEPHANT

*R*EVERSE-IMAGED IN A WEBCAM window, Penny fussed with her hair and moved in and out of the kitchen light, grimacing.

Is that *how I look?*

"It's the terrible thing about growing old," the actress Jessica Tandy said. "You look like shit."

One more year and Penny Tholet would be able to test the Beatles theory of love: *Will you still need me, will you still feed me, when I'm sixty-four?* According to Serena, sixty-three was the new forty-six. But this whole DNA nightmare seemed to have aged Penny a decade and she was looking pretty goddamn ancient tonight. She set the edges of her hands at her ears and gently drew them back, smoothing the wrinkles in her face. She turned this way and that, considering her options. Maybe just a tuck?

A beep and a whoosh and Skype opened a second webcam window, revealing Aiden Tholet. Penny let go her face and waved. "Hola, querido."

"Hey. Do you have a cold or something?"

"No."

"You don't look so good."

Aiden's girlfriend appeared in the frame and gave his head a little shove. "Salvaje. Brute. That's not how you say hello to a woman, let alone your mother."

"Hola, Inez," Penny said.

Inez waved both hands and peered into the camera. "Disculpa, mamacita, we'll have your son try that again. Aiden, say hello."

"Hello, Mami," Aiden said, smiling between hunched shoulders.

"Bien, mi amor, bravo." Inez slid arms around him from behind and kissed his cheek. "The beast can be taught."

Penny was all laughter inside, but she kept her face mild. Aiden's romantic life was a secret vault within the guarded keep underneath the fortified fortress of his life. Getting merely one glimpse of a girlfriend was like sighting some rare, tropical moth. Inez had been in the picture close to three months now.

"You both look great," Penny said. "Aiden, are those new glasses?"

Aiden touched the trendy, light blue frames. "Yeah I need them to read now, and for the computer."

"You cut your hair, too."

"I cut it," Inez said. "¿Se ve muy guapo, verdad?"

Aiden touched the sandy locks that once grew in a neglected mane to his shoulders. Now he sported a shorter cut, deliberately and artfully tousled, along with a rather smart V-neck sweater. Penny kissed her fingertips. "Muy guapo."

"What's going on?" Aiden said, leaning on his forearms. Inez leaned on him, an arm slung around his shoulders.

"Well," Penny said, filled with reluctance. She wanted to sit and stare at this new, scrubbed-up Aiden, lounging under the drape of a steady girlfriend. "I wanted to talk to you about some… Well, it's not exactly bad news. I'm not really sure what kind of news it is."

"What about?"

"About Jude. And me. And Papi."

Inez glanced at Aiden, eyebrows furrowed, then back at the camera. "I'll make some tea," she said, getting up. "You two chat."

"What's the matter with Jude?" Aiden asked.

"Remember the DNA testing kit Serena sent you?"

"Sure."

"Well the results came back and they showed something we didn't expect."

Aiden reached for a pad of paper with one hand and a pen with the other. "In your DNA? What is it, Parkinson's? Some kind of cancer?"

"No, no. The results showed that Jude…" Her mouth was dry, she cleared her throat.

"What?"

"Jude isn't our son."

Aiden looked up from his writing. "I'm sorry?"

"Jude isn't our biological son."

He stared at her a long moment. Took off his glasses and stared some more. "Where'd you get him?"

Penny said nothing. After being Aiden's mother for twenty-nine years, she knew the first thing out of his mouth was often appalling. Tone deaf.

Inappropriate. Lacking compassion. Missing the point by a country mile. He didn't do it on purpose. He wasn't a cruel man. He was wired differently and had a flimsy filter. Penny waited for him to craft a different response, remembering the time it took for her to rewire her reactions to her youngest son.

"I don't mean…" He put his glasses back on, drew the pad and pen closer. "Sorry. Tell me what happened. What did the tests say?"

Penny told him. Fetched the result cards and held them one at a time up to the screen.

"Email me pictures of those?" He wrote every figure and percentage down. The family secretary, he liked lots of visuals, lots of information, detailed notes, bullet points and lists.

"So that's what we know," Penny said.

"Wow."

"Which pales into comparison to what we don't know."

"Well, it's not a day in the life of the Tholets without something happening to Jude." Aiden's tone conveyed a lifetime spent calculating the trials of each Tholet, down to the second, with an accompanying pie graph. "Hasn't he been through enough?"

Penny nodded, keeping eye contact across the ether. Aiden sank his chin onto a hand, mirroring Penny's body language. She couldn't sync with him on an intellectual level, but when they kept company, their physical posture often aligned.

"Wow," he said. "Wow, that's hard. I don't know what to say."

"It's hard to take in," Penny said. "I feel like it's happening to someone else."

Aiden blinked, his mouth moving around unspoken words.

"It makes no sense," she said. "I don't understand at all."

"What are you going to do?"

"I don't know, querido."

"Will you look for his…" Aiden paused, which touched Penny to the bone. He stopped and thought before using the word *mother* or *parents*. Paused to consider her feelings. "His people?" he said.

"I don't know. I think that's up to Jude."

"All right." He tapped his pen on the pad, scanning his notes. His brow wrinkled tight above the frames of his glasses. It bothered him when he couldn't provide an immediate solution to a problem.

"There's nothing you can do," Penny said. "I just needed you to know. Because it's a family issue and in my mind and heart, we're still a family. Jude is still our son and your brother. But this is incredibly upsetting. You needed to know in case he reaches out to you. Or you reached out to him and he didn't answer."

More likely the former. Reaching out to people was a skill Aiden was still mastering.

"¿Papi está in casa?" he asked.

"He was in the shower, let me see if he's out."

Wet-haired and fresh-faced, Cleon scraped up a chair to the kitchen table. "¿Qué onda, gordo?"

Gordo meant "fatso" or "fatty." It was Cleon's endearment for the lean Aiden, who walked between raindrops. Penny listened as Aiden caught his father up on work, a little puzzled. His Spanish sounded different. She couldn't put her finger on it, she didn't possess that kind of ear. Cleon and Jude loved to learn and mimic Latino accents. They could pinpoint a Spanish speaker's country of origin in four words.

"Gordo, where in the world did you pick up that terrible accent?"

"What do you mean?"

"You sound Argentinian."

Aiden's smile unfolded. All the more beautiful for its rarity. "My project manager is from Buenos Aires. I must be picking it up from him. Are you all right? With everything?"

"I don't know what right means," Cleon said. "So I don't know if I'm all of it. I'm just worried about Jude."

Aiden reached up for the mug of tea Inez brought. "When are you not worried, Pa?"

"I worry about all of you, it's my job."

"My mother had a saying about parenthood," Inez said. "You're only as happy as your least happy child."

❧

THE ELEPHANT IN THE room, of course, was that if anyone's DNA wasn't Tholet or Cambie, it ought to have been Aiden's. He wasn't the least happy child, but he often seemed the least familiar.

"Where did he come from?" Both Penny and Cleon wondered at this oyster of a boy. His solitary, guarded nature frustrated them to distraction, until he unexpectedly popped open and showed the shimmering pearls within.

As a baby, he was happiest when swaddled up like a burrito. The movement of his own arms and legs startled him to tears. The first sight of his reflection nearly traumatized the poor infant. You couldn't drag Jude and Serena away from a mirror, but Aiden avoided them with a vampire's aversion. Even as an adult, he often did a double take at his own reflection, as if he forgot he was there.

As the years of parenthood went by, Penny found Aiden's introverted manner a respite from her other children. Jude and Serena flung their love onto her, which meant they flung their troubles, their woes, their drama and pain into her arms as well, often with no regard for what already occupied them. Aiden kept the world against his chest. Penny had to watch him carefully, studying his manner and nuances like a map. She had to put more work into cultivating this difficult younger child. Take more time to understand him, delve more deeply beneath his unreadable surface. Aiden wrung the most effort from Penny, but when he came to her, leaned on her, put a problem into her palms or spontaneously embraced her, it rang a bell of maternal satisfaction and fulfillment seldom chimed by Serena or Jude. They ding-donged all the livelong day while Aiden stood apart like a church tower manned by a solitary monk, tolling his feelings on only the most momentous occasions.

"Where did you come from," Penny murmured on her knees at Aiden's bedside, watching him sleep. "You little fat thing."

She didn't smooth his hair or cheek. His sleep was sacrosanct and not to be disturbed. Aiden didn't so much get into bed as lie in state, always on his back, neat as a pin with ankle bones pressed together and hands folded on his chest. In the morning, you wouldn't know he'd been there.

It was easy to forget he was there. Jude needed this, Serena needed that. Jude and Serena. Serena and Jude. Born a few decades later, they would've been a social media trend and gleefully adopted one of those cutesy hashtag names given to celebrity couples. #Judena. #Serude.

To their credit, it would quickly occur to their generous hearts that their brother shouldn't be excluded.

#AndAiden.

Born a few decades later, perhaps Aiden would've been diagnosed as on the spectrum. Possibly. Penny doubted it. No label ever stuck to Aiden Tholet. Slim and sparse, walking between raindrops, he was simply their cosito gordo.

Their little fat thing.

CLE●N

*1*MAGINE YOURSELF.

An interrogation room with a metal bunkbed. You and another man tied to the side of the frame, a third man tied to the top bunk. The DINA is interrogating all three of you, taking turns to electrocute you one after the other.

This goes on through the night to the next morning.

No time to build a house and the stories of your life are slipping through your burned fingers.

(Lucy, Lucy...)

Stop that. Pick up the pieces. Start again because thou shalt survive.

Imagine yourself.

You're in a four-square-meter cell with six other men. You take turns sitting and lying down. Take turns using the corner designated as a toilet. The smell is unbearable. The cold is unbearable. The hunger is unbearable. The sound of screaming and moaning in the damp dark is unbearable. The thought of your wife—round, ripe, pregnant like a strawberry—not knowing where you are is unbearable.

But of course, that's bullshit. It's perfectly bearable compared to when they come for you and call your name.

(Lucy, my love.)

Then it's truly unbearable.

They beat you with their bare fists, their brass-knuckled fists. They beat you with batons. With chains. With things you can't even guess at when you're blindfolded and beaten. You're hanged by your feet and beaten. Hanged by your hands and beaten.

But the worst is the electricity.

It's like painting your skin with oil and then lighting a match. It's like staring into the sun. It's like swallowing the sun.

It's like nothing you can survive.

But you must. You have a mandate.

Start again.

Imagine yourself.

You're thrown back in your cell. Once the door clangs shut, you feel footsteps and soft hands.

(Lucy?)

Your compañeros hold you, take your blindfold off. You're streaming sweat. The thirst is a beast. Water on your lips and then, dear God, you're helped to lie down and the filthy floor is so cool.

Your compañeros help you. You help them when they return from the torture. But you don't bond your forces with theirs to create a community within which to endure.

Uncle Louis's way cannot be your way.

You begin to build a new palace.

It has one floor, one wing and one room. No furniture. Only pure white space. A blank canvas.

No stories live in this palace. Only one song.

The password is not stell dir vor—imagine yourself.

Of course not. You've been a fool. You've translated it wrong all this time.

(I'm sorry, Lucy.)

To enter the fortress, to endure and survive, you must picture yourself.

You roll up your sleeves. You'll have to hurry before they call your name again.

(I'm coming, Lucy…)

THE ONLY ENTERTAINMENT

*J*UDE'S STOMACH GROWLED, LOUD enough to make Tej pick up his head.

"You hungry?"

"Nah." Then his stomach growled again, calling him a liar. He'd skipped dinner, hot-tailed from work to Tej's place and fell straight into the sack.

Eating's overrated, he thought, as his belly complained a third time.

Tej laughed. "Come on. I'll make you a sandwich."

"I'm fine."

"No lover of mine goes hungry."

The house was cold compared to the oven of the bed. Tej loaned Jude sweats and a fleece. In the kitchen, he poured out two lowballs of whiskey and made a poor man's reuben.

"Were you out in high school?" Jude asked.

"Not at all. And you know, I could've been. I had a great high school experience. I had amazing friends and I could've told any one of them I was gay. I had a posse of big, wide-open beautiful hearts and minds, and I trusted none of them."

Jude nodded. "I hear you."

"Not that they were untrustworthy. But people are human. I lived in a small, insular community. Everyone knew everyone and if a word, a hint, a *whiff* got back to my family, I was toast. Fear of my family kept me from being honest with my friends. I still get bummed thinking about it. All that time wasted on hiding. The potential for a deeper bond wasted." Tej turned from the stove, spatula pointing. "You should know up front that waste drives me batshit crazy."

"You're saying I should chuck all the ancient take-out containers before I let you see the inside of my fridge?"

"I think we should get tested before you go showing me your fridge. That's a big step."

A taut pause.

"Oh dear, are we having The Talk?" Tej said.

"My doc always runs a full STD screen at my physicals," Jude says. "I had one a couple months ago. If you want to see my results."

Tej had no end of snarky comebacks, but they never came when Jude expected them. Like right now. Instead of a zinger, Tej only gave a slow, considering smile that turned all the air in the kitchen soft and dreamy.

"You're so good," he said.

"Me?"

"No, the other guy I'm making a sandwich for."

Jude laughed. "I'm not doing anything."

"Yes, you are." Tej set the plate with the crispy reuben down. "Stick the results on your fridge door. I'll give them a glance. You want mine?"

"Leave them on your pillow in the morning."

"You plan on being here?"

"If you'll have me."

"Little late for that. Stop blushing and eat your sandwich."

Jude took a bite, his teeth sinking through soft ham and melted cheese and crisp, tangy pickles. It was, he reflected, the best damn sandwich he'd had in his life. And tonight was sneaking into his top five best nights.

"How are you with trusting people now?" he asked.

A roar of steam as Tej ran cold water into the hot skillet. "Better. I guess. Old habits die hard and I racked up way more years sabotaging the good shit in my life than I have trusting it. Little by little the balance tips. I hope."

"My habit is flight," Jude said. "I'm hardwired like a refugee, with a bag packed and a foot out the door. First sign of trouble, I head for the border."

Why am I telling him this?

If Phil had been in the room, his eyebrows would be on the nape of his neck.

"How are things with your parents?" Tej said, refilling their glasses.

"They're better," Jude said through a mouthful. "Thank you for asking. And I kind of want to talk about anything but them right now. Okay?"

"Sure."

"Translation: I want to talk about you."

Tej sighed. "Oh please let's not talk about me, said no gay man ever."

"Ever sleep with a woman?"

"Yes. Disastrously. But she was kind about it."

"Did you have any boyfriends in high school?"

"A few secret, terrified, experimental hookups. Luckily those guys were also kind about it."

"What about in college. Where did you go again?"

"Stanford."

Jude coughed mid-swallow. "For real?"

"Kidding. UC Santa Barbara. It was amazing. Even better than high school. I could be out with a capital O. Openly gay. I vividly remember the first time I said it in a group conversation. Just as a segue to another topic. 'Well, I'm gay, so the way I see it…' And my mouth goes on talking but I'm thinking to myself, *Holy shit, nobody blinked. That was like nothing. The sky is blue, water is wet and I'm gay.*

"So life was just incredible. Campus was full of LGB awareness and activism. AIDS fundraisers. Protesting Colin Powell coming to make a speech because he supported Don't Ask, Don't Tell. Road tripping to San Francisco Pride and marching with my people. I could hook up with guys without fearing for my life. I finally did have a boyfriend. I got to experience first love and making love. I got to obsess about a relationship instead of wasting time and effort obsessing about being outed." He scooped up a blob of mustard from Jude's plate and ate it. "I get particularly irritated at wasted obsession, by the way."

"What happened with that guy?"

Tej leaned back in his chair with a wide-elbowed stretch, fists at his ears and biceps popping. "He wanted to come home and meet my family. I said no offense, but no fucking way was I bringing a boyfriend home. He took offense and gave an ultimatum. Come out or we break up."

"Well, that's all kinds of unreasonable."

"Yeah. But here's the thing. I was in love. With him and with my life. I was in a place where I had it all. This is friendship. This is acceptance. This is inclusivity and tolerance and greater understanding. This is amazing sex and *this* is love. The world was a big, bright, beautiful ball of sunshiny rainbows and glittering unicorns, right in my hands. And I looked at it and thought…"

The legs of his chair came down, his elbows went on the table and his chin lowered into the cradle of his palms. "Can you guess what I thought?"

"You thought, *I better sabotage this myself before someone or something else can.*"

Tej extended a fist across the table. Jude bumped it.

"Exactamundo," Tej said. "I said to him, 'All right, come home with me, be my lover and wingman. We're coming out together.' And off we went."

"I already know it doesn't end well."

"Nope. Next thing you know, he's helping me box up my stuff and move out. Me being all I *told you so. I hope you're happy now.* He felt terrible but of course, now I was in full sabotage mode and making him the convenient villain. We were broken up within weeks. Because burn it all with fire. That'll show 'em."

"What did you do?"

"I couch-surfed where I could. Worked three jobs until I could go in on a shitty apartment with three other people. Hustled and survived. Drank whatever money was left over. Had meaningless sex because it was the only entertainment I could afford."

"You didn't go back to school?"

Tej shook his head. "Not to be Dickensian but dear old Dad cut me off without a shilling. After rent and food, I couldn't even afford community college."

"Jesus," Jude said.

At least I ran away from Canada with a matching set of luggage. I got compensated for my pain.

Penny put an invisible hand on his shoulder, reminding him pain was not a competition and Tej's story didn't diminish or dismiss what happened in Vancouver.

"Whatever you're smiling about," Tej said, "don't stop."

"What brought you to Seattle?"

"Followed a guy. As one does. Didn't work out but I liked the feel of the city. Plus I landed a tech job with benefits, which I liked even better. I could exhale. I joined the volunteer fire department. That led to EMT training. Which led to dispatch certification. Things just started falling into good places." He reached under the table, scooped up Jude's calves and put them in his lap. "Obviously the universe was preparing me to cross your path."

A cozy bit of time passed, during which Jude finished his sandwich, Tej rubbed his feet and the night easily slipped from the number five slot to number four.

"This is nice," Jude said. Softly. Not wanting to jostle the moment.

Tej pushed the sweats up Jude's left leg and his fingers ran along the scar. "Does it still hurt?"

"The scar?"

"The bone."

"Only when I'm upset or anxious."

Keep them eyebrows raised, Phil, he thought. *I got no filter on my quirks tonight. No idea why.*

"Weird how trauma literally gets into your marrow," Tej said. "Like all those triggers your father still has."

"Mm."

"So. I'll share that thunderstorms freak me out. I'm not a fan of fireworks, either. They remind me of the bombings. Remind my body, I should say."

"If I may understate, it must've been horrible."

"I don't have many clear memories of that time, but any loud booming noise instantly puts me into a mild panic."

"What about the dark?"

"The dark is not a friend of mine. Inside the bomb shelters, it was pitch. So black, your brain didn't know what to do. You would think you were seeing shapes and shadows, reach out a hand and touch nothing. It was a color darker than black. I didn't even know that was possible."

"What else?"

"Like your Dad, I don't do well at spectator sports or concerts. For me, it's not the venue, it's the event itself. All that heightened emotion and people screaming. Too many decibels. My body doesn't know the difference between terrified screaming and joyful screaming. It just knows the absolute value removed from a neutral tone of voice, recognizes it as abnormal and goes into survival mode."

"I'll remember that when Fourth of July rolls around."

"You plan on being here?"

"If you'll have me."

"I just want you to know that given the choice between going out to party and staying home with the door open, I stay home."

"That's cool. My clubbing days are behind me anyway."

"Glad we had this little middle-aged chat." Tej's big hands moved along Jude's leg, kneading and caressing. "How did the Condor find out about you and Feño? How did he track you down that night?"

"I'm not exactly sure. Maybe we got careless. Or he got suspicious and started following us around. Or a combination of the two. I really don't know. We came out of the woods one night and he was there with two of his posse." He shivered. "God, the feeling in my gut when I saw them standing in the parking lot. Like my entire life fell out my asshole."

Tej shuddered and held out a forearm. "Look. My hair is sticking up just thinking about it."

"Feño kind of mumbled to me, 'Run, Jude. I'll handle this. Get out of here.' But I didn't. Instead I took his hand. He startled a little, like he was going to pull away and run. But then he settled and squeezed it tight and we were in it together. Our *Thelma & Louise* moment. Instead of driving off a cliff, we stood there holding hands."

"Then what happened? After the attack, I mean. Don't tell me about your leg being broken, I'll have nightmares. Fast-forward."

Jude glanced at him. "You don't mind me talking about my ex?"

"My dude, I measure a slight difference between the ex you're friends with on Facebook and your tragically deceased first love." He leaned and pushed a fingertip into one of Jude's dimples. "I find little I mind you talking about, so spill it."

Jude told about the court case. The CCLA pushing the Tholets to go to trial and the community pushing them to keep quiet and settle. How push turned to shove and then to threats.

"Where was Feño during all this?" Tej asked. "Was he getting the same shit you were from the neighborhood?"

"He was sent away to boarding school. Which is what nice homophobic people call conversion therapy."

"Shut. Up."

"His family did not come to play."

"Honest to God, they put him in conversion therapy? Or did he go willingly?"

"Willingly in the sense he went to make peace and get things to blow over as fast as possible. He told me he'd go, he'd fake straight. Then when the heat was off, supposedly, we'd…"

"Skip town?"

"Something dramatic like that."

"Did you see him before he left?"

"Night before. He snuck out of his house and into mine. That was the last time."

"Never again?"

Jude shook his head.

"You mean ever? You never slept together again?"

"No."

All the teasing drained out of Tej's face. He was pure, stunned compassion as he looked at Jude and said, simply, "Shit."

"Yeah. He left and everything went to shit. The bullying started. The harassment. The threats. The phone calls. The letters. The graffiti. And then the blood."

"What blood?"

"Someone filled the windshield wiper fluid reservoir of my father's car with blood. Taped a note to the inside of the hood. *Infected with HIV. Now you can share AIDS with your faggot son.* And we—"

Tej put up a silencing hand. After a moment, the hand folded into a single pointing finger. "That took effort," he said. "That's not a random, spontaneous act of hate. Someone put a lot of thought into it."

"I know."

His palm turned up to the ceiling. "How much fear and loathing do you need in your heart to not only come up with that kind of plan, but actually implement it?"

"Right? It was so deliberate, so calculated and masterminded, it was almost more violent than my leg being broken."

"You left town afterward?"

"Within a month. The situation was untenable and the whole family was affected. My sister was born in lotus position. Her feet don't touch the ground, and she was having night terrors about the house burning down. Then my brother developed this weird phobia about the telephone."

"From all the prank calls?"

"Mm. To this day, it's a chore getting Aiden to answer the phone."

"Your parents must've been freaked out of their minds."

"It was unsustainable. We were gone within a month."

"And Feño?"

"Feño stayed and converted. The next time I saw him, it was to say goodbye for good."

THE OTHER CHEEK

"WHAT ABOUT US?" JUDE said.

"You and I are finished," Feño said. "It's over. It's done. I came here to say goodbye."

"And just like that, you're straight?"

"It was a phase."

"Oh spare me."

"I got it out of my system. It's nothing I am anymore."

"Bullshit."

"I'm in a different phase of my life."

"You're gay."

"Shut up."

"You're gay, Fen. You can't pretend or pray it away."

"What the hell do you know about it? You weren't there. You don't know the work I did."

"The work denying yourself to please your parents?"

"The work finding myself. Finding God. Finding the way. Putting away childish things and figuring out my family is the most important thing to me."

"Childish things. So fucking me was basically a game of duck duck goose?"

"It's not me anymore. I have a bigger purpose now."

"What, getting married, pumping out some kids and having a boyfriend on the side? Gonna cruise the altar boys at Sunday mass?"

Feño seized two handfuls of Jude's shirt and slammed him back into the wall. Held him pinned there while the toe of one foot pressed into Jude's shin. Precisely. Expertly. Knowing the fault line along the bone where it hurt under pressure. Their eyes burned, unblinking. Their bodies burned, poised on an edge.

"How bad do you want me right now?" Jude said.

Feño's lips drew back from his teeth and he didn't answer.

"Want me to turn the other cheek," Jude said. "Or turn both of them?"

The fists in Jude's shirt tightened. Feño's jaw twitched with the effort to suppress a comeback.

"I know you," Jude said. "I know you better than anyone. And I know you want me."

"Shut up."

"You're hard for me. I don't even need to look down."

"Shut. Your mouth."

Jude's finger drew down the placket of Feño's zipper. Tracing the bulging outline. "Told you."

Tears filled Feño's eyes.

"Why are you doing this," Jude whispered, making his hand soft and gliding it up Feño's side. Around his back and pressing between the trembling shoulder blades. "You don't have to do this."

"It will *kill* my mother," Feño said through his teeth. "You don't understand how she relies on me to—"

"To be something you're not? She's the parent, you're the kid, you're not responsible for her happiness and security. She has a husband for that."

"He's not her husband, he's her fucking master. Don't you get that either? I'm the only thing standing between her and three men who use her as a punching bag. I can't leave. And I can't stay and be gay."

"What happens when she dies?"

"Shut up."

"Nobody lives forever. At some point you—"

"Don't fucking *do* this to me, Jude."

"I'm doing nothing but loving you." Jude took Feño's face in his hands. "Come with me. I'm the most honest thing in your life right now. You can be yourself with me. We can find somewhere to—"

"I belong with my people. Not with you. This is done. You and I are finished."

"Maybe you're done with me, but you'll never be done with who you really are. You can stuff yourself into a new life but look me in the eye and tell me you'll forget what we had. Tell me you'll leave it behind like it meant nothing. Look at me. Look at *you*, you were hard within thirty seconds of seeing me. You'll never forget."

One last shiver went through Feño's body. His eyes went flat as death. "I'm already forgetting. In a few years I'll have to think hard to remember your name."

"AND THAT WAS IT," Jude said. "Gotta hand it to the guy, when he said done, he meant done. No word, no contact, no nothing. Next time I saw him, he was in a casket."

Tej's gaze was far away, his head slowly shaking. "What a waste of life."

Jude rolled his hand palm up on the table. Tej regarded it a long moment, then dropped his on it and said, "Seventeen years old. It must've killed you."

"It was such a total, complete rejection. Not just of my love but my identity. When I was working it all out in therapy, Phil said Feño abjured me."

"Abjure," Tej said. "Yeah. If there's a more apt word, I'd like to know what it is."

"It hurt so fucking bad. The kind of misery that changes you. Don't get me wrong, time heals and I carried on and I had boyfriends. But no one like Feño. And for a long, long time, I never let anyone that close to me. Figuratively and literally. I became a top and resolved to stay on top, stay in control, stay protected. Love could come into my life but it couldn't come *into* me."

Tej traced the outline of Jude's hand, not looking up. "You let me into you."

"I know," Jude said. "Which is kind of a thing. I mean, that night was so unlike me."

"How so?"

"I responded to an aggressive pick-up. I went home with a stranger. And I wanted him to top. I wanted to let him inside everything I was feeling." He smiled. "Let him take my sad song and make it better."

Ten years dropped from Tej's face. He looked like a boy at the gates of Disneyland.

"Whatever you're thinking about," Jude said. "Don't stop."

"I'm thinking not once did you feel like a stranger to me that night."

Jude nodded, skinless and pure and content. "Maybe that's why I keep coming back."

Because it feels like coming home.

Tej let go Jude's fingers. "Make a fist. Tight."

Jude did and Tej peered close, tracing along the network of blue veins beneath the heel of Jude's hand.

"What are you looking for?"

"The palmaris longus," Tej said. "It's a vestigial muscle absent in about fifteen percent of the population." He extended his own arm and made a fist. Two prominent tendons bulged up in his wrist. "See? The tendons sticking up show I have the muscle. But the inside of your arm is flat and smooth when you make a fist, so you don't."

Jude raised his eyebrows, not sure where this was going.

"In other species, the palmaris longus is used to retract the claws. I'm not sure if lacking the muscle means your claws are always out and you can't retract them when people are being nice. Or if they're stuck inside and you have to find other means to defend yourself." He looked up at Jude and smiled. "What do you think?"

"I think you're beautiful."

Tej's palms planed up Jude's forearms, dry and warm, leaving goose bumps in their wake. The night moved up to number three, turning the air thick and juicy in Jude's chest. A rush to the head as the blood in his body galloped due south.

"I haven't felt this way in a long time," Jude said.

"What way is that?"

"Only recently, I was saying to a friend I haven't felt high on someone since my teens. I was wondering if you only get one shot at that kind of euphoria. If it's exclusive to your first love. Or exclusive to being a teenager."

"Maybe that's why they call it high school?"

Jude laughed. "Maybe. But I think what I'm trying to say is… You make me feel the way I did before my leg got broken."

Tej's chin rose and fell.

"After the attack, something in me turned off. Or rather, it turned on. A new home security system. I'd get into relationships always knowing what my exit strategy was. I had to construct everything to keep from getting hurt, from what guys I picked to what we did in bed. But you showed up, picked me up, hit some kind of reset button on the system and I feel really…"

"Free?"

"Young." He exhaled, feeling his shoulders drop. "I feel young." He laughed under his breath to fill the silence. "And when you smile at me like that, I feel really good."

Tej took Jude's hand and pulled him up. Then pulled him close.

The night hugged itself and moved up to number two.

# THE HUNDREDTH TIME

*P*ENNY EMBARRASSED HERSELF BY justifying her son's existence, concocting the most absurd theories around the baby she delivered and the baby she left the hospital with. Having settled on a name long before the birth proved problematic: she tied her mind in knots referring to both boys as Jude. Then it became Jude and Not-Jude but she couldn't decide which was which. Jude 1 and Jude 2 felt downright cruel. Same with Jude and Jude Lite, she hated herself for even thinking it.

It's starting. I'm distancing my son already. I'm trying to figure out how to take his name back.

I can't take his name away, it's unconscionable.

But if he's not Jude, who is he?

He is Jude, he's always been Jude. He's mine. He's my boy. He's my son. He's…

She smacked herself out of it, demanded she get it together.

Jude is Jude and will always be Jude. End of story.

The baby she carried was her biological son. Until she learned his name, he would simply be Biological Son.

She stopped in the middle of the thought, her hand going to her mouth.

Until she learned his name.

Was he alive?

She assumed he was alive.

"Babies switched, report at eleven," she said behind her fingers. That *was* the scenario being entertained, wasn't it? A careless nurse, a chaotic hospital, an administrative glitch. A newborn baby put down in the wrong bassinet. It was a horrible, horrible accident.

Wasn't it?

Are you alive? Do you know who you are or who you aren't? Is your own mother pacing around, wondering what became of the baby she gave birth to in November of 1973?

Is she alive? Does she know?

"I'm so sorry," she whispered, still hiding behind her fingers. "I had no idea. If we hadn't taken that silly little test, I never would've known. We did it for fun. To see how many shades of white we were."

What did her biological son even look like? Was he a sandy Canadian in a brown-skinned family? A dark Sephardic son among Teutonic ancestry? Had he lived a life of ridicule and exclusion? Was he cherished? Was he safe? Was he loved?

Was he even alive?

I couldn't swear, Penny thought. *In a court of law with my hand on a bible, I could not swear my son was born alive.*

Jesus Christ, I couldn't even swear it was a boy.

I could've given birth to a girl.

Jude could be Serena.

But then who the hell would Serena be?

She put her face in her hands.

I have nothing to go on. How would I even start looking and what would I find?

Anxiety coiled like a snake in her stomach. If she reported this—*reported it to who for God's sake?*—would she be held accountable? Prosecuted for kidnapping? International kidnapping?

"I didn't know," she said aloud for the hundredth time.

And for the hundred and first time, a little voice answered, *Fool, how could you not have known?* Which sent her into the bungalow's crawlspace, dragging out photo albums and keepsake boxes. Going through innumerable pictures, looking for the time and place she screwed up and failed to notice her baby was not her own.

But once she had a gallery of her children spread across the living room floor she objectively and brutally decided no, she hadn't been an oblivious fool. Jude wasn't a carbon copy of either parent, but neither was Serena. Or Aiden. All three exhibited enough familial traits to be satisfying to the eyes. Jude had the dark Sephardic genes, Aiden had the pale Cambie sandiness, and Serena had a little of both. True, Jude's height struck everyone as an oddity, as did his blue eyes. His terrible nearsightedness was definitely an outlier in this 20/20 nuclear family.

Aiden just started wearing glasses to read, Penny thought. *And Uncle Louis couldn't see further than three feet from his nose.*

She stared at the wall of family photos, at the tall, nearsighted man who played credible piano and had an ear for languages. His cheeks were creased with dimples. The eyes behind thick, dark-framed glasses were hazel green.

"And he was gay," Penny said under her breath.

If homosexuality was something you were born with, why wouldn't it be an inherited trait?

No, she decided. She hadn't been blind. The day little Jude was fitted with his first pair of specs, Cleon laughed and laughed at the resemblance to Louis. This was the story and she had no reason to doubt it. Jude was her firstborn, her she-wolf cub and her war mate. She didn't want to know any other story but this. She didn't care.

Except she did.

Because when she sat at the kitchen table with pictures and papers, wondering who Jude was, she couldn't help thinking of a nameless, faceless woman, somewhere in the world, wondering *where* he was.

❧

WEEKS PASSED, NERVOUS NIGHTS spent falling down internet rabbit holes and bookmarking dozens of websites. Perusing forums for survivors of Operation Condor, looking for accounts of switched babies. Anything out of the ordinary going on at hospital maternity wards.

Anything. Any little fragment with edges that matched, or even sort of matched Penny's fragment.

Her heart rose when she made contact with a woman who was a nurse in Santiago in the seventies. She wrote Penny a long email:

> *I was still in school during the early months of the coup, but my older sister was a nurse at Hospital San Juan de Dios. I vividly remember the stories she told. It's vivid because she could rarely even get home from work. Either she didn't finish a shift until after curfew, or she was afraid to make the journey home by herself. My mother would be frantic every night, waiting for the phone call, waiting to know if my sister was staying or coming home.*
>
> *Anyway, the stories she told in the last months of 1973 were of pure chaos. People who'd been tortured and detained being brought in by family or friends. Or practically crawling in by themselves. Ambulances dropping off the living and dead they'd picked up in the streets and in ditches. And soldiers everywhere.*

In the halls, on the wards, outside operating rooms. Often for no reason than to just stand there and intimidate. Sticking a gun in your face if you dared to say, "Excuse me, can I get by."

When I started to work at Hospital Paula Jaraquemada, the chaos had morphed into a more systematic terror and I honestly don't know which was worse. We would find babies dumped at the hospital loading dock. At least one baby a week, no exaggeration. We'd assess its health and if it required no treatment, we'd send it to the Casa de Huérfanos. Those were the abandoned babies. Then there were the babies the soldiers brought in. In a section of the nursery, one line of bassinets was off-limits and guarded around the clock. I saw obstetricians signing birth certificates at gunpoint, for babies they hadn't delivered. Certificates pre-stamped with the seal of the Civil Clerk. Then the soldiers took the infants away. We were helpless. A doctor who objected was nearly beaten to death. What could we do?

Years and years later, of course, it came out that these babies had been born in detention centers. The regime gave them to military families who were childless. Or couples sympathetic to Pinochet. Many were smuggled to Argentina and placed with families there.

You should try contacting the AFDD—Agrupación de Familiares de Detenidos Desaparecidos. Or perhaps the Grandmothers of the Plaza de Mayo. They've done incredible work locating and reuniting children and grandchildren who were stolen during the Argentinian dictatorship. They might be able to help you. Also look into the Servicio Medical-Legal in Santiago.

I'm so sorry for what's befallen your family. I wish you all the luck in finding some closure to this.

THE NEXT RABBIT HOLE Penny fell down was the Church of Latter-Day Saints, which had indexed portions of Chile's civil registry, but only between 1885 and 1932. Forty years too early for Penny's purposes. But LDS also indexed Chile's cemetery records, and Penny searched the database for male babies born in 1973.

"Why only males?" she said aloud, hands poised above the keyboard.

Her baby could've been a girl. Should she cast a wide net and narrow it? Or a narrow net and widen it?

"Start with the simplest solution."

She was talking to herself a lot lately.

"Boys who were born and died in November of 1973. Search it."

Why are you looking for dead babies?

"Because I have to start *somewhere*."

Scrolling through the results, her eyes stuttered on one entry: Diana Cecilia Abarca Sepúlveda, died 15 Jan 1973

Sepúlveda. Same surname as Ysidro. As common as Smith or Jones, but it teased her.

Look at me. I'm a sign.

She exported the results into a spreadsheet. She sorted. Filtered. Narrowed it down to a list of eight male names before realizing all of them died in Valparaiso.

She scanned the "City" column, unable to believe. The database had no records of infant boy deaths in Santiago in the entire month of November.

How could that be?

She counted seventy-two infant boys buried in Santiago in January of 1973. Eight buried in June. Those were the only two months showing male deaths. January and June.

"Huh."

A big exhaled sigh. She still had no idea what she was looking for but this wasn't it.

Her brows furrowed at a cluster of line items at the bottom of her spreadsheet. Fourteen children with birth dates, but no death dates.

"What are they doing in cemetery records?"

Her cursor hovered over the name Patricio Agustín Muñoz Pino, born 14 November 1973 in Santiago. Eleven days before Penny gave birth to Jude. Or the baby she thought was Jude.

"Jude Lite," she mumbled, and then felt terrible.

She went back to the online results and clicked on the image attached to the record for Patricio Pino. It was scanned sideways so she had to put her ear on her shoulder to read it.

NACIMIENTO across the top section. The fields for Nombre, Apellidos and Fecha de Nacimiento filled out by hand.

DEFUNCIÓN across the bottom section—death. No fields filled out.

A general cemetery record for a male born in Santiago in November of 1973. But no death information.

Why would a cemetery record have no death information?

He was born and then he disappeared?

"Was he stillborn?"

She stared at the blank fields where parents' names ought to have been. Her head ached with frustration and uselessness.

"I'm trying," she whispered. "I'm trying to find you."

"Pen," Cleon said softly behind her. "Querida, it's time to stop. Come to bed."

"I don't know what to do."

"Shut it down now."

"I don't even know what I'm *looking* for."

CLEN

YOU BUILD A SIMPLE rowboat and paint it red. Your brush dips into candy-apple glossiness. Ribbons of crimson satin dribble off the rim of the can. The brush glides like magic across the pale boards.

Your boat must be on a river. At once you're provided with millions of mosaic tiles in every conceivable shade of blue, and you create a serpentine path across the floor, one cobalt, azure, turquoise or lapis square at a time.

Tangerine trees are brought from your father's nursery. You dig each one into its place beside the river, watering them with handfuls of glass tiles. The smell of paint is replaced with tangy citrus as the trees burst into bud, blossom and fruit.

Supplies of every medium appear and disappear as you demand. You take thousands of labels off jars of marmalade and decoupage them to the walls. Then you paint more tangerine trees over the labels, extending the orchard toward a horizon. See, you have no practical skills, but you've inherited an eye from the Tholets. It's intention that matters in this fortress, not execution. You know what it's supposed to look like. Your imagination and the Fab Four do the rest.

Behind one tree you paint a girl. You take a long time and a single-hair brush to put a million geometric shapes into the irises of her eyes.

But you need to hurry. It will be your turn soon.

Fabulous rolls of yellow and green cellophane unfurl across the floor. You fashion petals from wire, twisting and cutting and shaping before wrapping them into lemon and lime bouquets. Bales of thicker wire to make stems, and soon a tunnel of flowers arches over the blue mosaic river. The girl from the tangerine grove darts among them. She looks back, calling you.

They're calling you.

Her eyes have swallowed the sun.

Your hands are bound but your fingers curl to tap three drumbeats on your palm.

. . .

…
…
And you're gone.
(Lucy.
In the sky.
With diamonds…)

THE BORDER OF DIVINE

*J*UDE DIDN'T ASK TEJ to move in and Tej, whose housing was temporary, didn't hint he wanted to move in. They divided the nights easily, with the lion's share spent at Jude's place because he had to practice.

Tej watched Jude play piano with narrowed eyes and a wary expression. Musical scores fascinated and baffled him. He didn't understand how Jude could read the horizontal chaos of dots and squiggles and notations. Couldn't grasp how the right hand was in one clef—"The fuck is a clef?"—and the left in another, and Jude read both simultaneously.

"It's like reading French with your right eye and German with your left," he said. "That is insane to me."

He sounded almost offended by Jude's ability to read music.

"And why is it written sideways?" he said, arms crossed. "Why don't the lines—"

"The staff."

"Excuse fucking me, why isn't the *staff* printed vertically?"

"What do you mean?"

Tej gave the sheet music a quarter turn. "There. See? Now the left-hand part is, wait for it, on the left. And the right-hand part is on the right. Doesn't that make more sense?"

"No."

Tej's hands dropped to his sides. "The whole thing is bananas."

He puttered around downstairs while Jude practiced, occasionally calling up, "What's this? What are you playing now?"

"Glazunov," Jude called back.

Or Chopin.

Bach.

Satie.

Stravinsky.

Rachmaninoff.

Tchaikovsky.

Sometimes Tej turned the piano bench perpendicular to the keys so he could sit behind Jude at the short end. He wrapped arms around Jude's waist and pressed his cheek between Jude's shoulder blades, moving along with him through the phrases. "I like hearing the music through your body."

Jude leaned back on him, content to the point of speechless. Thinking, simply, *This is nice.*

He rarely had to set an alarm clock on weekday mornings anymore. He woke up to the coffee grinder whirring, either in his kitchen or Tej's, depending on where they spent the night. He lay in bed, listening to the scuff of Tej's slippers, the mumble of him talking to the cat (if they were at his place). Faucet running. Drawers and fridge opening and closing. Steamy, fragrant bubbling and more talking to the cat. The drag of a stirred spoon against the bottom of a mug. Three revolutions followed by two taps on the side, then the clink of the spoon on the counter. Always the same. Scuffed footsteps back to the bedroom and the gentle thump as Tej set the cup on the bedside table.

"Made you coffee, babe," he said, as if he'd never done it before.

"You did?" Jude said, as if this were a surprise. "You're the best."

"I know."

He shuffled to the shower while Jude stacked pillows, sat up and drank his coffee. Thinking, *This is nice.* Not overthinking. It took only a tiny bit of conscious effort to sit still and be a scientist of his own experience. Observe himself in his new habitat and record the facts.

The human likes another human. The human is happy. The human is not anticipating the end of a relationship, making a plan and assembling a bug-out kit.

This is nice for the human.

The experiment shall continue.

Tej fully embraced Full Frontal Fondue and added a little pre-party he called Pickle Hour. Tej had a *thing* for pickles. Jude was never allowed to throw away an empty jar because Tej would cram it with anything he found at the farmers' market, pour brine on top, stick it in the fridge and see what happened. Every week, he spread out his creations and let the squad judge.

Pickled grapes were a bizarre but surprising hit.

"These make absolutely no sense," Hewan said, three fingers deep in the mason jar, "and I can't stop eating them."

Pickled strawberries were a mushy disaster. Okra and carrots were divine. Watermelon rind, not bad. Peaches, orgasmic. Rhubarb...

"Let's pretend this never happened," Tej said, chucking the whole jar in the garbage.

Serena and Giosué stopped by, claiming it was just for a pickle and a glass of wine, then staying four hours. Often Mireille Khoury came. Sometimes with a date, sometimes with Samson, who turned everyone into a cutesy-poo moron.

"Just so we're clear," Jude said, pointing around the dog's fawning fans. "Miri has already altered her will to make me Samson's guardian."

"So if I'm found floating in Puget Sound," Mireille said, "Jude is your first suspect."

As she laughed and joked and sassed in company, Mireille's eyes were wistful on Tej, full of pride, but sadness. Tej, though, had nothing but love for his sister. He hugged her often. Cozied up to her shoulder and gave her the best of his charm.

Tej, Jude came to realize, had his family shit worked out. He clocked his hours on the couch. He battled his demons and made his peace. Yes, it still hurt. Yes, the sadness occasionally liked to come have lunch. Yes, the anger and hurt invited themselves for sleepovers.

No, they did not stay forever.

Tej had learned not to make his family's behavior into his character flaw, and he countered the episodic sadness with his work, his friendships and his obsession with hospitality. He liked to nurture and nourish people, which in turn nurtured and nourished him.

Hospitality was a religion with Tej. If you stopped by for six seconds, he poured you a glass of water. If you stayed longer, he set out cheese and crackers or a little sliver of cake. He always had something going on the stove or in the oven. Always had coffee or tea. He wouldn't entertain the idea of showing up at someone's house empty-handed.

"You are welcome here," was an oath, not lip service.

Jude wasn't aware he'd been learning by osmosis until Serena came by one day and, without thought, he put out plates and glasses and made a little nosh. All kinds of snacks and nibbles now occupied his fridge and cabinets, foods he'd never stocked before. Cheese straws, gourmet biscuits, salted nuts and dried fruit. Spiked seltzer and lemon sodas. Little something-somethings that could be offered to company.

"Well, this is genteel," Serena said.

"What?"

"Offering me food and drink like a grown-up."

He smiled, his face warm. "Guess I'm picking up Tej's good habits."

"Keep them," she said. "And keep him. He's sweet."

"He is."

"You guys are good together. You can feel it when you walk in."

When Jude next hosted Full Frontal Fondue, the cosmic Bert Gesundheit took a long, appraising look around the living room and said, "It's changed in here."

"I got a new rug," Jude said.

"No, I mean the energy is different."

"Oh."

"Drastically different. And you, my friend, your aura is unrecognizable."

"It is?"

"Dude, I've never felt you like this. You're purple."

"Is that good or bad?"

"It's enlightened. On the border of divine, if you know what I'm saying."

"Stop talking about our sex life," Tej said, coming by with a tray of drinks.

Jude blushed, because the nights were religious. Raucous with sex that peeled the sheets off the bed.

"You always look so surprised to see me in the mornings," Tej said.

"I guess I always figured when two guys fuck the way we do, one of them leaves when it's over."

"Fucking can't be for keeps?"

Jude shrugged.

Tej smiled. "Talking dirty can't be profound? Porn can't open your mind?"

"I don't know. When I met you, I had so many ideas and ways planted in my head and now they're gone. Uprooted, and what's left is a me I didn't know."

"You're having quite the year of self-discovery."

"I don't like some of it."

"Do you like me?"

Jude didn't have words to say how much, so he tried to show it with his actions and his music, and in the way he let Tej into his body. Again and again the SS *Thirtysomething Euphoria* came into port, carrying a cargo of indescribable riches. The sheets crept off the bottom corners of the mattress. Tej's hand crept along back of Jude's neck. Tej's hips in the small of his back. Tej's dirty mouth filling the air with things that made Jude feel clean.

THE WEIGHT IN MY LAP

"Jude's bringing Tej to dinner," Penny told Serena.

"Shut up. When?"

"Tonight."

"Pictures or it didn't happen."

"What should I make?"

"Well, from what I heard, the man will eat anything."

"That's what Jude said."

"*Mom.*"

Penny hung up smiling. One of parenthood's better set of problems was mortifying your adult children.

Over the years, through a dozen boyfriends, Penny learned Jude had a type. He dated slight, slender men, usually fair-haired. Penny guessed he gravitated toward the polar opposite of Feño Paloma. Or maybe they gravitated toward him, what did she know?

Tej Khoury was the polar opposite of Jude's type. Broad-shouldered and hovering a couple inches over Penny's tall son, he was darkly good-looking, wearing a carnal confidence like a second jacket.

He's bloody, Penny immediately thought, and then blinked at the kneejerk reaction. What the hell did that mean?

Along with his self-assuredness, Tej came bearing a tangerine cake—"It's his signature dessert," Jude said—and a bottle of Lebanese wine he said was from his family's vineyard.

"Do you get a discount?" Cleon said, uncorking it.

"Unfortunately, no," Tej said. "In fact, that bottle is stolen."

"Did you tell Tej about your sabotage missions in the liquor stores?" Penny asked Jude.

Tej raised his eyebrows.

"She made me a child activist," Jude said. "Raising awareness for what was going on in Chile. Big part of that was carrying out community sabotage of Chilean goods. So I'm like eight years old and going with Mami to the liquor store. And while she's chatting up the owner, I'm peeling labels off bottles of Chilean wine. Replacing them with stickers telling customers not to purchase the country's products."

"We had gatherings called penas," Cleon said, bubbling wine into four glasses. "All the kids would bring their stolen labels to show off."

"Like scalps," Jude said.

"No wonder my uncle made a killing in the seventies," Tej said. "All that guerrilla warfare against the competition."

"Liquor store missions were a lot more fun than standing outside grocery stores, handing out fliers and asking customers not to buy Chilean grapes."

"Here we are," Cleon said, handing out the drinks. "Jude, give us a toast?"

"Arriba," Jude said, and gestured for Tej to hold his glass high with the others.

"Abajo." All the glasses lowered.

"Al centro." Glasses put forward to clink.

"Y adentro." Everyone drank.

"Now I check out your cookbooks and make silent judgment," Tej said, sidling up to the shelf where Penny kept them. He glanced at her with a little smile. "I'm kidding."

"No, he's not," Jude said.

"I don't judge cookbooks, I steal them. Oh, hello, what's this?" Tej took down *Cucina Ebraica*, a tome of Italian Jewish recipes.

"My daughter's boyfriend gave me that one," Penny said. "He marked a page for me. Here. The Venetian fish soup. I'm supposed to try it."

"Tell me when you do," Tej said. "I'll bring more wine."

As Jude had said, he was different. Not so frustratingly shy or cloyingly deferential as the other men Jude brought to dinner. Frank. Curious. A pleasure to feed—he didn't compliment the food and then pick at it. Tej was genuine in his appreciation of the dinner, which was simply minestrone soup and good bread, but he closed his eyes at the first spoonful, his expression complex and expert.

"Did you roast the vegetables before you put them in?"

"Yes," Penny said. "You can tell?"

"Mm." He took another sip. "Especially the garlic."

He was, Penny decided, a lovely man. Her gaze kept caressing the couple through the meal, noting how their body language mirrored. They leaned crossed forearms on the table, biceps touching. Or, done eating, sat back in their seats, an ankle on the opposite knee. Tej put an easy hand on the back of Jude's chair. Jude said, "Hand me your plate, babe?" as he cleared the table.

They moved into the living room with coffee and cake. Cleon had made a dessert-digestif of terremoto, composed of white wine, pisco and pineapple ice cream. "Who's driving?" he asked the boys.

Jude raised a finger and Cleon set the snifter in front of Tej. "Jude can have a taste."

"That lethal, huh?" Tej said, digging in and taking a bite. His eyes bulged above the spoon. "Oh my God, call a cab."

"Puts hair where hair don't grow," Cleon said.

Typically at this point in the evening, Penny would ask Jude to play piano. She always loved his music, but often at these dinners, she did it to fill in and smooth over the awkward, exhausting gaps in conversation. No need tonight. Even the way Tej perused the family photo gallery and asked questions was unique. Off the bat, he zeroed in on Cleon's favorite picture.

"This," he said, pointing. "This is a Pulitzer Prize right here. Who are these guys?"

"My father and my uncle Louis," Cleon said. "Everyone thought Louis had perished in the Holocaust, but the Red Cross found him. That picture was taken the day Louis arrived in Valparaiso."

"Look at how they're holding onto each other," Tej said.

"They hugged so long and stayed so still, I thought they'd fallen asleep standing up."

"You were there?"

"You can see me just at the side. The little boy. That's me."

Tej peered closer. "Who are you with?"

"My sister, Gloria."

"Where does she live now?"

"She died in nineteen eighty-four."

"Oh, I'm sorry. Did she die in Chile?"

"No, in Canada," Cleon said. "But you could say she died because of Chile. She was married to one of Salvador Allende's chauffeurs. He was rounded up and shot in the first hours of the coup. Gloria fled for Peru but they caught her at the border. Two years she was missing."

"Pinochet had her in three different concentration camps before she got out and came to Canada," Penny said. "The picture just up and to your left. Yes, there. That's Gloria, maybe a year before she died."

"I see." Tej turned from the wall, arms crossed. "I lost a brother and a sister in Lebanon."

A beat of silence that seemed to expand, then contract down, drawing the four refugees of war close. Cleon lifted a hand and gestured to the armchair next to him. "Sit," he said. "Tell me."

Tej was four when civil war broke out in Lebanon. Like so many childhood survivors, his memories were chopped into pieces. His stories trailed off unfinished, with a shrug, an apologetic smile and, "But I don't remember much else."

He recalled the sounds of explosions, the taste of fear, the layers of black within the darkness of the bomb shelter.

"You don't like fireworks," Jude said, coming to sit on the floor between Tej's feet.

"I like them at a distance. I don't like being under them."

"Or thunder."

Tej gave a little shiver in his skin, shaking his head. "I hate thunder. A rumble in the distance is fine. But that biblical crack that sounds like the sky ripping open? I flip right out."

He told of his older brother, Raymond, who served in the Christian Militia and was killed in Beirut. "I remember him a little. Mostly I remember the funeral. All the screaming and crying. It was the first time I saw my father cry. I mean really weep."

The family left in 1978, after Syrians ruthlessly bombed the Christian neighborhood of Achrafiyeh and Tej's younger sister Lulu was killed.

"I don't remember it at all," Tej said. "It's shut up tight somewhere. Peeks out when I hear thunder, I guess."

Then he described a strange false memory he created, of carrying a dog with him on the flight from Lebanon. "We didn't own a dog. I didn't have a stuffed animal or anything like that. My sister Mireille looks at me like I'm insane when I describe it, but I swear to God, I had a dog with me." His arms curved around an imaginary pet. "I can feel it. It's so real in my head, the fur and the panting and the weight in my lap. Holding onto this dog. I swear it happened but..."

"I worry about that sometimes," Penny said. "That I made up false memories around the day Jude was born."

"You barely remember anything from when I was being born," Jude said.

"No, I mean what happened before."

Tej leaned and set down his snifter of terremoto. "Tell me?"

THE FIRING SQUAD

1

In 1973, the neighborhood of La Reina was only ten years old. The Tholets' street wasn't yet paved and only four houses were built on it.

"Nigel Rudd lived closest to the main road," Cleon said. "He was a British journalist. His girlfriend lived with him, Daniela Portales. Further down were the Silva-Merinos. The husband was an economics professor. His wife's name was…Fernanda?"

"Francesca," Penny said. "They had four children. Kitty corner across the street were the Godoys. The husband was Pablo, a civil servant. The wife was Trinidad. They had just one son."

"And then us," Cleon said. "Down at the end of the street. The double-lot of property. The main house and two efficiency bungalows. Across from us was Uncle Louis's plot of land."

"Where Ysidro had his new masonry workshop," Jude said.

With two journalists, a professor and a civil servant, the street was a raft of sitting ducks for Pinochet's hunters. By November of 1973, all the adult men had been arrested, except for Uncle Louis, Ysidro and Tatán.

"Why weren't they picked up?" Tej asked.

"Tradesmen often weren't," Cleon said. "It was the intellectuals who were viewed as the troublemakers. A city in revolt still needs the lights to turn on and the toilets to flush and the buses to run."

"And the dead to be buried."

On November 25, 1973, the soldiers came back to La Reina. Six or seven low-ranking grunts. A captain in charge.

"And Héctor Godoy," Penny said. "Pablo and Trinidad's son, who was in the army."

"Can you imagine," Jude said. "Héctor's regiment had arrested his own father. Now they were scoping out his neighborhood again."

"Jesus," Tej said. "What kind of position did that put him in?"

"A very bad one," Penny said. "It was obvious he was trying to protect his family because the soldiers pulled everyone into the street except Trinidad. It was me, Daniela Portales and Francesca Silva-Merino. The four children. And Uncle Louis."

"Ysidro wasn't in his workshop?" Jude asked.

"He'd gone to pick up a shipment of marble. Tatán was at work."

The soldiers lined the eight neighbors up against the Tholets' high garden wall. White-faced women and shivering, sobbing children on their knees. The *gringa* Penny and her round belly. And Tholet, *el judío*. The Jew.

The soldiers lined up as well. Raised their rifles and the captain gave the order.

A volley of shots. A cacophony of screaming.

And then uproarious laughter. The rifles were loaded with blanks.

"Jesus Christ," Tej said.

The children were hysterical. Daniela vomited in the street. The soldiers loaded up again, making a display of the ammunition, showing it was real this time. Jeers and taunting.

Penny knelt on the dirt road, one of Silva-Merino kids huddled against her round belly. Her other hand clasped tight with Uncle Louis's.

"I will never forget," Penny said slowly, "how Louis looked twenty years younger. Back straight. Face composed. Chiseled in stone. He whispered to me, 'Look at Héctor.'"

Héctor Godoy was following orders, but with a grim expression and a mouth pressed tight. His eyes flicking toward his mother's house as the firing squad assembled.

Rifles raised. The captain gave the order.

Tej's face was rapt, eyes wide. "And what did you... I mean, do you even remember what you thought or felt or..."

The potent terremoto dessert had softened all of Penny's edges and anesthetized the narrative. "You become so terrified, the fear turns inside-out and becomes apathy. Or ambivalence. Or enlightenment? I don't know. I was crying. I guess I thought, *This is it. This is how it ends.*" She tugged at her hair, shaking her head. "But honestly, that's a guess. It seems the thing to think, but it also sounds a little generic. I can remember the events, but I don't recall the emotion. When I tell the story, like right now, I often feel like I'm decorating it."

"You can never re-live or re-tell the story perfectly," Cleon said. "I think our genes are still coded to be oral historians and a story is only memorable if it's compelling. Enchanting or riveting. We'll always augment a part here, diminish a part there. Fill in the gaps with what probably happened when we don't know for sure what happened."

"So, the captain gave the order and obviously it was another fake-out?"

Another burst of laughter and jeering. Francesca's eldest son, about fourteen, pissed himself with fear and the soldiers narrowed in on him. Like a pack of wolves tracking a young gazelle, they separated him from the others and started roughing him up. Shoves and cuffs at first. Then they began beating him in earnest.

All of them except Héctor Godoy.

PENNY KEPT CATCHING HÉCTOR'S nervous eyes. Begging him with her own crazed ones.

Don't do this. Don't do this. Don't be a party to this. These are your people. We've never been anything but kind to you.

Then the captain noticed the exchanged looks. Noticed his young grunt's non-participation. He called, "You fucking the gringa, Héctor? She your old lady?"

"No."

"You're staring at her all moon-eyed. You fucking that socialist cow? Is that really why you fingered this block?"

"No."

The captain called another of his privates. "Ibáñez, get his mother out here. Let's see whose side they're on."

Héctor panicked. "No, leave her alone. I turned them in, didn't I?"

"Show me you meant all of them." The captain whipped out his service revolver and handed it to Héctor. "Shoot her in the head."

"She's pregnant."

"Is it yours?"

"N-no…"

"Good. Shoot the kid first. Big target. You can't miss."

Trinidad Godoy, Héctor's mother, was dragged out now, disheveled and screaming. Thrown down on her knees next to Penny.

"Choose," the captain said. "Your mother or the socialist bitch."

Héctor was frantic. "I can't—"

"It's easy. Watch." The captain pivoted slightly and shot Daniela Portales. All the women screamed.

Not a hair out of place, the captain offered the gun again to Héctor. "Now you."

"I can't."

"Choose."

"I can't."

Without a word, the captain placed the muzzle of the gun against the head of one of the Silva-Merino kids. His eyes cold and lifeless. His finger curled around the trigger.

"Héctor," Trinidad wailed, hands clenched in her hair.

Arms around her belly, Penny's mouth shaped her husband's name over and over.

Teeth bared and eyes wild, Héctor seized the captain's gun, aimed it at Penny's stomach and pulled the trigger.

❧

IT WAS RAINING OUTSIDE now. The four people in the living room went quiet. Cleon and Penny close together on the couch. Tej in the easy chair, Jude on the floor with his elbows draped on Tej's knees and Walter curled in his lap.

"What happened?" Tej finally asked

"Another fake-out," Penny said. "At the last second, he changed his aim."

Tej's chin raised a hair. "To?"

"He shot Uncle Louis," Jude said.

Tej rubbed his face. It was so quiet in the room, Penny could hear the rasp of his beard against his fingers. "I'm so sorry."

"Is that when Héctor hit you?" Jude asked.

"Someone did," Penny said. "I couldn't say it was him." Her hand went to the back of her head.

I remember the feel of gravel on my hands as I pitched forward.

The rush of fluid down my legs. I thought I'd pissed myself as well. But no, it was my water breaking.

And then…nothing…fragments of nothing…

I woke up. Turned my head and threw up.

Descanse, señora.

Look, señora. He has dimples.

"Did you ever go back?" Tej asked.

"To Chile?"

"I mean, to your house. After Jude was born. I mean…" His entire expression was miserable and his hands opened helplessly. "I'm sorry, I'll just leave my foot in my mouth."

"It's okay," Jude said, running his palms along Tej's kneecaps. "We're still figuring out how to talk about the Baby Formerly Known as Jude."

"I went back to the house once," Penny said. "With an armed guard from the Canadian embassy. He gave me twenty minutes to grab what I could." She pointed to the gallery wall. "I broke those out of their frames, let the glass shatter onto the floor. I was like a lunatic about not leaving them behind."

"And you brought your condor," Jude said.

Penny went in her room and fetched the carved figurine of an Andean condor off her bedside table.

"Cleon gave that to me as an engagement gift," she said, giving it to Tej.

"What's the significance?"

"First time we went away together was to Río Los Cipreses," Penny said. "To camp out and watch the condors."

"Uncle Louis carved it," Cleon said. "My first commission for him. He didn't even give me a family discount."

"Funny," Tej said, turning it over and over in his hands. "For better or worse, this bird seems to have followed your family around."

Penny smiled at Jude. "Este tipo aquí—vale la pena."

He's a keeper.

Cleon chuckled and Tej looked around at them, blinking. "What happened to Louis?" he asked. "I mean, tell me someone found him and buried him."

"Ysidro did," Penny said. "Louis is buried in the Jewish cemetery in Santiago."

"What happened to those other women from the neighborhood? And their kids?"

"Francesca and her children fled to Sweden. I don't think her husband was ever found. I believe Trinidad never left Santiago. And Daniela… She died."

"I used to be in touch with her boyfriend," Cleon said. "Nigel Rudd, the Brit. He got out, went to work for the BBC, then taught at the London School of Journalism. I run across his name every now and again. Or sometimes hear him on NPR."

"I never had any idea," Tej said slowly. "The first time I heard the name Pinochet was on Sting's *Nothing Like the Sun*. It had that song. 'They Dance Alone.'

About the Chilean women dancing in the streets with pictures of their missing men."

"I was fifteen when that album came out," Jude said. "Sting was always the man but when 'They Dance Alone' released, he became like a God in our neighborhood."

"I seem to recall it playing on a loop in your bedroom," Penny said, smiling.

"Papi, remember I showed you the YouTube clip? The *Desde Chile* concert at the Estadio. Sting sings the song with about two dozen Chilean women onstage, holding photographs of lost husbands and sons. And he dances with all of them at the end."

Cleon nodded, tugging at one of his eyebrows. "I remember."

"When was that concert?" Tej said.

"Nineteen ninety," Jude said. "Right after Patricio Aylwin became president."

"When did Pinochet die?"

"Two thousand six."

"And the son of a bitch never answered for any of it," Cleon said.

"I'm sorry." Tej set the condor carefully on the side table. "It's just…such a waste."

Jude looked up and back at him, then at Cleon. "¿Papi, le puedo mostrar a Lucy?"

Can I show him Lucy?

Cleon regarded the lovers a long time, considering. Then he smiled at his son. "Sí. Creo que la entenderá."

CLEN

*Y*OU SPEND A LONG *time on the ceiling. It's the most critical part of the room. Judaism has no graven images. No icons, no idols, no imagery, no artwork depicting God and the patriarchs. It has no goddess, either. You need one. Depicting your Lucy as a Catholic Madonna isn't good enough. You need older, stronger feminine power. You choose Pachamama, the Andean earth mother. You paint her with luscious curves and a pregnant belly like a full moon in the center of the ceiling. Her dark hair parts in the middle and flows out in all directions, creating a night sky.*

Like Michelangelo in the Sistine Chapel, you lie supine atop elaborate scaffolding. One at a time, you affix diamonds to Lucy's hair. You take tremendous care to make the sky perfect. It's no less than she deserves.

You lay down your tools and press your hands to the goddess's belly. Your child is within, turning like the moon.

(Papi's here, little one.

Here in the sky with diamonds.

I'll be gone soon.)

THE CEILING GODDESS

"HOLY SHIT, WHAT IS this," Tej said, stopped short in the doorway of the bungalow's third bedroom.

"This is how my father survived the Villa Grimaldi," Jude said. "He created a world in his head, and when the torture started, he went there. Wait, it's better when you see it this way."

He plugged in the strings of LED lights tacked along the juncture of walls and ceiling, then dimmed the overhead switch to low. Tej's head tilted back, his mouth parted at the simple, domed lighting fixture, now transformed into the pregnant belly of a primitive goddess. Her dark hair swirled in a whirlpool, her feet and hands joining the circle around the glowing life within her.

"Your father made all this?"

The ceiling goddess coiled at the epicenter of a magnificent mosaic. Individual colored squares started cerulean blue along the outline of her voluptuous body, darkening to azure, then cobalt, then navy, violet, indigo and deepest purple. Turning to black as they neared the walls.

"How did he..." Tej turned in a slow circle, still looking up. "What are these squares made of?"

"Paint swatches. He hit every hardware store, taking as many as they'd allow. When Home Depot opened up near us, it was like Mecca. He'd walk out of there with a shopping cart full, then spend hours cutting them down. He made the sky in separate sections, I think on pieces of MDF. They fit together like a puzzle."

"How long did it take?"

"Almost a year. Every square glued one at a time. Then he added all those rhinestones to make stars. When the sections were all finished and varnished, he hired some people to screw them to the ceiling. Then he made the goddess collage on another piece of backing, cut to fit around the light."

Tej's gaze slowly came down from the ceiling and noticed the collage on the walls. Drawings on scrap paper of all sizes, stuck haphazardly and overlapping. Their edges curling away from the sheetrock, like the peeling bark of birch trees.

"He couldn't talk about what happened in the Villa Grimaldi," Jude said. "But he could draw it."

Tej's free hand closed over his mouth and nose as his eyes swept left and right, taking in the tableaux of torture and interrogation. Prisoners bound hand and foot, being beaten with fists and sticks and chains. Men tied to bunk beds, wires trailing from their bodies to car batteries. Women being gang raped.

Tej crouched to peer at the Post-its lining the baseboards, each drawn with a mouse or rat. He stood again to take in a revolver spilling its bullets from the round chamber. Snarling dogs. Mouths open in silent screaming. Comrades slumped in one another's arms. Or crouched alone, curled around their despair.

One wall had no drawings pinned to it. Just one small leaf of white paper with the words *Louis made ten. I could make but one.*

"What does this mean?" Tej asked.

"I don't know," Jude said, straightening the curled edges. "Something to do with my great-uncle Louis. But whenever I ask Papi, he just shakes his head. The look he gets on his face is beyond sadness or grief. It's almost shamed."

Their voices had unconsciously dropped, as if the room were a library. Tej's feet barely made a sound as he approached the large platform centered precisely under the lighting fixture. Covered edge to edge with a diorama of a strange land.

"Reminds me of a model train exhibit I saw once," he said. "Except nothing like it at all. I don't understand. What is it supposed to be?"

Jude brought him to one corner. "Start here." He touched a trim sailboat painted shiny red. A single mast hung with a crisp white sail. A miniature easel sat in the hull and on it perched a small, gilt-framed mirror.

"I'm still lost," Tej said.

"What do you see in the mirror?"

"Myself."

"See yourself where?"

"On a boat?"

"Where's the boat?"

"Here." Beneath the hull was another mosaic, a thin ribbon assembled from fragments and wedges in all shades of blue. "On a river," Tej said, his finger tracking the line of blue as it serpentined before the red boat, starting a journey.

"Now put it together," Jude said.

Tej's brows wrinkled. "I see myself. On a boat on a riv— Oh my God."

"Get it?"

He moved along the edge of the diorama, eyes wide with revelation.

"See it now?" Jude said.

"I see it." Tej bent, gazing through the orchard of trees planted along the sloping, grassy banks of the mosaic waters. Each tree graced with dozens of tiny orange fruits. "Boat on a river. Tangerine trees." He looked up at the goddess overhead, smiling benevolently from her diamond-studded heavens. "This whole thing is 'Lucy in the Sky with Diamonds.'"

He beamed a smile that made Jude's chest pull apart with longing and pride and things he didn't have words for.

"He made a world based on the song?" Tej said. "And that's where he escaped when he was being tortured?"

"Yeah." Jude touched the figure hiding among the tangerine trees. A girl molded from clay, with unnaturally large eyes meticulously painted in geometric shapes.

"This is incredible." Tej's hand hovered above the bower of flowers arching over the river, making them rustle. Each was crafted from wire and covered with yellow or green cellophane. "This belongs in a museum. An exhibit. When did he make all this?"

"He started when I was a freshman in college."

"Why then?"

"Well." The room had no chairs, so Jude sat on the floor, back to a papered wall. "After I left for school, my mother had a bit of a breakdown."

"A bit? Or a colossal breakdown?"

"Colossal. Once I was safely out of the nest, everything that had happened hit her. Starting from when I was born up until my leg was broken. The bottom just fell out from under her. She actually ended up hospitalized for a few weeks. And it was a massive wake-up call for Papi."

"Like it made him contemplate what would happen if she were gone?"

Jude nodded. "Also, she was digging into the really painful parts of her life and you know how it is with therapy—you can't selectively unearth issues. You dig up one and you dig up all of them. Not to tell tales out of school, but I think my parents' marriage had some bedroom problems. PTSD and the meds decimated my father's sex drive and…" Jude waved away what wasn't his business. "Anyway. He started going to counseling like he was finally serious about it. He and Mami went to a therapist together, too."

"Were they in their fifties by that time?"

"Late forties."

"Still. It's huge that they went. Lot of people are set in their ways by that stage of life." His hand gestured toward the diorama. "That's when all this happened?"

"It started with the drawings. Papi's psychiatrist is from Argentina. Her family was caught up in that country's political terror and she knew exactly where Papi was coming from. She spoke his languages. She got him to tell the stories behind the sketches. Literally put them out in the open, pin them to the walls, let them be seen. He'd never done that before. He collected the testimonies of so many survivors. He wrote four books about dozens of Chileans' experiences under Pinochet, but never his own.

"So, once he hung all this shit up on the walls, his therapist asked how he survived it. Where did the strength and mental fortitude come from, how did he find the means to stay alive? And finally, Papi answered that question." Jude pointed to the sky.

"He'd never told anyone about this song-world? Not even your mother?"

"No. It was secret. Not a shamed secret but I think…"

"Holy?"

"Kind of. It was a secret the way knowing how to breathe is secret. Or the way you walk around with a constant inner monologue is secret. Nobody shares every stream of consciousness thought in real time. We move to our own soundtrack, to our own background music of thought. 'Lucy in the Sky with Diamonds' is Papi's background music."

Tej went around the perimeter of the table, following the verses of the Beatles song. Expression charmed as his fingertip teetered the crowd of rocking horse people. Jude's gaze followed, a secret of his own on the tip of his tongue. "You know, not a lot of people have seen this room."

"Mm." Tej was examining the fleet of taxis collaged from newspapers. Each had a sunroof through which emerged a clay torso. Where heads should've been was a poof of cotton-ball clouds. Tej looked up at the ceiling, his mouth moving around silent lyrics.

"What I mean is, I've never showed it to a boyfriend."

Across the diorama, Tej stared for a beat. "Never?"

"No." Jude got up and went to him. "It's not only me asking Papi if I could show you, but him saying yes. He said 'Creo que la entenderá,' which means, *I think he'll understand her.*"

Their fingers twined and squeezed. Tej's free hand closed over his mouth and nose as his eyes made a slow circuit around the room and back up to the ceiling.

"Why this particular song?"

"My mother's real name is Lucille."

"For real?"

Jude nudged against him. "Don't ever call her that. I mean it. Only my dad is allowed."

"Well, shit, I wonder why." He pointed at Lucy's round, electric belly. "So she's not some random goddess, she's your mother."

"Mmhm."

"And she's pregnant with you."

"Well. He thought it was me."

Tej squeezed his eyes shut. "I'm sorry, I keep doing that."

"It's all right." Jude put both arms around him from behind. "I keep doing it too."

Tej exhaled roughly. "I'm beyond honored you showed me this. It's unbelievable. The ceiling and the diorama blow my mind, but what's on the walls is breaking my heart and your parents are the sweetest people and… I'm just so fucking sorry."

"I know you are." Jude leaned on Tej's hard, warm body. Rested their temples together, twining their fingers on top of his chest. "You grew up in a war. Your mind didn't make a secret world to hide in, it made a dog for you to hold. I think that's how Papi knew you would understand."

THE BEGGARLY QUESTION

*J*UDE'S RESEARCH LED HIM down all kinds of rabbit holes and he followed every tunnel. Not knowing what he was looking for made everything curious and full of potential.

Tej's offhand comment from the other night—*For better or worse, this bird seems to have followed your family around*—made Jude curious about the Andean condor, the largest flying predator in the world.

"Damn, that is ugly," Tej said, looking over Jude's shoulder at the computer screen.

"Technically it's a vulture."

"I don't know, man. In terms of spirit animals, I think you can do better."

Jude disagreed. True, when photographed up close, the condor had a hideous mug and a hunchbacked silhouette. But in flight, with its wingtips touching the edges of the sky, the bird could only be called majestic.

"El Cóndor pasa," he said.

"Isn't that the Simon and Garfunkel song?"

Jude looked it up and discovered the tune was written in 1913 by Daniel Alomía Robles, based on folk music from Peru. Simon and Garfunkel put their own words to it.

He listened to the song on a loop while he was at the gym, but if a message were within, he wasn't receiving it.

"Then again," he said to Phil. "Simon and Garfunkel wrote it in nineteen seventy, three years before the coup, so…"

"Well, speaking of messages," Phil said. "My son's AP English class is reading *Jude the Obscure.*"

"Really?"

Phil got up and went to his desk. "I was helping him with some homework and came across a quote. I'll be damned if Thomas Hardy didn't have you in mind when he wrote it." He handed Jude a slip of paper.

> *The beggarly question of parentage—what is it after all? What does it matter, when you come to think of it, whether a child is yours by blood or not?*

"Wow," Jude said. "That's... Wow."

"My words exactly."

"Can I keep this?"

Phil gestured assent.

Jude read it one more time before slipping it in his pocket. "You ever hear of the Grandmothers of the Plaza de Mayo?"

"That's the organization that locates missing children in Argentina?"

Naturally, fucking Phil had heard of everything.

"They've identified over two hundred missing children," Jude said. "Actually found about fifty of them and reunited a couple dozen with their families. Plus they've found about a hundred grandchildren. Just by DNA testing."

Phil raised his eyebrows.

"I'm having a hard time finding an equivalent organization of abuelas in Chile. It seems like Argentina took lessons from Chile on how to commit atrocities, but it doesn't seem like Chile has taken any lessons from Argentina on righting the wrongs. Well, no, that's unfair, they have. I found a lot of websites commemorating Los Desaparecidos and an inquiry form to fill out. But those were all grassroots. The government doesn't seem to be stepping up as much. The whole online operation seems clumsy and primitive compared to Argentina's interface. It's so much more *defeated*."

"Did you fill out the inquiry form?" Phil asked.

"Not yet."

"Why not?"

"I suppose 'I don't know' would insult both of us?"

Phil smiled. "Well, we can go through the back and forth of you saying it, me pressing you, you pushing back, yadda yadda until finally we get down to it. Or we could just get down to it."

"I haven't yet because I still feel in shock."

"That's perfectly fair. Do you know what basic first aid for shock is?"

"What?"

"Keep the victim warm and elevate their feet."

"Which means?"

"You need to keep your feet above your head right now. Which means doing more and thinking less. If your biological parents fled Chile with your mother's baby, the only way to find them is going public with your DNA results on the ancestry website. If your biological parents were disappeared, you'll have to engage a Chilean organization to help you."

"And neither will yield any results unless someone from my biological family is making an identical effort."

"True."

A long moment of silence.

"I wonder if anyone's looking for me," Jude said softly.

Phil nodded. "It's a beggarly question."

Do more and *think less.*

For the sake of doing something, Jude added Cleon's parents to his online tree: Felix Tholet and Miriam Greenberg.

"Did you ever meet them?" Tej asked.

"Sure."

"When? How did they get out of Chile?"

"They left years before the coup and went back to Austria."

"Did you visit them?"

"Once. We did a family trip. The first time they came to Vancouver was when my Aunt Gloria died. My father's sister. He told you about her at dinner the other night."

"Did she live in your house?"

Jude shook his head. "She had her own place for a little while, but her physical health wasn't good and soon it became clear her mind was…" He pressed fingertips to his brow and exploded them outward. "She was in a nursing home the last couple years of her life. My grandparents came for the funeral and stayed almost a month."

"What were they like, what did you call them?"

"Oma and Opa. It was weird seeing them at first. Aunt Gloria had been this frail, meek invalid and my dad had all the problems with his legs and his physical health in general. But here come my grandparents who are in their seventies, hale and energetic, standing up straight on strong legs. Opa was down on the floor with me and Aiden, horsing around in a way my dad never could. And Oma was… Man, she was wonderful."

Tej brushed his knuckles along Jude's jaw. "Your face just went all moony."

"I really liked her a lot."

Jude's whole mind went moony, fixated on the memory of Miriam's voice and hands. Her face had drifted beyond his reach, but he remembered her funny, German-accented Spanish. "Yudchen," she called him, with a tousle of his hair. Yudchen or Yudlein. Little Jude. But it was her hands at the forefront of recollection, poised on the keys as she and Jude sat side-by-side at the piano, playing a duet. Holding a crochet needle and teaching Serena to make granny squares. Helping Aiden—four years old and already a researcher—trace countries out of the big atlas and label them carefully with capital cities.

Miriam's hands turning pages as she read aloud from a Spanish translation of *The Hobbit*. Her hands sandwiching one of Cleon's as he rested. Brushing the hair back from her son's brow as if he were a child with a fever. Miriam holding a weeping Penny in her arms, one wrinkled hand rubbing a circle between Penny's shoulder blades, the other cradling Penny's head on her shoulder, fingers buried in her hair. Rocking and murmuring in Spanish, German and the universal shush-soothe language of mothers.

"She'd lost her own daughter but she was practically holding Mami in her lap. Because Mami needed a mother." Jude sighed. "These are my memories. They're my stories."

"They'll always be your stories," Tej said. "These will always be your people. This is your family and family is so much more than blood."

"I know."

"But."

"But." Slowly Jude changed the status of Cleon and Penny from biological parents to adoptive parents. "See, just picking from a dropdown menu feels like betrayal. One click literally makes me feel like a shitty son."

"You," Tej said, sliding arms around Jude from behind, "are an extraordinary son."

Jude shook his head. "I don't want to be anyone else's son."

Tej held him tight. "You're so good."

"I'm not."

"You are. Trust me, I know good."

Feeling loathsome and ungrateful, Jude created another set of parents for himself and chose "biological" from the dropdown. Unknown married to Unknown, Jude's box dangling from the dotted line joining man and wife. He arbitrarily subtracted twenty-five years from 1973 to make an estimated birth year of 1948, in the assumed location of Santiago de Chile. He added four grand-parents, all called Unknown, with "Spain or Italy?" as their assumed, estimated, hypothetical shot-in-the-dark birthplaces.

He sat back, gazing at his two-trunked family tree. One side fruitful with names and dates and history. The other barren. Just empty pink and blue boxes and question marks.

Is someone looking for me?

So many people in the world. Name. Date of birth. Date of death. Every dotted line between boxes was a connection. A relationship. A marriage. Every person's leaf came from two leaves above. Child-parent-child-parent, backward in time, ad infinitum.

The exponential connections were staggering.

"The history of mankind is like one big love story," Jude said, staring at his solitary blue box at the bottom of the inverted pyramid.

"You ever stop to think how many fucking people there are?" Tej said. "Not just right now but in the entire history of humanity."

"I know."

Millions and millions of accounts registered on this website, all with their boxes and dotted lines and stories.

"The Y-chromosome replicates," Jude said. "Every father gives his son a perfect copy."

Somewhere in the world, a certain tree had a blank box labeled "Unknown," with a birth date in 1973. It sat there like a patient locked door and only Jude Tholet's key, with his specific DNA, would fit it.

What's behind that door, though?

Is someone looking for me? Waiting for me? Wondering about me?

"What if nobody is," he said. "What if nobody is looking for me and I go looking for them. And I blunder into their neat, ordered lives with the news I belong to them, but none of them are happy about it? The news ruins their story. What if they always knew I was somewhere out in the world, but it was a dirty little secret and they hoped I'd never turn up?"

"Well—"

"Or what if they're delighted. What if it's a miracle to them. What if I bring an incredible amount of joy and resolution until they find out I'm gay, and then…"

"God, man, I know."

"Then they turn their back on me."

Or break my leg.

Throw rocks through my window. Spray-paint faggot *on the sidewalk. Fill my car's windshield wiper reservoir with blood. Then run me out of town.*

Tej's arms tightened around him and the side of his face pressed tight to Jude's. "I don't blame you. I don't blame you one fucking bit for contemplating that scenario. I don't."

"I can't do it again."

"I know. But listen. Play it through. You're not seventeen, you're a grown man. If they reject you, you fall right back into the loving arms of your real family." His finger reached to touch Penny and Cleon's boxes. "This family. These people will never let anyone hurt you ever again. Your father will bludgeon them with his prosthetic leg first."

Jude laughed.

"Then your mother and Serena will dismember the corpses and your brother will hide the pieces in various off-the-map locations around the world. The Tholets do not come to play."

"Oh my God." Still laughing, he hung onto Tej's forearms.

"And for what it's worth, any of them who survive that first line of defense will wish they hadn't, because they'll have to deal with me. Nobody fucks with my boo."

Jude turned his face into Tej's neck. "Am I your boo?"

"Damn right. I'd kill to have you find me all over again."

"Okay then." Jude drew in a ferocious breath, exhaled and reached for the mouse. "Jude the Obscure is going out there."

He toggled the settings of the family tree from Private to Public.

❧

"TELLING YOU, MAN," JUDE said to Phil. "I am all over the place."

"Can you unpack that?"

"I built my tree and made it public, then practically ran away from the computer. *Don't tell me, I don't want to know.* But every hour I'm checking the website and getting all huffy. *No matches? Nobody? What am I, chopped liver?*"

Phil laughed. "How dare nobody look for me when I'm so reluctant to be found."

"It's like a PhD in passive-aggressive."

"How are you feeling otherwise?"

"No otherwise. Just all over the place. But I wanted to ask you something. My mom has been considering hypnotherapy."

Phil's head tilted. "For?"

"To see if she can find some of the lost memories from the day I was born."

"I see."

"My dad and I don't want her going to some quack, though."

"No, you want someone certified. I know a woman in Kirkland who does excellent work. Seattle PD often uses her with witness testimony. If your mom went anywhere, I'd rather it be her."

"Will you give me her contact info?"

"Sure. I'll drop a line and do a little intro, so she'll know to look out for a call."

"Thanks. It's really weighing heavy on Mami that she can't remember. I don't know if hypnotism will do anything, but I think she'll feel better knowing she did everything she could."

"In competent, professional hands, it certainly couldn't hurt."

"Cool."

The last thirty seconds of the session ticked away.

"How are things with Tej?" Phil asked.

"They're good. I like how it's going along. I like him." Jude exhaled. "I really like him a lot."

THE GEOGRAPHY OF SADNESS

"*T*HAT YOU?" JUDE CALLED.

"Does another guy have a key to your place?" A clattering jingle as Tej threw his keys down, then shuffled to where Jude sat at the dining room table. He rubbed his palms hard over his face and exhaled.

"Tough day?" Jude asked, leaning back in his chair.

"I took a suicide call."

"No shit. Really?"

"From the Aurora Bridge."

The legs of the chair came down and Jude got up. "You all right?"

"Yeah. It's just... Yeah. I need a drink."

"Sit down. Take your coat off."

Jude popped two beers and grabbed an unopened bag of potato chips. "How many suicide calls do you get?"

Still wearing his coat, Tej drained half the beer in two swallows. "This was my second. First time, it was a guy contemplating. He had no plan, just the ideation. This was someone right on the edge, looking over."

"What do you do? You're trained for that, right?"

"Sure. You have cheat sheets around with basic steps, but you can't be an automaton, you have to feel the guy out, get him to talk to you." He killed the rest of the beer and plunked the bottle on the table. "Woof. That went down fast."

"Here." Jude pushed his bottle across. "How long were you on with him before police got there?"

"Ten minutes. He kept saying, 'Tell my sister I love her. Just tell her. Remember you gotta tell my sister. Don't forget.' So I grabbed onto that and got him to talk about her. I said, 'She sounds really important to you, can you tell me why? When was the last time you saw her? What did you do together?' It kept him talking. Kept a connection going."

He brushed his hands off on his jeans and finally shrugged out of his jacket. "He got agitated when the cops and fire department got on scene. That's when I really started sweating."

"Do you handle this all alone, is anyone with you?"

"My supervisor was standing by. Couple of other co-workers came close. They don't get involved or take over, they just keep eye contact with you, nod, make little gestures. You know."

"I do nothing that is close to knowing, but okay."

Tej smiled and dug in the potato chip bag.

"So they got him down?"

"Yeah." A tremendous exhale. "Which is the hard part. When the call ends. You have this intense moment with someone and then it's over and most of the time, you don't know what happened. It's hard to shake it off. Your mind starts making up the rest of the story, trying to close it up." He killed the second beer and belched. "So. Let me piggyback on your lack of closure. What you got going on here?"

Jude had printed out satellite images of the city of Santiago, taped them together and spread the makeshift map out on the dining room table.

"I'm just trying to get an idea of where things were happening when I was born," he said. "See, this is Hospital del Salvador. My mom was taken here after she gave birth. At some point in this hospital, her baby and I were switched."

"You assume."

Jude looked at him. "Well, yeah. Where else would it have happened?"

Tej hitched his chair closer. "Where was your parents' house?"

Jude's finger drew a line almost directly east. "Out here. In La Reina."

"So maybe a ten- or fifteen-minute drive?"

"Sure."

Tej shrugged. "Lot can happen in fifteen minutes."

"What do you mean?"

"I don't know. I'm just seeing a parade and raining on it."

Jude uncapped a Sharpie and marked the Tholets' neighborhood. He made an H on top of Hospital del Salvador. "Over here is Estadio Victor Jara. It was called Estadio de Chile in seventy-three. My father was taken here first. This is the Estadio Nacional, he was released from here six weeks later. In between…"

His finger glided east again, back toward La Reina, and made a little circle. "La Villa Grimaldi." He capped the black pen. "So those are the places where my parents were. Pinochet had other detention centers in Santiago." He took a red Sharpie and made circles on the map: London 38, José Domingo Cañas House, La Venda Sexy.

"Venda Sexy?" Tej said.

"You don't want to know what went on there."

"Not in my current state of mind, no. Tell me later."

"I have two theories. One, the simplest, my biological mother was in the Hospital del Salvador at the same time as Mami. Human error. Baby in the wrong bassinet. The old switcheroo and here I am."

"Or?"

"Or my biological mother was in one of these detention centers and gave birth to me there. Then I was brought to the hospital."

Tej's brows wrinkled. "So what is this map supposed to do?"

"I don't know," Jude said. "I wish my brother were here, he's good at this kind of stuff."

"Well, wait. Okay. I think I see where you're going. If you and your mother ultimately ended up here together... Wait. Back up. If Penny lived here in La Reina, why was she taken all the way over to this hospital? Are there no hospitals in La Reina?"

Jude tapped the map and drew a circle with the red pen. "Hospital Militar," he said. "It served the armed forces and didn't start treating civilians until 1996. And with a military coup going on, it would've been the last place Ysidro and Tatán would want to take her."

"Okay, so the next-closest option was del Salvador."

"And if my real mother gave birth to me while she was detained, you'd think the detention center would be close to del Salvador. Right?"

Tej's head bobbled back and forth. "In a rational world. From what you describe, things were anything but rational at the time. Still, let's go with it. If you ended up at this particular hospital, assume you were born somewhere close by. So either of the stadiums qualify."

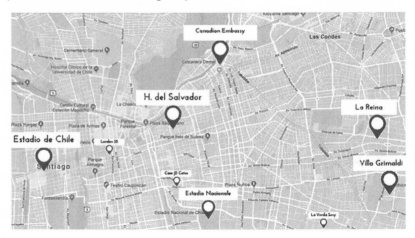

"Or London Thirty-Eight or Casa José Domingo Cañas," Jude said. "Except they weren't fully functional in seventy-three."

"The stadiums, then."

"Yeah. I started looking back through the testimonials my father collected." Jude indicated the stack of books on the table, all now dog-eared with a fringe of colored Post-its sticking out the top. "In the Estadio Nacional, the field and gallery were used to hold men, while women were in the swimming pool locker rooms. The interrogations were carried out in the velodrome."

Tej's thumb fanned open one of the books. He stopped at a random page, read a little, then closed it again. "Not for me right now."

"I'm sorry, I'll stop talking about this."

"No, I'm fine listening to you, I just don't want to read it. Go on, what were you saying?"

"I've been skimming these but I didn't find any accounts of women giving birth. But I went online and I found this." He pulled his laptop close and jiggled it awake. "It's a forum for survivors of political violence in Central and South America. I found this post…"

> "…My mother was arrested in Santiago during Pinochet's coup. She was held three months in the Estadio. Horrible, horrible things happened there. She helped another woman give birth on the shower floor in the swimming pool locker room…"

"Hello," Tej said.

"I know. I got all wigged out reading it."

"Have you contacted the poster?"

"It's over a year old."

"So?"

"She might not have this email anymore."

"And she might." He glanced sideways at Jude and his smile was soft. "Are you wigged about taking a step? Or do you not know what to say?"

"I don't know what to say."

Tej drew the laptop closer. He clicked the username to make an email message pop up, then began typing. Jude read over his shoulder:

> Hello. I'm trying to find my biological parents. I was born in November of 1973 in Santiago. I have no idea if my mother was detained or not, in the Estadio or not, but your mother's story caught my eye. I know this is random but if your mother

remembers any details about that woman, please let me know. My
email is below. You can also call or text me at the phone number.
I really appreciate it. Thanks so much.

"How's that?" Tej said. "Short and to the point. Send?"

Jude breathed in. "Send."

Before he could change his mind, Tej's index finger clicked and it was done. It was out there.

The first step taken.

"You don't know whether to shit or wind your watch," Tej said, sliding a hand up Jude's forearm to his shoulder, giving him a little shake.

"I guess I'm doing this."

Tej shrugged. "You saw something interesting and you're making a simple inquiry. That's all."

"That's all."

Tej slid the laptop aside and pulled the taped-together map closer. "This reminds me of when I first started as a dispatcher. I didn't have the boundary thing down yet. Nobody does when they start. You're a permeable membrane, every call is personal. Each emergency puts a dent in your frame and if they go south, they take a piece of you with it. It takes a while to build defensive distance. Anyway. I used to keep track of the locations of the bad calls, and when I got home, I'd map them. Like this. A geography of pain."

"Why?"

"Not sure. Looking for patterns, maybe? Or it could be that lack of closure thing I was talking about. When the call disconnected and I was left without an ending, I'd literally stick a pin in it."

"Hm."

"I thought it was my weird little thing, but I found out a lot of dispatchers do it. They drive through Seattle and instead of taking in the scenery, they're picking out locations and remembering calls. That apartment building was the overdose. That corner was the knife fight. That intersection had the T-bone. In the alley behind that bar was the rape."

"The geography of pain," Jude murmured, looking at the labeled locations across the city of Santiago.

"Soon you can't go anywhere without connecting it to a call. So I stopped plotting disaster and made a new map. I only pinned locations of calls that had a good outcome. Like if I guided someone through CPR and it was successful. Or coached a woman through labor."

"You did that?"

"Once. The ambulance got there before full-blown delivery, but she was hanging onto me over the phone. It was a trip."

"My sister once helped a woman deliver a baby on a bus."

"When?"

"About two years ago."

"No way, I remember that."

"Shut up." Jude leaned back a little. "You took the call?"

"No, but a baby being born gets talked about at the proverbial water cooler. It's exciting. It's positive. You're precipitating life, not fending off death. If it happens in your call center, you kind of own a piece of it. With every telling and retelling, you even feel like you were there. You know? Like *we* did it." He smiled. "That was your sister? Far out."

"The universe dropping hints."

"The coy bitch." Tej ran his hand over the terrain of Santiago. "Anyway, my man, I hope we can make some of this geography turn to joy."

My man settled soft on Jude's ears.

"I like we," he said.

THE LOCKER ROOM

*T*EJ AND JUDE CAME to spend a Saturday at Alki Beach. Cleon took them kayaking on the Sound, he in his single craft and the boys in the double-seater.

The boys, Penny thought. *I'm doing it again, aren't I?*

They fell asleep on the couch, their heads in one corner, Walter curled between. Penny wanted to put blankets over them, smooth Jude's hair and bask in his contentment. She made an apple pie instead, filling the house with spice.

Now Tej was moving around her kitchen as if he'd been born there, laughing and joking as they cooked and filling Penny with a wistful nostalgia. Two ends of a circle joined. Her home again harboring young, hungry lovers.

Jude sat at the kitchen table with his laptop, ankles crossed on a neighboring chair. His hair wind- and sleep-tousled, his cheekbones a little sunburned. The picture of health, but Penny noticed he kept Walter in his lap, repeatedly picking up the dog and rubbing his face against the soft fur, sighing heavily. Cleon sat across, reading the paper and glancing up at each heavy exhale.

"¿Qué onda, hueón?" he finally asked

Eyes on the screen, Jude pulled at his bottom lip. "Nada."

"You still thinking about that dream you had?"

Now his head bobbled back and forth, his gaze circling the ceiling in admission. "I can't shake it off."

The night before, he'd had a vivid, disturbing nightmare of a locker room. Tiled shower walls splashed with blood, vibrating against the echo of women screaming and babies crying.

"I don't ever remember a dream where I could smell something," he said. "But the scent of chlorine was all in my nose and mouth. My eyes were watering from it."

He woke up thrashing and yelling, one of his flung hands whacking Tej in the face.

"I can't get it out of my mind. I keep stopping and sniffing, like I can still sense the chlorine." As if to block out the remembered stench, he lifted Walter up to his face again.

"It was pretty intense," Tej said, coming to the table and refilling everyone's wine glass.

"More than intense, it felt like a memory." Jude put up a hand. "Yes, we all know I have an active imagination. I'm highly impressionable. My subconscious is always working overtime. True. Still…"

"It was disturbing," Penny said. "It felt personal."

"It felt like yours," Cleon said.

Jude's smile was wry above Walter's domed head. "I want to say it felt like a memory, which is so freakin' dumb."

"Look out," Tej called. "Coming in hot."

He heaved the big stockpot off the stove and carried it to the sink, where Penny was set up with a second stockpot and a cheesecloth-lined colander. A cloud of savory steam dampened her face as Tej poured, straining the onions, celery, carrots, garlic and fish bones. Leaving behind a gorgeous golden broth.

"Look at that," Penny said.

"*Smell* that," Tej said.

"I want to eat that," Cleon said. "Is it done?"

"Not yet," Tej said. "Pen, what's next?"

Penny dropped her glasses on her nose and consulted the recipe for Venetian fish soup. "Sauté the minced garlic and parsley. Add pepper flakes if using."

"We are using."

"Add the grated ginger if you want that North African-inspired Livornese touch."

"Oh, we want it."

"Add the white wine and saffron, if using."

"Who doesn't use white wine and saffron?"

"Tej," Jude said. "Check it out, I just got an email from that woman. The one I found on the Chilean forum."

"The one whose mother was in the Estadio?" Penny said.

"Yeah. She wants to call me."

"Right now?" Tej asked.

Jude looked at Penny. "Would that be okay?"

"Of course," she said.

"Why wouldn't it?" Cleon said.

"Well…"

Cleon folded the paper and put it down. "You know, we're just as eager as you to get to the bottom of this. You don't have to hide the looking or the finding from us."

"You're not going to offend us if you get curious," Penny said. "Or even consumed."

He looked at them, transparent and torn. Trying to balance every step forward on this strange journey with a look behind that said, *I haven't forgotten you. This doesn't mean I don't love you.* How could Penny blame him, when she herself was generous with encouragement while her hands wrung anxiously, wanting and waiting for those backward glances. Needing them. Thinking, *Go find your people but please, don't forget where your home is.*

Jude's phone rang. His eyes made a nervous circuit around the table and Penny nodded.

"Answer it, querido."

He put it on speaker. "Diga."

"¿Es Jude Tholet?"

"Sí."

"It's Roberta Cáceres. How are you?"

"Good, thanks so much for calling me." Jude held the dog against his chest and put the phone down on the table.

"Can you hear me all right? I'm at my son's soccer game, the cell service is kind of sketchy."

"I can hear you fine," Jude said, looking over at Tej. "But would you mind speaking English? Someone's listening who doesn't speak Spanish."

"Sure. So, I'll apologize up front that I don't think I can be much help to you. My mother died five years ago."

"Oh. I'm sorry."

"She didn't talk much about what happened to her during the coup."

"Did she ever say the name of that woman who gave birth in the locker room?"

"No. My God, we never even thought to ask."

"I was born in November. When was your mother detained?"

Roberta gave bitter laugh-sigh. "She was picked up off the street on September eleventh. Day one. She was in the stadium from September to December. She was out of the country by Christmas, I know that for a fact."

"I see."

"She would tell the story about the pregnant woman only to a point, and then stop and shake her head, saying, 'I don't want to talk about it.' She'd even put her hand over her mouth, like the words were just too terrible."

Across the table, Cleon was nodding. Minute twitches in his jaw and cheeks, his eyes never leaving Jude.

You have no idea, Jude, Penny thought. *You won't ever fully know the depths of how he adores you. What it meant when he set you like the moon in a diamond sky. He doesn't love you more than he loves Serena and Aiden. He just loves you differently.*

"She had a tough time when I was born," Roberta was saying. "It was a long, drawn-out labor that wouldn't progress. She'd give up right in the middle of pushing. Or even refuse to push. Like she was afraid to give birth, you know? Afraid to let me out into the world, she was so haunted by what she'd seen in the locker room."

Penny folded her hands around her mouth and nose, the hair standing up on her forearms and nape. Knowing with every fiber of her being that Roberta's mother carried that fear until the day she died.

My baby's going to be born so afraid.

The thought was quick and keen, like the flick of a scalpel. Darting across her mind and skipping away. Elusive and tantalizing, not quite hers. Like the fragment of a song lyric or poem.

Who said that? My baby's going to be born afraid. What's that from?

"Anyway, that's all I can really tell you," Roberta said. "I'm so sorry I can't be more help."

"No, no, I appreciate you taking the time," Jude said.

"I haven't thought about this in a while. When did I post that message, a year ago? Maybe now that it's in my head again and I've talked to you, some little detail will come to the forefront. If it does, I'll call you right away."

After thanking her, Jude hung up. They all sighed. Tej brought over bowls of the Venetian fish soup, each garnished with a toasted round of bread topped with a dollop of pesto.

"Soul food for four," he said. "And we need it."

Penny smiled at him as she took her bowl, thinking, *My baby's going to be born so afraid.*

Each bent a head toward the feast and inhaled the fragrant steam. Jude to smother the scent of chlorine. Cleon to feed a father's love. Penny to coax a fleeting thought into coming back. Tej because he loved good food.

CLEÓN

A BACKHAND ACROSS YOUR FACE *reminds you you're not gone yet. Captain Villarroel empties six bullets from his revolver onto the table, puts one back and points the muzzle at your head.* "What do you know about the weapons?"

"I don't know."

The revolver clicks. No bullet.

"Where are the guns?"

"I don't know."

They insist you have knowledge of Plan Zeta, a plot to kidnap the family members of military personnel.

"What are the plans?"

"I don't know."

Click. No bullet.

"We know Plan Zeta is the signal for the counter coup. When is it being implemented?"

"I don't know."

Click. No bullet.

"Where are the weapons for Plan Zeta stashed?"

"I don't know."

Click. No bullet.

You have two chances left.

(I'm going to die, Lucy.)

The captain puts the revolver on the table and snaps his fingers at two lieutenants. They haul you out of your seat and drag you to La Grilla—the metal bedspring leaning against the wall.

Your hands and feet are bound. The electrodes are placed.

Villarroel holsters his gun and smiles. "When I get through, you'll wish I'd shot you."

You're ready though.

The room is ready.
Three drumbeat taps of your fingers on your palm.
…
…
…
And you're gone.

THE CROSSED ARMS

*J*UDE THREW BACK HIS head and came, then dropped his brow on Tej's nape and came harder. Tej bucked and writhed in the circle of his arms, hands going to fists on the wall above the headboard, his speech dissolving into babble.

"God, you're so good. Jude, you're so good. Baby, you don't know how good you are…"

Jude hung onto him, falling into the swirling patterns beneath his clenched eyes. Rocking their bodies through wave after wave. Mouth sucking a circle on Tej's skin. Salty and sweet. Burning hot on his tongue even as his body shivered into cool stillness. Their slick, sticky fingers wove together, holding on tight.

"Jude. Man…"

"I got you." Jude locked his trembling knees as Tej's body shivered one last time. His damp head tilted back, lolling on Jude's shoulder.

"I can't feel me anymore."

"I got you," Jude whispered. "Let it go."

"Christ. My legs."

"I got you. Easy now." Jude turned Tej around and lay him down on his back. "You okay?"

"I'm okay. *You* are insane."

"Be right back." Light-headed, Jude had to grab the edge of the dresser until the fuzziness passed. He stumbled toward the bathroom, tied off the condom and chucked it, then pulled a towel off the rack.

Tej sprawled on the bed, golden and magnificent, forearms flopped over his face. One knee bent up, the other leg long. Ribs rising and falling in deep breaths. His nipples beaded tight and the hair on his chest and stomach sleek with sweat.

Jude ran the towel along Tej's skin. "You are fucking beautiful, man."

Tej garbled something incoherent, his voice blissed-out and slurry.

"You want to try that again in English?"

Another mosh of sound and the crossed arms opened. Jude crawled up and fitted his body alongside. A leg across Tej's thigh, an arm over his chest. Their fingers twined again. They both sighed.

"I don't know why you gave me that bullshit about sucking as a top," Tej said.

"Because I do suck at it."

"If that's sucking, I'm a dead man if you improve." He slid fingers into Jude's hair and gave his head a shake. "God, baby, you did that so good…"

The fuck is this? Jude thought through the humming buzz in his brain. *I don't like being called baby. I don't like being petted and told I'm a good boy. I don't need praise and encouragement in bed like it's a new skill I'm learning…*

Now Tej's hand moved soft and slow along Jude's brow and temples. "So good."

But with him, I fucking love it.

"Say that in French," he asked.

"You're so good? Tu est si bon."

"What about in Arabic?"

"Anta jayyedun jiddan is the literal translation. To a lover you'd say enta betjannen."

"Enta bet… Wait, what?"

"Forget it, you'll hurt yourself. Say it in Spanish."

"Eres tan bueno."

"Tan bueno. I like how that sounds. Tan bueno for the win."

"Bueno." As his mouth released the word, Jude's soul shook with a strange desire, wanting to be good—to be better, to be the *best*.

"Let's do this all night," he said. "I want to keep doing this. All fucking night."

Tej licked his lips slowly. His mouth opened and shut. When it parted again, the words were tiny, tight and shy. "I love making love with you."

"I love that you love it."

Tej slid his hand into the damp hair at the back of Jude's neck. Ran his lips across Jude's crown. Hooked his heel around the back of Jude's calf and pulled him close.

"Yeah," he said. "Let's just keep doing this."

Jude was enormous with feeling. Exploding at his fingernails and eyelashes, clamoring for a way out.

"You know what else I love?" Tej said.

"Tell me."

"When you call my name, looking for me."

"Hm?"

"If I'm in another room and you call out because you have a question or you need something, you call Tim. You only do it when you're looking around for me. But like you're not even thinking about it."

"I don't even remember when I started doing that."

"It's a little dopey thing but I just dig it. Tim belongs to long ago. Not many people call me Tim these days. I like you being one of them."

"I like when I call for you and you answer, 'Yeah, babe?' You make it sound like one word. Yahbay."

"Yahbay." Tej chuckled. "We're inventing a new language. Tejuleon."

"Judantej."

They were laughing together, but all the feeling inside Jude was too small for his skin. Emotion rushed for the easy egress of his throat. He was choking with it. "Something I want to tell you."

"Mm?"

"It's going to sound weird. It's going to sound insulting, but I swear it's not."

A loopy chuckle in Tej's chest. "Okay."

"Sometimes when I'm with you, I feel like crying."

He surfed up and down on Tej's deep, expectant breath.

"It's nothing you're doing. It's not the way I feel about you or us. It's..."

"Take your time."

"It's... See... After my leg was broken, I stopped talking. I stopped... I stopped. I wasn't sad, I wasn't angry. I didn't cry. I didn't rage. I didn't act out. I stopped feeling everything. Just shut down."

He twirled a bit of Tej's chest hair into a tuft, twisted it tight. Tej gentled the fidgeting fingers and said, "Keep telling me."

"After a while I thawed out. Turned back on. I found my voice. I found my anger and my rage and I acted out a shit-ton. But I didn't cry. I still don't cry. So when I say I feel like crying when I'm with you, it's because I can."

Tej wormed from beneath and rolled to face him. Jude rolled too, and they lay for a long quiet minute, breathing and staring. Tej's hand on Jude's face, thumb moving beneath his dry eyes. Jude held still and let himself feel like crying. The feeling was what mattered. The actual tears were beside the point.

"A lot of things in my life are stressful and confusing right now," he said. "But you're not one of them. I'm going around not knowing who I am, but when I'm with you, I feel the most like myself."

They rested in each other's gazes, Tej stroking Jude's face. "You're so good."

"I'm not doing anything."

"Yes you are."

They dozed with the bedside lamp still on. Kneecaps touching, forearms in a pile, resting in the breeze of each other's long breaths. Their hands woke first, lazily touching. The caressing woke up and became kissing. Soft and slow, then harder and insistent.

"I'm doing you this time," Tej said, kicking the covers away.

"You think?"

"Yeah."

The wave began to crest again as they kissed like thieves. They rolled this way and that, touching and rubbing, limb piling on top of limb. Co-captains of the *SS Chasingforty Euphoria*.

Flinging himself against Tej's straining body, Jude had no more nostalgia for back seats of cars and ghosts of 80s pop songs. Handprints on steamed windows had nothing on Tej's fingerprints in his skin. His body wanted this bed. His ears wanted Tej's edgy soundtrack with its bass riff so down in tenderness and trust, the words could be filthy and Jude wouldn't stop singing along.

"Whatever's making you smile like that," Tej said. "Whatever's making you this way tonight, don't even think about stopping."

Jude pushed Tej on his back and reached long for the bedside table drawer. "You ever top from the bottom?"

"No."

"Liar."

Tej's wicked laugh coiled above the pillows. "Get up here and fuck my cock."

Jude was so hard, he was dizzy. His head full of soft, tender thoughts while his body surged and sparked like a blown transformer. "All right," he said, tearing open the condom packet. "But remember you asked for it."

"Baby, that was begging."

The laughter faded as Jude rolled the condom on Tej, who wore his gates-of-Disneyland expression, the whites of his eyes shining in the dark.

"Oh man, I think I'm gonna hate this," he whispered.

Electric with want, Jude put a knee on either side of Tej's hips. "Too late."

A pulsing, anxious beat as he guided Tej inside him. Tej hissed a breath through his teeth. Then Jude sank down and both men let out a ferocious, growled exhale.

"Oh God, don't move," Tej said, fingertips digging into Jude's hips. "Don't move don't move don't move."

Jude's mouth and body strained against the dark, neither speaking nor breathing. A wave of heat rushed up his spine and over the crown of his head. As he gave way and let Tej in deeper, the night broke in a stream of salty wet down his face.

"Stay like this," Tej said.

"This," Jude said, finding his voice and feeling a tremendous shift in the universe.

Am I who is this?

Something once backward and upside-down, now righted and pointing in the true direction.

This is who I am.

He pulled along Tej and pushed down again. Time bubbled up in his chest and dissolved in his throat. The tears slid down his laughing face and danced between their kiss.

"Baby." Tej slowly canted his hips up as he pulled Jude's mouth in. "Cry if you want to. I know what it means."

Jude was crying, but out of freedom, not sadness. Crying because it felt so fucking good to be him. Because he could harbor himself by holding his lover down. Let Jude out by letting Tej in.

So let it out and let it in.

Hey, Jude. Begin.

He slid his hands up Tej's arms, twined their fingers and pinned them to the mattress. He moved on Tej, shifting this way to go faster, angling that way to go deeper. Taking control of the boat's helm and fucking like he meant it. Filled up with heat and want. Filled up with the one truth within the mystery of his birth: this was how he was born to love.

"Tim," he called softly. Over and over against his lover's body, he called, "Tim…"

He wasn't looking for anything. Only saying what he'd found.

THE MORNING WAS COOL and grey. Jude poured a cup of coffee, added milk and sugar, stirred and tapped the spoon on the rim twice. He shuffled back into the bedroom and set it down on the side table.

"Made you coffee," he murmured.

Tej's one eye opened. "You did? You're the best."

Jude fixed his own mug, sat down at his desk and jiggled the screen awake. He read over his notes and checked the website. He took a fortifying sip. An even more fortifying breath. Then he dialed the Chilean number.

"Servicio Médico-Legal de Santiago, buenos días."

"Buenos días," Jude said. "I'm looking for information on how I can locate my missing relatives…"

HEY, JUDE

"Take a sad song and make it better."
—John Lennon and Paul McCartney

THE GARDEN

"**A**RE YOU ALL RIGHT?" Jude asked Penny.

She sighed. "Stop asking me. I'm fine. You look a wreck."

Jude looked at his father. "How about you?"

"You know I'm a wreck. Ask me again and I'll kill you."

Jude smiled at his shoes and flexed his cold fingers. The communal waiting room was chilly, or maybe he was just nervous. He got up and wandered by the three closed doors, reading the plaques beside each one, ending with the hypnotherapist.

> Dr. Rachel Mezeritz, Ph.D.
> Licensed Clinical Psychologist
> Certified Clinical Hypnotherapist

Penny had already met Mezeritz for a consultation, during which they discussed her past history, her present situation and future goals. All week, Penny had been practicing the relaxation techniques that would be used in the sessions.

"They're really wonderful," she said. "Even if I don't remember a thing when all is said and done, I have some great new tricks for not losing my mind."

"Meditation makes your ass look fabulous," Jude said.

Today would be the first attempt at memory recall and, not knowing what to expect, Penny wanted both Cleon and Jude present.

"Call me Rachel," the doctor said, shaking all their hands. She looked to be in her late sixties, with an uncanny resemblance to Carole King. Her office was long and narrow, and she situated Jude and Cleon at its far end by the windows.

"This is just for the induction phase," she said. "Reason being that family members can be impressionable to the regression and end up going places they'd rather not."

Cleon raised a finger. "I believe you mean me."

She smiled. "We need you to stay in the present today."

He dug in his sport coat pocket and brought out his phone and ear buds. "I came prepared."

Penny got comfortable on the chaise section of the L-shaped couch. Shoes off, feet up. Rachel dimmed the lights a little, then sat in the armchair.

"Become aware of your breathing," she said, "and notice how your abdomen rises and falls with each breath."

Jude took a long breath of his own.

Don't hurt her, he thought as he exhaled. *Don't scare her. Don't take her somewhere she can't come back from.*

"Now take a long, slow, deep breath. In through your nose, all the way down into your stomach. Hold the breath for just a moment, and then exhale through your mouth. Allow your breath to carry away all stress and tension as the air floods out of your lungs…"

Jude tried to watch without listening, but afraid he might go somewhere he didn't want to, he pivoted his chair toward the window, took out his own phone and buds and listened to some music.

He jumped in his skin when Cleon tapped his arm and tilted his head toward the couch. They were ready. Heart thumping, Jude took a seat by Penny's feet while Cleon sat next to her.

"Penny, I want you to take me to a place in Chile where you are perfectly content," Rachel said. "Let your mind go back. Let your senses remember. Sight. Sound. Smell. Touch. Even taste. But above all, contentment."

"All right," Penny said, as if agreeing to meet for lunch.

After a few beats, Rachel asked, "Are you there?"

"Mmhm."

"Tell me."

"I'm in the garden."

"Describe it. Let yourself narrate. I'm a stranger, I've never seen this. Tell me."

"My house in La Reina. It's a double lot of property. Half used to be my father-in-law's nursery. It closed when he returned to Austria. Whatever stock he didn't sell he put into the ground. Fruit trees. Flowering shrubs. Drifts of flowers. He always told me to plant in groups of three and five. Repeat colors over and over, drawing the eye ever onward. A garden walk should be a journey. A story. Slip in things to look at. Places to sit. The point should be to meander and rest. Meander and rest."

"What do you hear?"

Penny's chin tilted up and to the right. "The wind. Hummingbirds. The Beatles."

Rachel smiled. "Who's playing the Beatles?"

"Ysidro, across the road in his workshop."

"What song?"

"'All Together Now.'"

"What do you smell?"

A deep inhale. "Roses. Honeysuckle. Flowering almond."

"What can you touch?"

Penny's hands lifted off the throw pillow in her lap. The fingers curled and touched her palms, then stretched out again and rested. "Dirt on my fingers. I've been pulling weeds. There's a strong breeze today. The sun is hot on my shoulders."

"Can you taste anything?

A little chuckle. "Gum. Mint chewing gum. I'm so nauseous."

"Why?"

"I'm having a baby."

"When are you? What year is it?"

"February. Nineteen seventy-three."

"February is springtime in Chile?"

"Summer. It's all upside-down."

"How do you feel?"

"Happy."

"Take a moment," Rachel said. "This place and this feeling are going to be home base. We'll begin and end here. Whenever you encounter a painful memory that's too much, we're going to return to this place in the garden. Return to safety. All right?"

"All right. There's a bench where I can sit."

"Good."

Penny smiled and half sang, "Sitting in an English garden, waiting for the sun."

"I'm sorry?"

"The line from 'I am the Walrus.' Ysidro chiseled it into a big paving stone." Penny's hand lifted, gesturing out and down. "It's over there, by the poppies."

"Will you take me inside the house now? Narrate as you go."

She prompted Penny through the guided tour, asking for details of sight, sound, smell and touch. Penny described doors and windows as if they were before her. Roof tiles and rugs. Furniture. Bookshelves. Throw pillows. Jude's eyes flicked between his parents, watching Cleon's reaction. How he closed his eyes and nodded. Wrinkled his eyebrows or chuckled. Murmured, "That's right." Or corrected, "No, no, that painting was upstairs."

"Where are we now?" Rachel asked.

"In the kitchen." Penny's entire face smiled, as if reuniting with a long-lost schoolmate.

"Is something special about the kitchen?"

"Something is always special about the kitchen. Everything happens in here."

"What's happening now?"

A reflective pause. "I'm sitting at the table, peeling potatoes."

"Is anyone with you?"

"Uncle Louis."

"Describe him to me."

"Nineteen seventy-three, I guess Louis is about fifty-five."

"Fifty-seven," Cleon said quietly.

"He looks much older though. Tall. Thin. Thick glasses. The kindest face but it's haunted. Sweet smile with dimples, but behind it is a deep sadness. He's beautifully dressed. Always. Even when he's sculpting and covered with stone dust, he has a style." Her hand touched her throat. "A scarf tied at his neck. He has three dozen. A different one every day."

"What is he doing now?"

"Reading bits of the paper out loud." A pained but affectionate giggle. "His Spanish is terrible."

"How do you feel?"

"Oh God, hungry. So pregnant and hungry and…" The color rose up in her cheeks and Cleon looked away, the corners of his mouth twitching.

"Let's move forward in time a bit," Rachel said. "Just a few months."

"All right."

"Tell me when."

"June. The coldest month. The garden beds are bare. We spend a lot of time in the kitchen. I'm so hungry. Everything tastes so good. Louis reads the news about Tanquetazo. The putsch. Colonel Souper led a failed coup against Allende. It's almost July now. The rainiest month. I'm blue and down and heavy. The air feels heavy. The news isn't good."

"Where are you?"

"In the kitchen. Helping my neighbor Daniela with her eyes."

Cleon made a startled "Hm" in his chest, chin rising, as if suddenly recalling something long forgotten.

"What happened to her eyes?" Rachel asked.

"She went to the Plaza de la Constitución for a protest. It was a women's protest, against the rising costs of food and fuel. I almost went, too, but the day of, I was too tired. The women were dispersed with tear gas. Daniela's at my kitchen table. I'm bathing her eyes."

"We're moving close to September now," Rachel said, her voice rising. "Closer to the hard memories."

"Yes."

"Take a moment to dial into your state of relaxation. Your body is in the here and now. Your husband is with you. Your son is with you. The memories are painful to recall but they cannot hurt you. Anytime you wish, we can go back out to the garden where it's safe. All right?"

"Yes."

"The danger is over. It's safe to remember. Remembering will not hurt you."

"All right."

"When is it now?"

"September eleventh," Penny said. "Cleon called me a little after nine, said the armed forces had taken control of the country and declared Allende deposed. They'd taken over all of Santiago except for the city center."

A long stretch of silence.

"What's happening now?" Rachel asked.

"Daniela and Fernanda and Louis are in my kitchen. Ysidro comes from his workshop across the street. We're listening to Radio Portales. It goes dead. Radio Corporación isn't broadcasting either."

"The air force bombed the antennas," Cleon said quietly.

"Radio Magallanes is still live. In the afternoon, we listen to Salvador Allende make his farewell speech. You can hear gunfire and explosions in the background as he speaks. It's over. How can this... He's done. It's done. The city's under a curfew. The radios are silent. The TV news channels are off. Cleon calls one last time. He doesn't dare come home that night, he sleeps at the office..."

Minute twitches under Penny's skin. Winces and flinches in her face. Fingers curling and clenching. Tears collecting along the edges of her closed eyes.

"When is it, Penny?" Rachel asked.

"October."

"Where are you right now?"

"En casa."

"Will you speak English for me, please?"

"Sorry." Penny shook her head a bit. "I'm at home."

"I want you to speak in English when you remember. English is now. Spanish is then. Speak in the language of now while you remember then, all right?"

"Yes."

"What room are you in?"

"All of them. I'm pacing around the house."

"Who is with you?"

"No one. They've gone to look for him."

"Who is they?"

"Uncle Louis. Ysidro. Tatán."

"Who are they looking for?"

"Cleon."

"Where is he?"

"Gone. He didn't come home. He hasn't called. No one is answering at the newspaper. None of his colleagues pick up the phone. Not at their offices. Not at their homes. I don't know where he is. I've never not known where he is."

"How do you feel?"

One of her hands began to glide up and down the throw pillow, tracing a remembered curve of her belly. "I'm so scared. The world's gone crazy. I'm so afraid. My baby's going to be born so afraid."

"Basta," Cleon murmured.

Enough.

Penny's head tilted a fraction toward him. "I'd like to come back now."

"All right," Rachel said. "Let's go out to the garden. Back where it's safe. Narrate me from wherever you are out the door. Describe it."

She prompted for sight. Sound. Touch, smell and taste. Guiding the return journey to happiness and safety, pointing out buoys of happiness, until Penny was sitting in an English garden, waiting for the sun. Back in safety. Back in the here and now.

Penny opened her eyes and smiled as she let out a long breath.

"How do you feel?" Rachel said.

"Goodness, it was so vivid. And so lucid. I thought it would be more dream-like but I felt perfectly awake and...*there.*"

The doctor brought her a paper cup of water. "Take your time. Let's make sure none of your awareness was left behind. It's important you feel safe and in the present before you leave."

Penny drained the cup and set it down. Her hands rubbed along her forearms, her expression astounded. "When I was sitting on the bench, I could actually feel the sunshine." She laughed a little. "Look at me, I'm checking to see if I got burned. It was that real."

"Lo hiciste bien," Cleon said, running a hand along the cap of her silvery hair.

She smiled at him. A little hitch in her voice when she said, "¿Tuvimos una casa preciosa, po?"

We had a beautiful home, didn't we?

Jude watched them, picturing the house and garden. Filled with a bittersweet affection. These were his parents.

But that beautiful home in La Reina had never been his.

THE NIGHT BEFORE

*T*HE SECOND SESSION'S INDUCTION went much quicker. Jude didn't
even get through a song before Rachel beckoned him and Cleon to the couch.

She repeated the visualization of the garden, affirming it as a place of happiness and safety, and the haven they'd return to whenever Penny wished. Then
Penny narrated them into the house.

"Where are you?" Rachel asked.

"In the kitchen?"

The doctor's chin tilted. "Are you sure?"

"Yes."

"When is it?"

"October. Nineteen seventy-three."

"What's happening?"

Her body seemed to gather itself, as if she were stepping off a high diving
board. "Cleon's been arrested. He's in the Estadio. Fernanda's husband and
Daniela's husband were also arrested. Everyone is terrified. Nobody can believe
what's happening. How could this have happened? We fought a war so things
like this couldn't happen."

A long pause.

"How do you feel right now?" Rachel said.

"I'm… It's so hard not knowing where he is." Penny's voice was different.
Younger. A few levels up from girlish, a few down from matronly. Filled with a
panic that made Jude clench his fingers hard.

"I'm afraid," she said. "All the time. My baby's going to be born afraid."

"What day is he born?"

"November twenty-fifth."

"I want you to take me to the night before."

"All right."

"Where are we?"

"In the kitchen."

"Who is with you?"

Uncle Louis was at the table. His face grim and stoic, Penny said. No doubt re-living things he'd already survived in Europe. Perhaps wondering if he'd failed to read signs he of all people should've seen coming.

Ysidro Sepúlveda at another chair. Estranged and disowned from his people, all his love and allegiance was now heaped on the Tholets. Especially Penny. They were close in age but she was a mother figure to him. With Cleon detained, Ysidro silently declared himself the man of the house and followed Penny everywhere, her safety now his ultimate concern.

"And Tatán," Penny said. "God, he's so upset tonight. The government is sending him to odd locations around the city."

"I don't understand?"

"He's an undertaker. But he also works for the city coroner. And he's being sent to places…" Her hand cupped her mouth and she drew a long slow breath.

"Take your time," Rachel said.

"He's picking up people at the Estadio Chile and the Estadio Nacional. He's picking up the dead. People who've been tortured and killed. Bodies in horrible shape. Things he can't un-see. And tonight…"

The hand lowered from her mouth and rested on the pillow in a fist.

"What happened tonight?" Rachel asked.

"Tatán picked up two dead children. And a baby. A newborn."

"From where?"

"One of the stadiums. And it's not the first time."

"It's happened before?"

"Yes. It's the third time since September he's collected the bodies of dead children. They were tortured to death in front of their parents. Tonight is the second time he's been given a newborn baby."

"Alive?"

"Yes. Both times he took it to the orphanage. La Casa de Huérfanos. He's crying into his hands, saying it's only going to happen more. More dead children. How many pregnant women are being detained? If they survive, how will they know what happened to their babies?"

Her breath grew short and choppy in her throat, the distress evident in every line of her face.

"My baby is going to be born so afraid." Her voice was thinner than a razor's edge, honed and keen, slicing the quiet of the room until it bled.

"Penny, I want you to get up from the kitchen table and go out to the garden," Rachel said. "Take me with you. Narrate your steps."

Back into the sunshine and safety. Noting sights and sounds and smells.

Back to the here and now.

Penny opened her eyes. "Goodness," she said in her normal voice. "I forgot I remembered that night."

THE THIRD SESSION.

Induction into the haven of the garden. Then sensory narration into the house.

"I'd like you to take me to November twenty-fifth," Rachel said. "Nineteen seventy-three."

"The day the soldiers come," Penny said.

Jude had been dreading this, but in contrast to the second session, Penny rather calmly narrated the events that took place in the street. The account was brisk and matter of fact. Almost journalistic.

Because she's told this story before, Jude realized. This wasn't recollection of something forgotten but a history recitation. He himself could practically tell it along with her, word for word.

"And then," Penny said, a hand going to the back of her head. "Something hits me. Right here. I feel like my eyeballs fly right out of my face. I fall forward and…" Her hands flew out in front of her, bent sharply at the wrist. "The gravel in the road digs all into the heels of my hands. I collapse straight down on my stomach. This tiny pop inside. Like a balloon. And then all… Is that water rushing down my legs? Oh my God, I've peed myself. No. Wait…"

Her outstretched hands went to her nape again. Then slowly dropped to the pillow in her lap. She went intensely, eerily still.

"My head," she said. "God, my head…"

Cleon's hands tightened around the curve of his cane. Jude's hands steepled over his mouth and nose.

I'm being born now.

No, he's being born. Her baby. Her and Papi's first child.

"Penny, can you hear me?" Rachel said.

"Mm." Her body pitched from side to side on the couch. Head turning this way and that. Licking her lips. Clenching her fists.

"Penny, where are you?"

"On the floor." A long pause. "By the couch. My water's broken and…"

She sucked in a sharp gasp through her nose.

"What's happening?" Rachel said.

"The baby's coming." Her voice teetered on a precarious edge. "It's happening so fast. I can't stop it." Her head whipped up and to the left. "The lights."

"What about the lights?"

"The power's out again. We have no light."

"Who is with you?"

"Ysidro and Tatán. The lights are out and… The phone's dead. The soldiers cut the lines."

"What's happening now?"

Penny's mouth opened but she didn't speak. Jude felt the first rumblings of panic and later he would look back with admiration at Rachel's professional skill. Her voice never faltered. If anything, it only grew more assured as she tried one prompt after another, never showing the slightest frustration or sign of giving up.

Recollection came in stuttering bursts, from the oddest of places. Rachel asked for a scent memory and Penny answered, "Wet leather."

"Leather?"

"Tatán is holding my hands. He's wearing a leather wristwatch. I bite it when the contractions hit."

Penny's arms folded back, a hand at each shoulder, twined with invisible fingers. "I'm holding onto him. I keep biting on the band of his watch. Oh my God, I bit him that time. I'm so sorry."

A long interlude of restless quiet when Penny didn't respond. Jude's shirt was stuck to his back with sweat. Cleon looked like a piece of sculpture, he was so rapt and focused on his wife. His hands never relaxing their grip on his cane, as if he'd bludgeon anything that dared disturb this moment.

"Anything you can hear or see or feel, you tell me," Rachel said. Her tone was pure pleasantness. None of this was a concern or a bother.

"Ysidro wants more towels," Penny said. "He can't find them."

Time stretched like taffy as she threaded fragments of memory like beads on a string.

"I hung the towels on the line."

"It's too much."

"I can't do this."

A long silence then. When she spoke again, it was in her present-day voice. "All my life, I've been in awe how brave Jude is. He's such a courageous soul and it's miraculous, because he was born into such terror."

And like a switch being thrown, she was in the past again. Back in the terror.

"Can you hear anything?" Rachel said.

"I think I'm going to die."

"Can you hear anything, Penny?"

No answer.

"Can you feel anything?"

"I'm so thirsty." Penny's reclined body seemed to soften into the couch cushions. "It's over?" she whispered.

Rachel leaned forward a little. "Is the baby born?"

Jude went cold all over.

Penny licked her lips. "My head hurts so bad."

"Can you hear anything, Penny?"

"Es un niño."

"Who tells you?"

"Ysidro says it. Tatán says it right by my ear. Es un niño."

"Do you see it's a boy?"

"Oh." The tiniest sigh under her breath. "It's a boy all right."

"What else can you see?"

Penny didn't speak, but her arms slowly rose. They extended, ready to receive, then they moved toward her body. One crossed above her chest, hovering. The other at her shoulder, cupped.

"Ese pobre bebé."

Her body trembled, breathing hard. She was exhausted. Her voice whispered a mother's soothing croon: "Pobrecito."

"Is he crying?" Rachel asked.

No answer. All glances exchanged when a little laughter filled the space between Penny's long, labored breaths.

"What's happening now, Penny?"

"The boys can't find the scissors," she said, shaking her head. "What is it with scissors? They never want to be found. They sit right under your nose until they're needed, then they disappear."

Silence.

"Is the baby crying?" Rachel asked.

No answer.

"Is the baby breathing?"

Silence.

"Can you feel anything, Penny?"

"He's so warm," she whispered. "Goodness."

"He?"

"Yes."

"Is it a boy?"

"Yes."

"You're sure?"

"Oh yes."

"Is he alive?"

Silence.

"Where are you now?"

"Nowhere."

Silence.

"Penny, where are you now?"

"The hospital."

"What's happening?"

Penny's hands went to her head. "Oh my God, I'm going to die."

Cleon made a little sound in his chest, like the involuntary yelp of a puppy whose tail had been trod upon. Rachel's eyes flicked to him and blinked.

"Penny, let's get up out of bed and go into the garden."

They returned to the sunshine, hummingbirds, Beatles songs and honey-suckle.

Penny opened her eyes and exhaled.

"How do you feel?" Rachel asked.

"Fine. I feel fine now, but... I don't think I've ever been as terrified as I was that night."

She leaned her head on Cleon's shoulder and closed her eyes.

"Te amo," he said, letting go his cane to take her hands. "Te amo tanto, querida. Lo siento mucho."

I'd kill for them, Jude thought. *Give me the chance, I'll go back in time and kill every fucking person who did this to my parents.*

THE HOLLYWOOD MOMENT

*P*ENNY HAD TWO MORE sessions with Dr. Mezeritz, but nothing new fell from the folds of her memory.

"The head injury could have erased them," Rachel said. "And then your subconscious came in to finish the job, simply to protect you."

Penny nodded, still reclined on the chaise. A cup of water in one hand, the other holding tight to Cleon's. His eyes were closed, his mouth buried in her hair.

"It may be you never have a satisfying answer to this," Rachel said. "You probably won't have a Hollywood resolution moment. The proverbial Perry Mason courtroom gasp."

"You mean our plot device problem won't get a plot device solution?" Jude said. "How dare it?"

Rachel laughed. "Well, what you may get, and what I suggest you prepare yourself for, is the most satisfying narrative constructed from the pieces of information you know. A narrative you can believe in. A narrative that's the closest thing to the truth. A truth you can accept in your heart and say, 'This is probably what happened. This I can believe happened.'"

"And," Cleon said. "Dot-dot-dot. Who are we going to be now?" He smiled at Rachel's puzzled expression. "Family motto."

"Personally," the doctor said, "I hope you do get the Hollywood moment that puts all of this to rest. Fatalistically speaking, if you don't, perhaps there's a reason. Perhaps it would be more devastation than resolution. Perhaps a greater divine order is protecting you."

"I can believe in that," Penny said. "I think I have to."

Rachel looked at each family member with eyes that were unprofessionally bright. "Realistically...I am so moved by your story. And I'm truly sorry for what happened."

THAT AFTERNOON, JUDE, CLEON and Penny got on a Skype call with Isabella Eberhoff from the Medical-Legal Institute in Santiago.

"This is certainly an unusual case," she said. "We've been working a decade to compile a database from the DNA of human remains, but this will be the first time I hope we don't match someone to it. Meaning I want your biological child and Juleón's biological parents to be alive somewhere."

Isabella would send the Tholets new collection kits to submit to the database, along with forms authorizing release of their contact information, in the event a match was made. She was patient and competent with their questions and expressed a genuine fascination in the story.

"Your friend who worked for the city coroner would have unbelievable tales to tell," she said. "Within days of the coup, the morgues of Santiago were overwhelmed with the dead. Hundreds of them unidentified."

Bodies piled up in offices and corridors of the morgue, eventually spilling into the streets outside. Family and friends wandered the horrifying stacks of humanity, by now in varied stages of decomposition. Desperate to find their loved ones in the growing charnel.

"The workers within Santiago's Civil Registry and the Medical-Legal Institute were working under indescribable pressure," Isabella said. "Any examination of the dead was frantic and sloppy. Doctors called them 'economic autopsies,' doing the bare minimum. The Civil Registry took no fingerprints of the deceased. As a result, important details that could've helped with identification were lost forever. This is why the discovery and exhumation of Patio Twenty-Nine was so important."

The Patio was located in a back lot of Santiago's General Cemetery, she explained. Here the cemetery workers were ordered to bury over two hundred bodies. Yet unlike the mass graves of other genocides, where a large number of bodies were dumped together, the corpses of Patio 29 were buried in twos and threes, in individual graves.

"And they were marked," Isabella said. "Which is another peculiarity. Most of the cemetery workers were Catholic. They were compelled to mark each grave with a cross made of metal, inscribed N.N. No name."

What should we name our boy, Penny thought.

It had been a long day. Jude went home. Cleon wanted to go out on the Sound and clear his head. Penny took to her bed, holding a pillow to her breast.

He's so warm.

My goodness.

She cradled both the pillow and the memory of the precious, damp skull nestled in her palm. The little face in her neck.

Is he crying?

Is he alive?

What should we name our boy?

Hey, Jude…

Her arms held the pillow tight. Tears stung her eyes as she whispered, "Don't be afraid."

You were made to go out and get it.

Her face crumpled. She buried it in the pillow and wept.

CLEÓN

*T*HE NEWSPAPER TAXIS ARE *fun. You fold them like origami and if you find an article with your byline, you affix it to the car door like an advertisement. The cabs are carefully placed on the shore, beyond the bridge by the fountain.*

You paint smiling human faces on rocking horses before the timer dings on the oven. The pies are set out to cool, each topped with a golden-edged swirl of melted marshmallows. You scoop up the excess to make clouds, shading them with the newsprint ink collected on your fingertips.

They're calling you.

It's time to go.

. . .

. . .

. . .

And you're gone.

THE LOCKS

*O*N THE LAST DAY of June, Tej's mother died in California.

"I'm so sorry," Jude said when Tej hung up the phone.

His shoulders flicked up and down. "Yeah," he said. "Yeah, it's... Yeah."

Jude put arms around him, but Tej half-twisted away.

"Sorry, I need to...just be alone in my head right now."

"All right."

"Think I'll go for a run."

"Good idea."

Tej went to change and Jude cleaned up the kitchen.

"Do you want me to look at flights for you?" he called.

Tej emerged from the bedroom, untangling his ear buds. "What?"

"I'll look at flights for you. I have a ton of miles I can transfer if you need them."

"Flights to where?"

"California"

Tej's voice raised. "Why the fuck would I be going there?"

"For the funeral?" Jude said slowly.

"I can't *go* to the funeral, you moron," Tej yelled.

"Dude, what the—"

"Christ, do you even get it? My father, my sisters, my aunts, uncles, cousins— they don't want to see me. When I say I'm disowned, I'm not being fucking romantic. It means my presence isn't wanted. I'm dead to them. Mireille is all I got."

"I'm sorry," Jude said. "I didn't mean to—"

"I have no family. You have two. Jesus, if I found out my parents weren't my own, I'd be tearing the *world* apart looking for the real ones. I'm kicked out of my mother's funeral and I get to watch you feel sorry for yourself. I'm fucking sick of it."

Jude stared as Tej stormed out of the townhouse, letting the door slam behind him, hard enough to make the floor rumble under Jude's feet.

"Okay then," he said. He went back to cleaning up, oddly unfazed. The outburst wasn't aimed at him. He was just the convenient target standing between Tej and a craptastic situation filled with a world of pain.

Jude ran a damp hand through his hair, sighing. "Christ, man…"

He picked up his phone and texted Tej: *I'm sorry.*

Read appeared beneath the text bubble, but Tej didn't respond. Jude let him be and dialed Mireille's number.

"Hey, I heard the news," he said. "I'm so sorry."

"Oh, God, thank you," she said. Her voice was a little shrill but she wasn't crying.

"Can I do anything? Do you need help getting a flight? A ride to the airport?"

"No, my girlfriend came over, she's arranging all that. I'm just kind of wandering around in a daze."

"What about Samson?"

"Oh. Um…"

"I can take him."

"Would you? We can drop him off on the way to the airport."

"That's miles out of your way. I'll come get him."

"Jude, you are a prince."

"It's not a problem." He reached for a pen and paper. "Tell me, what's the name of the funeral home?"

He called a flower shop and had a bouquet sent. "No, no card," he told the florist.

On the way to Mireille's apartment, he stopped at a chocolatier and bought a quarter pound of dark-dipped apricots. Because they were Mireille's favorite and because Tej wouldn't want Jude to show up somewhere empty-handed.

When Mireille opened her cabinets and fridge and put out plates, Jude didn't protest, knowing hospitality comforted her like prayer. He sat at her table and Samson climbed into his lap.

"Remember no grapes, no chocolate," Mireille said, pouring mint tea into cups.

"I'll just have to feed you love," Jude said, cupping the dog's handsome face in his palms. He hesitated, then said, "Tej kind of stormed out. He's not answering texts or calls."

Mireille sat down, sighing. "I'm not surprised. In any tense situation or crisis, he'll go extremely silent and extremely solitary. It's what he does. Ever since he was little. He copes by being quiet."

"Tej, quiet?" Jude said.

He expected laughter but Mireille's face was full of sadness as she nodded. "Has he told you about Lebanon?"

"About the war and when you came to the States? I know the general story. I know your brother Raymond was killed, and your little sister."

"Lulu was killed the day we were supposed to leave Beirut."

Their father had already left for the States, Mireille told him. Securing sponsorship and passage and paperwork. Salome Khoury would follow with her five remaining children. Tej was seven. Lulu was six.

"They were only eleven months apart," Mireille said. "Each thought the sun rose and set on the other."

The morning they were due to leave Beirut, the Khourys' house in Achrafiyeh took a direct hit from Syrian bombers.

"Lulu was blown apart," Mireille said. "Literally. Her dismembered body landed in Tej's lap. They had to pry it out of his arms."

"Fuck," Jude said softly. "The dog."

Mireille's beautiful eyebrows raised. "You know about that? How he fabricated a false memory of holding a dog?"

Jude nodded, conscious of Samson's warm, loyal weight in his arms and lap. He imagined it cold, dead and lifeless. Limbless.

"He didn't speak for two years," Mireille said. "In any language. Didn't make friends at school or in the neighborhood. He stuck to my father like a burr and Papa was so gentle with him. He took Tej along everywhere. To work. Errands. Room to room in the house. Always saying, 'It's all right, Tim. You don't have to talk unless you want to. You talk when you're ready. You'll feel better about talking someday. You keep me company. It's nice to be quiet together.'"

Not many people call me Tim these days, Tej had said. *I like you being one of them.*

I love that you call Tim only when you're looking for me.

"I didn't know he and your father were that close at one point," Jude said.

"After Raymond died, Tej was my father's only son. All the clichés—his pride and joy, apple of his eye. It took a long time for Tej to find his voice again and when he decided to tell the most important thing about himself, my father threw him out."

"Now he never stops talking," Jude said.

"No. No one and nothing will ever silence him again." She smiled. "He'll come back around. Filled up with piss and vinegar."

"He can come back and be quiet, too."

"Maybe he doesn't believe that yet."

"Maybe I need to be better at letting him know."

Finally Mireille stopped playing with the box of chocolate-dipped apricots and took one out to eat. "You're both so good for each other. I'd feel a lot worse about leaving Tej in Seattle this week if you weren't here."

❧

TEJ CAME BACK, LOOKING like a crumpled candy wrapper. "I'm sorry."

"Stop," Jude said. "You don't have anything to be sorry for."

"No, I apologize. I lost my shit."

"The shit loss was warranted."

Tej looked down at the dog. "Why is Samson here?"

"I took him for Mireille."

Tej looked even more lost.

"I called her. To see if I could do anything. I said I'd take him."

Silence as Tej put that together. He walked to the window and looked out, his back quivering.

Jude slid arms around and rested his head on Tej's nape. "She told me about Lulu. And your dad. How you stopped talking."

Tej nodded.

"I'm so sorry."

They stood quiet and still a long time, Samson leaning against their legs.

"I got a good life," Tej said thickly. "I have no desire to check out. But man, sometimes I wish I was never born."

"Don't say that."

"I didn't ask for this. I didn't ask to be gay. I made a lot of shitty choices in my life but being gay wasn't my decision."

Jude rocked them side to side. "I wish I knew where you were. Those years after you were thrown out. I wish I knew you then. I could've been your friend. I would've been."

"Thank you."

Jude held him tighter. "I'm sorry."

"I talk a big game," Tej said, fingertips lightly touching Jude's wrists. "I want what I want and I go after what I want. But I don't like to...need people."

"I know."

"I've been walking around. Terrified I couldn't come back here. That my big mouth wrecked everything."

"What? No. Come on, man, we know each other better than that."

"I thought I set it all on fire. I was fucking shitting a brick, coming back here to say I was sorry."

"Hey, you came back," Jude said. "Typically this is the point where you throw a grenade before someone else can."

Tej chuckled through his nose. "I still figured the locks would be changed."

"I'm not your father."

He seemed to crumple and shrink in Jude's arms. Jude turned him roughly and crushed him to his chest. "I'm not him. I'm not them. That door stays open, you say whatever the hell you want, whenever you want. I am so fucking sorry about everything."

"I'm so tired, man."

"I know. Come sit down. I'll make you something to eat."

TEJ STAYED MOODY AND distant in the weeks after his mother's death. His clever sass and snark developed a sharper edge. He became a shiv. Jude gathered all his patience and compassion and benignly ignored the pissy attitude, skirting the blade until he began to realize Tej was deliberately going out of his way to goad him.

"Look, do you want to talk about what's wrong," Jude said, "or do you want to bicker about stupid things?"

"Don't shrink my head."

"Why are you always picking a fight with me?"

"I'm not picking a fight."

And round and round it went. Tej was angry all the time. Even angry in bed, topping with an aggression that once made Jude quit in the middle of sex.

"Easy, man," he cried, his body and feelings hurt.

Tej seemed to snap out of it then, going pale as he put hands on Jude and said, "Shit, I'm sorry. I'm sorry, are you all right?"

"I'm fine," Jude said, wincing toward the bathroom. "But God, it's like I don't know who you are lately."

Tej's mood turned inside-out and he went docile and solicitous. Almost cloyingly so. Still not himself to the point where Jude started stretching out his workday longer to avoid the evenings. Checking on his pre-packed bag and passport and confirming where the nearest border was, because perhaps it was time he was going.

Or, he thought, *dot-dot-dot, I be someone else this time. Give this relationship the time, because it's nice and I like it and I like him, even if he's being weird right now.*

He might even be trying to give me a reason to flee. Before I think of one myself.

One night it occurred to him: *He might be wondering if I even notice what he's doing.*

"I see you over there," he said.

At the other end of the couch, Tej looked up from his laptop. "What?"

"I see you."

I see what you're doing.

Tej's brow dropped, the way it always did when he was on the defense. A muscle in his jaw flickered, and then went soft. All of his face went slow and soft. One side of his mouth smiled, but it was his real smile. Back after a long trip.

He lifted a palm. "Hi."

"I see you," Jude said, then went back to his score.

The knotted air between them loosened and let go. They crept back toward each other and Tej finally put some of the pain he hid inside into words.

"I miss my mother," he said. "I've been missing her for a long fucking time."

He didn't get to say goodbye.

He'd always hoped for a reconciliation.

To be perfectly frank, he'd hoped his father would kick off first. "Then she'd be free to see me and talk to me."

"It's such a waste," Jude said.

Tej pressed his mouth into a line and closed his eyes. "I'm sorry about the things I said. About you having two families and feeling sorry for yourself. I didn't mean it. Truth is, I'm jealous."

"It's all right."

"No, it's not."

"I know I talk too much about DNA and the research and all that. If it's hard for you to listen to, I'll dial it back."

"No, that's just it," Tej said. "I wish you'd let me do more."

THE HAVEN WITHIN

*T*EJ TOOK OVER JUDE'S ancestry account, going through the list of DNA matches, the fourth through eighth cousins and the logjam of messages in Jude's inbox.

"How do you want me to word these replies?" Tej said.

"I don't know."

"Generic reply that you're still figuring things out and don't have much to offer but you'll keep in touch?"

Jude sighed. "I hate to lie, but the truth is so fucking complicated."

"The truth is all we gots, my friend." Tej thought a moment, typed something, then turned the screen.

> *Hi, I'm replying on behalf of my partner whose account this is. He was born during the 1973 military coup in Chile and he has more questions than answers right now. We'll be in touch if we discover any definitive information about his birth family. In the meantime, if you know of any relatives who immigrated to Chile from Spain or Italy, please let us know.*

"That's good," Jude said. "Perfect."

"Gives the problem back to them."

"I like the *we* part." Jude ran fingers through Tej's hair and tilted his head back. "Thank you for doing this," he whispered against Tej's mouth.

"Thank you for letting me."

Tej got into it, becoming an amateur geneticist and genealogist. One day Jude found a Post-it stuck to the bottom of the computer screen: a list of surnames in Tej's handwriting.

"What are these?"

"I'm keeping track of the surnames from your DNA matches. At least the ones who had family trees linked."

Jude put the list down, picked it up again. Put it down. He couldn't yet put a *name* on all this. The idea spooked him. Made his feet cold. As Tej's interest increased, Jude became more uncertain and indecisive about making contact with any of the cousins.

And then they were bickering again.

"Jude, come on. You don't have to replace your parents. Whatever you find, you can weave it in. Layer it on top. It's a chapter in the story. And the story is never finished. You're never done, you should never be done."

"I know, man. It just feels like so much to lose."

Day after day, Tej went from platitudes to pronouncements, piling onto Jude's last nerve.

"You haven't lost anything, your family just got bigger. Man, I'd fucking kill for a second chance like you're getting."

"Don't start that guilt trip again," Jude said, tired and snappish tonight.

"Are you going to obscure this or reveal it?"

"Now you're making literary references? Really?"

"Are you going to take a sad song and make it better?"

Jude slammed the refrigerator door. "Do *not* bring the fucking Beatles into this."

"Let it under your skin, then you can begin—"

"Shut up."

"You were made to go out and get it. Stop hiding already."

"Knock it off," Jude cried. "This is my sad song, my skin and my story. I'm fucking sorry about what happened with your family but you can't hitch a ride on mine."

It escalated into a heated shouting match and once again, Tej walked out, not even bothering to close the door behind him. Jude slammed it himself, then went upstairs and banged on the piano for an hour.

Tej texted once: **I'm staying at my place tonight.**

Out of fucks to give, Jude replied: **K.**

He slept fitfully. Waking up to a silent apartment with no mug of coffee on the bedside table filled him with a shamed sadness.

I'm sorry about last night, he texted. **Can we talk?**

Ten lonely minutes passed before Tej replied: **I'll call you later.**

All that long, rainy day, Jude was painfully conscious of his silent phone. Typically he had six or seven texts from Tej before noon. At least one being a proposition or a dick pic. Nothing today.

He missed it.

He had lunch at his usual table at the Utter Chaos Café. Took a picture of the empty chair across from him and texted it to Tej with the caption, **Wish you were her.**

Oops.

HERE, he quickly typed and sent. **Wish you were HERE. Not her. Jesus. I swear I'm not bi. LOL.**

Nothing.

I'm sorry. I miss you.

He'd been out of touch with the guy for less than twenty-four hours, but an uneasy desperation was starting to creep along his limbs.

I feel like shit, he typed. **I'm sorry. I want to talk to you so bad. I want to LISTEN to you, I mean. Call me. Or at least take a picture of you giving me the finger. I deserve it.**

Nothing.

He sighed, hoping the record reflected he tried.

Tej was late getting to Jude's place. Really late. Weirdly late. Then alarmingly late. He wasn't answering his phone. Texts weren't registering a *read* status.

Where are you? Jude typed into the ether, his mind composing all kinds of scenarios. On the kitchen counter, his little TV was turned to the news, showing footage of a horrific car crash in Houghton. A passenger car blew a red light at an intersection by the I-405 overpass and drove into cross traffic at eighty miles an hour. Eleven people were dead. Emergency response and rubbernecking made traffic back up and snarl for miles in all directions.

Maybe Tej was caught in the jam and his phone battery died.

Of course, Tej worked far south of 405 and had three chargers in his car at all times.

Jude knew these things.

Dude, you okay? Where are you?

No answer.

He's disappeared, Jude thought. Then he went cold all over.

Something's wrong.

He paced and tried not to panic as he called around their now-combined circle of friends. Nobody had heard from him.

He kept texting. **Where are you? I'm starting to freak a little.**

He was starting to freak a lot. Something happened. He was sure of it. Something happened to Tej. He was gone. Sick or hurt. Missing.

Disappeared.

The word was like a two-by-four in Jude's chest and he had to get the fast fuck away from that thought.

He picked up the phone again. Thought for a beat, then typed: **Tim. I'm looking for you.**

He paced, feeling like the pupil of a tough, karmic history lesson.

Oh man, Papi, I'm sorry. I get it now. This is what it was like for you, every time I didn't call home or wasn't where I was supposed to be.

Tej knew those things.

He knew them damn well.

Was he doing this on purpose?

"Jesus," Jude said, a hand dug hard in his hair. "Man, you better not be fucking with me right now."

Timothée, he typed, using the full name *with* accent mark, to show he was serious. **I'm looking for you. If you're trying to sabotage this… If you're trying to force something to happen, I'm telling you now—I won't let you. If you don't come home to talk about it, I'm going out there to find you.**

Nothing.

Answer me. Please. Or I'm getting in the car.

A surge of adrenaline in his stomach as *read* popped up beneath the text.

"Motherfucker, what is going on," Jude mumbled, thumbs busy over the keyboard.

I know you read that. Are you all right? Talk to me. What's going on?

He jumped in his skin and nearly dropped the phone when it rang. "Hey," he said. "Where are you?"

A rush of noise.

"Tej?"

"Hi."

"Where are you?"

"Walking home." His voice was utterly monotone, as if Siri were transposing for him.

"What's wrong," Jude said gently. "Talk to me."

"Did you see the news?"

"What news? The accident in Houghton?"

"Yeah. I took the call."

"What call?"

"From the passenger car. The brakes seized up. Or something. They were out of control. They couldn't stop the car. It was accelerating without them."

"Oh my God."

"I took the call."

"Where are you? Come here. Come home."

"They neared that intersection, they were screaming. 'We got a baby with us. We have an infant in the backseat.'"

"Where are y—"

"They couldn't stop the car."

"Tej…"

"They didn't hang up. I couldn't do anything. I heard them go through the light."

"Come here. Come here right now. Or stay there, I'll come get you. Just tell me where you are."

"No one in that car is alive. They found the baby's car seat fifty feet away."

"Tim, where are you?"

"They never hung up. The audio will be out there soon." A string of shrill chuckles. "There's my fifteen minutes of fame, huh? A nine-one-one soundbite on Facebook."

"Hey."

"No one in that car is alive."

Jude picked up his voice and sliced it through the maniacal laughter. "*Hey. Tell me where you are.*"

A long beat of confused silence.

"I'm standing outside?"

Jude strode to the window, pushed aside the curtain. Tej stood across the street, shoulders stooped in his trench coat, phone pressed to his ear.

"What the…?" Jude walked out into the rain, his own phone absurdly at his ear as he crossed the street. He shoved it in his pocket as he stepped onto the curb. "Babe, come here."

Tej stared back at him. "They couldn't stop," he said into his phone.

"It's all right." Jude took the device out of Tej's hand, hung up and put it in his pocket as well. "Come inside now."

He took Tej's hand.

"Come on now. Come inside with me."

His arm stretched out as he began to walk. For a moment it seemed Tej wouldn't follow. But then he did. Stunned and docile.

"Come inside," Jude said, getting an arm around him now. "Today's done. You don't have to do anything anymore."

Once inside, he swiftly turned off the oven, silenced the TV and dimmed the lights. He put Tej in his bed, then made him tea. It went cold on the bedside table as they lay together, Tej shaking uncontrollably in Jude's arms. Teeth chattering, muscles quaking, his fingers in a death grip on Jude's shirt.

"This one got me bad," he whispered.

"I know, I've never seen you like this. Hold onto me."

"I can't stop hearing it. The way they screamed they had a baby."

"Just hold onto me, I got you."

"I couldn't hang up. They were driving into death, they had no choice. I had to stay. I owed it to them."

"You're incredible. I would've hung up and hid. I could never do what you do."

One of Tej's hands made a clawing motion at his ear. "It's like I keep reaching to pull off the headset. I keep trying to shut it off and I can't stop hearing it."

Jude took the hand and tucked it between them. "I got you."

"I feel like I'll never get it out of my mind."

"You will. Turn your head, put your ear on my chest. Like that. Listen to my heart. Okay?"

"I can't."

"Listen to my heart. Focus on the beats. Tap them on my body. Do it."

Tej's fingertips began to drum on Jude's side. Lub-dub. Lub-dub.

"Listen to me breathe," Jude said. "Listen only to my heart."

Lub-dub. Lub-dub.

He inhaled and exhaled slowly, consciously keeping his pulse calm and countable. Pulling Tej into sync with him. Little by little, Tej's body softened and the fingers on Jude's arm went limp.

"I got you," Jude said, rubbing his head. "You're in my house now."

Tej ran his wet face along Jude's shirt and nodded. Jude held him tight, pressing kisses in his hair.

"You're in my house now," he said. "Nothing's allowed to touch you anymore. All that pain is outside, and it'll have to come through me to get to you now."

Tej kept nodding.

"The day's done," Jude said, kissing him. "You can do no more. You're in my house and I take care of you now."

Tej exhaled. "Keep talking to me."

"I don't know anyone better than you," Jude said, wrapping his arms around Tej's head. "You're like a fucking angel out there."

"I feel so bad."

Jude flipped the comforter over them like a giant wing. "Ángel," he murmured into Tej's hair, the Spanish word a downy exhale with no hard edges. "Ángel, estás en casa. Estás en *mi* casa."

This angel wasn't a cherub with a halo but a seraphim with a sword. An avenger. Fighting for people's lives, then coming home broken and bruised, singed feathers dripping behind. Too tired and used-up to even fold his wings back down.

Jude ran a hand down Tej's spine, smoothing invisible feathers. Tucking them back within because today was done and there'd be no more flying or fighting.

You're in my house now.

This was the dogma within the religion of hospitality. It wasn't about food. It was about sanctuary. The haven within a home.

"You're the best person I know," he said. "You don't have to do this day anymore. You just stay here with me."

Curled in Jude's arms, Tej fell into a short sleep. He woke up hungry but didn't want to cook. Jude made him an omelet. Tej ate it quietly. He didn't want to talk. His eyes were shadowed and every line in his body drooped with exhaustion. He fell back into bed, folding Jude's arms around him from behind.

He twitched violently in his sleep once. Mumbled something that sounded like, "It's the color darker than black."

"What, babe?" Jude said.

But Tej was asleep again.

Jude held him all night, his arms moving through the years of Tej's life, starting with the little boy in the pitch-dark bomb shelter. The child who transformed his sister's dismembered body into a dog he could hold. The teenager mistrustful of anything good in his life, quick to sabotage before anyone or anything else could. The young adult thrown out of his home, into the color darker than black, unable to judge the sound of joy from the sound of terror, only the absolute value removed from normal.

Jude fell asleep holding this man who wouldn't be silenced. Who wouldn't show up empty-handed. Who answered the calls for help and refused to abandon a family driving straight into death. The man who poured a glass of water if you dropped by for six seconds because *you are welcome here* wasn't lip service.

He woke in the wee hours, his arms still holding all of Tej's life, all his facets and fears, knowing now he never wanted to let it go.

This is what I want.

This is my house and when he's in it, it's a home.

This is my story and he's part of it.

This is me, who is better because of him.

"Timothée?"

He was soft and still, his breath a whisper on Jude's chest.

"Tim?"

Tej's chin tilted up. His lips faintly smiled when Jude's fingertips touched them. "Yeah, babe?"

In his sleep-filled voice, it sounded like yahbay. The first word of their invented language.

"I love you," Jude said.

A long moment passed.

"I love you." He ran a thumb along Tej's cheekbone. "I'm so in love with you."

The moment clasped its hands, squeezed them in a tight fist of longing. It trembled, vulnerable and humble.

"See," Jude said, and swallowed hard, scared to death. "See, this is where I hope you love me too."

Tej said nothing.

"Because I know I make it hard, but I really, really want you to love me too."

Tej drew in a breath and let it out in a whispered rush. "Holy shit I love you too."

Jude went limp. The world collapsed and died as they pressed foreheads and palms together. "Whenever you tell me I'm good, it makes me want to be better. Not make it so hard."

"It's easy," Tej said. "So much other shit is hard but baby, this is so easy."

"You're the best person I know."

They were in each other's arms then, hands crawling through their clothes and sliding along their skin. It was a fast, fierce loving. Savagely tender and when Jude came, he *arrived*. Burst forth into his life with a mighty *I am here.*

This is my house.

You are my home.

Holding Tej tight, Jude shivered into stillness, feathery yellow patterns swirling behind his closed eyes. "Estás en mi casa."

"Eres tan bueno." His arms crossed over Jude's back, hands in his hair. They rolled down and curled into each other again, drowsy chuckles softening into sighs.

"Promise me something," Jude said.

"Anything."

"When you have another day like this, and you will, you come home to me. Or you tell me where you are and I'll come get you. All right?"

"All right."

"I don't just want to be your lover. I want to be your home. Your nine-one-one. I'm your call now. You make it and I will answer."

Tej's lips brushed his one more time. "Where am I again?"
Jude held his hands. "You're in my house."

⸺

WHEN JUDE TRUDGED INTO the bathroom the next morning, two Post-its were stuck on the mirror.

> *"At first I did not love you, Jude; that I own"*
> —*Thomas Hardy, Jude the Obscure*
>
> *"At last I do love your ass, Jude; that I also own."*
> —*Tej the Out There*

THE PRUNES

*T*EJ STOOD BEHIND JUDE at the dresser mirror, reaching arms around to fix his bow tie. "Nervous?" he asked.

Jude's shirt collar fit perfectly but he still felt like he was choking. "Yes."

"You're going to kill it."

"If I don't drop dead first."

"Look at my boo. Making his world premiere."

Jude exhaled slowly, trying to calm his heart. After months of Giosué making jokes about knowing people in the bad sushi business, he'd finally called in a favor: the undefeated Dae-Hyun Cho was felled by a vicious stomach bug. Jude was going on in his place. He'd be playing in the pit for *Ballet Imperial* and *Raymonda Variations*, then he'd be onstage for Jerome Robbins' *Dances at a Gathering*.

He better not fuck this up.

"You are nineteen kinds of gorgeous," Tej said, brushing his hands out along Jude's shoulders and down his arms. "When this tux is on the floor tonight, you'll be twenty kinds."

Blushing, Jude bumped back against him. "My folks will meet you in the lobby. The tickets are under your name at the box office." He exhaled a final time and put on his glasses.

Tej handed him his spare specs. "Keep these nearby. Don't take any chances."

"Thanks."

"Do not break a leg. And do not think about me sitting in the audience commando."

Rocketing through the pre-show jitters, Jude tried not to think of anything but the music. Filing into the pit with the other musicians, he tried not to second-guess himself. He adjusted the stand and his reading light, checked to make sure the TV monitor showing the stage was perfectly in his field of vision. For most of *Ballet Imperial*, he'd be watching the screen, not the conductor, shaping the music to the principal dancers. Someone might be ahead of the music with adrenaline. Someone else might be lagging behind from an injury, or just having an off night. They might misjudge their spacing or timing and need a phrase stretched a few beats to cover. Jude knew how. He knew these scores. He knew these dancers. He knew what to do.

And there would be zero chance of him falling backward off a platform.

The conductor entered the pit to generous applause. He bowed his head in thanks before turning to the orchestra. Just before giving the downbeat, his gaze caught Jude's and he winked.

Jude's nerves were stretched and screaming right until he reached the first solo passage of *Ballet Imperial.* Then, as happened once before, on a long-ago night against a chain link fence, he left himself. But instead of his mind fleeing the scene, his body quietly stepped aside and got out of the way. His hands, arms and feet disappeared. His entire consciousness narrowed to the distance between the piano stand and the monitor, framed by the dark edges of his glasses. Notes and dancers. Music and movement.

Time and place slid out of context. When the ballet ended and applause filled the theater, Jude stared down at his fingers still on the keys, wondering who the hell had been playing for the past half hour.

The gorgeous Hungarian piano solo in *Raymonda Variations* came out of his hands like a gypsy lament. The female principal smiled at Jude in the monitor and though he knew it was a trick of the eye, he smiled back, making the solo into a pas de deux. The ballerina took three curtain calls and during intermission, found Jude backstage and kissed him.

Then it was *Dances at a Gathering*, and from his seat at the onstage Steinway piano, Jude slipped back in time to parties from his youth, when he created instant, smiling community from a single pop tune. He played eighteen Chopin pieces now, composed and confident among friends singing along with their bodies. Halfway through the ballet, a piece of his sheet music floated to the floor. A smile stretched his face as his hands played on from memory.

"Let it go," he whispered to his page turner.

Something had to fall down tonight.

And it wasn't me.

The cast took bow after bow, then the dancers beckoned Jude onstage to bow with them. Ushers walked out with flowers, including a bouquet for Jude. He scanned the auditorium and its ovation but couldn't pick out his people.

They were obscured.

But he knew they were there.

AFTER A WHIRLWIND OF kissing and hugging and congratulations, Jude and Tej went out for a late supper and drinks at the bar where they met the first time. Coasting on the glory, Jude got thoroughly plowed.

Puh-LOUD.

He pulled Tej outside to the brick wall so they could recreate their first kiss.

"I love you so fucking much," he said into Tej's neck.

Tej, only slightly less wrecked, laughed into Jude's hair. "You are so in my house right now."

They went home, had disgustingly great sex and passed out. Jude woke up hungover and parched, but satisfied with the previous night's accomplishments and smug about how good his tux looked on the floor. Tej made him a giant bloody Mary. He sucked it down, chased it with two Advil and a liter of water, then went back to bed and slept the day away.

"Get up," Tej called around three o'clock. "Otherwise you'll be bouncing off the walls at midnight."

"Stop talking."

"Want another bloody?"

"I said, stop talking."

Tej opened the drapes. "Why don't you get up and go to the gym. You'll feel better."

Jude opened one eye. "Why don't you go scrub your ass so I can eat it?"

Tej laughed and left the bedroom. "I'm going food shopping. Try to find your humanity before I get back."

"Hey." Jude sat up. "You're going to waste that line? That was a *great* line."

"One of your best, babe," Tej called as the front door closed.

He lay back down, hurt. "Scrub your ass so I can eat it. That was a fantastic line, I can't believe he didn't hop on that line..."

He hoisted himself vertical, eyeballs clanging. He pulled on gym clothes and went to work out as gently as possible. After sweating out the last of the alcohol and showering off the sweat, he walked back into his kitchen a presentable human. And a hungry one.

"Don't go snacking," Tej said from the stove. "This will be ready in half an hour."

"I just need a little something-something," Jude said, ravenous. "I'm about to eat my arm off."

"I got those almonds you like. They should be right behind the bag of prunes."

"Prunes?" He took the bag out of the cabinet and waved it teasingly.

"What?"

"Who eats prunes willingly?"

"I do. Prunes are the bomb."

"That's one way of putting it."

"You have to look beyond that aspect. They're an extremely elegant delicacy."

"They're a broom."

"Take the fucking almonds and get out of my kitchen."

Jude went upstairs to practice. Slowly the townhouse began to smell rather delicious. A heady, spiced aroma beckoned coyly from around corners, refusing to be identified or ignored.

"Dude, are you baking something?" Jude called down the stairwell.

"No."

"What smells so good?"

"You'll find out."

They ate on the coffee table. After the plates were cleared, Tej came back to the couch with a little dish. He held it mysteriously out of sight and said, "Open your mouth and close your eyes."

"No way. That's how your dick ends up in my mouth."

"C'mon. You know if I'm going to put *that* in your mouth, I want you watching."

Jude did know. With a blush and a sigh, he tilted his head toward Tej, eyes closed and mouth open.

A cold spoonful. Vanilla ice cream, followed by a warm, spiced chewiness that filled his mouth like a glug of heavy port. Heated with ginger, heady with cinnamon, syrupy through the clean vanilla.

He opened his eyes. "Wow, what is that?"

"That?" Tej said, sitting down. "Is a stewed prune. A la mode."

"No way."

Tej ate a spoonful, eyes fixed on the TV.

Jude ran his tongue along his teeth, looking for the last drops of syrup. "That's amazing."

"Mm."

"Let me have another bite."

"No."

"No?"

"You don't deserve prunes. You hurt their feelings."

"Please?"

"No."

Jude rolled off the couch to kneel between Tej's feet. "Please?"

Tej leaned to look around Jude's body, eating deliberately. Deftly he held the bowl and spoon out of reach as Jude made a grab for the dessert. "No, you don't get any more."

"I was wrong," Jude said.

"Mm."

"Utterly misinformed. I made a snap judgment and I apologize unreservedly. To you *and* the prunes. May I have another taste?"

Leaning back, knees wide, Tej slowly pulled the spoon along his tongue. "What's in it for me?"

"You get to be the plate."

Tej's brows flicked upward as he scooped a bit of dessert and held it out. "Set the table."

Tej fed him. He fed on Tej. Sweet and rich. Cold and warm. Spice and skin.

"Wow, I love prunes," Jude said, filling his mouth again and again.

"I love you," Tej said softly.

Jude's phone rang.

"Swallow before you answer that," Tej said, still breathing hard, eyes closed.

"I'm not answering it," Jude said, pulling his shirt over his head.

"Could be the theater. Needing you to go on."

He unbuttoned his jeans. "Don't care."

Tej's eyes glanced sideways, then he sat up a little. "Dude, it's a Chilean number."

Jude scowled, took the phone and swiped at the screen. "Diga."

"¿Juleón Tholet?"

"Sí."

"It's Isabella Eberhoff with the Medical-Legal Institute. I have some news."

Jude sat back on his heels. "News?"

"About your lab results."

Both his head and body were trying to exit the scene simultaneously. He licked his lips. "All right."

"So the lab matched your—"

"Wait," he said, putting a hand on Tej's leg. "Do you speak English?"

"Of course."

Jude switched. "I want my partner to hear this, I'm putting it on speaker."

"No problem," she said. "Can you hear me?"

"Hi," Tej said, smiling as he tucked himself away and zipped his jeans. "We can hear you."

"So, Juleón, the lab team matched your DNA sample to human remains found at Patio Twenty-Nine."

"You mean the lot in Santiago's General Cemetery?"

"That's right."

"What do you mean, matched?"

She spoke slowly. "Your DNA markers match with two other profiles in our database. Both were taken from remains found at Patio Twenty-Nine. Indicating you are related."

"All right."

"Are you breathing?"

"I think so. Related how, who are these other profiles?"

"Jude," she said. "They're your parents."

Tej clapped a hand over his mouth, eyes wide.

Jude sat on the floor. "Say again?"

"Your biological parents were among the remains recovered from Patio Twenty-Nine."

His heart turned sideways. He looked down, expecting to see his chest bulging. "Are you sure?"

She laughed. "Yes. Ninety-nine-point-six percent sure, to be precise."

"You mean… This is real?"

"It's real. Markers on your Y-chromosome and mitochondrial DNA conclude you are the biological son of Eduardo Gabriel Penda and—"

"Oh my God, wait," Jude said, scrambling to his feet, spinning in circles, looking for a piece of paper.

"—and María Clementina Vilaró," Isabella said. "Take a breath."

"Oh my God," Jude said. "Wait, say that again. Say those names again. Wait, let me get a pen. Wait."

"Take your time."

"Oh my God."

"Breathe, honey." Tej handed him pen and paper and turned around so Jude could write against his back.

Eduardo Gabriel Penda, Jude wrote. *María Clementina Vilaró.*

"Women traditionally keep their maiden names in Chile," Isabella said. "She would've gone by Vilaró. Or perhaps Vilaró de Penda."

Jude stared at the names, his heartbeat at his temples, peripheral sparkling with yellow glitter. "Is there any other information about her? I mean, about them?"

"Yes. But perhaps you'd like to hear it all from your brother?"

Prunes and ice cream churned in Jude's stomach. "My... What?"

Tej's mouth slowly shaped "Oh my fucking God."

"These remains were identified last year by the Pendas' son, Alejandro, who escaped to the United States. His profile with us includes a statement of release."

"Meaning what?"

"Meaning if you still have that pen, I have permission to give you his contact information."

THE NAMES

"JUDE, THIS IS JUST unbelievable," Penny heard herself say. Her face was numb and her lips tingled. As if she'd been slapped.

Cleon leaned on his elbows, hovering over the phone on the kitchen table. "It's a miracle," he said slowly.

"I can't take it in," Jude said. "I'm shaking."

"Did you call him? Did you talk to him?"

"No, I called you first."

To say goodbye, Penny thought.

A harsh scrape as she pushed back from the kitchen table and walked to the sink, trying to get away from herself. Backed into a corner of the countertop, arms crossed tight over her middle. Cleon's hands had slid on either side of his head, fingers in his white hair. He lifted his head with a deep breath, face wet and shining. He reached a hand to her, beckoning.

"Are you there?" Jude's voice called.

"We're right here," Cleon said, his hand reaching further. He drew Penny tight to his side and put both arms around her waist. He was trembling.

"I don't know how this makes you feel," Jude said. "I don't even know how I feel right now."

Penny forced herself to say something. "It's unbelievable."

All the while thinking, *It's over.*

It's over.

It's official.

He's not our child.

She didn't think it would really turn out this way. The odds were stacked against them. The thread of Jude's DNA would never slip through the eye of the needle hidden in Chile's database. Not this easily and not this soon.

"Can I tell you their names?" Jude asked, sounding so small and tentative.

Penny put a hand beneath her collarbones.

Her name?

The question hit dead center of her chest and her heart closed around it, cradling it close like a treasure. Her head cleared, she could feel her face again.

She has a name.

For months she'd been contemplating a woman at a kitchen counter, staring at papers and pictures spread before her. Or perhaps staring at nothing, because she had nothing to go on in her endless, answer-less quest to find out what happened to her baby.

That woman had a name.

That woman was dead. She and her husband murdered. Their bodies interred in a mass grave, marked with crude metal crosses reading "N.N." No name. It was a defiant act of resistance by Catholic cemetery workers. Literally forced to bury their government's atrocities, they refused to accept anything was normal about it. They marked the graves, hoping for a time when the bodies could be reunited with the names.

The time was now.

And. Dot-dot-dot. Who are you going to be?

Penny moved from the circle of Cleon's arms and sat again.

She has a name.

You've held her image in your head all this time. Now hold her name. Hold it tight. This is your compañera. Your sister-compatriot. Your she-wolf in arms. You are her surrogate.

She drew the phone closer to her. Pulled Jude closer to her.

None of this is your fault. You're not responsible. But you can honor the responsibility of knowing her name.

"Yes," she said. "Tell us."

CLE◉N

Umberto Alva slumps against *your shoulder. He's only nineteen years old. He's afraid he won't live to see twenty. His weight pains you—you're sure your ribs are broken and the other day you coughed up blood. You can barely lift your arms after yesterday's session when you were hung by your wrists. Umberto lifts them himself and drapes them across his shoulders. Thus you hold him, humming John Lennon's "Imagine" like a lullaby. Umberto can't hear you—his interrogators beat his ears with their open hands so often, he's gone deaf. But his head rests above your heart and he can feel the vibration of your voice as you warble Uncle Louis's lazy version.*

"Imagínate la la…"

Your other compañeros slump around the cell. Out of the original six, four are left, so everyone can sit. Everyone still wears the clothes they came in, but no shoes. Footwear serves a different purpose in here: you shit and piss in your shoes and throw the waste out the window. You're lucky you were wearing good, solid shoes the day you were arrested. You're lucky you have a window.

The Villa Grimaldi is never silent. Weeping, moaning, shouting, shrieking. You didn't know a human voice had such a range. You never guessed agony and terror could manifest in so many sounds. If a man is electrocuted hard enough, he screams like a woman. If a woman is raped long enough, she bellows like a man. And children…they don't sound human anymore.

They're calling you.

It's time to go.

…

…

…

And you're gone.

THE SAME

*J*UDE CALLED SERENA AND Giosué, who fell out of their chairs. He called Hewan and Bert, who screamed at the news. He texted Aiden, who replied: **Wow. Cool!**

"Wow, cool?" Tej said. "That's it?"

"Cool with an exclamation point," Jude said. "Which means it was sent with a world of heightened emotion and excitement behind it."

Tej laughed. "You know him best."

Which made Jude pause and think, then dial his brother's number to talk personally. But, as expected, he got voicemail. Aiden didn't like answering the phone.

Jude knew these things.

"Hey, it's me," he said. "I wanted to talk to you. I need to hear your voice. Call me when you can, po? I miss you. ¿Vale, hueón? Hasta luego."

He hung up and resumed pacing with his scrap of paper. It was ten o'clock at night on the east coast, where Alejandro Penda lived. Jude couldn't call him now.

Could he?

"Uh, yeah," Tej said. "Shit doesn't start happening until ten."

But Jude didn't. Not right away. He paced around, staring at the names.

Eduardo Gabriel Penda.

María Clementina Vilaró.

He read them again and again but couldn't connect. He sat at the computer and entered the names carefully into the blank boxes of his family tree. Making a little grouping of four. Mother. Father. Two sons.

"Penda," he said under his breath, trying it on.

My last name is Penda. This is my DNA. This is my family.

What would they have named me? Who was I supposed to be?

He touched his brother's box. Alejandro Penda. He imagined himself at a party, introducing his sibling.

Hi, I'd like you to meet my brother, Alejandro.

Ten-thirty and he still hadn't called. He kept whirling the name around his mouth. The same way he got fixated on Giosué all those months ago.

Did his brother go by Alejo? Alé? The Americanized Alex?

What did he look like?

He paced, mumbling, "I can't believe it" over and over.

"Dude," Tej said. "Call and you'll believe it."

"What do I say?"

"Introduce yourself. Say, 'This sounds crazy but I think I'm your brother.' If he hangs up on you, call Isabella back and get *her* to call him and verify everything. Or hell, I'll call him. Give me the phone."

"You are so fucking brave, man."

"You want me to? I will. Give it."

"Yeah. No." Jude picked up his cell. "No, I'll call." His finger literally shook as he punched in the number. "Christ, look at me."

"I can't take my eyes off you."

Jude squeezed his eyes shut as he held the phone to his ear. A little bit away, as if it were on fire.

"Holy shit," he mouthed without a sound.

One ring.

Two.

Oh my god oh my god oh my god oh my god…

The third ring broke in half. "Alex Penda."

He's real, Jude thought.

"Hello?"

"Hi," Jude said. "Alex, this is…" His voice stopped, swiftly as if his vocal chords were sliced. His mouth moved but nothing came out.

I am going to pass the fuck out.

"I'm sorry, I think you got cut off," Alex said. "Who is this?"

"My name is Juleón Tholet. I got your number from Isabella Eberhoff at the Medical-Legal Institute in Santiago."

Silence.

"Chile," Jude added, stupidly. "She called me because… Because you and I…"

The silence continued on the other end of the line. It was so quiet it was *dead.*

"I mean," Jude said. "She said our DNA is…the same?"

"The same," Alex said.

"Our DNA matches."

"Okay." A beat. "Wow."

"I know. She gave me your number. I mean, she had permission to."

"I signed the release."

"That's right."

"So. Wait. Are you a cousin?"

"No, I think I'm your brother."

Tej grabbed his hand hard. The silence on the line was deader than dead now and through it, Jude's heart pounded like a cannon.

"Are you there?" he said.

"Oh my God," Alex said.

"I submitted my DNA. She called me a little while ago saying I had a match."

"Oh my God, wait. Wait. You're saying that... Wait, what did she say?"

"She said my DNA showed I was... I mean, I don't understand all the technical words but it's the Y-chromosome that matches. You and me, our Y-chromosomes match. And both of ours match the male bone fragments you identified as your father."

"Oh my God."

"Which means your father is my father."

"Are you fucking *kidding* me?"

"Isabella said you identified the bones last year."

"Yes."

"Those are your parents?"

"Yes."

"So...that means I'm your brother?"

Alex's voice cracked open. "Yes."

"I'm your brother? This is real?"

"Oh my God..."

"This is happening?" Jude stood up. Then sat again.

"Wait," Alex said. "Oh my God, I don't believe this. Wait. Jesus Christ, what's your name?"

"Juleón. Jude. I'm called Jude."

"Jude."

"Yes."

"Where are you?"

"In Seattle."

"I mean, where *were* you?"

"With my parents."

His voice raised. "How did *they* get you?"

"We're still trying to figure that out. They think I was switched."

"What do you mean, switched?" Open hostility in the voice now, making Jude panic and scramble to his feet again. Tej was scribbling on a sheet of paper and holding it up.

KEEP IT SIMPLE.

"Listen, let me start from the beginning," Jude said, pacing. "My father is a Chilean citizen. His parents were Austrian Jews and they fled Hitler in the late thirties. He was born in Santiago. My mother is Canadian. Her father was a civil engineer and he worked on designing Santiago's metro system, so she ended up living there and working at the Canadian embassy. She met my father, they married in seventy-two and my mother was seven months pregnant when Pinochet took over."

"Mine too," Alex said, his voice still tight.

"My father was arrested during the coup and… Wait, do you speak Spanish?"

With a bark of laughter, Alex cried, "¡Hueón, por supuesto que hablo español!"

Of course I speak Spanish, you moron.

Feeling a little hysterical, Jude switched. "My dad was in the Estadio de Chile, then he was transferred to the Villa Grimaldi for six weeks. My mother got roughed up by soldiers and one of them rifle-butted her in the head. She went into labor and gave birth to me on the floor of her living room. Wait, not me. The baby we thought was me. I'm sorry, my brain is reeling. I still can't extricate myself out of this story. She gave birth in her house and then was taken to the hospital. Her skull was fractured and she had a severe concussion. When she was finally conscious and lucid again, they brought the baby in to her. But it was me."

"Okay."

"Do you understand? She gave birth to her baby at her house, but left the hospital with me. Not knowing I wasn't their son. She had no idea her biological child was…"

"Where?"

"We don't know. We didn't know any of this until last October, when we did DNA kits for fun. My sister won them in a silent auction, we did it for laughs, already knowing what the results would be. But when the kits came back, my parents, sister and brother all matched up, but I was this crazy blend of Italian and Spanish. My father is Jewish, but I had no Jewish ancestry at all. None. We thought it was a mistake. We took the test all over again but it came back the same way. Nothing matched. They weren't my real parents."

"Jesus Christ."

"And then," Jude said. "Oh God, there's so much to tell."

He looked helplessly at Tej, who, lost in the Spanish, just held up his sign higher.

"My father was fucked up in the Villa Grimaldi. Six weeks of beatings and torture. The DINA guards dumped him in the street and drove over him with their jeep. They broke every bone in both his legs. He never walked normally again."

"Jesus, I'm so sorry," Alex said, the tight, angry knot of his voice finally unwinding. "I don't understand how this... Never mind, go on. Your father was released, what then?"

"We got on a ship in Valparaiso and sailed back to Vancouver, where my mother's father lived. We stayed there until I was seventeen and then we moved to Seattle. This was my life story. I had no reason to think otherwise. None of us did. When my parents found all this out, when they found out their baby was taken or switched or given away, they—"

"But where *is* their baby?"

"We don't know. We only started looking. I just found you tonight."

"Oh my God, what the fuck happened?"

"Where are you, where am I calling?"

"New York. I live about two hours north of Manhattan."

"How did you get out of Chile?"

"I had an uncle in the States already. We had our papers all ready to leave but then my father was arrested. First him, then my mother. Our mother. Jesus, I can't get my head around this."

"Right? I'm freaking the fuck out. So, they were arrested but what happened to you?"

"I hid in the apartment."

"Alone?"

"Alone."

"How old were you?"

"Ten. Almost eleven. Papi got out somehow. He came back for me and took me to the American embassy. He made me leave without him because he needed to look for my mother. I never saw him again. Never knew what became of him and Mami until last year when my DNA matched up with the remains they found at Patio Twenty-Nine."

"This is *crazy*. Are you married?"

"I'm married. My wife's name is Valerie and we have a daughter."

"I have a niece?" Jude practically shouted it, with no idea why this struck him as miraculous.

"I can't fucking believe it," Alex said. "I've been wondering about you my whole life."

"I had no idea. I'm sorry." As the words left his mouth Jude was swamped, *inundated* with a remorse that didn't seem to belong to him, yet it squatted in his heart and took up defiant residence.

"Wondering if that baby survived," Alex was saying. "If I had a sibling in the world who didn't even…"

"Alejandro, lo siento." Jude sank to one knee. Then to both. "I didn't know."

"I can't believe this."

"I'm sorry." He couldn't understand why he felt like an utter failure.

Tej crawled over. He put his back to the couch and pulled Jude between his knees like a bobsledder, squeezing Jude between his legs and holding him tight against his chest.

"I got you," he whispered. "It's all right."

"Alejandro, lo siento mucho," Jude said, and then he couldn't anymore. He wasn't crying, he was just unable to go on. His fingers opened and the phone nearly toppled. Tej caught it just in time.

"Hi, my name's Tej, I'm…" A pause. "Alex?" Another pause. "Hello?"

A long pause now. And then Tej started laughing softly. "Hi, Val. It's nice to meet you. I know, right? It's unbelievable. I know. I'm crying, too. No, no, tell him to take his time. We could use a minute over here and— What's that? A minute *and* a drink, no shit. This is incredible…"

 THE SHAPE

*P*ENNY CRIED WHEN JUDE called her back. She put Cleon on speaker and he cried.

Serena cried. Hewan and Bert cried.

Tej was a *mess.*

Jude was dry-eyed and numb. And wondering what the hell was wrong with him when an email came in from Alex.

> *Jude,*
>
> *Last year, when I got the call that ~~my~~ our parents' remains had been identified, I thought I knew what "surreal" meant. When I read the DNA report, when I finally held those urns and touched those ashes, I thought nothing would ever shock or surprise or shake me up again.*
>
> *Wrong.*
>
> *This is the most surreal night of my life. I can't stop shaking. I can't stop saying "I can't believe it." I keep walking around the house, twitching and telling the furniture, "I can't believe it." The dog is looking at me like I'm nuts and Val's putting orange cones around my desk.*
>
> *God, I don't even know how to explain what's in my head tonight. I've been wondering about you my whole life. If I'd had the first clue what happened when you were born, I would've never stopped looking. I would've taken the world apart. But of course, I had no clues. I couldn't begin to look. But I never stopped wondering.*

You have been with me every day of my life since I was eleven. I rarely talked about it, rarely voiced it aloud, but every day, I imagined you. Both as a brother and a sister. I wondered if you were out there. I wondered if you knew who you were or if you had even the slightest feeling you didn't quite belong where you were. Mostly, I just hoped to God you were all right. Every day of my life. And it's like a whole new life starts tonight.

I don't know if you'll ever know what it means to finally find you. I can't believe it.

I cannot. Fucking. Believe. It.

Attaching a picture. Christ, it was like I was creating a dating profile, the way I agonized about which one to send. Finally Val threw me out of the chair and picked it herself. Story of my life. I can't wait for you to meet her and Deane. I can't wait to meet you. You.

Holy shit, you. Are you real??

This is insane.

Please send me your picture. I won't sleep until I see your face. Who am I kidding, I might not ever sleep again...

A JPEG file was attached.

"Holy shit, look at that," Tej said.

At the first sight of his brother, Jude didn't burst into tears. He *exploded*. His entire life—his birth, his name, his height, his near-sighted blue eyes, his dimples, his broken bones, his blood, his genes, his DNA... It all socked him like a punch to the heart and came pouring out his eyes and nose. He cried until he thought his face would fall off.

"Look," Tej was still saying, one forearm crossed around Jude from behind, the other pointing wildly. "Would you fucking look at that?"

Jude's gaze was clogged with tears but he had no trouble seeing himself within Alex's face. In the shape of the forehead and the line of the eyebrows. How the ears stuck out a little. The dimples. The tilt of the eyes behind glasses and the curl of the smile.

My God, it's my smile.

He opened the other attachments. Snapshots in black and white or faded Kodachrome. Then Jude fell apart all over again, trying to simultaneously reach out and embrace his people while holding onto the loyalty to his people.

Constantly choosing from a dropdown menu of vindication and guilt, joy and sadness, wonder and shame.

Here was Clementina Vilaró, dimpled and devilish.

"Her smile," Jude cried. "Look at it. Look at her. Both me and Alex have our mother's smile."

Mami, I'm sorry, not you, you're my mother you're always my mother, but...

Here was Eduardo Penda, tall and bespectacled, with an air of shyness.

"Look at him. Look at his eyes. That's my father. I look like just like my *father.*"

Papi, my compañero, you're my only father and I don't want to be anyone else's son, but...

But.

But look.

Look at them.

"I can see it," Jude said. Over and over, picture after picture. "I can see me. Jesus fucking Christ, do you see it?"

"I see it."

As they gaped over the shots, another email came in from Alex: *This is the one and only family portrait. August 1973. (I'm ten.)*

In the attached picture, Alex stood between his parents, mugging for the camera. Eduardo's arm was around his shoulders. His head tilted a little toward Clementine, who was pregnant.

"Oh my God." Jude barely breathed as his finger reached to touch that round belly. An overhead light switched on, lighting up an Andean Mother Earth in a diamond sky. Her arms legs and hair swirling around the glowing orb of life she carried within.

"Jesus, that's you," Tej said.

Over and over, Jude's fingertip traced the arc of his mother's stomach.

There I am. I'm in there. I'm right there.

THE BROTHERS

*T*HEY TALKED EVERY DAY. Emails and phone calls and texts. Pictures going back and forth, life stories told. In between, they endeavored to re-examine the research and the clues and the history, trying to determine where Jude could've been born.

"My father was arrested on October tenth," Alex said. "Our father, I mean."

"Let's just leave the pronouns alone," Jude said. "I won't be offended if you won't. We know who we mean."

"He was arrested and taken to the Estadio Nacional. Four days later, maybe five, the soldiers came in the middle of the night and took my mother. The date is a little fuzzy in my head because I wasn't paying much attention to time."

"Of course not."

"When I tell the story, I say I was in the apartment alone for a week. Was it precisely seven days? I couldn't say. But my father came back and found me. He took me to the embassy and handed me over. I arrived in the States on October twenty-fourth. I had to surrender my Chilean passport when I became an American citizen, but I know for a fact the entry stamp was dated the twenty-fourth. It's on all my legal paperwork."

"The birth date on all my papers is November twenty-fifth," Jude said. "I'm not going to stop celebrating, but I'm trying to accept the fact it might not be my actual birthday."

"I hear you. I'm trying to manage expectations. The chances of us finding a piece of official documentation showing when and where you were born, are slim to none."

"Do you have any knowledge of your parents' whereabouts after you left the country?"

"My father's assistant, Milagros, kept in touch for a while. There was one sighting of Papi back at the Estadio Nacional. And one of my mother at the Villa Grimaldi."

"When was that?"

"Maybe at the very end of November? I definitely remember it being after my first American Thanksgiving. I read the letter from Milagros sitting by a Christmas tree."

They looked it up on the Internet—Thanksgiving 1973 was on November 22nd.

"I could've been already born," Jude said. "Clementina could've given birth to me in the Estadio. Then I was transferred to Hospital del Salvador while she was taken to Villa Grimaldi."

He told Alex about the conversation with Roberta Cáceres, how her mother witnessed a woman give birth in the swimming locker rooms of the Estadio. The recurring nightmare it triggered, with its vivid imagery and pervasive smell of chlorine.

"Or you could've been born in Villa Grimaldi," Alex said. "We just don't know."

"But the Villa is all the way out in La Reina," Jude said. "If I was born there, wouldn't it make more sense for me to be taken to Hospital Militar, which was five minutes away?"

"True," Alex said. "You're right."

Frustration like a beast roared in the silence, constantly upsetting the pieces Jude was trying to assemble into a truth he could live with.

What the hell *happened*?

But then, inevitably, it would occur to one that he was actually, for real, talking to the other.

"I don't believe I found you," Alex would mutter.

Or, "I can't believe this is happening," Jude would say.

They nearly always talked on speakerphone, Alex's family chiming in as they passed through. Tej wandered in and out, interjecting, chatting, contributing. Jude couldn't have made it clearer they were lovers and partners and Alex made no comment, other than to ask how long they'd been together and how they met.

"I want to meet you soon," Alex said. "I want this to happen."

"I might bring Tej with me," Jude said.

"I want him, too."

JUDE AND TEJ WALKED out of the baggage claim and into the throng of
waiting chauffeurs and loved ones. Tej had the video on his phone running.
Jude was sure he was going to pass out any moment. His eyes swept the crowd,
seeing everyone and no one. Then his eyes locked onto teenage girl he recognized from pictures and video calls. With one hand, she held her phone high.
In the other was a hand-lettered sign:

¡¡TIO JULEÓN!!
!!UNCLE JUDE!!
(!!HOLY SHIT!!)

"Dude," Tej mumbled. "This is the most amazing thing I've ever seen in
person."

The girl was flanked on one side by a blonde woman and the other by...

"Oh fuck me," Jude whispered, walking toward his brother, now the only
face he saw. A stunned, half-open mouth. Eyes swimming with tears. Dimples
winking in and out of sight. Arms held wide and glasses dangling from one
clenched fist.

"Por Dios, no me lo creo," he said, shaking his head.

Look how tall he is, Jude thought stupidly. He let his backpack topple off his
shoulder onto the ground and walked straight into the embrace.

"Oh my God," Alex said, dropping his glasses and holding Jude's head in his
hands. "Jesus Christ, I don't believe it."

"I can't believe it," Jude said, tossing aside his own glasses now.

Two pairs of myopic eyes stared. They kissed each other's faces—left cheek,
right cheek, left again. Then stood wrapped in arms, hands fisted tight in jackets
and shirts.

I can feel your heartbeat, Jude thought.

"I knew it," Alex whispered. "I knew you were alive. I knew you were somewhere."

"¿En serio?"

"No." A sniffling laugh. "I'm full of shit, I had no idea. I believed it was possible but I figured the chances were nil."

"I can't believe it and I'm standing right here."

*I can feel your heartbeat. A heart pumping blood. Blood filled with cells. Cells
containing millions of strands of DNA.*

And all of it matches mine.

303

"I keep thinking about the last time I saw you," Alex said. "I mean, sort of you. After our father was arrested, I slept with Mami in her bed. Right up next to her big belly."

Your heart against my heart. Born of the same woman.

"I'd put my face against it all the time. Hear a million things going on in there. I couldn't see you but I could hear you. That was the last time… Ah, fuck, here I go again. I'm going to be crying for a year and a half, I swear."

Jude squeezed him. "I'm sorry."

"You don't—"

"Just let me be sorry."

"It's not your fault. None of this is your fault."

"I know," Jude said. "I don't understand why I need to say it, but I do."

"It's all right."

"I had no idea. I had no fucking idea who I was."

Jude the Obscure.

"Mine," Alex said, roughly taking Jude's head again and pressing their brows together. "You're mine and I can't believe I found you."

"I didn't know I was lost."

Hidden in plain sight.

"Come meet my wife and daughter."

Deane, Val and Tej stood in a circle of held hands and arms around shoulders, chattering and laughing like they met in kindergarten.

"Cosita, ven aquí," Alex called.

"Holy crap, Dad, you have a mini-me." Deane gave Jude a hug thick with perfume. "Look at him."

"Look at me."

"I'm Deane."

"Hi, Deane," Jude said, swiping his soaked face on his sleeve.

"Her middle name is Vilaró," Alex added.

"And I'm Val," the blonde woman said. "My middle name is Holy Shit."

"We're keeping her," Tej said. "She's my best friend now. Dibs. I touched her."

Val whacked his shoulder as if he were a little brother, then opened arms to Jude. Her embrace smelled more subtle. A hand touched the back of Jude's head as she rocked both of them side to side. "You have no idea," she said. "No idea what this means to him."

"I want to find out."

"I can't thank you enough."

"I didn't do anything."

"You did *the* most important thing." She held him away and mopped the tears dripping down his face again. "You let yourself be found."

⁓

THE TOWN OF GUELISTEN spread like a picture postcard on the east bank of the Hudson River. Alex led a walking tour through the pretty streets, showing Jude the house where their uncle Felipe Penda lived. Followed by the house where Val grew up and where Alex had been taken in after Felipe's death, raised and loved like a son.

"So were you two fooling around in this house?" Tej asked, looking up at the windows.

"No," Val said, as Alex said, "Yes."

"You liar, it was never *in* the house," she said.

"The intentions were in the house," he said. "Totally counts."

"You're so full of shit."

"I love how-we-met stories," Tej said.

Val caught Jude's eye and inclined her head toward Tej. "Where'd you find this one?"

"In a bar."

Tej sighed. "Our story is so boring."

They turned onto the main street, which appeared lifted from a Norman Rockwell painting with its brick buildings, flapping American flags and charming train station. As they walked along, Val pointed out the scale models in each window. Every store and shop had a miniature version of itself, creating a parallel Main Street.

"My mother made these," Val said.

"All of them?" Jude said.

Tej peered closer at an intricate, scaled barber shop model. "She was like a professional…miniaturist? Is that a word?"

"She had a dollhouse gallery on the top floor of that building," Val said, pointing. "Which my great-grandfather built."

"It's called the Lark Building," Alex said. "Val's sister owns it."

They passed Val's place of business, Deane Fine Tailoring. Next door was Lark's Wine Bar & Tapas. Last was a bookshop and coffee bar called Celeste's.

"Named after Great-Aunt Celeste," Val said, opening the door and letting out an indescribable perfume of coffee, chocolate, paper and ink. "This was her shop."

"Val brought me here the day we met," Alex said. "We went out walking the dogs together. I barely spoke English but somehow, we had a whole conversation. Then I came into this place and got all bummed out." He glanced at Jude. "Papi's bookstore was just like this. Tables and comfy chairs and books. A pot of coffee always going. People gathered. Soon as I walked in, I was back in Chile, back with him. I lost it. And I didn't know how to explain."

"He dropped the leash and walked out in tears," Val said. "Of course, I was only twelve, so I took it personally and got really mad at him."

Tej laughed. "Did you follow him out?"

"No, I went home and sulked. But Aunt Celeste came over later that night and brought me a Spanish-English dictionary." She leaned and rubbed her nose against Alex's temple. "My siblings and I kidnapped him, took him out for ice cream and started over."

They sat at the long bar and were served by Val's younger sister Trelawney Lark, a beautiful, elfin woman with cropped blonde-white hair and a captivating, genderless face. Between them in age was their brother Roger.

"Wait," Tej said. "Roger Lark. The Treehouse Guy? On HGTV? *That* Roger Lark?"

"None other," Trelawney said.

"My mother loves that show," Jude said, resisting the umpteenth urge to clarify *mother*.

"We get that a lot," Val said.

"I love him," Tej said. "He's such a lunk. Is he coming to dinner? Say yes."

Trelawney smiled. "Sorry, he's on his honeymoon."

He snapped his fingers and shrugged. "Knew it was too good to be true."

"This place is great," Jude said, spinning on his stool to take in the shop. "Put a piano in here and I'd never leave."

"There's a piano in Lark's," Trelawney said, gesturing toward the wine bar on the other side of the wall. "Come to happy hour tonight and play a set."

So they did, and Jude sat at the keys, taking requests from Meatloaf to the theme from *The Flintstones*. He pulled out all the Billy Joel hits, then played "Hey, Jude" the way he liked it best—with an enthusiastic crowd singing along. Drinks held high, swaying and na-na-ing the vamp, one or two brave souls improvising the falsetto scat line. The whole time, Alex sat right next to him on the bench, with a slightly territorial air. The same way Aiden Tholet, on a long-ago night, claimed the spot next to Jude's body and would not move. Because a brother swearing "I will be there" was no more lip service than Tej declaring, "You are welcome here."

Alex's voice was nicely on pitch and the way he occasionally harmonized seemed unconscious. Jude started a sneaky experiment, telling Alex the key of a song before playing it, casually throwing in music theory as he improvised between ditties. After an hour, he covered Alex's eyes with one hand and played a note. "What's this?"

"C," Alex said.

Jude played another.

"E-flat."

A third.

"G?"

"Dude." He took his hand away. "You have perfect pitch."

Alex's dimples flickered. "Is that a genetic trait?"

"It is now."

⟡

DEANE HUGGED AND KISSED Jude goodbye before heading to bed. She had to be up early to drive back to the University of Vermont.

"Thanks for taking the time off," Jude said. "It means everything."

"I wouldn't miss it." She screwed her index fingertips into his dimples. "I cannot *believe* what a mini-me you are." She smiled big enough to make her own, single dimple show.

"Oh," Tej said. "That reminds me. Alex, hold out your arm. Make a fist."

Alex looked puzzled but complied.

"He's looking for the palmaris longus," Jude said.

"I don't have it." Alex ran fingertips on the inside of his wrist, which was smooth and flat. "I can't retract my claws."

Tej looked fast at him. "I don't believe you said that."

"Deane doesn't have it either."

Deane held out her smooth arm. Jude held his next to it. Tej and Val put their fists in, both showing the raised tendon beneath the heel of the hand.

"Genetics, man," Tej said. "It's a crazy thing."

Val turned in as well. The three men had a nightcap, then Tej went up to the guest room. Leaving the brothers in Alex's study, telling stories, looking at family photos and touching the Penda artifacts. An antique dagger Eduardo had used as a letter opener. Two cardigan sweaters Alex had pulled on when he was hiding in the closet in the Santiago apartment. One on top of the other. Creating the haven of his parents' arms the only way he could. He was still wearing them when he was pushed through the gates of the American embassy. Still wearing them when he deplaned at JFK airport, where he was collected by his uncle.

"Tell me about him," Jude said, looking at the photo of Felipe Penda. He sat on some porch steps, smoking a cigarette. Slick and dapper. Wingtip shoes and a sweater knotted around his neck. Like a young Ricardo Montalbán.

"He was loving, generous, intellectual, cultured," Alex said. "You may have noticed I don't really have the quintessential Chilean accent?"

"I did notice," Jude said. "You're not as mushy."

"That was Felipe's doing. He was a linguistic snob, always on my case to enunciate and use correct grammar. Looking daggers at me if I used po or hueón."

Jude wagged a finger. "Watch your language, young man."

"It was his one hang-up in terms of being a disciplinarian. In all other aspects, he was a hopeless guardian. No practicality whatsoever, but then again, Papi was pretty impractical, too."

"He was?"

"Oh yeah. He'd walk out of the house with two different shoes at least once a week. He constantly lost keys, lost his wallet, lost his glasses. Easily distracted by shiny things. He'd put water to boil on the stove and walk away for an hour. Mami was the field general. She had her finger on the pulse of everything. Unfortunately, Felipe didn't have anything equal to her."

Jude smiled above his phone. He was texting a picture of him and Alex hugging in the airport to his parents. Adding the caption, *So this happened…*

"If Felipe was useless," he said, "who ended up raising you?"

"The Larks," Alex said. "Val's family." His face went soft, and a little dopey. "I wasn't in the country twelve hours when Val came into my life. She and her brother and sister became my best friends. Her parents treated me like another son and when Felipe died, they became my legal guardians. The Larks were my family. Are my family."

But you never stopped wondering about me, Jude thought. *Every day for all of your life, wondering what became of the baby your mother was carrying when she was arrested.*

"I legally changed my name to Lark-Penda after Deane was born," Alex said. "It's her surname. It's on the mailbox."

"Lark," Jude said. "You literally were taken into a nest."

"A group of larks is called an exaltation," Alex said.

"Hm?"

"Nothing."

Jude's phone pinged with a text from Cleon: **_It's happened before, sweet boy._**

Right after came a picture. Or rather, a picture of a picture from the family gallery: the shot of Louis and Felix Tholet hugging on the pier at Valparaiso.

"Cabrón," Jude said softly. "Alejo, mira ésto."

Alex looked. "Who is it?"

"My grandfather and his brother. Great-Uncle Louis. It was taken the day he arrived in Valparaiso. This little boy here is my father."

Jude swiped between the two photos, taken sixty-three years apart. The composition was eerily identical between the two sets of brothers. From the tight, tangled embrace, to the hands on heads. In the Valparaiso shot, little Cleon Tholet stood wide-eyed and wondering. In the New York shot, Deane Lark-Penda wore the same amazed expression.

"That's crazy," Jude said, the hair prickling up on his forearms.

Alex nodded, a hand cupped loose over his mouth. "I'd say that's kind of like…destiny?"

EL CÓNDOR

*A*LEX TOOK JUDE TO Guelisten Cemetery to see the graves.

Jude sat on little bench, staring at the Pendas' headstones and unable to connect to the chiseled names. "It still doesn't feel real. I mean, it doesn't feel... It doesn't feel. I'm still standing outside looking in."

"You're connected to the intense emotion of the story," Alex said. "Caught up in the dramatic arc, but you can't quite believe it's yours."

"Yeah. Exactly."

"Val said that last night."

"She's great. You picked a winner."

Alex chuckled. "She picked me."

The day was gorgeous. Blinding sunshine in a pristine blue sky. Above a ridge line of trees, hawks were catching thermals and spiraling lazily.

"El cóndor pasa," Jude said.

"Hm?"

"The hawks over there. You ever see an Andean condor?"

"Sure. When we'd go skiing in the mountains. We took a trip to Patagonia once and I saw a ton of them."

Jude steepled his hands over his mouth. "All the political upheaval in South America was called Operation Condor."

"I know."

"The guy who broke my leg? He was the school baseball star. Sick pitcher. He had a seven-foot arm span and they called him El Cóndor. It's an historical irony I don't particularly appreciate."

Alex drew and let out a long, pained breath. "Me neither."

Jude glanced at the tight muscles in his brother's jaw and indulged in some revisionist history. Alex jumping a chain link fence and coming to Jude's rescue.

Chasing down and tackling Juan-Mateo Díaz. Picking up the dropped bat and taking a few practice swings before breaking the Condor's legs...

But that would mean erasing Aiden from the story. Aiden sitting bedside in the hospital, his sleeping head by Jude's hip, his fingers closed tight around Jude's wrist. With no manner of coaxing, pleading or ordering that could make him move until Jude woke up.

These are my stories, he thought, sighing. *I can't let them go. I don't want them to change.*

I don't want to pick between brothers.

"You all right?" Alex said softly.

"Yeah. Just trying to let the condor pass."

"Not to be a nerd, but the Andean condor is technically a vulture."

"Not to be a nerd, but I knew that."

"Did you know vultures have three different group terms? A group in flight is called a kettle. If they're in trees or on the ground, it's a committee. And if a group is feeding, they're called a wake."

"Well aren't you a font of useless information?"

"Papi knew all the group terms for animals. He taught them to me. It was a game we played."

They went quiet. Jude chewed on Alex's easy use of Papi. Took a taste of his ownership in the word. Nothing. *Papi* belonged to Cleon.

"A group of condors is called a scarcity," Alex said.

"Good," Jude said. "The less of them the better."

Alex cleared his throat and got up. He picked at the grass around the base of the stones, fussing, pulling out weeds. Jude looked at his brother. Eleven years older. Greying and mature. This brave, resilient human being who lived a haunted life, wondering what became of his people.

"I wish I could tell you that I always had a feeling something was wrong," Jude said.

"What do you mean, wrong?"

"That I didn't fit in or felt some essential piece of me was missing or...I don't know."

"Hearing you grew up a misfit would not make me feel better," Alex said. "At all. I mean, yeah, of course I wondered if you even had an idea you were someone else's child, but rarely in a way that meant you were unhappy or ostracized or unwanted. Those kinds of scenarios could make me lose my mind. If I couldn't ever find you, then I just prayed, *begged* you had a good life and you were loved and safe." He gestured toward the gravestone. "That's what I always believed would put their hearts at rest."

"I understand. But at the same time, I don't know why I feel so strongly that I let you down somehow."

"You had no idea. This literally all happened before you were born. Hours after you were born. You didn't have a consciousness yet, let alone a memory."

"I *know*. And yet it's there, stuck in my chest and making me feel like apologizing. Atoning. I feel like I should have… I don't know. This guilt I feel is hard to explain."

Alex nodded slowly, then stood up. A long sigh as he stared at the silver granite where bone fragments were buried. Bones that told the truth.

"Believe me, Jude, I get it. Guilt's been a friend of mine my whole life."

Jude got up and stepped closer. Behind and a little bit to the side of his brother's tall frame. Feeling so small and unworthy, he slid his hand into Alex's.

"No fue tu culpa, Alejito."

It wasn't your fault.

Alex glanced down at their twined grip. His fingers squeezed a little. "It's nice to hear someone call me Alejito again."

They stood still, holding hands. Letting Clementina and Eduardo see their sons. Jude closed his eyes, imagining wispy, spectral hands rising from beneath the ground. Touching their faces. Ascertaining. Could it be true? What was lost was returned to them?

Are these our boys?

Are we together again?

Hold still. Let us see you. Let us claim you.

Yes. It's you. We see you.

It's all right now.

All is well now.

Jude opened his eyes. "I'd like to go to Chile someday," he said. "See where I come from. If it's possible, I'd like to go with you."

"We can do that."

"Is your house… Our house still there?"

"It's there. I'll take you to Chile. I'll show you everything."

Jude hesitated. "My parents… I mean, Cleon and Pen—"

"Your parents," Alex said. "Look, I don't want you to stop calling them that, I don't expect you to transfer Mami and Papi to people you don't even know. Cleon and Penny are your parents and I respect it. I'm fucking grateful for it. I'd like to meet them and say so."

"You're not angry?"

Alex freed his hand and put an arm around Jude's neck. "The people to be angry at are out of my reach."

Jude nodded and started over. "My parents might want to come to Chile, too. They've never been back. But something in my gut tells me it might be time."

"Es hora de dejar pasar al cóndor."

It's time to let the condor pass.

 THE SHAME IN HER VEINS

*A*FTER THIRTY-SEVEN YEARS, THE Tholets were going back to Chile. It was all arranged. Alex was coming to Seattle with his wife. They'd stay a night, then the six of them—Penny and Cleon, Jude and Tej, Alex and Val—would fly to Santiago together. Jude said if they were going to do it, they may as well fucking do it, so he booked the flight first class both ways, wouldn't take anyone's money and wouldn't listen to any protest.

"This is my gift back to the divine order," he said. "I'm taking the sad song and making it better."

"Mami, are you nervous?" Serena asked.

"No," Penny said, truthfully. "I'm excited."

In the weeks since Jude had connected with his brother, Penny had found peace in reflecting on Clementina Vilaró, embracing her as a soul sister. When she did her meditations and visualized the garden in La Reina, she patted the bench and asked Clementina to sit with her. She pretended they walked arm-in-arm through the flowers. Or sat at Penny's kitchen table, going through photos and keepsakes of Jude's life. Watching him grow and evolve. When Jude forwarded a picture of Clementina, Penny printed it out. She kept it on the kitchen windowsill, lighting a candle beside in the evenings. She brought her compañera little offerings—pretty pebbles picked up on the beach, a gull's feather, a perfect dahlia bloom.

"Papi, how are you feeling?"

"I'm nervous but I'm ready." Cleon's smile faded as he put a hand on his most serene child's cheek. "You look so tired. You feel all right?"

"She's working hard," Giosué said. "Big project."

Serena waved the concern away. "Tell me your itinerary, what things are planned on this memory tour? Are you going to look up any old friends?"

They tried. With Tej's help—"I'm an expert stalker"—they combed the internet, Santiago phone directories and social media, looking for anyone from their circles. Cleon did make contact with a couple high school classmates, but neither lived in Chile anymore.

"No matter," Cleon said. "We'll be there during a significant week. September eleventh is the anniversary of the coup. September eighteenth is Chile's independence day. Lots to see and do."

"Apparently Alex tracked down the people who live in his old apartment," Penny said. "He went by the building when he was in Santiago a few years ago, but didn't go upstairs. This time, he wants to walk into the lion's den."

"That'll be intense," Giosué said. "Will you go to your old house?"

"We plan to."

"We didn't do any reconnaissance though," Cleon said. "We'll just barge in."

"Are you nervous about meeting Alex?"

"Of course not," Penny said. "I've seen his pictures, seen him on video calls. I feel like I know him."

She was utterly wrong about this.

When the day came, she and Cleon were antsy with excitement. When Jude texted he was parking the car, they came out of the house, down the walk and waited at the gate.

One look at Alex Penda in person and Penny cracked in half.

One head-to-toe sweep of his tall, built frame.

One glint of the sun off his glasses.

One glimpse of his wide, dimpled smile.

"Oh dear God," Cleon murmured.

As the in-the-flesh resemblance dawned on her, Penny broke.

And then she fled.

She ran across Alki Boulevard to the beach, blinded by horrified tears. Ducking behind a lone tree by the guardrail, hands pressed over her mouth. Eyes bulging and streaming.

I took another woman's son.

I took a woman's child away from her.

I took this man's brother.

I left him to wonder all his life.

I did this.

Jude caught up to her, breathing hard. "Mami?"

She pressed her hands harder to her mouth, shaking her head.

"Mami, what is it?"

She moaned against her palms. Her legs buckled and Jude caught her up. "It's all right."

"I can't."

"Mami, it's all right."

"I can't look at him. I can't bear it. I can't…"

"Shh, take a deep breath."

She was hysterical. Irrational. What the hell was wrong with her? "What do I say to him? How do I explain?"

"Mami, you did nothing wrong."

Alex was coming toward them and Penny shrunk back, hiding in Jude's arms. *Don't look at me don't look at me don't look at me…*

"Are you all right?" Jude's brother asked.

At the sound of his voice, Penny shied like a frightened colt, nearly breaking free and making a run for it. Jude's arms tightened.

"Hey, hey, Mami, it's all right."

"I'm sorry," she cried. "I can't stay."

"No," Alex said. "No, please. Please don't."

"I'm so sorry." She writhed and strained, looking anywhere but at her son's brother. The shame in her veins was utterly foreign to her. "Don't look at me."

"It's all right," Alex said. "I promise."

She peeked up. He held out his hands to her, palms to the sky.

"I'm sorry," she said.

The hands beckoned. "Please."

Shaking her head, she extended her trembling fingers.

"It's all right," he said. "Come here. It's all right."

His hands were warm. They held her life. She felt like a stray dog being coaxed into shelter and a vague recollection stirred in her swirling mind, remembering Alex Penda was a veterinarian.

"Don't be afraid," he said.

He had beautiful, mint-green eyes, damp at the edges. A quick smile and his dimples flickered.

"I'm so sorry," she said, even as a calm began to trickle down from her scalp. Much like the entranced relaxation in Dr. Mezeritz's office.

Alex put his hands on her shoulders. Then on her face. He held her forehead to his. "Thank you."

"I had no idea, please believe me."

"I believe you." He was hugging her now. A hug so much like Jude's. "Thank you. I can never thank you enough."

"Oh my God." She relaxed into his embrace. "I'm so sorry."

"There is nothing, *nothing* to forgive but if you need to hear it, I forgive you. I forgive everything. All of it."

She was crying again. "Oh my God."

"Basta," Cleon was there now. Last to arrive, but first to calm her down. "Come here, my love."

She was passed off and buried her face in his chest. "I'm so embarrassed."

"Shh. You had no idea how you'd react."

"I'm so ashamed."

Three male voices protested but she held up a silencing hand.

"I know I have no reason to be, but I can't help it. What did I do? I know I didn't do anything, but I can't help it. I didn't know I was taking him from—"

"Nobody here took anything from anyone," Alex said. "Things were taken from us."

"We were stepped from the path of normal life," Jude said.

Alex gave Penny a handkerchief. She wiped her eyes and blew her nose. They went inside where Valerie Lark was helping Tej, Serena and Giosué put out a magnificent spread and huge drinks. In her turbulent state, Penny couldn't form an opinion of Alex's new sister-in-law beyond *She's a lovely woman.* Both she and Alex were unquestionably lovely people. Gracious, compassionate, solicitous of everyone's fragile emotional state. Attentive in front of the family photo gallery and curious about the Tholets' saga.

The two families didn't just come together, they dissolved like sugar in water. Despite the sweetness, Penny stayed rattled and off-balance the rest of the evening. Slipping away to cry in bathrooms and pillows.

What's wrong? What's wrong with me?

She breathed. She used all her relaxation tricks. She affirmed. She chanted. Then she slipped into the bathroom or bedroom to gasp again.

What if whatever's wrong can't be made right?

She splashed her face with cold water over and over, but stayed flushed with heat, her heart refusing to slow down and walk.

Do I need to go to the hospital? Am I having a heart attack?

Val kept pressing water on her, garnished with paper-thin slices of cucumber and lemon. "Stay hydrated. You'll feel worse if you don't."

Cleon went quieter and stiller than a painting. Apologetically turning up his palms and gesturing to Alex and Jude, his smile bewildered. "I have no words," he said over and over. "I don't believe what I'm seeing."

Penny had never seen him look so small.

Don't get small. Don't disappear.

She refilled her water glass and sat next to Alex. "I feel so strange."

"I know." He rubbed a hand on his chest. "I can't seem to exhale all the way. This is like the happiest time of my life and I feel kind of…wretched."

She laughed, and because he was lovely, she rested her head on his shoulder and closed her eyes.

This doesn't have to be hello or goodbye, she thought. *It doesn't have to be taking sides or choosing teams. My family. Your family. It can be our family. The pool is big enough for everyone. The wall is big enough for more pictures.*

Nothing made her feel better.

"You want half a Xanax?" Alex mumbled. "I was thinking of taking one but I'll split it with you?"

Like two teenagers sneaking off for a joint, they slipped into the kitchen and split a little helper. There, Penny showed Alex her shrine to Clementina on the windowsill.

"I'm trying to separate the feeling of being responsible from a conscious decision to behave responsibly," she said. "Finding out her name and seeing her face gave me something to connect to. I talk to her while I'm washing dishes. I tell her stories about Jude's life. Stories about my life."

"I love that," Alex said softly. "I just want all this to bring peace to everyone. Everyone both living and dead. When Jude came with me to the cemetery and we stood in front of the grave, I felt like… *Here he is. I found him. He's all right. You can rest easy now. No more wondering and worrying. He's right here, he's had a good life, he was safe and he was loved and we found each other.*"

Then they were blubbing again and Alex was passing her his handkerchief. How could you not like a man who carried a handkerchief?

Gradually, the Xanax sank fingertips into Penny's muscles, took the edge off her anxiety and finally gave her exhales a bottom. It let her peer beyond the fog of nervous confusion, wanting to see how Cleon was handling everything.

He was gone.

"Where's your father?" she asked Serena.

Serena glanced at the easy chair, but only Walter was there. She looked around. "I don't know."

Penny found him in the bedroom, sitting on the bench by the footboard, doing nothing. One trouser leg hitched up, his prosthetic leg on the floor. Looking cut in half, broken and lost.

"I'm sorry," he said. "I can't take anymore. Everyone is wonderful, it's a beautiful night but I can't…" He put a hand over his face and his other palm flew up, pushing at her presence. "Give me a minute. Go back to them."

She took a step toward him instead. "Querido."

His palm spread wider. "Don't. I love you but… Just go. Please."

Penny went back to the living room. Her party face in shambles, she gave up the honest truth. "He hit a wall. I think my tank is empty, too. Why don't we call it a night?"

Everyone grabbed cups and plates, insisted she not do a thing to help and go straight to bed. With matriarchal privilege, she kissed and hugged, said goodnight and did just that. Cleon was already under the covers, waiting. Rolled to his side, wanting her heartbeat against his back.

"I couldn't look at Alex anymore," he said. "I'm sorry."

"Don't apologize."

"The resemblance is uncanny. Up until now, it didn't seem real. My mind wasn't fully onboard. Even when Jude shared Alex's picture, the resemblance was obvious but it still didn't register. But seeing him today in person. Flesh and blood. Three dimensional. My God, he smiled and I nearly fell over. My heart broke."

Penny's throat was raw and chafed. She'd been crying all day but nothing had loosened in her heart.

My heart is breaking.

My heart is under attack.

"It got to me," Cleon said. "Jude really is another couple's son. It doesn't change how I feel but it changes…something."

"I don't know why I feel so ashamed."

"I can't stop thinking about Alex's father. Their father. I feel accountable to a man I never met and do you know, I might have met him. He owned that bookstore on the Plaza San Margarita. I knew that place. That lair of students and activists and cigarettes and coffee and causes. I know I went in there at least once. One book on my office shelves was bought there. Eduardo Penda could've sold it to me. Could've poured me a cup of coffee."

"I could've passed his mother on the street."

"She was in the Villa Grimaldi. I might have seen her. I might have heard her screams in the night. I could have been feet, inches away from Jude being born…"

He was crying. He rarely cried. He coasted above such violent emotions.

"I could've been there," he said between sobs. Which was untrue and unfair. Irrational. But sometimes you felt what you felt and nothing could assuage it.

"I could've known. I could have seen her. I could have let someone inside but the palace only had one room. There was only room for one. I'm not Louis. I couldn't do it his way. I couldn't make room for ten. Only one. If I saw a baby lying on the ground, I would've stepped over it. I would've passed Jude by…"

This was the cue for Penny to go strong and solid and stoic. To give him the floor and let him have his turn. She couldn't. They were talking past each other now, fear upon fear cascading out and piling up on bed like throw pillows.

"What if he's looking for us?" Cleon said.

"What if he isn't?"

"What if he had a terrible life?"

"What if he has no idea?"

"I wonder what he looks like," he said. "I wonder where he is. I wonder his name. I wonder if he's even alive. I wonder if we passed on the street, would he do a double-take. Maybe Aiden, in his all his travels, passed him by. They could've exchanged a glance somewhere in Patagonia or Peru or Argentina and thought, *Wow, look at that guy, we could be brothers…*"

"Where is he," Penny sobbed into his shoulder. "Where did he go, what happened to him?"

"Goddammit." Cleon let out a frustrated roar, dragging his hands down his face. "I just want my fucking *life* back," he cried. He shoved her weight off and rolled over. "They took everything from me. They can't have my son, too."

Then he grabbed her and dragged her on top of him. They clawed and clung, weeping.

My heart is breaking.

"They can't have him, Lucy," he said into her hair. "They can't take him from me."

She clutched him as if he were the only thing she had left in the world. At that moment, he was. He'd built a sky and set her like a goddess at its zenith, her belly filled with lit-up hope. He gave her diamonds. He gave her children. He gave her the best and the worst of himself.

"How much more do they think I can take?"

He was holding her hard, with those hands that could crack walnuts or place a thousand delicate paper squares into a mosaic. Arms that could hoist him and his wheelchair aloft or paddle effortlessly to Bainbridge Island and back. The barrel chest enclosing his fragile heart. The scars from brass-knuckled fists, chains and live wires. The mouth that held back so many secrets while it encouraged others to tell their stories.

"How much more, Lucy?"

They usually took such care making love. Not tonight. Their angry passion had no use for their imperfect, aging bodies. It turned them inside-out, threw off clothing and caution and they fucked like the world was ending. Collapsed into naked sleep with the tear-tracks still wet on their wrinkled faces, not caring if they ever woke up again.

THEY WOKE UP AGAIN.

They got out of bed carefully. Limped to the kitchen and chuckled through sheepish, blushing glances. They made big omelets and bigger bloody Marys. In the afternoon, they took the two-seated kayak onto Puget Sound. Cleon clipped his Bluetooth speaker through the buttonhole of his jacket and played the Beatles from his phone. Their paddles dipped and sliced as McCartney sang "Let it Be."

This is the hand we were dealt, Penny thought, breathing in the cool damp air. *Who are we going to be now?*

They took Walter to the kennel, then came home and packed their suitcases. Assembled their papers and passports and tickets. Got ready for bed. The phone rang: it was Serena, with Giosué on another extension.

"I'm pregnant," she said. "Almost four months. We wanted to wait through the first trimester. We had the ultrasound this morning."

Penny and Cleon stared at each other.

"It was beautiful," Giosué said in a thick voice. "Perfect little head, little arms and legs. Turning and kicking. It was magic. You could see all four chambers of the heart. You could see everything."

"Well, almost everything," Serena said. "No gender reveal. But Mami, if it's a girl, I want to call her Giulia. For your mother, but with a G to make it Italian."

"If it's a boy, we thought maybe Ringo," Giosué said.

Now Cleon roared laughing and Penny sat down on the bed, her mouth open. "Oh, querida," she finally managed. "What an un-revolting development."

Then they were all laughing.

"I wanted to tell you before you left," Serena said. "Something to take with you. And if this trip to Chile doesn't put anything to rest or you find more questions than answers, then it's something to come home to."

"You are the sweetest, most serene child," Cleon said.

"Isn't she?" Giosué said.

"Wait until I go into labor," Serena said. "I'm calling in *all* the crazy."

"I'm going to be a grandmother." Penny stood up, then sat down again. "Oh my God, I can't wait. When?"

"February."

"What a gift," Cleon said. "We love you both."

"I'm so glad we didn't know until now," Penny said. "It's perfect. Just perfect. I'm putting it in my carry-on luggage."

She moved on soft feet the rest of the night, smiling into the steam of the shower. Staring through her reflection as she brushed her teeth, creating vistas of grandparenthood. Her arms bundled the towel to her chest after she dried her face, imagining a baby to rock.

A girl, she thought. *I'd love if it were a girl. Giulia.*

Then the scene shifted to Cleon sitting at the kitchen table with a little boy in his lap, sharing a strawberry milkshake. And she loved that, too.

"I'm so happy," she said in bed. "More than happy. I feel so *relieved.*"

"What a gift." Cleon clicked off the light and rolled toward her. "So tell me again, who's the hottest grandfather in Seattle?"

"I believe that's you."

He kissed her neck. "I'm not convinced."

She laughed. "You can't possibly be looking for a repeat of last night."

"No. Yeah. Sort of."

"Sort of."

Well…" His fingers ran through her hair. "Maybe a little slower this time?"

CLE◉N

EVERYONE IS BRUISED AND broken. You're all marked with burns from elec-trodes and cigarettes. You've been spit on, pissed on, even ejaculated on. Every one of you has stared down the muzzle of a revolver and heard an empty click. You're all starving on a diet of hatred, rage, pain, grief, fear, distress, frustration, resignation, powerlessness, bitterness, and disappointment.

A portion of disappointment is reserved for yourself. You of all people. You're the grandson of Jewish refugees. The nephew of a concentration camp survivor. A jour-nalist reporting on human suffering. You looked at the grounds of Pisagua with your own eyes, and still you didn't believe your own country capable of such cruelty.

The sadistic glee of the interrogators doesn't surprise or shock you anymore. When you think you've heard every atrocious act that could possibly be committed upon a human being, one of your mates comes back from interrogation with something new. Something worse. Something more heinous. Your mind has no more ability to process the accounts. You listen but you don't hear. You open your arms, but the door to your palace stays closed and barricaded. It only has room for one.

You, Carlos Luis Tholet.

Thou shalt survive by building a castle in the sky with diamonds.

They're calling you.

It's time to go.

. . .

. . .

. . .

And you're gone.

THE TOWER

"**W**HAT'S WITH THE DOGS?**" Jude said, their first morning in Santiago.

Everywhere he looked, from his vantage point at the outdoor café, he saw dogs. Dozens of them. Grouped on street corners like Sharks and Jets. Sitting daintily at crosswalks, waiting for the light to change. Prowling beneath tables for crumbs. Snoozing under benches. Flirting with passers-by. Curled belly-up in puddles of sunshine.

Alex smiled as he stirred his coffee. "I arranged them for you. You like?"

"They're all strays?" Tej asked. "They just live here?"

"Close to half a million."

"They're called quiltro," Cleon said. "Or perros callejeros."

"It was like this when you lived here?" Jude asked.

"It's always been like this."

"They're everyone's pets," Alex said.

His smile was just short of beatific. In the short time knowing him, Jude learned his brother was something of a Dr. Dolittle. Not just a skilled veterinarian but a veritable animal whisperer. Especially with dogs. He'd charmed the grouchy Walter in six seconds and Jude would lay money that if Alex were introduced to Samson, Mireille Khoury would be out of a pet. By the end of breakfast, no less than five quiltros were piled around the legs of his chair. He leaned back in his seat, arms crossed as he surveyed the plaza, and a little bird flew in and perched on the chair back. Alex turned his head, expression unfazed as he said, "Hello."

The bird ruffled its feathers, as if showing off a new dress.

"¿Qué onda?"

The bird gave a short cheep, then flew away.

The three couples made loose plans, with events they'd do together—exhibits and museums and memorials—and excursions that were more private. Val's sole request was to go to La Chascona, home of Chile's beloved poet, Pablo Neruda. Alex had his date to see his old apartment. Cleon wanted to go to the Jewish Cemetery. Penny wanted to visit the old house in La Reina. Tej just wanted to explore the food.

Jude didn't know what he wanted. His whole life, Chile had loomed large in the background. A distant, mythical land of beauty and violence. Now that he was here, he wondered if the romance of the family narrative had gotten the better of him. The city was beautiful and he couldn't look at the surrounding mountains without his mouth falling open. Yet he felt strangely ambivalent. A little detached and lost.

Maybe I'm just jet-lagged.

"Let's go to the Villa," Cleon said after breakfast the first morning.

"The Villa Grimaldi?" Jude said. "Now?"

"Now. If I don't go straight back to La Reina, it'll be looming over the whole trip like the angel of death. Let's just go and get it over with, and then go see the house."

What Jude assumed would be the culmination of the trip ended up being the overture. They'd rented an SUV that could seat all six comfortably. Tej drove east out of the city with Jude navigating.

"I don't recognize anything," Penny said over and over, craning out her window or ducking to look across through Cleon's side. "It's so built up. La Reina was basically still a ranch when we lived there. Our street wasn't even paved. Now it's a suburb."

Tej turned off Tobalaba onto José Arrieta. A high, red brick wall loomed up on the passenger side, broken by an arched entrance, fit with a heavy, grilled door. The number 8401 at the apex. A large sign to the side:

Museo De Sitio — Parque por la Paz
VILLA GRIMALDI
Ex Centro Clandestino de Detención Tortura y Extermino

Lugar de memoria y promoción
De los Derechos Humanos

"Look at that," Cleon said under his breath. "Just look at that."

He was leaving the parking lot before everyone was out of the car, his uneven gait barely stopping to look both ways before crossing the street. When they caught up to him, he was paused in the arched gate, a hand on the concrete. A gladiator entering the arena.

With his cane and Panama hat, he looked like Hemingway, Jude thought. He reached for his phone to take a picture but stopped. It seemed cheap. Irreverent. Today wasn't a social media post. He made a sudden decision to do this the old-fashioned way. Be mindful and present and conscious about taking it all in. These would be his first memories of Chile. He'd pay attention to the act of remembering.

"Vámos." Cleon walked into the courtyard. An open, green space spread out before them, bisected with paths. Birds darted and swooped among the trees and flower beds.

"This way," Cleon said, heading straight ahead, toward a tall, red tower in a corner of the park. "That's it."

Val fell into step beside Jude. "That's where he was imprisoned?" she said quietly.

"I have no idea," Jude said, looking around.

"They were all locked in a fucking tower?" Tej murmured.

"Look," Cleon said, pointing to a swimming pool, lined with pale blue tiles. Leaves and debris collected in its corners. "Children of the DINA would come swim in the evenings. You could hear them shouting and laughing from the cells."

Jude stared, imagining the surreal juxtaposition. The screams of the tortured against the sound of kids splashing and horsing around. Sick, broken prisoners locked up in their own filth and misery, while healthy children dove into cool, clear water.

They walked closer to the tower, which rose up like a squared barn silo. A plaque nearby informed it was a replica of the original tower, torn down in the 1980s in an attempt to cover up the atrocities. The tower was painted red with white trim. Each side had three narrow windows at the top.

It made no sense to Jude.

"How did they fit all the prisoners there?" he asked Cleon.

"They didn't," Cleon said. "This was where the torture took place."

"Oh."

At the base of the tower were two concrete steps leading up to an opened double door.

"Are you going in?" Jude asked.

A foot on the step, Cleon looked up to the top of the tower. He peered within at the exhibits. "No," he said, then smiled at Jude. "I choose not to go this time."

He turned to face the park. Their party had split off and was meandering through the sights. Val and Penny stood together in the park's exact center. A circular plaza built around a fountain. The water jets were turned off, revealing the inlaid mosaic flower.

"Is it recognizable?" Jude asked.

"The original villa is gone," Cleon said. "See where the ground is excavated over there and the steps are exposed? It was right there. The cells were inside old wine cellars and outbuildings. Or new ones were built freestanding."

All around the dry fountain, tourists sat on the low wall, everyone quiet and contemplative. The open space was filled with a hallowed yet peaceful sadness.

Yes, it said. *Yes, this happened. Sit a moment and think about it. Give it your attention.*

Cleon took Jude's arm and they continued on the path, walking toward the corner opposite the tower. A pair of heavy iron gates were set into the brick perimeter wall. They were closed. A plaque told visitors this was the main entrance of the Villa compound. Prisoners were driven through and dumped out here. The gates were permanently locked now. A large concrete sculpture of a leaf blocked the wide, black doors, ensuring they could never be opened again.

"Is it a leaf?" Jude walked around to get a different vantage. "Or a flame?"

Cleon poked at the edge of the sculpture with his cane. "Point is it's growing. Not dying." He pushed back his hat and looked around, taking it all in.

"You all right, Papi?"

"I don't know what I am."

"Same."

"It's surreal. And strange. Seeing it out here in the sunshine. Rearranged and made beautiful. It doesn't match my memory, which I guess is ideal."

"You had the right idea, starting out with this."

Cleon drew a deep breath and held it for an unusually long time. Then exhaled slow. "Remember when Dr. Mezeritz said we may never learn the whole truth? That the best we'll get is a story made from pieces of truth?"

"A story that's the closest thing to the truth. A story we can believe in. I remember."

Cleon nodded, eyes narrowed at the giant leaf blocking the compound gates. "I believe you were born here," he said. "I believe we were here at the same time. Me and Clementina Vilaró. We never saw each other, but we heard each other in the night. I believe this. I was transferred here from the Estadio because it was necessary. It was important I be present when you were born."

His gaze met Jude's then. "I have nothing to back that up. I couldn't take it to court. But it's the story I've assembled from bits of truth. And I like it. It feels good in my heart."

Jude blinked, pressed his mouth hard and fought to hold himself together.

"Everything that happened to me," Cleon said, "happened so you could be my boy." He took Jude in his burly arms and held him tight. "Do you hear me, hueón? It happened for a reason."

Jude nodded.

"Everything happened so you could be my boy." He ran his cheek along Jude's hair. "¿Sómos compañeros?"

"Compañeros," Jude whispered. "Por siempre."

Cleon kissed his face. "Let's go see the rest of it."

They walked by a huge cube made from plates of copper and balanced on an edge. Inside, Tej and Alex stood looking at cases displaying large pieces of rusted metal.

"Railroad ties," Alex said. His arms were crossed tight, his face a closed fist. "They were used to weigh down victims thrown out of airplanes into the Pacific Ocean."

"Christ," Jude said, holding his own sides.

"This was always my recurring nightmare. All my life I had bad dreams about my parents being thrown out of planes. It's why I hate flying so much."

Jude half smiled, recalling how Alex had unapologetically knocked back two Xanax during the flight safety talk and was out cold as they taxied to the runway.

"Telling you though, soon as their remains were identified and I knew for certain they weren't rotting away on the ocean floor, the dreams stopped."

Jude kept holding his sides as he read about María Ugarte, one of the many murdered victims who disengaged from their deadly anchors and washed up on Chile's shores, revealing another layer in Pinochet's sadistic terror. Other dissidents were thrown from planes inland. Even today, women were searching the Andes Mountains and the Atacama Desert, looking for remains of their disappeared ones. Even today, they were still finding fragments of bones and teeth and bringing them in to be analyzed, hopefully identified.

There but for the grace, Jude thought, freeing an arm to slide it around his father's hunched shoulders.

"Te quiero, hueón," Cleon said, not looking up from the display case.

Val put her head inside. "Here you are. Come see something."

One section of the park was a rose garden memorializing the women of the Villa Grimaldi. A riot of white, red, pink and orange making concentric circles around a bubbling fountain. Stuck into the ground between blooms were oval markers, each with a woman's name. After visiting Chile a few years ago, Alex had sponsored one for his mother. Val and Penny found it by a cluster of bright coral blooms, the name etched in pretty script:

MARÍA CLEMENTINA VILARÓ

"Would you look at that," Cleon said.

Alex crouched down and brushed off the surface of the marker, digging the dirt out of the letters. Jude stayed still. Feeling he should be helping. Feeling it wasn't his place. Feeling absolutely no connection to the name or the memorial.

He just felt like shit.

"A clementine is an orange," Tej said.

"Hm?"

"Nothing, I'm just making an absurd connection to tangerine trees."

Jude took his hand. "Come walk with me."

Fingers twined, they ambled toward a memorial wall etched with the names of victims, offerings of red carnations heaped beneath. They kept holding hands as they moved along the tributes, and Jude could feel gazes follow. Eyes darted off as he looked up. Sideways glances lined with either benign curiosity or defensive hostility. One middle-aged man curled his upper lip and rolled his eyes as he looked away.

I was born here, Jude thought, his fingers tight between Tej's. *Right here. In this place. Think what you want, glare all you want, but I'm standing here with my lover. How you feel about it won't make us lose any sleep tonight. We both survived things you can't imagine. Pull any shit and my father will bludgeon you with his prosthetic leg.*

The Tholets don't come to play.

"Whatever you're smiling about," Tej said. "Don't stop."

They went into a freestanding building, its walls hung with sketches made by former detainees.

"Wow," Tej said softly. "They're like the ones your father drew."

The sketches were on blank paper, lined paper, scraps of paper and one on what looked like a brown paper bag. They were penciled, charcoaled and ballpoint penned. A prisoner tied spread eagle to a metal bedspring. A guard sitting with a machine gun at the end of a long hall of closed, bolted doors. Four men huddled in a space that could barely hold one. Five men blindfolded and shackled, trudging in a snake, each with a hand on the compañero ahead of him while machine-gunned guards looked on. A prisoner comforting a cellmate in a corner.

A room with a bunkbed, a chair bolted to the floor, and a long table with instruments of all manner of torture.

"God," Jude said. "I never doubted his stories. Never. But seeing these… They're the same. They're all the same things he drew."

"It confirms everything."

"It was real. Remember he talked about people being born storytellers. Always embellishing or filling in the gaps. But he drew it just the way it happened. They all did."

"He should…" Tej shook his head. "Forget it, I have no right to say what he should do."

"He should send his sketches to be included here?"

Tej went on shaking his head. "Never mind."

Jude slid his hand along the back of Tej's neck. "I always mind."

THEY WERE QUIET ON the drive to the old house. In the far back of the SUV, Alex had his head on Val's shoulder, his eyes closed. In the middle row, Penny and Cleon held hands, looking out their respective windows. From the front passenger seat, Jude reached behind, his hand wanting in. Fifteen fingers tangled and squeezed.

"Everybody for to hold hands," Val said softly, like a Russian countess. It was a little mannerism that Jude was growing fond of. He smiled at his sister-in-law. The corners of her eyes and her nose crinkled back.

"Is this it?" Tej said, leaning on the wheel.

"Buena Vista," Cleon said. "The world's most boring street name."

Penny laughed under her breath. "It has sidewalks. Oh my God, it has *blocks.*"

"Wait, Jude, this isn't right."

"Number twenty-one," Jude said. "This is it. It's on the wall."

"But we were the cul de sac."

"Not anymore," Tej said, pulling to the curb. "As Tolkien says, the road goes ever on."

Out toward the mountains, Buena Vista continued onward. The Tholet's double lot of property now sat on a defined street block, walled on all four sides. A miniature estate in the suburbs.

"Oh my God," Penny said, stepping from the car. She turned in a slow circle. "It's so…"

"Changed," Cleon said, holding onto Tej's arm as he got out.

Penny pointed across the street. "Look. Ysidro's old workshop. It's a café."

"Why don't Val and I go there and get a table," Alex said. "Since you're ringing the bell unannounced. Best keep the party small."

Not only was the party small, it was short. The owners were away and had rented the house to an American couple for the week. They apologized, saying they didn't feel comfortable letting people onto the property, as it wasn't theirs. The Tholets didn't press it. They were tired after the morning's events. The husband went inside to get the owners' business card. Cleon pocketed it, thanked them, and he and Penny peeked at what they could through the wrought iron gates.

"It's not a functioning nursery anymore," he said. "Just a house with a beautiful garden."

"Nothing just about that," Penny said.

They laughed at having to look both ways before crossing the street to the café, where Alex and Val had taken seats outside.

"Look at these tables," Val said. "Didn't you say your friend was a mason?"

All the café's tables were made from big slabs of marble and granite, mounted on iron stands. Some had lines chiseled along the edges or motifs in the corners.

"Would you look at that?" Cleon said, running his fingers along the unfinished designs.

"The stone is everywhere," Tej said. "Look at the pavers on the patio."

"Look what's between them," Jude said, pointing out the tiny chips of white, gray and pink. "I wonder if this was all Ysidro's leftover stock. Left behind."

"Buenas tardes." A burly, mustached man in a long apron came out and began tossing napkins down on the table.

"Are you the owner?" Cleon asked.

"Yes, sir."

"How long?"

"Took over from my father about five years ago."

"When did he open this place?"

Penny smiled, softening the interrogation. "We used to live across the street."

"No kidding? My dad opened in nineteen eighty-eight. This lot was abandoned, the building falling down. It used to be a... what do you call it? A place that makes gravestones."

"That's right." Cleon ran a hand along the tabletop. "Did you make the tables from what was left behind?"

"You wouldn't believe it, señor. The lot was a jungle of weeds and vines, with a bloody fortune of stone hiding underneath. We're talking mausoleum-grade granite. Unfinished headstones and statuary, left behind and abandoned. We couldn't believe it hadn't been scavenged off."

"You didn't happen to know the man who worked here?" Penny asked. "He was called Ysidro Sepúlveda?"

"The family were all memorial masons," Cleon said.

The owner thought a moment, then shook his head. "Sorry."

"No matter, hueón."

He clapped his hands and rubbed them together. "So. Hungry? What can I get you?"

"What's good?" Tej said, a marketplace gleam in his eye.

The owner matched it. "Everything."

"Then bring us that."

He brought ice-cold beers, appetizers of tomato, avocado and corn kernels piled on sopaipillas. Grilled eggplant on toasted bread. Skewers of beef and sausage. The good food filled up the emptiness inside Jude. The beers and the sun overhead made his eyes prickle with fatigue. All around the table, yawns were being stifled.

"I think I for to take leetle nap," Val said, sinking her cheek onto a hand.

"I take big nap," Cleon said.

As they left the café, Tej bent and picked up some chips of granite from in between the paver stones.

"Souvenir," he said to Jude, pocketing them.

It was good to stumble into the air-conditioned hotel room and fall onto the crisp, tight bed. Tej pulled the drapes shut and took his clothes off, which was good, too. He took Jude's clothes off, which was even better. They took each other, giving their best, and a while later, when Jude curled around Tej's big, warm body and drifted off, he was out of superlatives.

 THE SEAHORSE

*T*HE NEXT MORNING, ALEX and Val went off on their own to see Alex's old apartment. The Tholets took the car and drove northwest to Recoleta and the Cementerio Israelita.

"I've wanted to do this for years," Cleon said as they walked into the cemetery's little outbuilding. "I should have. It's long overdue."

Penny took his hand. "It's time."

"Buenos días," the man behind the desk said. "¿Puedo ayudarle?"

Cleon took off his panama hat. "I'm looking for my uncle's plot. Louis Tholet. Died November twenty-fifth, nineteen seventy-three."

"Spell the last name for me?"

Penny's heart beat fast as the attendant tapped on his computer. For an anxious moment, she was positive the name wouldn't be found. Louis wasn't here after all.

Ysidro promised, she thought. *But was he able to arrange it? Did he and Tatán flee before he could make Louis a stone?*

The man clicked the end of his pen and drew a pad of paper close. "Section nine," he said. "Row fourteen. Plot number sixty-two."

"Oh my God," Penny said, relief now running warm and wet down her face. She turned back to Tej and Jude, waving fingertips at her streaming eyes. "Look at me."

"Were you worried?" Jude said.

"Yes, but I didn't know how much until now."

In his backpack, Jude carried some supplies he'd picked up at an art store— rice paper and thick black crayons and masking tape, so they could make a rubbing of Louis's stone. The cemetery had no benches, but the attendant offered two compact, folding camp chairs.

They walked outside, eyes screwing up at the bright light. It was another hot, bluebird sky day. The sun beat down on the rows of gravestones, stretching in long, bleached white rows.

"It has a weird uniformity," Tej said as they walked along the narrow path between markers. "I mean how the stones are different heights and widths, but they're all squared off and minimalist. You look at it as a whole and it's like a piece of modern art. Cubism or something."

Penny's heart had kicked up again. Her eyes swept along Hebrew lettering. Stars of David. Clusters of pebbles along the tops of the stones, showing visitors had been there.

"Aquí está," Cleon said under his breath.

LOUIS JACOB THOLET
03. 08. 1916.
25. 11. 1973.

Yesterday, Cleon had coasted above the intense emotion at the Villa Grimaldi. Today, the enormity sucked him down into the maelstrom. Or perhaps he sank willingly, for this had been a long time coming. His face crumpled and the look in his eyes could only be described as shame. He was late. Terribly late.

It happened quickly. A keening moan rumbled in his chest. His hat fell one way, his cane the other. His hands came to his face, shoulders shaking, legs swaying. Tej popped open one of the camp chairs, set it close to the headstone. Jude helped Cleon into it.

"It's all right, Papi."

Cleon wept. His face leaned against the white marble, the fingers of one hand digging into the chiseled letters. The other arm hooked around, palm spread on the stone's top, as if cradling a head to his shoulder.

Tej backed away and went invisible. Jude broke open the other chair but Penny ignored it. She knelt by Cleon's feet, put arms around him and buried her face in his neck. She rocked him through the storm, her own tears wetting down his collar. Pressed beneath grief that had waited thirty-seven years for them. Humbled in the presence of a promise kept. Reduced to a jumble of memory and adjectives, Louis's face winking in and out of blurred vision. *Dear, dear, darling man. Courageous and resilient and gentle and haunted and lovely, the loveliest man...*

"Oh my God," Cleon said thickly.

Penny handed him a hunk of tissues. He mopped his eyes and nose. Laughed a little and looked up at the stone. Sank his face into a palm again. "Por Dios, tío, lo siento."

"Shh, he loved you."

"It took so long."

"It was time. This is the time. It's not too late, it's never too late."

Penny reached fingers now to trace the letters, chiseled straight and true and precise. The star of David crowning Louis's name. The border of thin, precise lines outlining the inscription.

Thank you, she thought simply.

The boys came back, pulling bottles of cold water out of Jude's backpack. When Cleon was calmed down and dried up, he inched his chair back so they could get to work. They taped the paper carefully to the stone. Each took a turn with the crayon, rubbing it sideways to bring out the engraving. When it was done, Jude rolled up the paper carefully and taped it. "We'll find an office store and have it shipped home in a tube," he said. "Or get the concierge to do it."

"We need to leave stones," Penny said, looking around the paths.

"Here," Tej said, digging in his pocket. "I picked these up yesterday. At the café." He held out a palm and showed some chips of granite. Remnants from Ysidro's workshop. "It seems kind of appropriate."

"It's perfect," Penny said, taking one.

THEY MET ALEX AND Val at a restaurant near the hotel. From their faces, it was clear they hadn't had a sob-less morning either.

"It was unbelievable," Val said.

"The family who lives there was incredible," Alex said. "I can't get over it. I thought it would be a hello, goodbye, a quick look around, thank you so much. They made a…a *thing* of it. They were waiting in the lobby with flowers."

Val showed the bouquet of roses peeking out of her shoulder bag. "We went upstairs and they'd made breakfast for us. Homemade chocolate empanadas. The best cup of coffee I had in my life."

"Show them the other thing. Check this out."

From her bag, Val drew a piece of honey-colored wood. Two inches wide by six inches long. She passed it around.

"What is it?" Tej asked.

"It's a piece of the floor," Alex said. "From inside the bedroom closet, where I hid after my parents were arrested."

"Shut up," Jude said, taking it.

"Can you believe it? They *pulled out* a piece of the closet floor to give to me."

"Who does that?" Tej said.

"I cried my face off," Alex said. "It was ridiculous."

Jude unrolled the rubbing from the cemetery and showed it off. A round of pisco sours was delivered. They toasted and drank.

"These are different," Val said to Tej. "Did they put ginger in? Do you taste it?"

"I do, it's a nice twist."

By now they were used to Tej finding the best things on the menu. The waitress put down a huge cast-iron bowl, filled with vegetables and seafood.

"Po, bonita familia," the waitress said, setting down a stack of plates by Penny's elbow. "Are these all your children?"

Penny started to explain who was who, then stopped. "Yes," she said, looking around the table. "All mine."

❧

AFTER LUNCH THEY WENT to the Museum of Memory and Human Rights. Tej paused by the walkway to the outdoor amphitheater, struck by one half of a giant pair of glasses, the lens shattered.

"What does this mean?" he asked Cleon.

"They symbolize Salvador Allende's glasses. They were found in the wreckage after Pinochet's men bombed La Moneda. One of the lenses shattered. Just like this. They found his shoes, too. The blast blew them right off his feet."

As with the Villa Grimaldi, their group split up and rejoined through the exhibits, broke apart and then wandered back to find each other. "Come see this," they said. "Come over here and look at this."

Penny stood a long time before a giant map of Chile, marked with hundreds of dots where atrocities took place. Her brow knitted tight as she read how Pinochet used the country's diverse geography to his cruel advantage. Prisoners were tortured with the heat in the Atacama Desert, and with the cold in Antarctic Patagonia. Chile's miles and miles of coastline was a convenient graveyard where thousands were disappeared.

Alex was fascinated with an exhibit showing the seahorse as a symbol of Chilean resistance. When museum founders began collecting artifacts and testimonials of the coup, they continually came across the image of the seahorse. They found it in drawings, letters, carvings on cell walls.

"It was the drains," Alex said. "Most of the drains in Chile were covered with a metal grille with a seahorse in the middle."

"That's right," Cleon said. "Of course."

"The prisoners were blindfolded all the time. They could only look down under the bottom edge and see a bit of the floor. And when they were taken to bathrooms, they saw the drains. It became a symbol."

"I'll be damned."

"I had no idea," Alex said. "I've never heard of this before."

Val put her chin on her husband's shoulder. "Sounds like someone's getting a new tattoo soon."

Looking thoughtful, Cleon pulled at his chin. "I may join you."

THEY FINISHED AT THE Estadio Nacional, surreptitiously tagging onto a guided tour. They walked through Escotilla Número 8, where male prisoners were kept. People leaned toward the walls, squinting, deciphering the writings and carvings left in the concrete. They moved down a long corridor connecting the locker rooms, the walls hung with photographs and testimony. Graphic depiction after graphic depiction piling up until all at once, Cleon stopped. The crowd moved around him as he looked down at Penny.

"I'm done now," he said. "I've seen enough."

"All right," she said.

"Let's get some air."

They backtracked, slipped away and out to the Gradería de la Dignidad—a section of the stadium preserved as a memorial. Carefully gated off, the original wooden bleachers still intact. Here Penny and Cleon sat, staring across the turf, sharing a bottle of water and breathing.

"There's only so much you can take in," Cleon said.

"Of course. It's been a long day."

"But it's been good. I'm glad we did this. I'm glad we did it in this company." He drew in a long breath and exhaled slow, falling a little closer to her. "I really like the idea of that seahorse. As a tattoo, I mean."

She gave a big sigh of her own. "I suppose you're old enough now."

"Sixty-three years with no ink is a good run."

She leaned her head on his shoulder, closed her eyes and sing-songed, "You're going to be a grandpa."

He laughed into her hair, rubbed his nose along her temple. "I know. I keep that right in my pocket."

"Penny?" Alex had appeared at the hatchway. "Jude wants you to see something. He says it's important."

"Go," Cleon said. "I'll be here."

She went down a few steps, then turned back. "Right here?" she said, pointing to the floor.

He put his hands atop his cane and his chin atop his hands. "This exact spot."

"Don't you dare not be where you say you are."

"I'll call you if I move one seat over."

She followed Alex back down the long corridor, past the photographs and displays, to a place where the walls were hung with hundreds of bronze plaques, each inscribed with names. Jude stood before one, arms crossed tight, eyes shining behind his glasses. When he saw Penny, he gestured toward the coppery square with his chin.

Paloma, Arturo Velásquez
Paloma, Cristian Andrés
Paloma, Oliva Teresa

"Oh God, look at that," she whispered, taking in the names of Feño's father, brother and sister. An eerie blank space separated Oliva from the next name, as if a name were missing.

"I keep reading it and reading it," Jude said. "I don't know why, but I feel like Feño's name should be here with them. Is that crazy?"

She wormed her hand into the crook of his elbow. "He was a victim of all of this, too."

"It's like whoever submitted the names left a space for him."

"No," Penny said slowly. "I think it was Graciela. And she left the blank line for herself."

CLEN

*U*MBERTO IS CRYING IN *your arms.*

Mario is slowly thumping his head against the wall.

Héctor does nothing. His eyes are closed. He might be dead or asleep, you don't know. You care, but you don't. Your palace only has room for one.

Your compañeros are giving up hope. You, however, are building a train station out of culled memories from your one summer in Europe, cramming it with architectural details. The oily fragrance of plasticine evokes kindergarten days. You only had primary colors back then. Now a rainbow of shades is at your disposal to create an international cadre of porters. You don't meet your own eyes as you fashion their ties from delicate shards of mirror glass. Your gaze is fixed on the girl at the turnstile. The colored chips of her eyes spiral into stained-glass rosettes. She points toward the ceiling.

It's almost time to be gone.

You nod at her, your chin brushing Umberto's dirty hair.

(I'll be there soon, my love.)

They're calling you.

It's time to go.

. . .

. . .

. . .

And you're gone.

THE EXECUTION

*A*FTER DINNER, CLEON AND Penny went to their room, saying they were exhausted. Jude, Tej, Alex and Val found an outdoor bar with live music. They ordered a pitcher of sangria. Tej and Val ordered another, then got up to dance.

Munching the alcohol-soaked fruit in his glass, Jude's eyes roamed hungrily over his lover. The backward tilt of his head and his hips catching the beat. How the smile flashing in his beard growth was for Val, for the band, for the night. Sweat glistened in the hollow of his throat. The muscles in his back and arms bulged in and out of sight through his loose white shirt. All the women on the floor were openly ogling him.

You like that? Jude thought. *I sleep with it.*

Alex's focus was downward, his thumbs busily tapping on his phone. He went still, reading the replies. Then rolled his eyes and shook his head before replying.

"Who are you texting?" Jude asked.

"Deane." A long, troubled sigh, and he put the phone down.

"Boy trouble?"

"Are there other kinds of trouble?"

Jude leaned back in his chair, hands laced behind his head. "Tell her to text me. I'm kind of an expert in boys."

The joke fell flat. Alex flicked one shoulder as he finished what was left in his glass.

"It's cool she talks to you about it," Jude said.

Alex half-smiled. "Yeah."

"Is this her first love?"

"No. No, that was a different kind of trouble."

"How so?"

Alex ran fingertips across his brow. "She met a great guy. A winner. He was terrific in every aspect."

"What's the trouble?"

"He's her first cousin."

Jude brought the legs of his chair down. "Oh. Had they never met before?"

Alex began to answer, then sighed again. "Long, complicated story short, no. They'd never met."

"I see."

"We didn't treat it like a scandal. It was a shock, but we figured if we lay down a restraining order or something dramatic, they'd only be more compelled to run off together. Or something dramatic. We took a 'love each other and see what happens' approach. They loved each other, saying being cousins didn't make a difference. But after about a year, it did. It resolved itself, but it was heartbreaking to watch." He gestured at the phone on the table. "She's moving on but some-times it rears up and bites her."

"And she texts you. That's awesome. I mean, awesome for her. Sucks for you."

Alex blew out his breath and nodded. "Parenthood. It ain't for sissies."

Jude picked a fat blackberry out of his glass and ate it. "You know, I read somewhere once that siblings and close-cousins are actually born hardwired to be attracted. To instinctively see the ideal partner and mate in each other. It's only being raised in close proximity that disconnects the instinct. Literally rips out the wires and lays down new ones that make the attraction taboo."

"Huh."

The devil on Jude's left shoulder prodded him with its pitchfork. "I mean, not for nothing, but if I didn't know you were my brother, I'd try to get your number."

Alex laughed. Sort of. His expression was hurt. Sort of. But then Tej and Val were back at the table, breathless and sweaty and laughing. Slamming another glass of sangria and dragging Alex and Jude out to dance.

As he rocked and swayed and shimmied in Tej's enthusiastic grip, Jude felt the collective female gaze downshift to a resigned fascination, while the collec-tive male gaze narrowed in suspicion.

I was born here, he reminded the world. *I'm in my home with my man and what you think won't make me lose sleep tonight. Pull any shit, my brother's got my back.*

Turning under Tej's arm, Jude came face to face with Alex's gaze. It wasn't hostile, but it wasn't quite a look of got-your-back either.

Well then, suck my dick, Jude thought. Hating himself for it. But unable to keep from checking a strongbox in his heart, making sure his passport was there. Next to his packed bag.

UNSURPRISINGLY, ALEX AND JUDE were alone at the breakfast buffet the next morning, each ejected from the hotel room by a hungover mate.

"Think we can get a bloody Mary in a to-go cup?" Jude asked, hitching his chair in and unfolding his napkin.

Alex gave a tight smile and said nothing.

"You all right?"

"Yeah."

But he only picked at his food. Surreptitiously glancing sideways at Jude eating. The silence stretched taut and tense. An elephant took a seat and poured itself a cup of coffee.

Can we just get it over with?

"You looked kind of offended last night, when I made a crack about getting your number," Jude said. "It was a joke."

Of course, he said it just as Alex took a more enthusiastic bite of his omelet. His eyes bulged as he chewed through a reply. "I know."

"Okay. Wasn't sure if you…"

Alex swallowed his food. His gaze was hard grey. "I have zero problem with you being gay, if that's what you're implying."

"Not at all." Feeling foolish, Jude took a bite of bacon, which he didn't even want. Now the silence swelled like an angry pimple.

"Look, I'm sorry," he said.

Just as Alex said, "Our Uncle Felipe was gay."

A beat of silence like a challenge.

"Really?" Jude said.

"Really. And I'm bisexual."

The elephant slipped away as the brothers stared.

"Sort of," Alex said. "Right around the time Deane was having a thing with her cousin, I was having a…thing with my best friend."

Jude blinked. "Oh."

Alex smiled at his hands. "Just sharing."

"Well." He took a steadying sip of coffee. "How was that walk on the dark side?"

"Dark."

"Does Val know?"

"Mmhm." He was still faintly smiling, but Jude's keen ear heard the perfect pitch of a vulnerable pain.

So this is a brother laying his heart at your feet.

And who are you going to be?

"I'll listen if you want to talk about it."

"Not much to tell. He came into my life. He became an incredible friend to both me and Val. Then he told me he was bi. That I was more to him than a friend. And all at once, to my shock, I realized I felt the same."

"You never in your life were attracted to guys?"

"Never."

"Did you…?" Jude turned a hand over in the air.

"We came close. Then Val busted us and it was a fucking mess."

"For real? She caught you?"

"Red-handed." Alex closed his eyes against the memory. "It sucked."

"The kind of moment when your entire life falls out your asshole?"

The eyes opened and he laughed. "Oh my God, that's *exactly* how it felt."

"But you worked it out, obviously. I mean, from where I stand, your marriage looks tight."

"We made it back from Crazytown." Alex took a sip of coffee. "But man, it sucked. I sucked. Not my finest moment at all."

"It had to have been all kinds of bewildering."

"And violent." He looked at Jude now, earnest, intent and supplicant. "I had no idea an affair involved that kind of emotional violence. I didn't know *not* having an affair was so fucking violent."

"Do you still see him?"

"In person? Rarely. We talk, we're in touch. Shit, he was the first person I called after I got off the phone with you that night, so… It's not exactly estrangement but it's definitely distant."

"Gotcha."

"He's living with someone now. Maybe that'll narrow the distance. Someday."

"As far as attraction goes, are you writing it off as a one-time, random thing? Or do you accept this as part of you?"

Alex didn't answer for a long time. His mouth twisted, considering and rejecting words before he finally spoke. "It's hard," he said. "It's like a resource that will go untapped because I'm not going to cheat on my wife with anyone. Ever again. On the one hand, there's a lot of comfort in that resolution. On the other, it's a source of frustration. My mind thinks what it thinks and my body wants what it wants. By day, I don't actively think about it too much. But he likes to show up in my dreams at night and I can't do anything about that. I wake up rattled and some days it's hard to reset. It's just something I have to deal with."

"Some choices are simple to make but it doesn't mean the execution is easy," Jude said.

"Mm."

"What's his name?"

"Javier."

"¿Es chileno?"

"Dominicano."

"Is it hard to see him with his boyfriend?"

"It…arouses my curiosity."

Jude laughed.

Alex was blushing. "When we hooked up, neither of us knew what the hell we were doing. Now I'm aware he's gone down a road I haven't and he definitely knows what he's doing. So while I'm curious, I'm also a little intimidated."

"He wouldn't be blindly fooling around this time."

"No. So it's hard to see them, yeah. But Jesus, he's so happy. He got dealt a shitty hand in life and after everything he's been through, he deserves this."

"Circling back, you really feel like you identify as bisexual now?"

"Selectively," Alex said slowly. "Is it lame to need that modifier? I mean, it's only happened once with one particular guy."

"Hey, I give you a ton of credit. Not many straight men I know would be a quarter as open-minded."

"It's good to talk about it. I really don't have anyone else I can take it to. I mean, I tell Val everything, but under the circumstances…"

"It can't be *everything.*"

"No. And weirdly, the only other person I think would connect to how I feel is Deane."

"Why?"

"Because she loves her cousin."

"Ah," Jude said slowly. "I see what you mean."

"They've made their choice not to be together, but you don't flip a switch and turn it all off, right? It still is what it is and it's going to be something they struggle with. Not struggle. Live with. Knowing every now and then it'll show up in a dream or rear up and bite them."

"Makes sense."

"Still, she's my baby and this isn't for her ears."

"Only mine."

Alex gave him a long slow gaze. "I think if you weren't my brother, I'd give you my number."

Jude pretended to gag. "Sorry, I've been re-wired to find you gross."

THE LANDSCAPE

*N*OW THE CITY STREETS were festooned with red, white and blue for Chile's Independence Day. Loud, accordion-drenched music beckoned from around corners, along with the tantalizing smoke of a dozen barbecues. Perfectly sober to mildly buzzed to totally soused, the Santiaguinos sang, drank, and turned the rows of sizzling meat skewers called anticucho. Other vendors hawked mushroom and cheese enchiladas, or whipped up fruit juices and even the lethal terremoto concoction of pisco and ice cream.

After an hour in the jostling, carousing crowds, the Tholets and Pendas found a table outside a café at the edge of a plaza and stopped to rest. Tej, Val and Cleon wandered into a nearby bookstore. Alex crossed his arms and closed his eyes, face tilted up to the sun. A group of people in traditional dress began dancing by the fountain.

"Look, it's the cueca," Penny said.

Jude watched the paired-up men and women, each holding a white handkerchief. They circled one another with sideways, grapevined steps. When they met, they didn't touch, didn't hold hands. They shared ends of the handkerchiefs and exchanged flirtatious glances. A crowd slowly made a ring around them, hands raised by ears, clapping smartly to the beat.

Jude's phone pinged an incoming text. He glanced. Did a double take. It was Aiden.

To what do I owe the pleasure, he thought, smirking as he swiped the screen. He read two sentences, then began scrolling down, confused.

"Jude, what's wrong?" Penny said.

"Nothing."

"You look the way you did when you first read your DNA results."

He laughed. "Almost as shocking. Aiden just texted me."

"Our Aiden?"

"Aiden your brother?" Alex said.

Penny bumped Alex's arm. "You mean brother from another mother?"

A stab of silence. Alex and Jude looked at each other, then at her.

"Too soon?" she said.

Both men gave a simultaneous bray of laughter.

"Penelope, you bitch," Jude said, pretending to backhand her.

"She went there," Alex said.

She blushed as they affectionately pummeled and swatted her from both sides.

"Good lord, this is lengthy," Jude said, back to scrolling the fat wedge of text. "A whole paragraph. He must've been hacked."

"Aiden is what you'd call a terse communicator," Penny said to Alex.

"What does it say?"

Jude read it to them.

> *Out at a dive bar last night and met a guy who is Mapuche—native Chilean, with a little bit of Rapa Nui in his heritage, too. Real spiritual dude. Long, thin face. Intense stare and a crew cut so he looks like a Moai statue. Anyway, I kind of told him your life story and everything going on. And he told me some cool things about Condors. Their spiritual meaning, that is. I went back to find him tonight so he could tell me again and I could write it down exactly. And weirdly, he was coming to find me for the same reason. He said he had a dream last night and he had a message for you. He asked me to open voice recording on my phone, and the sound file of him talking is attached. I hope—*

Jude stopped reading aloud.

> *I hope you're okay. I think about you all the time. I mean it. I wish I could say stuff more easily. I don't like when things change. I want you to know this changes nothing. You're my brother and always will be.*
> *—A*

He looked up, his gaze damp around the edges. "That last part was just for me." He cleared his throat hard, opened the sound file and set his phone down on the table. He hit play.

"Hola, Julio, this is… ¿Qué? Po. Juleón. Disculpa. Does he speak Spanish? Of course. Hola, Juleón, po, me llamo Elicura Lienlaf."

Three heads bent toward the center of the table, hovering over the crackling line of the WAV file, heads tilted into Elicura's messy Spanish, punctuated by pos and cachais.

"El cóndor is the reigning hunter-king of the skies," he said. "He uses all of his senses to hunt for prey, find a mate, raise young and protect himself. But his keenest, most powerful sense is his vision. His ability to interpret what he sees in the sky is unsurpassed, po, and this visual prowess even spills over into his spiritual life.

"El cóndor's divine gift from the universe is interpreting the landscape of his mind, cachai? He looks at images and visions, understands the messages within and translates them into personal power, ultimately shaping his destiny.

"Part of el cóndor's gift is knowing how to interpret what he sees to his advantage. He knows the divine purpose of the universe is to follow the path of enlightenment and el cóndor does not settle for anything less. ¿Entiéndeme, hueón? ¿Cachai? He always takes the highest path.

"Po, your brother told me you were hunted by a condor in your youth. A predator who broke your leg and forced your people out of his territory. Banished you from his sky-sight. I fell asleep last night thinking about your story, and I had an intense dream about two condors fighting in the mountains. I believe it was a message, so I'll tell you and you do with it what you will, cachai?

"The boy who hunted you was not a condor. He was no king. He was a pretender to the throne of the skies. An imposter. He had no vision. No gift. No enlightenment and no path.

"You, Juleón, you are a true condor. Po, you are a king and the sky is before you. You have extremely powerful and interpretive vision. You know your divine path and your purpose. *No te conformes con menos.* Do not settle for anything less. This is not me telling you, hueón, but el cóndor himself. ¿Cachai? Bueno. Adiós. ¿Aiden, cómo paro esto? Ah, sí, sí—"

The recording abruptly ended, as did the music from the cueca. Applause echoed in the plaza.

"Wow," Jude said.

From its perch on the heel of her hand, Penny nodded. "I think a shaman just confirmed you were made to go out and get it."

Jude barely heard her. He was scrolling backward on his phone, looking over the landscape of his brother's text. A condor on the hunt, his predator eye homing in on the last line.

I want you to know this changes nothing. You're my brother and you always will be.
His talons delicately picked it out of the sky, interpreting the message within.
You're my brother and you always will be.
Jude glanced up at Alex. All the features inherited from Eduardo and Clementina mirrored back at him. And suddenly, it was there. So simple.
You're my brother, he thought, looking at Alex, then at the phone.
I don't have to choose between two paths.
The sky is before me and the sky is vast.
The sky has room for many true kings, as long as they know their purpose.
Aiden and Alex are my brothers.
And always will be.

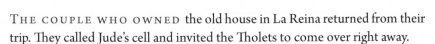

THE COUPLE WHO OWNED the old house in La Reina returned from their trip. They called Jude's cell and invited the Tholets to come over right away.

Penny kept a hand tight in Cleon's elbow as they moved from room to room. Noting new floors. A wall taken out or put up. Whether the layout of the kitchen, the living room, the bedrooms was the same or different.

Jude followed, detached and sullen, feeling suddenly and weirdly robbed of an experience.

I was never here. If we came before we took the DNA test, I could've claimed an in utero connection. But I have nothing, no history in this place.

I wasn't the baby my mother was pregnant with in this house. I wasn't the baby born on the living room floor.

I was never here.

Penny didn't become emotional until they went into the back yard, which spread out like a park, incorporating all the land that was once the nursery. Drifts of perennial foliage, fruit trees in bud, meandering paths.

"Look," Jude said, pointing to a stone bench. "It's your happy place."

She laughed and sat down. Posed for Jude's camera. Cleon sat beside her and Jude took more pictures, texting them to Serena and Aiden.

At the garden's far end were the two free-standing, one-bedroom bungalows, a paved patio area between. A pergola was built over the flagstones, thick with bougainvillea blossoms.

"That's new," Cleon said. "Looks like they have new roofs, too."

"Uncle Louis lived here," Penny said, peeking in one unit's window. "Ysidro and Tatán were in that one."

She walked off into the garden beds again but Cleon stayed, his expression blank.

"You all right, Papi?" Jude asked.

Cleon scratched his head under his hat. "I had no idea that October morning. I drove away from this house with no idea I'd never see it again."

"I wonder what happened to your stuff," Tej said. "Not just yours but all the stuff left behind by the ones who fled or were disappeared. Apartments full of lives. Food in the fridge, books on shelves, art on the walls, sheets folded in the closet. Toys. Soap. Pots and pans. What became of it all?"

Cleon slowly shook his head, eyes wide in his weathered face. "Stolen. Scavenged. Who knows."

"You can disappear a person but not their things."

"Not one thing of ours is here except the flowers."

"And the memories?"

Cleon turned slightly, surveying the beautiful property. "Those too."

Tej glanced at Jude then back at Cleon. "Can I ask you a question? You don't have to answer."

"Sure."

"What does 'Louis made ten, I made but one' mean?"

A strange mix of awe and annoyance prickled the back of Jude's neck. It was a ballsy question and pure Tej fearlessness. But even Jude didn't know what was behind the note pinned to the wall in the Lucy room. Why should Cleon give Tej an answer?

Louis made ten. I made but one.

"My uncle survived Sachsenhausen by joining with nine other men," Cleon said. "They made a minyan. A quorum. They survived by building a memory palace filled with stories. Ten floors. Ten wings on a floor, ten rooms to a wing. Each room filled with ten stories. They survived together, as long as they could. Louis was the only one to get out alive, and he became the steward of the palace. He made ten.

"When I was in the Villa Grimaldi, I tried it Louis's way. But I couldn't. I made one room. The room Jude showed you. I joined with no one else. My palace only had space for one. Me. Me alone." He took off his hat and fidgeted with the brim, smoothing and shaping it. "It always bothered me. And it was why I never wanted to come back to Chile. Not because of the ghosts in the Villa, or the ghosts at this house. Because I couldn't come back without going to the cemetery. And I couldn't go to the cemetery without explaining to Louis why I made one when he made ten."

"I didn't know," Jude said softly.

Cleon smiled at him. "It's time you did, then."

"You wrote all those books," Tej said. "You collected all testimonials and accounts and survivor stories. The books are palaces. They're your ten rooms."

Cleon smiled wider, then reached and put his hat on Tej's head. "Gracias, hueón."

"This was so generous," Penny said, walking over with the owners, a young married couple. "I can't thank you enough for making the time."

"It was our pleasure," Marisol Esposito said.

Her husband, Pedro, asked, "Do you need us to call you a cab?"

"No, we drove over," Jude said. "We had to park a few blocks away. Looks like the café across the street is having a massive barbecue."

"Oh yes. Independence Week is one big barbecue."

"I'll bring the car around," Tej said, walking off. Still wearing Cleon's hat.

"I'm so glad we did this," Penny said. "Inside was anti-climactic. No ghosts. And outside was spectacular. I couldn't ask for more."

"Come see us again," Marisol said.

"Any time you come to Santiago," Pedro said. "Nuestra casa es su casa."

"Hey, Jude," Tej called from the end of driveway. He was patting his pockets. "Jude, do you have the keys?"

"Jude?" Marisol said, just as Pedro said, "Did he just call you Jude?"

Jude nodded. "Most people do."

"Like the Beatles song?"

"Right."

The Espositos exchanged a long, worried glance.

"¿Qué onda?" Cleon said.

Tej came back over. "You have the keys?"

"It's just funny it's your name," Marisol said.

"Funny why?" Jude said, his heart kicking up a notch.

"Come look at something," Pedro said. He herded them to a far corner of the yard and a large weeping cherry tree, sagging with buds.

"It was here when we bought the house," Marisol was saying.

"And the previous owners said it was here when *they* bought the place," Pedro said.

"Nobody knew what it was, exactly."

Pedro pointed beneath the tree.

Jude's face went numb as Penny screamed.

 THE LONELY PEOPLE

AN OBLONG OF PINK granite was embedded in the dirt at the base of the cherry tree, faintly sparkling where the sun's rays touched it. Block serif letters chiseled into its surface.

HEY, JUDE
25.11.73
Buried Along With His Name

"Oh my God," Tej said.

The blood pounded behind Penny's eyeballs and squeezed her temples. Her vision tunneled around letters and numbers as remembered voices darted from one ear to the other.

"I left a little room," Ysidro said. "I'll add the date when he's born."

"That's my birthday," Jude said.

"It's a lament for lonely people," Tatán said. "They missed each other, missed a chance to have a connection. All the priest can do is make sure she's buried along with her name."

Penny heard Cleon behind her, hoarse and choked. "Jesus Christ, what did they do?"

"Careful," Tej said. "Lean on me if you need to. You all right?"

"Mami," Jude said, fingers tight in her sleeve. "How did this get here?"

"Pedro, can we get a chair?" Tej said.

Unable to take her eyes from the stone, Penny put a hand on Jude's shoulder. She put down one stiff, trembling knee. Then the other. Her palms tingled, recalling the warm slick curve of a newborn skull. The little face against her neck.

Es un niño, señora.

Is he alive?

Is he crying?

"Lucy…"

She blinked and looked back. Cleon was seated in a lawn chair, head in his hands.

"You know what this is?" Pedro asked, looking around the stunned faces.

"We thought it was for a pet," Marisol said. "The previous owners buried their dog here."

"No," Tej said, leaning over the back of Cleon's chair, holding him. "We think it's a baby."

"What?" Marisol cried. "No. Stop it, you can't be serious."

"¿Qué mierdas pasó?" Pedro said.

Penny looked back at the stone. Her fingers reached to touch the smooth surface and sharp, beveled edges.

All the priest can do is make sure she's buried with her name.

"It's safe to remember," Dr. Mezeritz said. "The danger is over. Remembering will not hurt you."

Penny remembered. She'd missed it before, but now the story fell open before her, etched in stone. The answer wasn't in the irretrievable memories from the day of Jude's birth. It was in the kitchen table talk from the night before.

Tatán. God, he's so upset tonight. The government has been sending him to odd locations around the city.

Jude sat in the grass beside her. "I don't understand"

He's picking up the dead. Bodies in horrible shape. Things he can't un-see. And tonight…

"He was out here all alone," Cleon said.

"You didn't know," Tej said.

"All these years. Left alone in the ground. Out in the rain and cold."

"It wasn't your fault."

Tonight Tatán picked up two dead children from one of the stadiums. And a newborn baby.

It's not the first time.

Twice before he's been given a newborn. Each time he took them to the orphanage. La Casa de Huérfanos.

Tatán Álvarez, that beautiful, tender soul. The romantic idealist who championed the lonely people. Standing graveside as a witness, because he believed nobody should die alone.

He's hunched at the table, crying into his hands, saying it's only going to happen more. How many pregnant women are being detained? If they survive, how will they know what happened to their babies?

"What the fuck is going on," Jude said.

My baby is going to be born so afraid.

The revelation boiled up into her throat, bubbled over in a raging grief that slashed like a hundred blades. "Oh my God," she cried through the barricade of her fingers. Then she was weeping from her guts. Pitching forward as if rifle-butted in the head, palms hitting the soft grass. Jude drew her off her knees and into the hard curve of his side.

"It's all right," he said, holding her tight.

Her heart burst open, running wet from her eyes to her mouth.

Is the baby alive?

Is he crying?

How many pregnant women?

How will they know what happened?

Jude curled his fingers in her rough hair and kissed her crown, rocking her. "You didn't know," he said. "It isn't your fault. You didn't know."

Fool, how could you not have known?

You forgot you remembered what Tatán saw.

He lamented the lonely people.

He thought no one should die alone.

He was given the dead bodies of children. He was given newborn babies.

"I'm sorry," Jude whispered. "Whatever it is, I'm so sorry."

They weren't switched in the hospital, my baby and Jude.

Tatán did it.

But how?

When?

"Come here," Cleon said hoarsely. "Lucy, please. Come here now."

CLEÓN

*T*HEY CALL YOUR NAME.

You're cuffed, blindfolded and put into a van again.

The palace comes with you. Behind your taped eyes, you fuss with details and make small repairs. Lay more tile in the mosaic river. Tilt cellophane flowers into better position. Fold new taxis. Pick ripe tangerines and hold them to your face. All the while your fingers poise over your palm, ready to tap three times and be gone.

You emerge blinking and bewildered into the bright lights of another stadium. Not the Estadio Chile but the Estadio Nacional, east of downtown Santiago.

Compared to Villa Grimaldi, this place is a hotel. You're allowed to shower with cold water and a scrap of industrial soap. You're allowed to sit on a proper toilet. You get new clothes and shoes and don't care much that they belong to a dead person.

You catch sight of yourself in a locker room mirror.

The man staring back is a thousand years old.

If you ever get out of here, will Lucy even know you?

The guards hand out chocolate flan. You and your compañeros wolf down the treat. Then as one, you vomit on your new shoes. The guards bray laughing, doubled over and slapping each other. You heave over and over, a puddle of human excrement at your feet, the smell in your throat and nose, the taste slimy and foul.

It's the final humiliation. You are nothing to these people. Your country has chewed you up and shit you out.

You try not to think about it. You can't help thinking about it. Every time you think about it, you vomit again. It's a long time before anything can get past your throat and stay in your stomach.

Never again, ever in your life, do you eat chocolate.

Next the guards hand out papers they demand detainees to sign—pre-printed testimonies of being treated well. It's not difficult to pretend your hands can't hold a pen. No trouble at all to feign misunderstanding or illness to avoid signing.

Your last blind ride is in a jeep.
After a winding, hour-long journey, the soldiers throw you out into the street.
You get one more beating for the road. You lose three teeth. Your spleen is ruptured.
Laughing, the guards climb back into the jeep and rev the engine.
Then they run over you.
Three bumps of the thick, dirty tires over your body.
And you're gone.

THE OTHER JUDE

*J*UDE FELT SICK AS he watched Penny crawl through the grass toward Cleon. His heart broke as she dragged herself up between his knees and fell against his chest.

He turned his head away, back to the pink granite stone. He couldn't pry his mind's fingers off the idea he was looking at his own grave.

No, not me, him. It was supposed to be me.

No, wait, it was never me. I was never here.

Was this baby born dead? Who buried him here?

Penny moaned in Cleon's embrace. "I didn't see it. I remembered what he said but I never put it together. I didn't *know.*"

Tej knelt by Jude, took his hand. "What does this mean?"

"I don't know," Jude said.

"How did they do it?" Penny cried. "When did they do it?"

They who? Jude thought. *She knows something. She understands it now. What does it mean?*

Cleon's fingers clutched at the back of Penny's shirt. His brow rolled side to side on her shoulder, as if saying *No, no, no. . .*

Penny sat back on her heels, dragging the backs of her hands across her face.

Marisol brought out mason jars of limeade for everyone, and a cold cloth for Penny's swollen face. Pedro brought more chairs. They sat and listened, pale and incredulous, as the Tholets told their story.

"You weren't switched at the hospital," Penny said, looking at Jude with red-rimmed eyes. "It must have happened before. Along the way."

"What must have happened?" Jude said, confused.

"Tatán knew," Penny said. "Tatán saw it. I remembered during the hypnosis. How Tatán was transporting both the dead and the living."

As Jude thought back to the sessions with Dr. Mezeritz, a map took shape in his mind. A taped-together, aerial view of Santiago. Landmarks circled in black. Superimposed with the image of Ysidro and Tatán, leaning against a hearse and laughing.

The memorial mason and the undertaker. The Kings of Death. The amateur midwives when Penny gave birth to Jude.

Not me, Jude thought. *The other Jude. This Jude. I was born somewhere else. Near or on the same day.*

The map pulsed. Pointing. Demanding he notice. Insisting he remember.

During the hypnosis session, Mami still didn't remember giving birth.

But she remembered talk at the kitchen table.

She remembered Tatán crying. He was distraught because he picked up newborn babies when he picked up the dead at strange places around Santiago.

"And Villa Grimaldi is less than ten minutes from here," he said aloud.

Villa Grimaldi, where the last eyewitness account put María Clementina Vilaró.

I really was born there, he thought, his mind in a whirlwind tour of the compound. The tower. The swimming pool. The excavated steps of the old villa. The permanently locked gates. The concrete leaf. The fountain. The rose garden.

It's true. I know it is.

I was born in the same place my father was imprisoned.

We were there together.

He was El Cóndor, king of the skies. Finding the hidden secrets and symbols in the landscape. Interpreting the message within. The scene unfolded before his myopic eyes, reflecting off the inside of his glasses.

Penny's baby was stillborn. The Kings of Death drove her and the dead infant to the hospital in Tatán's hearse. Along the way, Tatán must have made a scheduled stop.

"*A lot can happen in fifteen minutes,*" Tej said, looking at the map of Santiago.

Now the hearse carried a couple corpses and a live baby. An unconscious mother whom the Kings loved dearly. She became their family when their people turned against them. She had taken them in, opened her heart and her home, had them sit at her kitchen table. Now her husband was imprisoned. Her uncle-in-law shot in the street. Her child dead. The Kings had the means to keep her from becoming one of the lonely people.

Tatán acted like Eleanor Rigby and Father McKenzie were real people. It moved him that they missed each other. Missed their chance to have a connection.

He wouldn't have missed this chance.

The hearse pulled up to Hospital del Salvador. Ysidro carried in Penny and the baby from the Villa Grimaldi. The baby who became Jude Tholet. Tatán made his delivery to the morgue.

They brought Other Jude back here.

And buried him along with his name.

"But it can't be," Jude said, looking back at his parents. "Ysidro and Tatán couldn't have pulled off something like this."

Cleon turned his palm up to the sky and raised it back toward the tree. "Then what the hell is that stone doing there? Engraved with those words and that date?"

"Ysidro finished it," Penny said. "He told me he would. He left room for the date. He came to the hospital and promised he would bury Uncle Louis and give him a proper stone. He was telling me more. He added that lyric for a reason, don't you see?"

Desperation lined her face. She needed this to be the truth.

"It may be you never have a satisfying answer to this," Dr. Mezeritz said. *"You probably won't have a Hollywood resolution moment. The proverbial Perry Mason courtroom gasp."*

The most the Tholets could hope for was a satisfying truth built out of the pieces.

A truth that could never be verified, but a truth they still could believe in.

We'll never know, Jude thought. *We will never, never know what happened.*

But from everything we do know… It seems to be what happened.

I can believe this is what happened.

The Kings of Death switched me and my mother's stillborn baby.

They were two young, terrified lonely people. They were trying to make a sad song better.

Ysidro shortened Juleón to Jude and chiseled it into a scrap of pink granite. Not as a memorial, but as a gift. A private joke between him and Penny. A love letter. A thank you note. One of the million bits and pieces left behind when thousands of lifetimes disappeared.

He made it as a birth gift, Jude thought. *But it ended up being a gravestone after all.*

"It can't be," he said again. "No. Come on. It's just fucking *impossible*."

He stared at his parents, who looked helplessly back.

They all believed in this truth.

"Is there somebody we should call?" Pedro finally asked.

THE BORING EVERYDAY THINGS

*C*ALLS WERE MADE. TO the police. The authorities. Isabella Eberhoff.
All the correct bureaucrats alerted to the possible presence of an infant buried
in the Espositos' yard. But it wasn't a *Law & Order* hard cut to the forensic team
thrusting a spade into the ground. These things took time. Statements given,
affidavits made, reports filed. There was nothing to do but go home and wait.

"Love each other and see what happens," Alex said. He and Jude hugged a
long time in the Santiago airport, holding each other's heads.

"I'll see you soon," Jude said gruffly.

"I'll see you everywhere."

"This trip is in the top five things that ever happened to me."

Alex laughed, drew back and ran a forearm across his face. "For sure."

The families boarded their respective flights with their strange souvenirs. A
piece of floorboard. Some marble chips. A gravestone rubbing. A pink granite
headstone.

They went home. Back to work. Back to life. Jude printed out pictures of the
trip and hung them on his walls. He kept a framed shot of him and Alex on his
desk. He added names and dates to his family tree and started making cautious,
tentative contact with some of the distant cousins. Piecing together the other
side of his family history. Accepting it as one of his truths.

It was late October when the forensic team in Santiago began to dig, and
nearing Thanksgiving when Jude got the news.

"They didn't find anything," he said to Alex on the phone.

"What?"

"No bones underneath the tree. Only dirt."

"Nothing?"

"Nothing."

"Oh my God. I don't believe it."

"Me neither."

"Are you okay? You sound crushed, man."

"I'm devastated. I mean, it's nuts. I had no idea how much I had invested in this being the answer to everything."

"I'm sorry."

"We were so sure."

"So was I. It made so much sense."

"My mother is a wreck. It really hit her hard and I'm worried… I mean, it's like…" His voice gave out and Jude pushed the heel of his hand into his eyes.

"It's all right," Alex said.

"She just keeps taking it and taking it and…"

"I know. She doesn't deserve this. How's your dad doing with it?"

"He's not an emotional man by design. His meds keep him from being devoured by ghosts. But he's walking around blank-eyed and stunned. He looks like a refugee."

"Oh man. Jude, I feel terrible."

"They look old. For the first time, I can't deny their age. They've always been so hale and lively. Now they look frail to me and everything feels so fucking tenuous and unfair."

"I'm so sorry."

Jude gave a tremendous exhale that did nothing to alleviate the pressure in his throat and chest. "Anyway. That's the news. And I miss you."

Alex gave a short, surprised laugh. "I miss you, too."

"You know, Deane texts me. All the time."

"She does?"

"Yeah. Just to say hi. She tells me little things going on. She'll FaceTime me and introduce me to her friends. And I love it. Suddenly being an uncle makes me so happy. I love making this little relationship with her. I want her to meet my sister, I think they'd get along great."

"I love it too," Alex said. "I'm a huge believer in what Val calls 'the second circle.' When the shit goes down, you have your first phone calls, sure. But who's your second line of defense? And the third and fourth? Growing up, Uncle Felipe was my legal guardian but I always had the Larks as backup. When I became a father, I never wanted to hoard Deane and imply Val and I were the only ones she could count on. I wanted her to build concentric rings of community and have a ton of numbers in her phone. Different people she can take different problems to. Knowing you can be one of those phone calls now? Both you and Tej? It's…"

"It's a gift," Jude said.

"Yeah. And the world needs more gifts like it."

"We'll get together again real soon. I don't want years to go by between visits, you know?"

"I know. And news of your life—you, Tej, your parents, your sister and brother—I want to know that stuff, know what's going on. I want to know you had a dentist appointment. Share all the boring everyday things, I'll tell you when it's too much information."

"What are you wearing right now?"

"Jeans and a... Shut the fuck up."

"Talk slower."

"*Get* out of my face."

Jude laughed, finally feeling a little better. "All right, I gotta go. I'll call you soon."

"Vale, hueón. Say hi to Tej."

"I will. Hug Val for me."

"Love you. Adiós."

"Te quiero. Ciao."

⌒

JUDE'S THIRTY-SEVENTH BIRTHDAY WAS on Thanksgiving Day. Penny was still depressed and ambivalent to holiday celebrations. She didn't want to cook, didn't want to go anywhere. They came to her and Tej cooked everything, including his tangerine cake for Jude.

They sat in the living room with coffee and dessert. A fire crackled. Displayed on the mantlepiece was the pink granite stone, still a little green around the edges from decades in the earth. Penny and Cleon loved its memory and hated its mystery.

It was all they had.

"Have you named him?" Tej asked carefully. "I mean, do you privately call him something now?"

"Funny you ask," Cleon said. "We only just decided on Luis Felice Tholet."

"Named for grandfather and grand-uncle," Penny said.

"The botanist and the sculptor," Jude said.

"Does Luis have a diminutive?" Tej asked.

"Lucho, I suppose," Cleon said. "The little light. Which shouldn't be buried under a bushel but shine on to yadda yadda yadda. My New Testament is rusty."

Tej smiled. "Neither do men light a candle, and put it under a bushel, but on a candlestick; and it giveth light unto all that are in the house."

"Dig you spewing the scripture," Jude said.

"Don't throw a Bible gauntlet at a Maronite Christian."

"Challenge accepted."

"Play something, Jude," Serena said. She was curled up against Giosué on the couch, pregnant like a strawberry.

Jude was still working on his plate of tangerine cake, but with his free hand, he slowly played the opening line of "Eleanor Rigby." The C-major progression—*Ah, look at all the*—shifting into E-minor for the last four notes. *Lonely people.*

He picked out the verse melody. McCartney was such a freaking genius. He wrote in Dorian mode, a minor scale with a natural sixth degree. It showed in the mournful C-sharp as Eleanor first picked up the rice in the church, then again when she died there.

And was buried along with her name.

"Nobody came," Jude sang softly.

"Oh my fucking God," Serena said, rocking and rolling up from the couch.

"What?" Cleon said.

"You've got to be *kidding* me." She went to the mantle, pointing at the pink stone. "Oh my God, we missed it."

"Missed what?" Tej said.

"Buried with his name. Mami. It's right *here.*"

"What's right here?" Penny said. "What are you talking about?"

"Buried along with his name. His name is Tholet."

"Of course it is. And?"

Serena turned back, revelation in her eyes, her belly burgeoning with the next generation. "He's buried with Uncle Louis."

THE INFANT

*T*HERE HAD NEVER BEEN a pair of greedier, more jealous grandparents. During the hospital visits, Penny and Cleon glared at anyone daring to hold Giulia longer than ten minutes. They glared at each other, calculating intervals of cuddling down to the microsecond. Shameless martyrs, they suffered the indignity of Serena nursing the infant, then snatched her back.

Gimme. Mine. My turn.

"You are ridiculous," Serena said from her bed.

"You're goddamn right," Cleon said, hovering over Penny's shoulder. She sat in the sunshine, arms and eyes brimming. Her finger caught in the baby's tight fist, which she held against her lips.

"Stand by the bed," Giosué said. "I want a picture of three generations."

Serena moved over. "Get in here, Mami. Take to the bed."

Penny carefully squeezed beside, rested her head on her daughter's and smiled for the camera. The forgotten taste of joy was sweet in her mouth. Her heart sighed, finally soothed and restful for the first time since they returned from Chile.

Tej and Jude arrived, bearing gifts. Chocolates for Serena. A bag of McDonald's hash browns for Giosué.

"Oh man," he said, digging into the greasy sack. "Jude, you know how to make me eat out of your hand."

For Giulia, there were picture books and onesies.

"Cleon, check it out," Tej said, shaking one of the tiny garments loose and showing its silkscreened seahorses. "It matches yours."

Cleon reached to hitch up his right trouser leg, revealing the magnificent seahorse airbrushed on his prosthetic calf.

"Can I hold her?" Jude asked Penny.

"No."

"All righty then."

"You'll get a chance," Serena said, winking at her brother. "Mami has to pee at some point, right?"

"The baby comes with me," Penny said. "Girls always go to the bathroom together."

Cleon cleared his throat, glancing meaningfully at his watch.

"You hold your seahorses," she said.

Jude sat in one of the armchairs. "I have some news."

Penny gasped and blurted, "You're engaged."

An embarrassed beat of silence, broken by a snort of stifled laughter from Tej. "Um, no," he said.

"Not yet," Jude said.

"Forgive the abuela, boys," Serena said. "She has no filter when she's this happy."

"Wait, what do you mean *yet*?" Tej said.

"Oh Christ," Giosué muttered through a mouthful of hash browns.

"I have some news," Jude said loudly. "I got the call yesterday, but it was Serena's day so I waited."

"What call?" Cleon said.

"From Detective Arendt."

The residual laughter died off. The family drew close. Penny got off the bed and moved to sit by Cleon. "We'll hold her together for this," she said.

Arranging an exhumation had been a longer, more complicated and more bureaucratic operation than digging up the yard in La Reina. The Tholets needed to hire both an attorney and a rabbi to facilitate the process, which stretched out over the winter to the point where it went invisible.

"Two sets of bones were inside Uncle Louis's grave," Jude said. He drew from his inside pocket a printed copy of the forensic report and passed it around. "One set was confirmed to be an adult male. The other was a complete, almost intact skeleton of an infant."

The woven cradle of Penny and Cleon's arms tightened.

Jude went on. Forensic examination concluded no abnormal fractures or blunt-force trauma to the baby's chest or skull. Examining the latter, analyzing spatial geometry and suture boundaries, the coroner was confident the infant was either stillborn or died shortly after birth, but the cause was undetermined. He was slightly less confident the baby was male. DNA analysis would confirm, if they could get the bones to talk.

"They've sent fragments to the Medical-Legal Institute," Jude said. "From both sets of bones, so they can compare to Papi and Aiden. If it was a boy, they'd all have the same Y-chromosome."

"And what then?" Giosué said. "What becomes of the remains?"

"It's up to us," Jude said. "They can be reinterred in the Jewish Cemetery. Or, if it's time and it's what we want, they can come home. We could have Louis's gravestone shipped if we wanted." He got up and crouched in front of Penny and Cleon. He picked up one of Giulia's tiny fists and kissed it. "We can do anything. This is our family."

They'd wait and see. Hope the DNA within the tiny skeleton would wake up and speak to them. Recognize and claim them.

They held their breath and waited on the truth in the bones, knowing at the end of the day, the bones never lied.

CLEÓN

*Y*OUR HOSPITAL ROOM IS *so clean.*

They've shaved you to the skin, getting rid of the lice and fleas and caked filth. The sheets are cool and soft against your bald pate. Nurses and orderlies have gotten all the dirt out of you, with soap and water, carbolic, alcohol and saline. They clean under your fingernails and behind your ears, as if you're a child. Tubes whisk away all your waste, you don't even have to look at it.

So clean. Everything is so clean again.

As soon as you can sit up, the baby is put in your arms. Out of the ceiling light and into the crook of your elbow, Lucy's brightest diamond. A marshmallow fist closed around your finger. His kaleidoscope eyes are shut tight. You put your nose against his crown and inhale tangerines.

Juleón. Clean and whole in your arms. Heavy and warm on your chest. His smooth, hairless face up against yours, whispers of sweet breath on your skin.

Juleón.

You hold him for hours, your legs encased in plaster and porcupined with steel rods. When he's out of your arms, the pain rises up, the memories come out to play, the dirt creeps back in.

You're in bad shape, yet you make few requests of the hospital staff. Bring the baby. Let me hold my son. Give my son to me.

And no chocolate, please.

It appears on your lunch tray, foul and disgusting. Mocking your clean world and reaching filthy fingers toward Juleón's perfection. You keep the arm holding him composed while the other hand seizes the offensive dessert and throws it against the wall.

"No chocolate, please," you say. A world of threat within the polite tone. These people have no fucking idea who they're dealing with. You've seen things that would make them go mad. You've learned ways to break people and they'd be fools to believe you won't use them.

They have no idea the lengths you will go to keep this child safe.

They cannot imagine what you will do to protect your family.

The baby yawns against your angry heart. Your palm smooths his head of wispy, dark hair, running it this way and that. You kiss him. Smell him. Swear by him.

Juleón.

You are in his blood and bones. Yours is the back half of his name. It doesn't matter if you ever stand on your legs again. You will stand behind this boy and never let him out of your sight.

Imagínate.

Your eyes are drooping.

Picture yourself, on a boat on a river.

Your hand on Jude's shoulder as he sails past tangerine trees.

Your other fingers curl and tap against your palm.

. . .

. . .

. . .

And you're gone.

THE LAST NAME

*S*ANTIAGO'S MUSEUM OF MEMORY and Human Rights accepted Cleon's donation of his Lucy installation, sight unseen. They sent a curator to Seattle to supervise the dismantling of the ceiling and the diorama. Cleon was brisk and unsentimental as the light went out in Lucy's pregnant belly and the screws spiraled out of the sky panels. It was time. He wanted it gone. This room was going to be for his grandchildren to play in. He would come in here to shape the future, not the past.

Every piece was carefully wrapped and placed in shipping crates. Every drawing unpinned from the walls and smoothed flat in art portfolios. Once the rooms were empty, Cleon called in his children to spackle, patch and paint.

"Your daughter has made Papi into a tyrant," Jude said to Serena. "I hope you're satisfied."

"You and Tej better get a move on," she said. "I can't build this family tree all by myself, you know."

He glared cross-eyed at her, then glanced at Tej, who was plugged into his earbuds and methodically painting the window sashes.

"You guys would make some beautiful babies," she said. "I am just saying."

"Well I'm trying my damnedest every night but I just can't get him pregnant. I don't know what I'm doing wrong."

She bent to run her roller in the paint tray. "Out of hypothetical curiosity, if you had kids, what would you want their surname to be—Tholet or Penda?"

"Huh. Good question."

"You haven't thought about it?"

"I've thought about kids, sure, but the last name part didn't occur to me. He or she would be a Penda, though. I guess yeah, I'd want to include it somewhere."

"Penda-Tholet has a nice ring."

Jude glanced at Tej again. "Khoury-Tholet is nice, too."

Serena started painting again. "Can I say something sappy?"

"Can I stop you?"

"I've been thinking about the divine order. Things happening for a reason. People being born when they're supposed to be born, to the parents they're meant to have. Yadda yadda. It got me to thinking. I could've had an entirely different older brother growing up."

"You could have."

"Everything would've been different."

"Nah."

"I mean it. A lot of who I am is from being your sister."

Jude's roller stopped on the wall and he looked at her. "Really?"

By contrast, Serena was painting vigorously, her expression fierce. "Do you know I wrote hate mail to Juan-Mateo Díaz for years?"

Jude nearly stepped in the paint can. "Shut up."

"Swear to God."

"You wrote him while he was in jail?"

She nodded.

"Do Mami and Papi know?"

"Nope. I wrote a bunch of scathing letters to Feño Paloma's family, too. Which wasn't as satisfying as breaking their car windows with a baseball bat would've been. But I'm a peaceable person."

Jude stared. "I've literally never seen this side of you."

"I hate that family," she said. "I hate what they did to you and Feño. But. And…" She inclined her head toward Tej and smiled. "Who is he going to be now?"

Jude chewed on the question the rest of the afternoon. Looking at the divine order from his sister's vantage. Then taking one more step back and realizing the wheel she'd put in motion by bidding on DNA kits at a silent auction. If she hadn't won, the family wouldn't have spit into tubes and learned the truth. Without the shock of his revealed parentage, Jude wouldn't have stormed out of his parents' house and into a bar in Capitol Hill. Without everything he thought he knew about himself in question, he would've rebuffed the bold advances of a guy like Tej. He would've missed the chance.

But he didn't. All because Serena took a chance. The rest followed in divine order.

Everything that happened to me, he heard Cleon say, *happened so you could be my boy.*

He was still quiet and contemplative when he and Tej got home.

Tej rifled through the collected mail. "Letter for Señor Tholet," he said, handing over an air mail envelope. The return address read: *Servicio de Registro Civil e Identificación | Ministerio de Justicia y Derechos Humanos | Gobierno do Chile.*

"I know what this is," Jude said, working his thumb under the flap. He drew out and unfolded the heavy paper of his new birth certificate, printed under the seal of the civil clerk.

CERTIFICADO DE NACIMIENTO

Nombre: Juleón
Apellidos: Penda-Vilaró de Tholet
Fecha de nacimiento: 25 November 1973
Lugar de nacimiento: La Reina, Santiago
Madre: María Clementina Vilaró
Padre: Eduardo Gabriel Penda

"Wow," Tej said. "How's that feel?"

Jude looked over the certificate. He'd never use it in an official capacity. He was still a Canadian citizen, with Penny and Cleon's names on his Canadian birth certificate. He'd still travel on a Canadian passport and be a permanent US resident.

"It doesn't change anything," he said. "But it feels like mine."

"Happy re-birthday then." Tej reached, smushed Jude's mouth and kissed it. "This calls for cold beer and hot sex."

He went into the kitchen. Jude stood still, tapping the folded paper on his palm. Finally, he called, "Tim?"

"Yahbay."

"I was thinking…"

"What, you want the sex before the beer?" Tej clattered around in the fridge and came up with two bottles. He grinned as he twisted the caps and handed one over. "Too late."

Jude held up the certificate. "I'd really like one of these with your name on it, too."

Tej's brows pulled together. "Hm?"

"I mean, if you want to join the madness."

"The fuck are you talking about?"

Jude swallowed above a pounding heart. "See, I have this beautiful, whacko, unique and complicated family history. And I want you to be part of it."

Tej blinked.

"I'm saying I want to spend the rest of my life with you."

Tej said nothing.

"Like, I want to marry the shit out of you."

Silence.

"Hey." Jude put down the beer and the paper and took Tej's hands, suddenly nervous. Regretting the spontaneity and the joking tone, wondering if Tej wanted something more formal. "I don't have a ring, but…" He hesitated, then put a knee down. "Will you marry me?"

Tej just stared.

"See, this is where you say yes."

Tej's mouth opened slowly, then shut. He nodded.

"You can't possibly be speechless."

Now Tej slowly shook his head, lips pressed tight. His eyes were brimming.

"It's okay," Jude said, standing up again. "You don't have to talk."

Slowly Tej's head lowered onto Jude's shoulder and a shiver went through his body. "I am not fucking dressed for this."

Laughing, Jude held him away, looked him up and down. Crappy jeans, ripped T-shirt, both smudged all over with paint. Splatters in the hair of his forearms, worked into his nail beds, a dollop at the edge of one sideburn.

"You're beautiful."

"Christ, shut up," Tej said. "Just tell me where I am."

Jude slid a hand up the back of Tej's neck and threaded into his hair. "You're in my house."

EPILOGUE

*T*HE DAY WAS GLOOMY, with a stubborn sun attempting to squeeze through gaps in the cloud cover. Together, Jude and Alex sprinkled a bit of Luis Felice Tholet's ashes over the Pendas' gravestone, binding the two families forever. A short distance away, Tej and Val were by the Lark family plot, tidying up the markers, their laughter carrying on the breeze.

"Those two," Alex said, brushing off his hands. "It's like they were married in a past life."

"You want to come to our wedding?"

"The question is how would you stop me?"

They sat on the bench by the grave. Elbows on knees, hands clasped and chins on top. Like twins.

"Can I ask you something?" Jude said.

"Mm."

"You being eleven years older than me… Was that gap planned? I mean, did Lalo and Tina try to have kids between us?"

These nicknames were Jude's solution to the problem of addressing two sets of parents. A stubborn chagrin wouldn't share the *Mami* and *Papi* he'd used all his life for Penny and Cleon. Calling the Pendas by their first names felt disrespectful to Alex, who insisted it didn't matter. But Jude insisted it did, and began calling his birth parents Lalo and Tina, elevating the diminutives to honorifics.

"Mami miscarried when I was nine," Alex said. "I don't really remember if she was pregnant any times before that."

"Were you psyched I was on the way?"

"Oh yeah, I was excited."

"Did they know I was a boy?"

"No."

"Did they have names picked out?"

"Mami wanted Hernando. I wanted Leonardo after one of the Chilean football players. Papi wanted whatever we wanted."

"What about girl names?"

"I didn't pay any attention to those."

"Story of my life."

"Look," Val called. She and Tej were pointing up, heads tilted back. An enormous bald eagle was circling the skies above Guelisten.

"Holy crap, look at the size of him," Jude said, standing up and turning in a circle to follow the magnificent predator. "He's huge."

"She," Alex said absently, a hand shielding his eyes. "The females are bigger."

"Story of your life."

Alex slid his arm around Jude and ruffled his hair. "Te quiero, cosito."

Jude leaned into his side and let the Condor pass.

The clouds moved and the sun shone through, lighting up the afternoon like an Andean goddess's pregnant belly.

Jude the Revealed.

The sun on his face, the world under his skin and a hand on his brother's back.

His fingers ashy with bones that only told the truth.

His heart full of sad songs made better.

Acknowledgments

*L*ASHINGS OF LOVE AND gratitude to...

Susan Katz, who was this book's doula through a long and arduous labor. I couldn't have done it without you. No shit.

Greg Williams, who put his house in Alki Beach on the market, posted it on Facebook, and gave me a home for Cleon and Penny.

Peter David, who has an equal sign tattooed on his thumb. He shook my hand and Bert Gesundheit was born.

Hewan Tomlinson, who probably doesn't remember me, but I always remembered her name and I've been wanting to use it in a book for years.

JP, my fixed star in the sky.

Julie, who played a lot of Beatles this past year and gave me a good idea.

AJ, my cosito gordo.

My parents, because I don't want to be anyone's daughter but theirs.

Steve, who is my brother and always will be.

My grandmother, Lena Danese Schelper, who upon her diagnosis with pancreatic cancer, said, "Well, this is a revolting development."

Dr. Carol-Ann Galban, who told me, "You're only as happy as your least happy child."

John Joseph, who told my mother, "You don't have to do this day anymore."

Elizabeth Gilbert, who asked me, "And who are you going to be now?"

Aunt Evelyn, who gave me *Cucina Ebraica* for a birthday present.

Dr. Joseph Schippa, PhD, who advised me through the hypnosis sessions.

My towers: Tracy my cover designer and Colleen my formatter.

Daniella Chacón Araujo, for making the Spanish sit up straight and behave.

The Read & Nap Lounge, plus the beta readers and bloggers and reviewers who help get my stories into the world.

And to Alice Archer, who might be reading this and thinking, "Good girl."

All my books have a label of some kind: the first, the hardest, the best, the most important. This book felt the least like me. The adage goes that "every novel is a memoir, every memoir is a novel." But little of me is in *Condors*. It seemed I wasn't so much writing a book as answering a mandate. I wasn't the creator. I was the pipeline.

I believe ideas pick us to be made manifest. I believe characters are the spirit-energy of people's stories, looking around for a storyteller. And I truly believe something, someone, or possibly many someones, picked me to write *Condors* and asked my ego and bias and personal experiences to step aside.

Whoever they were, I thank them. It was a privilege. As with *Finches*, I knew there was a lot more I could get wrong than right. It's my sincere hope I got it right.

RECIPES

"I am too happy to write. I have to eat and drink with you, dear friends."
—Pablo Neruda

Sopa di Pesce Spina all'Ebraica (Venetian Fish Soup)

2 celery stalks, chopped
2 carrots, peeled and chopped
1 large onion, chopped
2 cloves garlic, left whole, plus 1 tablespoon finely minced garlic
2 teaspoons salt
About 8 cups water
2 ½ to 3 pounds assorted firm whole white fish, cleaned and heads removed and reserved.
3 tablespoons olive oil
3 tablespoons finely minced garlic
1 teaspoon red hot pepper flakes (optional)
2 teaspoons peeled and grated fresh ginger (optional)
1 to 2 cups dry white wine
Pinch of saffron threads (optional)
3 tablespoons tomato paste or 2 cups diced seeded peeled tomatoes (optional)
4 tablespoons minced flat-leaf parsley
4 tablespoons minced fresh basil
Small, coarse country bread slices fried in oil for serving

In a large stockpot, combine the celery, carrots, onion, whole garlic cloves, salt and water. Bring to a boil and cook for 10 minutes. Add the fish, reduce the heat to medium-low, and simmer for about 12 minutes. With a slotted spatula, gently remove the fish from the liquid. Remove the skin and bones from the fish and set the fillets aside. Return the skin and bones to the pot along with the reserved heads. Simmer about 30 minutes. Strain the liquid through a colander lined with wet cheesecloth and set aside.

Warm the olive oil in a deep sauté pan over medium heat. Add half the parsley and the minced garlic and sauté until the garlic is pale gold, about 5 minutes. Add the white wine. If using red pepper flakes, ginger, saffron and/or tomato, add them now. Warm the fish until heated through. Adjust seasonings to taste. Stir in the remaining parsley and the basil. Serve topped with fried bread.

Pickled Grapes

1 pound red grapes, preferably seedless
1 cup white wine vinegar
1 cup granulated sugar
1 1/2 teaspoon brown mustard seeds
1 teaspoon whole black peppercorns
1 (2 1/2-inch) cinnamon stick
1/4 teaspoon salt

Rinse and dry the grapes, and pull them carefully from their stems. Using a small, sharp knife, trim away the "belly button" at the stem end of the grape, exposing a bit of the flesh inside. Put the grapes into a medium bowl, and set aside.

In a medium saucepan, combine the remaining ingredients. Bring to a boil over medium-high heat; then pour the mixture immediately over the grapes. Stir to combine. Set aside to cool at room temperature.

Pour the grapes and brine into jars with tight-fitting lids (or cover the bowl with plastic wrap), and chill at least 8 hours or overnight. Serve cold.

Terremoto

Pipeño wine (type of sweet fermented white wine)
Pisco or Fernet Branca
Pineapple ice cream
Designated driver

Fill up a liter glass with Pipeño wine almost to the top.
    Add a small shot of pisco or Fernet Branca
    Top it off with a big scoop of pineapple ice cream.
    Call a cab.

Poor Man's Reuben

2 slices bread
3-4 slices ham
2-3 slices cheddar cheese
Generous helping of bread-and-butter pickles, patted dry on paper towels
Mustard and mayonnaise
Olive Oil
Lover (optional)

On a small plate, layer ham and cheese, folding to fit the shape of your bread. Microwave 40-60 seconds, until cheese is melted.

Heat olive oil in a skillet, lay bread slices side by side. Spread with mayonnaise and mustard. Layer pickles on one piece of bread.

With a spatula, scoop melted ham and cheese off plate and on top of the pickles. Close up the sandwich and press it down hard with a lid. Cook 1-2 minutes then flip, pressing down again. Slice on the diagonal and serve to your lover with cold beer and potato chips.

Or eat it yourself.

Cinnamon-Orange Stewed Prunes

1/2 navel orange or 1 tangerine
1/2 lemon (optional)
1/2 pound pitted prunes
1 cinnamon stick

Cut the citrus fruit in half vertically, and then slice it thinly, peel and all. Place the slices in a medium saucepan with the prunes and the cinnamon stick, and add water to cover. Bring the mixture to a gentle simmer, and cook over medium-low heat for about 30-45 minutes.

Remove the cinnamon stick and serve over vanilla ice cream.

Then apologize.

Tej's Tangerine Cake

For the Cake

1 cup (2 sticks) unsalted butter
3 cups all-purpose flour
1 teaspoon baking soda
1 teaspoon fine salt
2 cups granulated sugar
6 large eggs
2 tablespoons finely grated tangerine zest, plus 1/2 cup tangerine juice (from 6 tangerines)
2 tablespoons orange-flavored liqueur, such as Grand Marnier
3/4 cup low-fat plain yogurt
1 teaspoon pure vanilla extract

For the Glaze

1 1/2 cups confectioners' sugar
3 tablespoons tangerine juice (from 2 tangerines)

Preheat oven to 350 degrees.

Spray a 12-cup Bundt cake pan with Pam.

In a medium bowl, whisk together flour, baking soda, and salt.

Beat butter and granulated sugar on medium-high until light and fluffy. Add eggs, one at a time, beating well after each addition. Beat in tangerine zest and juice and liqueur.

With mixer on low, add flour mixture in three additions, alternating with two additions yogurt, and beat to combine; beat in vanilla.

Transfer batter to pan, smooth top and firmly tap pan on a flat surface to remove air bubbles. Bake until a toothpick inserted in center of cake comes out clean, 55 to 60 minutes. Let cool in pan on a wire rack, 30 minutes. Invert cake onto rack set in a rimmed baking sheet and let cool completely.

Whisk together confectioners' sugar and tangerine juice until smooth. Spoon glaze evenly over cake and let set 1 hour.

About The Author

A FORMER professional dancer and teacher, Suanne Laqueur went from choreographing music to choreographing words. Her work has been described as therapy fiction, emotionally intelligent romance and contemporary train wreck.

Laqueur's novel *An Exaltation of Larks* was the Grand Prize winner in the 2017 Writer's Digest Awards. Her debut novel *The Man I Love* won a gold medal in the 2015 Readers' Favorite Book Awards and was named Best Debut in the Feathered Quill Book Awards. Her follow-up novel, *Give Me Your Answer True,* was also a gold medal winner at the 2016 RFBA.

Laqueur graduated from Alfred University with a double major in dance and theater. She taught at the Carol Bierman School of Ballet Arts in Croton-on-Hudson for ten years. An avid reader, cook and gardener, she started her blog EatsReadsThinks in 2010.

Suanne lives in Westchester County, New York with her husband and two children.

Visit her at suannelaqueurwrites.com

All feels welcome. And she always has coffee.

Also by Suanne Laqueur

THE FISH TALES
The Man I Love
Give Me Your Answer True
Here to Stay
The Ones That Got Away

VENERY
An Exaltation of Larks
A Charm of Finches
A Scarcity of Condors
The Voyages of Trueblood Cay
Tales from Cushman Row

SHORT STORIES
Love & Bravery

Made in the USA
Middletown, DE
09 January 2020